THE GREAT AMERICAN
TILLY AND ELMER
NOVEL

Elmer Tilly Carol Hub Gary Tiffany

Rocky Dr. Ira Gold Betty Patti Prudence

GENE CLEMENTS

Cover Design and Illustrations: Gene Clements

Pickleworks Press
Sweet/Hot Editions

SERENDIPITY
Seattle Erotic Art Festival Literary Art Anthology - 2017

GOODE TIMES
Seattle Erotic Art Festival Literary Art Anthology – 2018

THE DOMINO EFFECT
Seattle Erotic Art Festival Literary Art Anthology - 2019

HOORAY, HOORAY, THE FIRST OF MAY
Seattle Erotic Art Festival Literary Art Anthology - 2020

See and order the complete collection of books about Tilly and Elmer, and others, at:

TILLYANDELMER.COM

Pickleworks Press
Sweet/Hot Editions

ACKNOWLEDGMENTS:

Needless to say, many people have helped me in my efforts to bring the shameful tales of Tilly and Elmer, and their education between the sheets, as well as in the park, at the beach, down by the "crick", in a wheat field during a thunderstorm, parked next to Old Man Smith's orchard, and at the "Dream-On Motel", to an indifferent public. I've mentioned some of these people in the acknowledgment section of other books and, so far, none have unfriended me on social media, so I'll take the risk of revealing their identities once again.

I'm always indebted to **Elizabeth Johnson**, who has now edited five of my books despite the fact that when she began with my earliest book, she found I had misspelled the very first word following the title. Nevertheless she persisted! Over the years she has saved me from more bonehead errors in the writing than I knew were possible. In fact, she gently steered me away from a dead-end path when I first began this book! Thanks Beth, yet again.

Tim Schellhardt, a good friend since high school who has enjoyed an illustrious career as a talented professional writer, editor, and newsman, also accepted the challenge of attempting to keep me on the straight and narrow; normally a hopeless, and thankless, task. Thank you, Tim! I'm thrilled that Tim would take up such a cause. He encouraged me at every turn in spite of the record number of errors he was called on to point out.

Several others who read portions of this work, and

didn't unfriend me as a result, should be mentioned with thanks as well, including **April Cooper**, who kindly pointed out that Tilly and Elmer could not have reached Iowa from Nebraska if I continued to report they crossed the Mississippi River in order to do so.

Thanks as well to **Chuck Herndon**, who pointed out many possible improvements to the text (which I skipped over) and noted a few things he thought I got right (on which I lavished excessive attention).

My wife **Ann** has heard me read all of my stories to her and never fails to laugh when I finish. I choose to believe this means she likes them. Thanks for that and for 53 great years so far!

CONTENTS

ABOUT TILLY AND ELMER

Some years ago, I began writing about Tilly and Elmer, an older couple from the made-up town of South Branch, Iowa. Tilly and Elmer have been married fifty years, still like each other, and know what to do about it. After a series of short stories recounting a few of their loving but usually funny sexual exploits as sexagenarians, I thought it would be proper (or amusingly improper) to write about their revisionist recollections of their high school courtship. This became a popular tell all about coming of age in the Midwest during the 1960's. Eventually these two storybook characters revealed to me their untold secret shenanigans after Elmer went to college in Northern Iowa, and Tilly left for nursing school in San Francisco. As one can imagine, they had wildly different college experiences, which led to misunderstandings and an era of estrangement, not to mention disdain, for one another. *The Great American Tilly and Elmer Novel* is the sad, delightful, kinky, enlightening, shocking, and amusing story of that period in their lives.

THE GREAT AMERICAN
TILLY AND ELMER
NOVEL

PROLOGUE

August 8, 1967 – Somewhere in Wyoming

Elmer slowly awoke from a dream in which a young female detective mercilessly interrogated him under an intense accusatory spotlight. She seemed convinced he was guilty of something; whatever it was, Elmer had an unsettling feeling she was right.

He cautiously opened his eyes. The blinding spotlight was actually the early morning sun shining through the windshield of his well-used 15-year-old Chevy pickup. Shielding his eyes, Elmer was surprised to find himself in a desert of some kind. He turned to look around and felt a twinge of pain in his neck; he had been sleeping in the driver's seat with his head tilted awkwardly against the side window.

As his thoughts cleared, he remembered that late last night the truck had begun to lose power and he had pulled off State Route 130 into an abandoned gas station at the edge of a small town, just west of the middle of nowhere. The town appeared doubtful; a dozen dilapidated dwellings and a tacky tavern that wouldn't open until noon, and where a long-haired, fresh-out-of-college kid in bell bottoms wouldn't be welcome anyway.

Elmer suddenly felt apprehensive. Where was Tilly? He looked down to find her curled up asleep next to him, her dusty bare feet against his thigh. At least she was still there, looking beautiful and innocent. Her long peasant dress was pulled up and tucked between her knees; her uncombed long brown hair was sweetly entangled with her left arm, which covered her face.

They had been sweethearts four years ago, back in high school, and he couldn't help remembering the delicious and delightfully dissolute things they had learned to do together in this very truck during their two years of do-it-yourself sex education. Evidence of their homework still discolored the seats here and there. Those had been the best days of Elmer's life, before Tilly had left for nursing school in San Francisco and he had departed for the State College of Iowa in Cedar Falls. EVERYTHING was different now.

Tilly and Elmer were beginning the fourth day of their confinement in his cramped truck on an unwanted road trip back to South Branch, Iowa, their former hometown. These days they couldn't stand each other's company for four minutes, much less four days. It hadn't gone well so far, and they still faced more dismal days of stony silence alternating with acrimonious accusations.

Elmer got out of the truck and slammed the door, awakening the already grumpy girl. He poked around under the hood for a few minutes and when he came back, she was fuming.

"Give me your panties!" Elmer said in the most unromantic way possible, although the thought of her panties brought the hint of a smile to his face.

Tilly gave him a look of loathing. "Are you kidding?" she hissed.

She turned away from him and said under her breath, "What an asshole!"

"Damn it, Tilly! I need them to fix the truck!"

"You need my PANTIES to fix the truck? How stupid do you think I am, Elmer?"

"I don't think you're stupid, but I doubt you're an expert on troubleshooting the fuel delivery system in a 1952 Chevy pickup. I would have used those pink panties Prudence left under the seat if you hadn't tossed them out the window in Winnemucca!"

PART I   DEPARTURE
CHAPTER 1   GO WEST YOUNG LADY

Every young bird leaves the nest
Not sure which direction is best.
Tilly's insistence
Insisted on distance
And she stretched her new wings toward the West.

July 14, 1963

"Did we ever hear who won the game last night?" Elmer asked as he steered the truck out of the "Sleeptite Motel" parking lot and into northbound traffic out of St. Louis.

Tilly snuggled up against him and laid her head on his shoulder. "I think we BOTH won!"

She giggled and gave him a kiss on the neck. "You're the best lover I've ever had!"

"I'm pretty sure I'm the ONLY lover you've ever had, Tilly!"

"Well, even so, I'm pretty sure no one else could make me feel as good as you do, Wiggle Bear!"

Elmer gave her thigh a squeeze in response.

"Why do you care who won the game?" Tilly asked.

"My folks think Bob and I came to St. Louis to see the ballgame, remember? I'd better at least know the score!"

Tilly gave Elmer's earlobe a little squeeze, a gesture that had come to mean, "I want to fuck you right now or I love doing it with you." This was especially effective when they were in public and would have to wait.

"Tell your folks the score was debauchery 1000, decency 0. I love being indecent with you!"

"I love how deliciously indecent you are too, Flash!"

Tilly turned on the radio and tuned to a local station. After some minutes they learned that the Cardinals had lost to the Milwaukee Braves 7-5.

"I'm glad we were rolling around in bed together instead of wasting time at the game!" Elmer asserted as though it might have been different if the Cardinals had won. He shifted into third gear, pushing Tilly's skirt up in the process since she was sitting as close as possible to Elmer and her legs straddled the floor mounted gear shift.

It had been six months since they had first gone all the way, but last night was the first time they had spent an entire night together. This was accomplished through a complicated plan with their friends Linda and Bob in which the girls' parents believed the girls would be driving down from South Branch and staying over in St. Louis after visiting an amusement park together. And quite separately the boys told their parents they were going to St. Louis to see the Cardinals' game, which would be finished too late for them to drive home until the next morning. Once out of town, the passengers changed places, and each couple spent a glorious and top-secret night together at the Sleeptite Motel.

Nothing was said for a while and Elmer thought Tilly might have fallen asleep. They HAD been awake most of the night after all. He was going to miss this, miss her, miss the way she looked up at him when they were naked together. He was going to miss everything about her. He thought back over their previous two years; how clueless he had been about girls and how she had sweetly showed him how to seduce her so he thought it was all his idea. He knew this was happening and loved her for it. Elmer hadn't had any concept of falling in love — until their first kiss.

He gave her shoulder a hug.

"What are we going to do Elmer?" Tilly asked softly, starting to cry.

"About what?" he asked, knowing full well what this was about.

"Don't worry Flash, everything will work out." He didn't sound convincing, even to himself.

August 3, 1963

Three weeks later, Tilly and Elmer made another trip to St. Louis, this time with Tilly's family, to see her off on a DC-8 to San Francisco. They left early in the morning and everyone, including Tilly, was in a somber mood. There was little conversation on the trip because

15

there wasn't much to say.

Tilly's parents hugged her and wished her luck in San Francisco as they waited for her plane to board at Lambert Field. Then, knowing that Tilly and Elmer needed a few private moments together, they took her little brother to the ice cream shop.

Mostly Tilly and Elmer hugged. There was a lot to say but nothing was said. Elmer reached into his pocket and brought out two small plastic boxes, each containing a necklace with half a heart that was broken in such a way that they fit together to make a whole. He had dashed into the gift shop and found them while Tilly was checking her luggage. He gave one box to Tilly and put the other one in his pocket.

"Fifty years from now, those will be in a frame over our mantle," he said as though he believed it.

"Wouldn't that be something!" said Tilly.

She kissed Elmer once more, looked at him with a mixture of hope and sadness, gave his earlobe a tug, and then went down the stairs to the ground level. Elmer saw her climb the moveable stairs to the door of the airplane, and then wave in his direction although he doubted she could see him from that vantage point.

And then she disappeared.

Tilly was awash in conflicting and complicated emotions as she stepped aboard the DC-8 that would, if everything went well, take her out West. This was her first flight, and, of equal concern, it was taking her 2000 miles from home to a place far different from South Branch, Iowa. And far from Elmer Talbot, the love of her life. She would be leaving the familiar for a new adventure; an adventure she was not so sure was a good idea at this moment.

She reminded herself, for the one thousandth time, why she had decided to attend nursing school in San Francisco instead of Des Moines. Her cousin Carol had put her up to it. She and Carol had enjoyed a great time together when her family visited Aunt Bev, Uncle Elliott, and Carol a couple of years before in Berkeley. When her cousin had written to propose that Tilly come to San Francisco and attend nursing school with her at UCSF, it seemed like a great adventure. Carol's enthusiasm for the idea was catching and to Tilly's surprise, her parents approved, especially when they learned there were scholarships available. She expected to eventually settle down with Elmer but there was no hurry. Her parents were fond of Elmer and thought they would be a good match, but their romance seemed to be proceeding too fast, and they didn't want the two to have to get married before they could attend college. Her mom and dad pointed out that a sojourn out West before coming home to Elmer would expand her horizons, and Aunt Bev would be just across the Bay so she would have family nearby if need be.

This all seemed great as a plan for the future, but now, strapped into a small seat in a huge metal object with a bunch of strangers bound for a strange and unknown place, it all seemed frighteningly real. Tilly looked out the window at the busy ground crew. When she saw them put her suitcase on board the die seemed to be cast. She closed her eyes, took a deep breath, grasped the arms of her seat, and imagined Elmer was holding her hand.

Soon she could feel the plane being pushed back from the gate. After what seemed like a long trip around the airport the craft stopped at the end of the runway and waited as if trying to get up the nerve to give flight a try. The powerful jet engines began to rumble and the plane shuddered as the noise reached a crescendo. After a pause, the aircraft abruptly lurched forward. This was it!

To her surprise, Tilly felt a bit of an erotic thrill as the huge plane accelerated dramatically toward either seemingly impossible flight or sudden death. She began to worry that, in spite of the speed of the lumbering jet, it would be unable to get off the ground, but when she felt the craft angle upward then leap into the air following a frightening final bump of the wheels on the runway, she felt exhilarated. Not only was she still alive, she was about to leave Iowa behind at five hundred miles an hour! Tilly was sad to leave home, but suddenly she felt like the world was hers for the taking.

She looked out the window to an unexpected view of the Midwest. Distances that took hours to traverse by car seemed like nothing from the air. She sat back and gradually released her tight grip on the arms of her seat. This was a new beginning — and suddenly she felt more than ready. Tilly put any fear of flying aside and stared out the window, except when the stewardess brought her lunch. She found the meal delicious and, feeling very independent and grown up, she ordered coffee afterwards. *"California is going to be great!"* she told herself, although not fully persuaded.

Tilly was again looking out the window intently as the plane began its final approach into San Francisco. Her delight at the vast urban landscape that was going to be her new home gave way to a momentary fear that the plane was going to land in San Francisco Bay. At the last possible moment however, the seawall and the end of the runway flashed under her and the huge craft met the runway with only a minor bump. *"Hello, California!"* she thought, tearing up a little.

The plane rolled up to the gate under a sign that informed her she had arrived at San Francisco International Airport. SAN FRANCISCO! She couldn't remember ever having felt so excited, especially when she saw her cousin Carol waiting for her. On the way to Carol's apartment, where Tilly would be living with Carol and her two roommates, Tilly was reminded of what a large and beautiful city San Francisco was. It was early in the afternoon and Tilly thought the city looked like a magical place with pastel-colored buildings arranged decoratively on the hillsides. She wondered how anyone got anything done here, since they must feel as if they're on vacation all the time!

As if to amplify the distance Tilly had traveled since morning, Carol chose a route that took them up the

Great Highway, along the Pacific Coast, on their way to the apartment. Tilly had never smoked marijuana, but she was as high on anticipation of her new life as if she had; a new life away from cold winters, parents who wanted to tell you every move to make, even a boyfriend who hoped you'd never change. Carol was pointing out sights along the way and telling Tilly outrageous tales of afternoons at nude beaches just down the coast, impromptu music in Golden Gate Park, and nights at Playland at the Beach. Tilly looked west, past Carol at the wheel of her Volkswagen Beetle, to the serene Pacific. She reflected on the fact that Horace Greeley's advice to young men, "Go West!", should apply to young women too!

On the way, Carol told Tilly about their roommates. Hub, who happened to be Carol's boyfriend, was a student at San Francisco City College. Gary was an artist and poet from Los Angeles who had been in San Francisco for about a year. Both were smart and idealistic, interested in politics and philosophy. She went on to describe several other friends that often visited or stayed overnight at the apartment. Tilly was barely able to contain her excitement about the future and her confidence that life was going to be quite an adventure in her new home. In a few weeks she would be beginning nursing school with Carol, which added another layer of excitement to her whole experience.

"Wouldn't Elmer be surprised to see me now?" she wondered. Tilly knew he would be a bit jealous of her

new freedom and her awaiting adventure, but, while she loved Elmer, he wasn't known for being wildly daring. Well, Elmer would just have to fend for himself for a few years until she returned to South Branch. She watched the sunlight sparkling on the tips of the waves rolling in toward Ocean Beach. *"IF she ever returned to South Branch!"* The thought surprised her and scared her a little.

Carol turned off the Great Highway and drove Tilly through Golden Gate Park on the way to their apartment in "The Haight". Tilly was curious about apartment living. South Branch featured only a few apartments, mostly in large older homes that had been divided into two or three units or residences upstairs from shops on the main street. Here most people lived in apartments and, as they left the park and plunged into the city itself, people seemed to be everywhere, out walking, laughing, and enjoying the afternoon's ambiance.

"Here we are!" Carol announced, pointing to one of the ubiquitous three story, vaguely Victorian-style, buildings forming a solid wall along the street. She drove on past.

"THAT was our apartment?" Tilly asked, turning to look back.

"That's it, home sweet home!" Carol enthused. "There's never a parking space close by so we'll have to try some other spots I know about."

She drove two blocks away and tucked her VW into a spot that was two-thirds a red zone.

"Won't you get a ticket?" Tilly asked.

"I doubt it," Carol said. The legal portion was longer than most cars, leaving a short distance available when a normal car was parked in the space. Carol simply let her car extend into the red zone, then covered up a bit of the painted curb at the leading edge of her car with a cardboard box she kept in the trunk that somewhat matched the color of the concrete. Meter Maids approached from the back and only had time for a quick glance at the front of her car as they passed. Usually they were fooled, and if not, Carol simply threw the tickets away. The possibility of a future reckoning didn't seem to bother her.

The girls grabbed Tilly's belongings and walked two blocks to the apartment Carol had pointed out, dodging small groups of young people in colorful clothing, laughing, smoking, sometimes stopping to kiss or hug one another. Now and then, a curious smoky smell would envelop them, and Tilly asked about it.

"Oh, that's grass," Carol said as though it was commonplace for people to smoke marijuana in public.

"I thought they would send you to jail for that!" Tilly said with concern.

"Well, you can put on a little patchouli oil, and then they can't tell. Besides, they can't jail everybody! And anyway, we never smoke pot..."

Tilly was relieved to hear this – until Carol finished the sentence, "...out in public!"

It was clear to Tilly that she had a lot to learn about her new home.

Carol directed Tilly to a short set of steps and a doorway located between a shop selling drug

23

paraphernalia and a liquor store.

"This is a very convenient location!" Carol teased.

The doorway opened to a landing and then to a stairway leading up to apartments on the two upper floors. At the top of the stairs a door on the right labeled 2A led to Tilly's new digs. Carol unlocked the door and ushered Tilly into a large space that functioned as a dining area and a living room. At the end of the room was a bay window overlooking the street. Opposite the door was a beat-up dining table that could accommodate six diners, surrounded by a half dozen unmatched chairs. A bar to the left of the dining area revealed an open kitchen beyond and next to the kitchen, a hallway led to the bathroom and two bedrooms.

"Welcome to your new digs!" Carol announced, kicking off her shoes.

Tilly did the same and took a quick inventory of the apartment. The first thing she noticed was that, apart from the secondhand dining table, no actual furniture was evident. The "living room" was furnished with four mattresses, stacked in pairs to make seating surfaces, covered with blankets and topped with a variety of pillows in paisley or tie-dyed fabrics. The walls were covered in decades-old wallpaper, peeling in places, and this was enlivened with psychedelic posters of musicians, Che Guevara, and leaf forms.

"I'll give you the grand tour," Carol said. "It won't take long!"

Just behind the kitchen was the bathroom. It featured a clawfoot tub, surrounded with a shower curtain on a suspended rod around the perimeter, a chipped pedestal sink, and a toilet whose tank was not attached but hung high on the wall and connected to the bowl with a chrome pipe. A cabinet held toiletries for the roommates. There was no lock on the bathroom door, but Carol gave Tilly the code – an open door meant available, a closed door meant keep out, and a door left ajar meant "come in at your own risk, I'm not doing anything that I don't want you to see, although you might not want to see it!" She let Tilly know that this usually meant someone was in the shower but who might throw open the curtain and emerge at any time.

The next room was a small bedroom, currently occupied by Gary. He had agreed to sleep in the living room once Tilly arrived so this would be her room although Gary would still keep his desk there and his clothes on the floor of his half of the closet. Her bed would be a mattress on the floor.

At the end of the hall was the last bedroom, modestly larger and shared by Carol and Hub. The furnishings consisted of a well-used desk whose surface was hidden by a stack of papers, books, and a set of bongo drums; an overstuffed chair; and a mattress on the floor with a hairy bare leg extending from under the covers. Carol explained that Hub's sleeping habits were somewhat random and that he'd probably be awake for dinner. Returning to the first bedroom, Carol made Tilly's bed with clean sheets and helped her find places for her things.

Next came a more detailed exploration of the kitchen. It was getting close to dinnertime and Tilly was especially hungry because she had begun the day in the central time zone.

"Everybody generally gets their own groceries and cooks whatever they want whenever they want it. You can use this shelf in the refrigerator. Now and then we cook together, usually on Sunday nights. We go shopping together, split the cost, and somebody makes their specialty, such as it is. But don't worry Tilly, I'm going to make you a special dinner tonight in honor of your arrival – calamari cooked in white wine!

Tilly had never heard of calamari, but it sounded Italian, so she was picturing a variety of pasta. "What's calamari?" she asked.

"Haven't you had it? You'll love it!" Carol told her. "It's squid."

Carol took a package of something that looked like slimy tubes of rolled, open-ended condoms, mixed with giant slippery white spiders, out of the refrigerator.

Tilly closed her eyes tight and experienced a little shiver. She had a lot to learn all right!

"Wait 'til I tell Elmer what I ate for supper on my first night in San Francisco!" she thought.

Carol began the cooking and once the wine was added, divided the rest of the bottle between two glasses, gave one to Tilly, and offered a toast:

"I'm so happy you're here, Corny! We're going to

have so much fun together. I can't wait to show you everything! You're going to LOVE San Francisco." The cousins hugged, taking care not to spill the wine.

"It's been fun and educational, already!" Tilly said, hoping that would still hold true after dinner.

As it turned out, Tilly found the calamari curiously chewy but liked it well enough to finish at least a small portion. Hub showed up in his underwear as they were eating and, after introductions were made and Carol admonished him to get dressed if he wanted to join them, Hub reappeared in a loose white shirt, bell bottom pants, and sandals. He then finished off the remaining supply of calamari, freeing Tilly from having to demur.

After supper, which Tilly was going to have to learn to call "dinner", Hub, Carol, and Tilly gathered in the living room to get acquainted. A gallon jug of "Red Mountain" wine appeared, and Tilly gave a summary of her life in Iowa, which represented an obscure and unimaginable part of the universe to the others.

Tilly's initial impression of Hub was that he was rather quiet and thoughtful, and fully in tune with the peace and freedom-loving lifestyle she associated with hippies, although he seemed more serious than expected. He was tall and thin, with curly black hair, flowing down around his face into a beard that he continually stroked when he was concentrating on something. He was in his second year at City College of San Francisco, studying philosophy.

During the conversation, Gary arrived with his latest

girlfriend, a young American woman with long hair, bedecked with beads, and dressed in a sari. Everyone was introduced including "Nama," Gary's partner.

"Namaste," she said, bowing slightly. The couple moved slowly and gracefully to a place on the mattress sofa, bringing with them an aura of marijuana, an aroma Tilly was becoming familiar with. The couple didn't fully participate in the conversation, preferring to display their affection for each other in spite of the company, and before long they disappeared into the bedroom that was to be Tilly's.

"I guess you're sleeping out here tonight after all, Cuz," Carol said. "Sorry. We'll work it out in the morning!"

Tilly was tired after an early morning and a long day, and without getting undressed, fell asleep on the living room mattress in spite of the sounds of late-night revelers drifting up from the street below.

Tilly was not used to Pacific time and awoke three hours ahead of the others. At least she had the bathroom to herself. Carol had given her a key to the apartment, so she ventured out in search of breakfast, feeling very grown up and adventurous! Almost no one was on the street. It was Sunday and Tilly found the corner grocery closed until later in the morning, so she returned to the apartment, borrowed a bowl of cereal from Carol's shelf, and sat down to write a letter to Elmer.

August 4, 1963
Hi Wiggle Bear,

As you can see, I made it to sunny California! Flying is
so groovy (see, I'm picking up the California lingo
already!)

She got this far in her letter before Carol came in,
clad in panties and one of Hub's T-shirts.

"You're up early!" Carol said. "I see you were able to
scare up some breakfast."

"I stole it from you – I'll get you a new box when we
get to the store."

"Don't worry about it!" Carol said. "Don't worry
about anything. We use each other's stuff all the time
and everybody contributes. It works out in the end!
Let's go for a walk this morning and I'll show you
around a little."

After breakfast, the girls embarked on a walking tour
of the Haight-Ashbury neighborhood. The street level
throughout was given over to small shops of all kinds,
grocery stores, liquor stores, booksellers, laundries,
restaurants, so called "head shops', clothing stores,
bars, bike rental establishments, drug stores and more.
Tilly noted that every block had more businesses than
the whole town of South Branch. Anything you could
want was available nearby; no driving twenty-five miles
to Mount Pleasant to get a copy of "*Walden* "!

Four blocks east of the apartment, to Tilly's astonishment, a grassy hill as tall as a skyscraper rose from the mostly flat neighborhood. This was Buena Vista Park, a rocky outcropping covered in trees and grass with hiking trails and spectacular 360-degree views of the entire Bay Area. Tilly wondered if this would be the tallest mountain in the state if relocated to Iowa. They climbed to a lookout point to survey the scenery. Toward the north was the Golden Gate Bridge, glowing bright orange in the morning sun. To the East was downtown San Francisco and the East Bay.

"That's my mom's house right there!" Carol laughed, pointing east. "See it?"

Carol's mother, Tilly's Aunt Bev, lived in Berkeley, now lost in a hazy gray until the morning fog lifted. To the south was the "Peninsula" and the San Francisco Airport, and looking west, pastel-colored houses, Golden Gate Park, and the Pacific Ocean. From this elevated perspective, Tilly was overwhelmed by the magnitude and beauty of San Francisco. Close up there were a few inconveniences in the city, but from here everything looked like paradise.

Tilly gave Carol a spontaneous hug. "Oh my god, Carol, I've never seen anything so beautiful! How do you stand it? I might start crying with joy any minute!"

Carol gave her a smile. "Thanks for reminding me! We get involved in trying to find a place to park and forget to look at this place sometimes! It can get routine after a while."

"It's not going to get routine for me after coming

here from Iowa! I'll remind you every day, Cuz! Oh, and one other thing, I'm going to need a new nickname — 'Corny' doesn't apply anymore!" Tilly said, breaking into a silly dance.

"I'm going to give you a few days to get fully infused with San Francisco, and then we'll think up a new nickname!" Carol said giggling.

The two spent the rest of the day exploring the sights of the neighborhood — from the houses where famous musicians lived and the best place to get a cheap meal to the regular hangouts of marijuana sellers. Carol introduced Tilly to the "Panhandle", an eight-block-long strip of parkland between Fell and Oak Streets. When they got to Golden Gate Park, they walked a short way into its eastern edge. Carol promised to take Tilly for a day's outing to explore the park the next day, but she let Tilly know that it would take more than a day to cover everything it had to offer.

They got back to the apartment at dinner time and, this being Sunday, Hub was doing the cooking.

"He's better in the bedroom than he is in the kitchen," Carol whispered to Tilly as they sat on the mattress sofa recounting the day's exploration. This reminded Tilly of Elmer and she was surprised that she hadn't thought of him all day. She resolved to finish her letter to him after supper. *Dinner!* she silently reminded herself.

Hub's offering of overcooked spaghetti topped with canned tomato sauce wasn't the best she had ever tasted, and when she and Carol had to clean up, they found Hub had used every pan in the kitchen and spilled half the ingredients on the counter or floor in the process.

"Hub better be REALLY good in the bedroom!" she giggled to Carol.

As it turned out, she couldn't finish her letter to Elmer because after dinner the four of them, and Nama, were going to a concert at a local bar where Hub would be playing bongos with an aspiring rock and roll band. This lasted until late, and Tilly was tired and a bit sloshed from drinking wine by the time they got back to the apartment. Elmer's letter was forgotten for the moment.

Elmer and Tilly mostly communicated through letters. Long distance phone calls were expensive, and neither was in a location where conversations could be kept private. Tilly was up early again on Monday and finished her letter to Elmer. In it she described the delights of flying, her drive with Carol along the coast, Buena Vista Park, Golden Gate Park, and her welcome dinner of "calamari", which she suggested he look up in the dictionary. She assured Elmer she loved him and signed with XXOO.

Letters usually took three or four days to get back and forth but, just two days later, a letter arrived from Elmer:

August 3, 1963
Hi Flash,

*Was it fun on the plane? I hope you've made it OK and
your apartment is nice. Is Carol showing you all
around? It must be beautiful there. Nothing much has
happened here, but you just left 3 hours ago so I guess
not much could happen. I miss you already. Your little
brother is already talking about taking over your
room! Ha!*

*Have fun but not TOO much! How are your
roommates? Tell Carol Hi for me.*

Love,
Wiggle Bear

Tilly was delighted to get a letter from Elmer even
though there wasn't any real news in it, and she
chuckled at the fact that she had answered some of his
questions before she had gotten the letter containing
them. Nevertheless, it was sweet that he wrote it as
soon as he got home from seeing her off at the airport.
She especially missed him at night, and it didn't help
that she could hear Carol and Hub pleasing each in the
adjacent bedroom.

The next few weeks, before the beginning of the semester, were thrilling and eye-opening for Tilly. Carol took her to the places young people in San Francisco hung out and introduced her to the latest incarnation of the Bohemian lifestyle that had been alive in San Francisco since the Gold Rush.

Carol also introduced Tilly to their upstairs neighbors, a white couple and a black couple, who were sharing the apartment. They were friendly and fun; it was only after Carol, Tilly, Hub, and Gary invited them over for dinner one evening that Tilly realized what everyone else knew and took for granted — that the two men were lovers, as were the two women. Tilly had never met anyone who was an acknowledged homosexual before, and she found their relationships surprising yet fascinating. Tilly chalked this up as another thing she had to learn here; don't apply stereotypes to people's relationships!

On Sunday, Tilly sat down to write Elmer about a selection of her latest adventures. Her letter included surprising details about their apartment and the Haight-Ashbury neighborhood and its denizens. She left out some details that she thought might upset him but threw in just enough to tease him a little about her male roommates and the sleeping arrangements, and signed with love, and hugs and kisses.

Tilly was, by now, well into her crash course on the San Francisco lifestyle! She was beginning to get used to the idea of seeing people her age, men and women, on the street or in the park dressed in loose, colorful clothing, smoking marijuana, and dancing in public. She definitely had never encountered any of these behaviors in South Branch! Tilly tried to keep an open mind about activities that were common here but would get someone arrested in South Branch. Still, seeing people smoking pot in public, or the idea of going naked on the beach would take some getting used to.

Elmer's next letter arrived on the following Saturday:

August 12

How was your visit to Golden Gate Park? Is it a big park? Is it next to the Golden Gate Bridge or what? It's so boring here without you! We've started working on a new garage for one of your old neighbors. Nothing is less interesting than building a garage. Whatever I end up doing for a career, it won't be building garages!

Eddie and I went to see the movie The Birds – it was scary! These birds start attacking everybody for no reason! Have you been to Bodega? Don't go there! I don't think it's that far from San Francisco, near the coast. And if you go outside and see lots of birds, go back inside!

Love,

Wiggle Bear

PS: Calamari is SQUID? Barf!

Tilly was a little disappointed in the lack of content in Elmer's letter, but she realized that nothing much happened in South Branch so there wouldn't be too much to talk about. Still, Elmer could have filled the extra space with romantic pronouncements or sexy innuendos, but maybe she just needed to encourage him a little. And she liked showing off how "California" she was becoming, even though it would take her a while to develop a serious taste for squid!

The chilly summer of San Francisco began to give way to a perfect fall: warm, sunny and delightful. Since Carol had first mentioned the idea, Tilly had been a little nervous about the prospect of going to a nude beach, an outing that she knew her new friends would invite her to on the first warm day. And with the weather warming up, there had been talk about going soon. Along with her nervousness, Tilly felt a little thrill. What could be more symbolic of leaving South Branch than going naked in public on the beach! If everyone else was naked, wouldn't you feel out of place if you had clothes on? And, of course, even though she loved Elmer, it couldn't hurt to study how he measured up to dozens of other beautiful naked men could it?

On the other hand, even though Tilly had not been

overly modest by Iowa standards, the idea of being naked in broad daylight with dozens of strangers seemed not only potentially embarrassing but somewhat creepy as well. Wouldn't people be having sex everywhere she looked? And what if all the other girls looked better than she did? And wouldn't they get arrested? Tilly could just imagine the local reaction if it were reported in the *South Branch Sentinel* that she had been arrested for indecent exposure out in California! She casually brought this up with Carol who assured her they wouldn't get arrested since they always went to Devil's Slide, a private beach, and that after a few minutes she would forget all about being naked and just enjoy the freedom of being outside with nothing on. She suggested to Tilly that she bring an old swimsuit; if she didn't feel comfortable getting naked at first, she could stay dressed or put the suit on.

"Tilly, this is California in 1963. You're free to do whatever you want to. If you want to put on a bathing suit you won't be the only one. But I'll bet you'll love the freedom of going naked outdoors," Carol told her. "Besides, it will give us a head start in anatomy class when school starts!"

The nude beach outing did seem interesting, and she was definitely "tripping out" on the freedom that California seemed to offer. The custom around the apartment was that, at a minimum, everyone wore underwear when they were in the common areas of the dwelling and, after a momentary catch of her breath the first time she saw Gary in his white cotton briefs, these occurrences became completely unremarkable. Nevertheless, Tilly had not yet begun to feel comfortable letting the boys silently critique her figure in nothing but her bra and panties, so she always threw a long T-shirt on over her underthings when on her way to the bathroom.

That bit of decorum would not apply at a nude beach, however. She decided to distract herself from worrying about this by writing to Elmer about Golden Gate Park and the prevalence of pot, throwing in a note about their plan to explore Devil's Slide Beach. Tilly decided against including the detail that their destination was a nude beach, and that their two male roommates would be going too. He was probably still getting used to the idea that his girlfriend was sharing an apartment with two men!

Sure enough, on Thursday the weather was beautiful and warm, and the foursome decided to head down to Devil's Slide Beach. Tilly was cautiously agreeable, although she couldn't help but wonder if the name "Devil's Slide" came from the potential slide of the naked beachgoers into the arms of the devil!

Despite her uncertainty, Tilly was bubbling with excitement when they parked the car and started down the dirt path toward the ocean. The beach was large and stunningly beautiful. To Tilly's surprise, even on a Thursday afternoon there were dozens of people there, most of whom were completely au naturel. The bathers consisted primarily of young people, but there was also a variety of families, mothers with kids, and older couples. Two or three fully dressed middle-aged men sat on the bluff above, forlornly observing the festivities.

Everyone on the beach seemed to be having a great time and Tilly began to relax and contemplate how natural she was willing to get. In the years since she was a small child, Tilly had seen exactly one man naked: her high school boyfriend, Elmer. And, in all those years, he was the only man who had seen her naked. Elmer seemed to like her body well enough, but for some reason the opinion of strangers seemed important to her at that moment, and she worried they would not give her perfect a 10 as Elmer seemed to.

Carol, Hub, and Gary spread out their towels and undressed without hesitation, as though it was the most natural thing in the world. Tilly stood awkwardly holding her towel and noted that Gary and Hub seemed to have no interest in watching her undress. To her chagrin, she found this disinterest in her potential nudity a little insulting. She also wondered why neither of the men had an erection since they were already in the company of dozens of undressed members of the opposite sex. Thinking back, she couldn't remember ever seeing Elmer naked when he DIDN'T have an erection. Tilly surreptitiously checked out the two men. Their sexual equipment seemed perfectly acceptable, not that she anticipated making any use of it, but there was no way she could compare them to Elmer since she had never seen him flaccid, as they were.

Tilly looked at Carol, who motioned for her to lay her towel next to her. Tilly did so, then stood next to the towel awkwardly. She had avoided comparing her figure to Carol's up until now, but her cousin's figure didn't seem particularly superior to her own. For that matter, her fellow beachgoers were for the most part completely average. Some were better-looking than others of course, but no one, apart from perhaps the lonely older men on the bluff, was focused on this characteristic. Everyone was just enjoying the beach, with or without swimming suits.

With this unexpected observation, coupled with the tranquil mood of the scene, Tilly's caution evaporated and she undressed, capping off her new declaration of freedom by throwing her panties into the air, intending to catch them on the descent, but having to chase them for ten yards when the wind caught them. She ran after them, her breasts swinging haphazardly, a feeling she had never experienced before. She had never felt so uninhibited and, when she retrieved the unruly undies, she held them up like a victory flag. When she returned, her friends applauded her successful effort.

Tilly lay back on the towel. She felt the warmth of the sand on her back, and the sun on her bare breasts. She closed her eyes and imagined all the nearby men secretly admiring her exposed charms. Tilly found this wonderfully erotic, a source of sexual arousal that she had never thought about. She could just imagine the reaction of the people back home, including her parents, if they could see her now. She wasn't too sure about Elmer.

"I'm not sure he would be up for this!" she thought.

On Monday, she got a somewhat "newsier" letter from Elmer:

August 21

You've only been in San Francisco three weeks even though it feels like three years! Don't tell me you're going to come home as a Beatnik! That will sure make a splash in South Branch Ha Ha! I'm not even sure what a Beatnik is but I hope you don't turn into one! Everything is still very boring here, but not for everybody I guess – it turns out Margery from our South Branch High biology class is preggers. I wonder what got into her! Ha Ha! It's the big summer scandal right now! I guess she and Todd were studying late last spring and learned more biology than they bargained for. They should have done more book learning and less hands-on practicing, I guess. They're getting married on Labor Day, but I suppose her personal labor-day will be around Christmas! I wonder if the kid will come out gift wrapped!

I really miss you! There are three weeks until I head to college – and I'm sort of looking forward to it. I don't know if I'm excited about going to college, but I can't wait to get out of South Branch.

I love you!

Tilly loved Elmer too! She had been too busy learning her way around and getting acquainted with her new friends to think much about the absence of Elmer and the dearth of sex she had been experiencing over the last three weeks. But the trip to Devil's slide and the letter from Elmer reminded her she would have to take care of herself in this regard for the next few months, until she went home to enjoy Elmer's company at Christmas. Suddenly, Christmas seemed far off, and she experienced an urgent need to please herself at the next opportunity. Tilly had rarely needed to take care of this on her own while she and Elmer were intimate nearly every day, but she began looking forward to enjoying the pleasure of masturbating without having to amuse Elmer as well.

After dinner, the foursome gathered in the living room as usual, to talk, drink wine, and, with the exception of Tilly, smoke pot. It was common for Hub and Carol to head for the bedroom early, even if they had dashed in for a quickie during the day, and once they finished in the bathroom, Tilly excused herself to "read" in bed. By the time she had finished her bathroom tasks, Carol and Hub already had a good start on their evening's pleasure and they never seemed to have sex with each other quietly, so their yelps, moans, and grunts of pleasure encouraged Tilly to please herself as vigorously as she wished.

Tilly possessed a menagerie of fantasies, nearly all of which featured Elmer in a starring role, and which involved replaying things they had done together. She quickly thumbed through the catalog and chose one of her favorites, the first time Elmer had made her come. Tilly removed her clothes sensuously as though she was teasing Elmer, then chose as her nightwear a long T-shirt and a pair of light blue cotton panties. This would allow her to remove them slowly as Elmer had done on the night last year in his truck after they had gone skinny-dipping that afternoon.

Tilly turned off the light, allowing the moonlight that made it down the small airshaft between the buildings to provide the dim illumination, and slipped into bed. On that summer evening, after they had seen each other naked for the first time at the swimming hole, she had pulled Elmer's pants down to mid-thigh in the truck and slowly stroked his penis, contemplating how strange and curious penises were. She began softly touching her belly and thighs as she remembered his rigid cock and the droplet of wetness that she could feel oozing from the tip. She had been sure she was about to find out what a boy's ejaculation was like, but as she gently stroked him, causing him to shiver and begin panting like he had just run a mile, he suddenly stopped her with the strange explanation that he liked it too much.

After a time, he had turned his attention to her, and after a few preliminary explorations, pushed her shorts and panties down to her ankles and began roughly thrusting his fingers in and out of her vagina. This was unpleasant and she wondered where he had gotten the idea that this was what girls liked. But once she placed her hand over his and showed him how to move his fingers very slowly up and down between her labia, essentially demonstrating how to masturbate her, he got the idea and brought her to a quiet but spectacular climax, her first time with a boy.

As she chuckled to herself that Elmer didn't even know what had happened at the time, she eased her T-shirt up around her neck, softly rubbing her nipples and enjoying the cool feeling of wetness beginning to saturate her panties. She now placed her free hand over her pubic mound and let the tip of her middle finger softly massage her clitoris through the silky garment. It had been too long, and she was reminded of how beautiful it was to feel this aroused and to take care of yourself.

Tilly was briefly startled by a squeal of pleasure from Carol in the next room just as she slipped her hand down inside her panties. Her hand became Elmer's hand as she slid her fingers along and across her slippery clit, making a marvelous mess of her panties. After a time, the panties became too restrictive and she threw off the sheet covering her and slipped them down around one ankle, then flipped them across the room with her foot. This allowed her to move her legs involuntarily as she approached her first orgasm in several weeks. She wrapped her legs around Elmer, in the form of her pillow who was now on top of her face and chest and as she imagined his climax, she joined him in a shivery and possibly vocal finale.

As Tilly recovered, she became aware of Carol and

Hub giggling in the next room and wasn't sure whether it was due to their own pleasure or if she had been squealing or calling out Elmer's name as she came.

"Oh well, it's not like they haven't kept me awake now and then."

Tilly curled up with her pillow and gripped the tangled blankets between her legs as she floated off into a dream about showing Elmer off at a nude beach someday.

Tilly wrote back to Elmer the next morning, expressing surprise about their friend's pregnancy and noting that she and Elmer had been lucky to avoid that outcome after forgetting to use protection a few times themselves. She included a teasing line about her own recent shocking behavior, which she didn't describe in detail, and expounded on how excited she and Carol were to be starting classes the next week.

Two weeks after the nude beach outing, classes started for Tilly and Carol. The night before, Hub entertained them with a bongo solo, and Gary read a toast he had written in their honor, as they sipped a few celebratory glasses of wine:

"As you two callipygian pigeons fly off to constellate outside the warm and comforting walls of apartment 2A, may you take with you enough nuggets of nugacity to counteract the flapdoodle of this crazy world of rules and

fools!

Tilly, our beautiful new friend – stay calm amidst the cacophony!

Carol, our beautiful old friend – hang on to your love of life through the uproar!

May you fly back home every night to an aerie where you can throw off the shackles and remind yourselves to be yourselves. Bring your newfound treasures home with you – we could all use more magic!"

Tilly didn't have a dictionary at hand, so she didn't know the meaning of every word, but she got the idea and was touched by the thought behind it and the obvious affection her new friends had for her.

As her classes got under way, Tilly once again experienced the thrill of taking a big step toward becoming a grownup – and as usual, it was accompanied by a hint of nervousness. She and Carol's fellow students represented a wide variety of nationalities, races, and cultures. Discussions outside of class with their new peers were interesting to Carol, who had grown up in San Francisco, but were a revelation to Tilly. South Branch was not at all diverse and she was fascinated with the new information, ideas, and customs she was hearing about from her new friends.

Tilly was amazed, and more than a little hesitant, about some of the ideas that these new friends espoused, but they all seemed smart and worldly, and she took everything in, testing her Iowa ideas against these new outlooks. Their outing to a nude beach had turned out to be fun, and her friends were right. She did feel free and, although she wouldn't be reporting the event in any detail to her mother, or her boyfriend, it seemed harmless enough.

Carol and Tilly spent a significant amount of time studying, especially at first as they were getting to know the system, but there was plenty of time for fun too. None of the roommates had an oversupply of money, so they didn't eat in restaurants often, but they sometimes indulged in a meal at the "US Restaurant" (about as ITALIAN as a restaurant could be), where you could live it up for under a dollar or have a burger further down Columbus Avenue at Clown Alley. South Branch had nothing like either of these and Tilly felt herself falling in love with nearly everything about her new town.

Before long, another letter came from Elmer:

September 3

Have fun in your classes! It will be nice to have Carol with you so you can figure it out together.

My folks are taking me up to State College on September 14. Classes start the next week, but I don't know when. I guess I should figure it out soon huh?

So – as soon as you're out of my sight, you start
studying the "anatomy" of muscle men at the beach?
And I haven't so much as looked at another girl since
you left! Of course, once you left South Branch, there
was no one left in town worth looking at so …

That just makes me miss you even more! Seriously, I
don't think you'll become a drug addict, but I hear a
little experimenting can lead to hard drugs without
you being aware of it – don't do that!

Tilly was excited to tell Elmer about her classes and
wrote back the next day to tell him how much she loved
her classes and all the new ideas she was hearing from
the wide diversity of people she had met.

On the weekends, the four roommates enjoyed
hitting the road in Carol's VW Beetle, and while the
weather was still warm, they planned to explore every
beach within fifty miles of San Francisco. Even though
it was the custom to wear swimming attire on most
beaches, Tilly was amazed that many beaches were so
large that if the roommates walked a quarter mile
beyond the more crowded sections, the few people in
evidence were usually nude. On one of these trips, they
explored Point Reyes, a vast, windswept area north of
San Francisco dotted with dairy farms and spectacular
beaches. Abbotts Lagoon and Kehoe Beach became their

favorites and if they walked north a short distance, they found themselves the only occupants of miles of spectacular beach front. Everyone loved the feeling of being alone in these places, and no one, including Tilly, saw any reason to keep their clothes on. Her roommates didn't find the experience unusual, but Tilly was abuzz with her new freedom and compared it favorably with her outdoor experiences in Iowa.

Finally, in mid-September, Elmer arrived at State College and wrote to Tilly about it:

September 14, 1963

Hi Flash,

I'm glad you're having fun in San Francisco, but not too much fun, I hope! I just arrived today – mom, dad, and Alex drove me down, well, Alex wasn't driving of course. Ha Ha. I miss you too! It's been 41 days since you left, and I think about you every day. And every night, ha, ha!
I guess I'm looking forward to classes starting next Tuesday but I'm a little nervous about how hard it's going to be. Especially if I'm thinking about you all the time. Anyway, I can't wait to see you at Christmas time!

My roommate seems nice but I'd rather you were my
roommate!

Love,
Wiggle Bear

By now, Tilly was an old hand at college life, and she was excited for Elmer to experience the same widening of perspective that she had encountered. She knew he was smart enough to succeed, but she wouldn't have described him as "scholarly" and hoped he'd become as engaged in broadening his knowledge and exploring new ideas as she was. She wrote to him on the 22nd, inquiring about his classes and the new people he was meeting at State College.

Elmer had written to her the same day she wrote to him, and his letter arrived four days later:

September 22. 1963
I've had 4 days of classes and I'm already 3 days
behind. OK, maybe it isn't that bad.
I'm getting to know my roommate a little, but he's a
brainy type and spends most of his time studying – I
suppose I should do the same. On the other hand, I like
sitting around with the other guys in the dorm
shooting the breeze. We get together in somebody's

room and talk about our old girlfriends mostly. Some
of these guys were a lot crazier than we were if they're
telling the truth, which is questionable. I don't brag on
you too much, I just smile and get a hard-on. I hope
none of YOUR roommates are reading this! Ha Ha!

I Love you,
Wiggle Bear

Tilly didn't find this too encouraging and was slightly annoyed that Elmer was spending his time bragging about her, instead of taking advantage of the new opportunities before him. She was a little flattered and a little embarrassed about the topic of Elmer's discussions with his buddies, but she began to fear that the State College of Iowa wasn't as lively and forward looking as the University of San Francisco!

Both Tilly and Elmer were busy by now and it was almost two weeks before Tilly heard from Elmer again:

October 2, 1963
OK, I survived the first month of college. I'm getting
into the swing of college life, hanging out, bull
sessions, parties and, oh yeah, studying. I've been
thinking back to 2 years ago when we had our first
date. I still can't believe I got up the nerve to call you
but I'm sure glad I did! Especially when you grabbed

my dick halfway through the movie, whatever it was. I
knew right then that you were the girl for me!

Tilly continued to parse Elmer's letters carefully for hints at how serious he was going to be about college. For the first time, she began to feel a hint of concern about the future of their relationship. She loved him of course, and love conquers all, but it dawned on her that by the end of four years of quite different experiences they might no longer have that much in common.

Tilly wrote to him to encourage him to keep up with his classes and suggested that it would be hard to catch up if he fell behind. She also teasingly reminded him that their first date was to see the movie "Blue Hawaii" and to deny, once again, that she had deliberately fondled his genitals during the movie but noted that he didn't object when she did it a few months later.

She got Elmer's response on October 21:

October 16
Dear Tilly,
I just saw my first Halloween decorations of the year
here. It appears that Halloween is a big deal at State
College of Iowa! I might go as a pirate – I probably
still have my old Pirate costume – I don't think it was
too badly damaged when you pushed me off the porch
a couple of Halloweens ago.

Do you still have your fangs? You should wear them to
dissuade any guys who might want to kiss you!
I hope you're still having fun but not overdoing it on
the Halloween parties!

Love,
Elmer

Tilly chuckled about what was shaping up to be a rousing Halloween in San Francisco. She wondered what people would wear on Halloween since they appeared to her to be in exotic costumes every day. The decorations were minimal, but the parties were outrageous. Tilly covered this phenomenon in a brief note to Elmer on the 21st.

A letter from Elmer arrived a few days later:

October 25
Dear Tilly,
Today was the first big mid-term in English. We had
to write an in-class essay on the most exciting thing
that happened to us in the last year! I had several ideas
and you were the central character in all of them! But
none of them were appropriate for an English class
essay! So, I wrote about going to St. Louis to see the
Christmas decorations last winter. I was a virgin then,

remember? I really wanted to write about Christmas day when your family was in Chicago and you and I were in your bed! But I thought my hand might be shaking too much to write!

OK, now I'm really missing you. I hope you're behaving yourself and won't be doing anything too scary on Halloween!

Love, Elmer

Whatever concerns Tilly had about Elmer's activities, or lack of activities at State, she loved remembering the excitement of their first months together as a couple, not to mention all the other firsts they delighted each other with. This nostalgic indulgence, aided by Elmer's letter, put her into a very romantic and melancholy mood, especially since everyone around her in San Francisco was involved in a romantic and sexual relationship, while her romantic partner was two thousand miles away. She settled in on Halloween night and wrote Elmer a long, romantic letter, then snuggled in with her pillow, wishing it were Elmer.

Over time, both had become used to the routine of school, study, and outings with their new friends and were busy digesting new ideas and learning to live away from home. They missed each other, but there were plenty of things going on to distract them from dwelling on it. Tilly was always delighted to get letters from

Elmer, although she had noticed that Elmer's letters were written in a somewhat "rural" tone that she hadn't noticed before.

Time flies when you're having fun, and time was flying for Tilly! As the weather became rainy and cool, the roommates spent more time together, often discussing philosophy or politics. Both Hub and Gary were from Southern California, and both had friends in Los Angeles and San Diego so, as complaints about the rain came up, a plan to vacation together in the summer by driving down the coast gradually took shape. Tilly had never been to Los Angeles, a mythical place for many in the Midwest, and she was anxious to go. Her roommates thought it would be fun, and it would be an essential kindness to introduce their untraveled friend to the pleasures of the coast and points south; after a while, it was taken for granted that the trip would be an exciting part of their summer of 1964.

Hub's band sometimes played for tips at local drinking establishments and Gary began self-publishing his poetry by giving away mimeographed copies of his work. By now, the foursome thought of themselves as a family, and this resulted in an obvious increase in the understanding they showed for each other, as well as an increase in friendly arguments around household tasks. Their increased familiarity with each other sharpened their teasing and lessened their cautions about touching one another affectionately or dashing into the bathroom without clothing.

By Thanksgiving, the weather in San Francisco had turned rainy and chilly. Tilly laughed at her roommates who wrapped up in sweaters and down jackets when the temperature dipped below 60, while it was below zero in Iowa. On the other hand, it was chilly inside the apartment too, unlike Iowa where houses were frequently overheated in the winter, so the roommates often looked like monks as they moved around, clothed in a heavy blanket from head to toe.

Tilly and Carol spent Thanksgiving in Berkeley with Carol's mom and after they returned to the apartment, Tilly called Elmer on the phone when she knew he would be home. They talked about the biggest national news of the year, the Kennedy assassination; Tilly was distraught about the event; Elmer was surprised it happened but not greatly concerned. They shared inconsequential information about their activities, expressed their love for each other, and looked forward to reconnecting at Christmas. The phone call had a slight tenor of former lovers who reconnect and experience a brief period of uncertainty as to the intensity of their current relationship. This gradually disappeared during the call and their customary intimacy returned although Tilly couldn't become too verbally graphic about their activities of last summer because her roommates were nearby.

Christmas 1963

Tilly had planned to come home for Christmas and Elmer was anticipating a private, romantic, reunion. He was disappointed when this plan was dropped due to the cost of flying and an unusually cold and snowy December in Iowa, which made flying problematic.

As a Christmas present, Elmer sent her a T-shirt from the "State College of Iowa" that was far too big for her and which she used around the apartment as a humorous night shirt and cover-up. Hub and Gary made gentle fun of her when she wore her "Iowa" shirt, usually by humming the line "they all ran after the farmer's wife" from the "Three Blind Mice" nursery rhyme, but both Hub and Gary always made sure to mention that it made her look sexy in spite of the logo.

The roommates had, by Christmas, developed an affectionate, teasing, and flirtatious relationship with each other, and the teasing, when it came to Tilly, usually involved a reference to her Iowa roots and how hot the "farmer's wife" was. Tilly was not embarrassed about her home state and correctly took their teasing as a sign of affection. Now and then, when she was in a playful mood, she would suggest that she'd "cut off their tails" if they DIDN'T chase her! Without any particular discussion or intention, Tilly's San Francisco nickname became "Iowa". This seemed to fit, and Tilly rather liked it because she didn't mind representing an exotic locale like Iowa among her friends.

She had gotten Elmer a Christmas present too – a necklace featuring a number of medallions etched with depictions of San Francisco landmarks. By this time, Tilly had gotten used to seeing men wearing necklaces and thought it would look sexy on him. She knew that

that would be a new look for a man in Iowa, but she imagined, incorrectly, that Elmer could wear it and teach conservative Iowa about the new fashion in men's jewelry. Elmer thanked her for the gift but hid it in the bottom of his sock drawer and never wore it.

Although Tilly missed Elmer, in truth she was not too disappointed to stay in San Francisco over Christmas, even though it didn't feel like Christmas. There was no snow, and the day was bright and sunny. But it would be cold in Iowa and she didn't look forward to answering questions about her living situation or new friends in San Francisco. The roommates put up a tiny tree and shared gag gifts with each other. The house gift was a bottle of wine that was modestly higher quality than "Red Mountain" and the four finished the bottle while singing Christmas carols off key. Tilly's roommates enjoyed smoking marijuana now and then, and once the wine was finished, Hub produced a "lid" of grass and rolled a joint as a continuance of the Christmas celebration. Tilly had, so far, opted out of participating in this unlawful ritual, but her roommates indulged in pot smoking a few times a week and, as far as she could tell, apart from making them hungry and relaxed, none had suffered any ill effects or taken up the use of hard drugs. Of course, her friends always invited her to join them, but they didn't want to make her uncomfortable by pushing her to indulge. This afternoon, the same invitation was issued and Tilly, slightly tipsy from the wine and in love with the world, her friends, and San Francisco, decided to join in. They instructed her in the technique and, after a few tries, Tilly was able to indulge without coughing. At first, she didn't see any difference in her mental state, but after finishing half a bag of potato chips, and beginning to giggle and dance around her friends, she thought perhaps the marijuana was having a small effect after all. She noticed a feeling of exhilaration and an enhanced awareness of how much she loved her friends and decided that pot wasn't the evil drug it was reported to be.

The eventful Christmas celebration was reprised in the apartment a few days later on a rainy New Year's Eve and the group, in their relaxed mode, began joking about the idea of New Year's resolutions. Various indecent propositions were floated about the kind of pleasurable trouble two men and two women could get themselves into together, but this, while tempting, was a bit too far out for Tilly. And Gary, whose girlfriend Nama was spending the holidays in Southern California felt that he should remain faithful to her, at least for now, so any suggested scandalous shenanigans were tabled for future consideration. When this discussion concluded, Hub and Carol, who had undressed each other under the blanket on the mattress they were sharing, arose and departed for their bedroom, attempting unsuccessfully to cover their nakedness while under way with the uncooperative blanket.

When Tilly and Gary had finished laughing at the

chaotic spectacle of their naked roommates attempting to walk while "embracing" and, at the same time remain covered with a blanket that kept falling off, their conversation returned to New Year's Resolutions. Gary was an artist as well as a poet, and he encouraged Tilly to get a sketchbook and resolve to use it to keep a journal of her thoughts and to begin drawing as a means of encouraging herself to look closely at things. She knew that Gary was rarely seen without his sketchbook nearby and she decided this would be a useful and fun habit.

The roommates hadn't gotten Christmas presents for each other officially, but Gary had, in an attempt to help Tilly understand his curious poetry, gotten her a copy of "Octopus Frontier", a book of curious poetry by Gary's friend, Richard Brautigan. Tilly found most of it silly or indecipherable, but she was curious about it and asked Gary to explain what the poems were about. Gary told her he had no idea what his friend's poems were about, but he offered to read some of his own.

"I'd like that!" she said.

Gary picked up his sketchbook and thumbed through it.

"How about this one?

"We wake up cold and shivering. We wrap up in each other and now we're shivering again."

"What do you think?"

"It sounds like the relationship is fading and you didn't make each other warm enough. Is that the idea?" Tilly asked.

"That's one possibility. Or maybe we were shivering with desire!"

"Wow. That's simple but it makes a person think!"

"That's the idea!" Gary said. "Want to hear one I wrote about you?"

Tilly was flattered and very curious. "Sure!" she said.

"I hear you talking in your sleep. You're giggling about something and I hear the word 'Iowa'."

"Why was I giggling?" Tilly asked.

"You tell me, you were the one who found something about Iowa funny!"

"Or sweet!" Tilly said.

"I love your poetry, Gary," Tilly told him. "I've always thought of poetry as basically nursery rhymes, kind of silly and shallow. But yours are very thought provoking."

It was a chilly night, and they pulled a blanket around them and began a long conversation about poetry, life, and love. Tilly was amazed at Gary's wide knowledge on many subjects and his ability to put forth philosophical questions and provide arguments for each side. She was not used to conversations that were as richly challenging as this and she loved Gary's scholarly bent and his ability to think critically about many subjects.

"These discussions traditionally conclude with wine!" he told her, getting up and going into the other room to retrieve a moderately expensive bottle of wine he had been hiding in his closet. They didn't have any official wine glasses on the premises, but Gary brought in a couple of ordinary drinking glasses from the kitchen. They sipped the wine, which was much better than their usual stock and twisted their legs together under the blanket for still inadequate warmth.

Both were horny as minks, but Tilly still felt her relationship with Elmer was only in a pause because they were both so busy. And she thought it was too soon to jump into bed with another man, but she knew her patience would run out before long. Gary felt somewhat the same about Nama, but he had a feeling she would be taking up with an old boyfriend and staying in LA after the holidays were over. As it was, they finished the bottle of wine and nearly went to sleep on the sofa snuggled together under a mound of blankets. It was too cold to really sleep, and after a while, Tilly unsteadily got to her feet and headed for the bedroom.

"Going to bed?" Gary mumbled.

"Yes, and you're coming with me," she said. "But just to be clear, you're not COMING with me. It's just too cold to leave you out here and we'll both be warm if we take this blanket into my bed and add it to the supply."

Gary was too cold to put up an argument, which would have only been perfunctory anyway, and they wobbled off to bed. As much as each wanted to stay awake and consider the precedent they might be setting and the future implications of enjoying each other's company, clad in their underwear under a pile of blankets, each went right to sleep. This led to a slightly embarrassing moment the next morning when each discovered they weren't in bed alone, but both laughed out loud when Gary said, "I'd like to stay and wiggle around in bed with you, but I have to get up and write a poem about a man with an awkward but understandable erection."

Tilly regarded the protrusion under his briefs as he got out of bed. "You'd better get started. I imagine that poem will require a long, hard effort!"

Winter 1964

In mid-January, Carol and Tilly began their second semester of nursing school. Both were excited, because they would be getting actual hospital experience for the first time, working with patients, and seeing how the world of medicine really worked. They were also busy with friends, poetry readings, concerts and the beginnings of political activism. Tilly, who, like Elmer, had not given politics a lot of thought, was becoming aware of the world situation and the underlying unfairness of the American political system. Judging from Elmer's letters, and things she had read, her Midwest friends were still unaware of and uninterested in the shortcomings of democracy as practiced in America.

To Tilly's surprise and delight, the rain turned the city green and verdant; flowers began blooming in February. Tilly, in her occasional letters to Elmer or calls to her parents, innocently mentioned how beautiful the flowers were, pretending not to know that the temperature was below zero in Iowa. Visits to the beach were on hold until late spring, but the music scene in San Francisco was bubbling and Hub, who kept careful track of the latest news on this topic, kept them informed about the latest inventions and the current concerts, many of which they attended. Tilly, who had not been a close follower of popular music before she came to San Francisco, was amazed and delighted by what she began to realize was a new generation of musicians that would change the music scene far into the future. She began to drop the names of upcoming bands in letters to Elmer, as though everyone knew about these new sounds, but, while she told herself she was teasing him, she was, in some way, showing off how "with it" she was, in comparison to hopelessly uninformed Midwesterners. She pictured Elmer as unchanged since she had last seen him, but these tiny cuts were gradually communicating the slow dissolution of their relationship.

After a brief flurry of flirtatious letters back and forth around Valentine's Day she hadn't been motivated to write to Elmer. She always seemed to have something else she had to do, or she simply forgot to write him when she had a free moment, after which she always felt a little guilty.

Tilly masturbated regularly, especially when Carol and Hub were loudly getting it on. She noticed to her surprise that she now fantasized about more than just remembrances of things she had done with Elmer. These days she imagined having sex with Gary, or even joining Carol and Hub in their bed. She didn't remember turning away from her earlier fantasies and wondered how long she had been masturbating without imagining Elmer as her partner. She hadn't had sexual relations with Elmer, or anyone else, for six months, and she wondered for the first time how long she could resist what seemed like attractive opportunities. If Nama didn't come back from LA, or even if she did, Gary might be a candidate for the role of "intimate friend", or perhaps some of the men in her classes would like to try a roll in the hay, Iowa style. Tilly had also begun to notice, especially after their nude beach adventures and the increasing casual approach to nudity around the apartment, that she was somewhat turned on by exhibitionism. Her bedroom window looked out into an air shaft that was shared with the building next door, and although the neighboring apartment didn't offer a view directly into her bedroom, someone there could, if they moved to the right position, look down through the upper corner of her window onto her bed.

She hadn't seen anyone looking out, but now and then she liked to "accidentally" leave the curtain partially open and imagine that a handsome man was watching her masturbate. And doing the same thing himself.

As if to exaggerate her lack of intimate companionship over many months, Tilly was surrounded by lovers who were outwardly affectionate with each other, especially after a bit of pot, and when Carol and Hub were getting it on in the bedroom next door, Tilly felt sadly left out of the lovemaking. Lovers in the park weren't making a secret of their affection for one another, and the two couples upstairs could hardly make it all the way upstairs before they were all over each other. Gary was waiting for Nama to come back from Los Angeles, so he at least had a possibility. With Elmer's letters diminishing in frequency, which she interpreted as a dwindling of his affection for her, the idea of taking on a new partner seemed more and more acceptable.

Until that happened, Tilly became more creative with her masturbatory fantasies. She had come into contact with new friends who openly discussed sexual subjects that she had never thought about or never even knew about in some cases. The two homosexual couples lived just upstairs, and discussions of multiple partners, orgies, bondage, and sadomasochism were common. Nudity and semi-public sex weren't unheard of in Golden Gate Park, and of course by now she had become an aficionado of nude beaches where she could indulge in exhibitionism without the slightest of guilt feelings.

Spring 1964

By spring, she and Carol were beginning to put some of their learning into practice in a hospital, and to see that their work was helping real people. This was rewarding for both of them. Even though it was not on the curriculum for this semester, the two women read up on sexually transmitted diseases and Carol began taking "The Pill" which at that time was only approved for treating irregular menstrual periods even though its contraceptive function was well known. One of the curious perks of working in a medical setting was that they were able to obtain free condoms – provided as "samples" from supply houses and these were, as a result, never in short supply around the apartment.

Tilly and Gary had developed an increasingly friendly and flirtatious relationship, but Gary was still thinking about Nama, who assured him she was coming back to San Francisco at some point, and Tilly still felt that she and Elmer were a couple even though their connection was gradually unraveling.

The spring brought the rainy season to an end, and the foursome began regular trips to Devil's Slide and other nearby beaches on the rare days when the weather was warm enough. They went roller skating in Golden Gate Park, picnicking in Buena Vista Park, they often spent evenings at Playland at the Beach which was a short drive, or a long walk, away.

All this thrilled Tilly. She loved having sex with Elmer but the general tone surrounding that activity among her Iowa peers had been that it was secret, immoral except in specific circumstances, and something that only bad girls engaged in before they married. And any kind of unusual sex, no matter how harmless and playful, was taboo. In light of her new information and a more relaxed local culture, Tilly began to experiment with everything in her imagination. She fantasized about tying Gary to her bed and having her way with him, and him trying the reverse on her. She imagined both male roommates pleasing her while Carol held her in position. Since fantasy was free, she even tried on the idea of joining the two lesbian girls upstairs and learning how they managed their physical pleasure together.

As wild as Tilly's thoughts had become though, she was still an Iowa girl at heart, and the idea of actually carrying out any of these ideas, apart from taking up with a new man, was still scary and, for that matter, quite unlikely. For now.

One Tuesday in March, when Hub brought the mail upstairs, he flipped Elmer's latest letter to Tilly across the mattress-paved living room of their apartment.

"Here you go Iowa, a letter from 52 Pickup."

"Be nice Hub, he's a sweet boy!"

Tilly crossed her legs, twisted a long strand of brown

hair around her index finger, and leaned back against the wainscot to read Elmer's letter.

Friday, March 13, 1964

Dear Flash,

You must be having a lot of fun in San Francisco – you haven't written me a letter for a month at least! How is school? Is it hard? I'm very busy. I have an Econ test tomorrow, but I keep thinking about you and hoping you're doing OK. I miss you. It's sunny here, but still cold. Can you believe spring is only 8 days away? I can't wait. Mostly I can't wait because that will mean summer is just around the corner and we'll be back in South Branch together for 3 whole months. Did I mention I miss you? I had to get a new battery for my truck; the winter was really bad, and I didn't get to drive it much, so it didn't get charged up like it should have. How is Carol? Tell her "Hi" for me. I hope I get to meet her sometime. Is she showing you all the exciting parts of San Francisco? I hope they aren't TOO exciting, ha, ha. You and Carol are probably hanging out with all those Charles Atlas types at the beach.

I'm learning a lot in my classes! Maybe when we get out of college, I'll go back to South Branch and start a business as a contractor or something. You can be the

*bookkeeper, but it will be a hard job since I'm sure
we'll be millionaires. Or at least thousandaires. We
could build a fancy house down by the creek, maybe
next to the spot where we always go skinny-dipping.
We could just go out the back door and go skinny-
dipping any old time – as long as the kids weren't
watching! Well, I guess I have to get back to economics
if I'm going to get rich. Please write! Even if it's just a
short letter. I really want to know what you're doing
out there! I miss you!*

Love,

Wiggle Bear

"Any big excitement in Iowa?" chuckled Gary.

"Elmer's truck froze to death and he misses me."

"I'll bet he mostly misses your tits!"

"Cut it out, you two!" said Tilly, tearing a blank page
out of her sketchbook.

She took a toke on the joint that Hub handed her,
then passed it to Gary, and began a letter to Elmer:

March 21, 1964

Hi Elmer,

*Sorry I haven't been good about writing to you lately,
but I've been really busy. I started keeping a journal*

but it's mostly little drawings and things. No, you can't see it! It's private and the drawings are not very good anyway, but they express my inner feelings so that makes me happy. I'm finding out lots of cool things; it's so exciting but laid-back too. I mean in school and everything.

Last week we went out for a drive around the city. We stopped at Fisherman's Wharf and looked at the tourists. They are so funny! They think it's going to be warm in San Francisco and they are shivering in Hawaiian shirts and shorts when it's 50 degrees out. I just got the pictures back. Carol, Hub, and I are going to spend the summer driving down the coast to San Diego. We'll camp out and just go wherever we want; it will be so groovy! I think Big Sur is really going to be a blast. Carol has friends in San Diego, so we'll camp out in their backyard whenever we finally get there. I hope the three of us and all our camping gear can fit in Carol's VW Beetle. I'm sure we can squeeze in somehow! It doesn't look like I'll make it back to Iowa this summer, but I'll send you pictures if I can find a drug store to get them developed. I miss you too.

Love, Tilly

Tilly enclosed a photo and sealed the envelope.

Tilly was surprised Elmer didn't respond to this letter, and she saw this slight as just another sign he was losing interest in her.

Summer 1964, Gary

As soon as school was out for the summer, the foursome began serious planning for their summer trip down the coast. The trip would have to be low budget; none of the roommates had an abundance of money, except Hub, who came from a wealthy family. Gary lived hand-to-mouth by selling cartoons and, occasionally, stories to a local newspaper as well as taking other odd jobs now and then. The two girls had money from home, but their allowances weren't lavish. That meant they would be camping, having picnics, and being naked on beaches whenever they could.

Carol's Volkswagen was crowded with just the four roommates, and with even their abbreviated supply of camping gear it was packed. It's so called "trunk" in the front was filled with sleeping bags, the rear seat contained Tilly and Gary as well as clothing and a small tent. Another tent and a small bag of clothing occupied the small space under Hub's legs on the floor in front of the passenger seat.

Their first destination was Santa Cruz where they planned to enjoy the Santa Cruz Beach Boardwalk and find a camping spot somewhere nearby in the evening. The weather was beautiful during the days but chilly at night and on their first night camping, at Monastery Beach, a beautiful and secluded spot south of Carmel, they celebrated the first leg of their journey by building a campfire and drinking wine until singing silly camp songs seemed like a good idea. In keeping with their custom, they doffed their clothes at the beach whenever possible, but once the sun went down, the ocean air became cooler, and they reluctantly got dressed. By bedtime, it had become quite cold, and while each of them had a summer sleeping bag, it became clear that breaking out the tents would be required. Hub and Carol, of course, shared a tent that was designed for a single person, which didn't bother them, but Gary's tent was equally small. It was clear that everyone had to be in a tent, so Gary and Tilly snuggled into his. Rather than each occupying a separate sleeping bag, they decided to unzip both sleeping bags to make two quilt-like blankets, snuggle together in their underwear, and wrap both sleeping bags around them.

"We should meet like this every night!" Gary proposed. He hadn't had sex with another person since Nama had stayed in Southern California after Christmas, and Tilly had done without even longer. Not only that, but she hadn't heard from Elmer for quite some time, and she took this as a sign he no longer cared about her, especially since she had gotten a letter from Linda, her friend from high school, letting her know that Elmer was back in South Branch for the summer and had been seen dining with one of the girls at the Burger Shack on multiple occasions. Maybe he had acquired a new girlfriend and hadn't bothered to tell her about it.

The sounds of lovemaking reached their ears from Hub and Carol's tent.

"Well, I'm still cold, I think it would be appropriate to snuggle together, just for warmth of course," she said with a laugh.

"I'm all for that," Gary said, wrapping his arms and legs around her.

Tilly had been hugged by lots of men over the last year, but never in a situation quite this intimate, and it felt good. Gary was shorter than Elmer, and a bit heavier, but the slight softness of his body felt good and warm against her. They cuddled for some time, involuntarily moving their bodies against each other to enjoy the intimacy and human touch. This wordlessly evolved into a flirtation using only affectionate touches.

"Gary?"

"Hmm?"

"Why are we wasting time not kissing?"

Gary answered this inquiry by rolling over on top of Tilly, taking her face in his hands, and kissing her as though he might never have another opportunity. This immediately exploded into a frenzy of kissing and rubbing of one another's extremities, and, as though the dam had suddenly broken, they quickly moved to fondling, squeezing, and massaging each other's most sensitive areas. Fingers slipped under waistbands, Tilly's bra was magically unfastened, and Gary's erection could be felt against Tilly's thigh.

"Are you going to fuck me right now?" Tilly asked.

"Or are you going to keep me waiting all night?"

"I'd love to fuck you right now, Iowa, but there's a little problem."

"What?"

"I don't have a rubber; you should have told me this was going to happen!"

"I stashed some in the car – I'll go get a dozen or two," Tilly said, laughing.

She wiggled out of the sleeping bag bundle and the tent, feeling Gary's kiss on her belly as she crawled over him, and sprinted stark naked across the beach to where the car was parked. Unfortunately, it was locked; she would have to run back and get the key from Carol. Now freezing, Tilly ran back to the two tents, but from the sounds emanating from Carol and Hub's tent she decided not to interrupt their uncompleted assignation.

Tilly poked her head into Gary's tent. "The car's locked, Gary."

"Damn it!"

"Get ready for plan B," she said, crawling into the tent headfirst and stopping halfway into the tunnel of sleeping bags when her face got to Gary's midsection. Astride her delighted partner in a sixty-nine position, she managed to pull her knees far enough into the tent to get everything but her feet inside while aligning her swollen sex with Gary's tongue.

Their suddenly beneficial friendship began right away and was initiated with two minutes and eighteen seconds of delicious and wiggly oral sex before they both reached convulsive climaxes. Since their mouths had been occupied, the culmination of their first tryst was rather quiet, but when they could move again, Tilly backed out of the tent, kissing Gary and giving him a taste of his own medicine on her way by. Gary followed her outside and they chased each other around the two tents, dancing and yelling nonsense to the dark Pacific Ocean.

They used a stick to enliven the still flickering campfire and were joined by Carol and Hub, who had finished their frolic and were eager to know what was going on. The looks on Tilly and Gary's faces told them everything they needed to know. A joint appeared. Hugs happened. The foursome celebrated being alive together in this place at this moment. Eventually things quieted down, the innuendos and giggling ran their course, everyone realized that sitting by the fire naked only warmed your front half, and the campers returned to their retreats and concluded their first day on the road with goodnight kisses and high hopes.

After that first night at Monastery Beach, Tilly and Gary made sure they had a generous supply of condoms in their possession when they went for a private "walk" down the beach, and when they snuggled together in their zipped-together sleeping bags. As the group made their way south, the nights on the beach got warmer, tents were unnecessary, and, although Tilly was quite hesitant at first, Gary insisted they fuck on top of the sleeping bags. Even though it was night, there was moonlight, and now and then other nighttime beachgoers would happen by, usually pretending not to notice, but sometimes stopping to watch briefly, or encourage them with a delightful or off-color comment. This nearly public lovemaking became a thrill for Tilly who soon embraced the practice since it was very un-Iowa. She also found herself enjoying Gary's sometimes demanding moods, as long as he didn't force her to go beyond her expanding limits.

The trip down the coast continued in slow motion. The foursome would find a nice beach or park, stop for a picnic; then a nap; then a swim; often a sexual romp in the dunes or the woods; drinks, dope, and dinner; and then bedtime.

This continued for several days, and Tilly was introduced to a number of places she had heard of but couldn't place on a map. Some of these places she remembered from movies, and from time to time she felt like a Hollywood celebrity hobnobbing with the rich and famous, although she knew she was neither. San Louis Obispo, Pismo Beach, and Santa Barbara were all exotic places to her, and she enjoyed keeping her friends back in South Branch up to date on her worldly travels.

Occasionally she would send a picture postcard to Elmer, with a detail-free note of the "Having fun in the sun, wish you were here!" variety. Elmer read them, fruitlessly looking for an expression of affection, and then turned his thoughts to the local girl who would soon be supplying HIS summer fun.

Gary and Tilly spent as much time as possible making up for the three months when they could have been having sex together but weren't. In addition to every evening on the beach or in the woods, this included making out in the back seat of Carol's Volkswagen — titillating, and occasionally shocking, the occupants of the front seat.

Tilly had been slow to let go of her Iowa ideas and embrace the San Francisco culture, especially when it came to romantic relationships. But a year had gone by and in Tilly's mind, Elmer had abandoned her. She was ready to leave every scrap and trace and whiff of South Branch behind and join the new age. She had loved San Francisco from the beginning, and now she was ready to make love to it. At first, all the intellectual musicians and poets she came into contact with had seemed a bit too silly, self-important, and serious. Now she began to discover a depth of thinking and understanding that she had missed at first. Their political ideas made sense as she began to pay more attention to the news. And what she first took as a somewhat effeminate style, in contrast to the men she knew in rural Iowa, she now began to see as a confident throwing off of stereotypes and a joyful thoughtfulness and gentleness that would change the world.

She thought of Elmer, formerly the love of her life, tooling around in his old pickup truck, thoughtlessly pounding nails every summer into thoughtlessly designed houses, cruising thoughtlessly through his first exposure to real life, attending to basketball and balderdash, deliberately avoiding any difficult questions and letting any new ideas pass him by.

At first, Tilly had found Gary's poetry silly, but after he had begun to read them to her, and point out the questions they raised, she began to see his writing in a different light. Whenever she and Gary weren't preparing to have sex together, having sex together, or luxuriating in the afterglow of having just finished having sex together, Gary was writing or drawing in his sketchbook. Now his poems were sometimes specifically directed to her; most of these he kept just between them. Gary would memorize and recite these special poems to her out of the blue when they were out of hearing distance of others. Some were so sweet that Tilly was moved to tears. Other times they made her wet between her legs.

During parts of the trip, Carol and Hub felt like parents trying to get their distracted children to look at the spectacular scenery as they were engaged in a game in the back that they found more interesting. Gary cupped his hand around Tilly's ear:

"You're in a teasing mood. I'm trying to cook dinner and you're not helping. You're just arranging pieces of fruit to look like genitalia. You pick up two bananas and nod your head to the side. We'll have dinner later."

Tilly began to giggle. Carol and Hub knew better than to ask why, just smiling at each other.

"WOW! Nothing's nicer than necking naked with a naughty nursing student. I'll be your homework any time, Baby!"

More laughter.

"Come on, you two! Either tell us the joke or enjoy the view of the ocean!"

"WOW! Nothing's nicer than necking naked with a naughty nursing student. I'll be your homework any time, Baby!"

"Okay, that IS funny," Carol, and especially Hub, agreed.

Once the travelers reached Sothern California, they were able to crash in the apartments or camp in the backyards of Hub, Carol, or Gary's friends. One of Hub's friends was staying in his parents' Santa Barbara beach house for the summer, and each couple had their own luxurious bedroom overlooking Santa Barbara and the unpacified Pacific. The roommates stayed for several days and apart from when someone had to venture downtown to resupply the liquor cabinet or during sit-down meals indoors, no one in the household wore clothes during their sojourn in paradise. In fact, after this weekend, Tilly began following the San Francisco custom of going braless nearly all the time, and she often found it convenient to dispense with panties as well since they were in the way of several activities she was becoming especially fond of.

Hub's friend had two perfect female companions living with him and the entire company more or less circulated between bedroom time with their current favorite, swimming or sunning at the pool, or food and intoxicants around dinnertime. Due to the newness of their relationship, Gary and Tilly didn't fully participate in the flirtation and sexual games that often happened on the terrace after dinner, although they liked to retire to their upstairs bedchamber and please each other while observing the festivities from their balcony. All the men, and at least one of the host's girlfriends admired Tilly and, while canoodling with multiple partners seemed like going too far, she loved the attention. Even though she had never been sexually attracted to other women, Tilly did note that having someone who wanted to apply suntan lotion to one's backside, like the host's blond girlfriend insisted on doing for her, would have its advantages. Apparently, there were things girls knew about pleasing one another. Things that no boy she had ever been with was aware of.

Tilly and Gary spent the majority of their time in bed. Now and then, they spontaneously jumped up and chased each other around the bed like five-year-olds, although their motivations were very adult. They imagined themselves lord and lady of the manor, misbehaving in the master bedroom while the servants took care of the remainder of the household. Their bedchamber had a private bathroom and they showered together, staged sword fights with their toothbrushes, and generally verified the delights of living together in a state of playful domesticity.

Naturally they had to rest from their erotic exercise regimen now and then, and during the time outs, Gary was inspired in his writing by the thrill of Tilly. One morning he was busy while Tilly was still sleeping, and he woke her up by whispering in her ear:

"I'm thinking about popcorn while I wait for you to wake up. The flame under me is making me sizzle and wiggle. I'm about to pop thinking about being covered with your warm, salty, butter!"

Tilly climbed on top and turned up the heat. An hour later, Tilly returned to bed after her shower and Gary was ready again:

"Watching you step out of the shower makes me realize the error of Plato's allegory."

"What?" Tilly asked. She knew Plato was an ancient Greek philosopher, but the specific details hadn't been on the curriculum in South Branch.

"As I remember it," Gary told her, "Plato postulated that every object we see is an imperfect example of some underlying perfect form of the object. In his allegory of the cave, he likens us to prisoners in a cave who can never see real objects but only their shadows on the cave walls. But you, Matilda Williams, are the perfect form of the world's most beautiful woman and I can see you! Thus, Plato's theory is disproven."

Tilly was impressed and delighted. She rolled over and kissed the tip of Gary's penis.

"I think you're right; sometimes we can experience the perfect form of physical objects!" Tilly concurred.

Out of nowhere she thought about Elmer and

momentarily wondered if he knew what Plato's "Allegory of the Cave" referred to.

Next up was Santa Monica. The troop planned to stay with Carol's high school friend who was now a student at Santa Monica College. Unlike their Santa Barbara accommodations, she occupied a small two-bedroom apartment. Her roommate was away, so the newly arrived foursome squeezed into the extra bedroom and the living room. Gary and Tilly unrolled their sleeping bags on the living room floor at night and, after putting up with the late bedtime caused by Carol and her friend reminiscing about the old days, made love as quietly as they could once the others had retired. Trying to be quiet was excruciating and delicious but not entirely successful. They enjoyed each other's company as always, and their spontaneous sounds were often camouflaged by the sounds of what seemed to be a continuous party going on upstairs.

They visited the Santa Monica Pier, Muscle Beach, and splurged at a couple of nice restaurants. Tilly made certain to send Elmer a postcard of Muscle Beach to tease him. Or possibly show off her West Coast worldliness. One night, Tilly and Gary walked down to the beach, bought a bottle of wine on the way, and sat by the water in the half moonlight, drinking wine and feeling delicious. Even though there were a few people enjoying the beach, they removed their clothing below the waist – and waded into the water on the assumption that their naked parts couldn't be seen. They slowly and sensuously copulated standing waist deep in the dark water where their lower halves couldn't be seen, and passersby could be expected to assume they were just kissing. They got away with this, although not every passerby was fooled, and they were lucky to find a break in the beachcomber traffic when they could exit the water and restore their lower garments to their original locations. They hugged and giggled all the way back to their sleeping quarters, and this event became legendary between them as their "Muscle Beach Moonlight Moment".

Variations of these experiences reoccurred in Laguna Beach and San Diego. All in all, they were away from San Francisco for over a month. The trip was delightful in every way, especially for Tilly and Gary, whose flirtatious friendship exploded into a full-throttle sexual relationship during the trip. This continued in a somewhat less urgent manner once they got back to their Haight Street apartment, and the apartment now settled into a domestic scene with two romantic and loving couples in residence.

Chapter 2   Fall in Cedar Falls

As Elmer confronted the world
And the flag of his future unfurled
The safety of love
Ceased to fit like a glove
And the fortunes of life tossed and twirled

Fall 1963

Once Tilly had flown off to San Francisco, Elmer felt forsaken. He was mildly excited about going to State College, but the highlights of his existence were Tilly's letters. These he read over and over, parsing them for details of her new home and hints of her enduring affection for him. Since the San Francisco idea had first appeared, Elmer feared she would forget him once she got to the big city.

Elmer had missed Tilly as soon as he saw her get on the airplane and wrote her a letter as soon as he got home asking about how her flight went and how she liked her new apartment. He knew a letter from Tilly would take several days to get to him and if she had written when she first got there, her letter would arrive on Wednesday. By the time it finally arrived on Friday, he was beginning to worry.

August 5, 1963
Hi Wiggle Bear,

As you can see, I made it to sunny California! Flying is so groovy (see, I'm picking up the California lingo already!)

I don't get what makes planes fly, but it's so much fun to look down and see everything so tiny. It sure shows you everything in a very crazy way. You should fly out and visit me! Ha!
Carol picked me up and we drove along the Pacific coast – it's so beautiful. I wish you were here! I miss you!
You wouldn't believe there's a mountain two blocks from our apartment! Carol and I went there today and climbed to the top where you can look out over the whole city. It's really beautiful, I wish I could show it to you! I have to go – Carol is going to take me to Golden Gate Park today!

I love you so much!
XXOO Flash

PS: You'll never guess what I had for supper (I mean dinner) on my first night in San Francisco! Carol fixed Calamari as a "Special Treat!" It tasted OK, but I wish I hadn't known what it was beforehand! I'm going to make you look it up in the dictionary – you'll be shocked! It may take me a while to get used to San Francisco, but I love it so far!

Elmer was thrilled to get Tilly's letter. Even though he knew she loved him, and of course he loved her, he was a little concerned she might just disappear out west. He assumed she had arrived, there hadn't been news of an airplane crash. Still, in the back of his mind, he had worried that she would vanish into thin air in some inexplicable way.

Parsing the contents carefully, Elmer tried to read between the lines of Tilly's note. To begin with, it was shorter than he expected, and she had waited two days to write it. He was anticipating a several page-long letter that outlined her movements and impressions in detail, but this was something she had dashed off quickly, probably between partying with Carol and her friends. Second, while he was interested in her experiences in California, he was considerably more interested in how much she missed HIM. She did mention missing him and all, but he felt a bit let down to find that was not the principal subject of the letter. And his initial reaction to the comment about flying out to see her was to think she was showing off her newfound worldliness. After further consideration though, he decided she was just enthusiastic about air travel and wanted to share it with him.

He decided to wait a day or two before writing back to indicate he wasn't spending every waking minute thinking of her, even though he was. His second letter to Tilly inquired about her visit to Golden Gate Park, which Elmer was unfamiliar with. He reported that he and Eddie had seen the movie "The Birds" and he warned her against traveling to Bodega Bay. He complained about how boring his summer construction job was and, in fact, how boring everything was in South Branch was since she had left for San Francisco. And he expressed a disinclination to try calamari, now that he had looked up what it was!

As he had the previous summers, Elmer had a job with a local contractor in South Branch and this gave him a nice tan and a modestly muscular build, at least as compared to his normal appearance. He thought back to the previous summer when he and Tilly had sneaked into a house he was helping build late one night. They had made love on the plywood floor of the newly framed-in bedroom, christening it before the new owners had a chance to move in. Tilly had loved his muscular body and didn't hesitate to let him know how aroused it made her. Now that Tilly was gone, he felt his daily workouts on the job were wasted, although he did occasionally imagine that there would be girls at the State College of Iowa who would have to deal with their disappointment when they discovered that he had a girlfriend in California. He expected that just the fact that he had a girlfriend who lived in such a place would give him an additional dollop of attractive mystery.

Tilly's next letter arrived a few days later:

August 11, 1963
Hi Wiggle Bear,

I'm having so much fun here! Classes will be starting in a few weeks so that will probably be the end of the fun though! Ha Ha!
It turns out our apartment is in the middle of the Beatnik part of San Francisco. It's certainly a lot different than South Branch that's for sure. Our apartment is on the second floor and we look right down onto Haight Street. People are out there having parties all night long! At least I have a bedroom mostly to myself that's toward the back of the apartment, so the noise doesn't keep me awake.
I like my roommates so far. Hub is Carol's boyfriend (they share a bedroom!) and then there's me and Gary. Don't worry, we don't share a bedroom. He sleeps in the living room.

I love you.
XXOO Flash

Elmer was happy for Tilly and was glad she was having fun in San Francisco. Still, San Francisco didn't seem like Elmer's kind of place at all; people right outside your house partying all night long? And the idea of Tilly living in the same apartment with two young men sounded very ominous. It was inconceivable to Elmer that a woman and man could live together without eventually engaging in sex!

"…and then there's me and Gary!"
"Don't worry, we don't share a bedroom…"

"Sure, but you've only known him a week! What about next week?" Elmer thought.

Elmer had spent a total of one entire night with Tilly during their two-year love affair, and by now she had spent almost two weeks with this muscle-bound stranger!

His mind was on Tilly most of the time, but he was already beginning to feel cautious about what to say to her. Mostly his letters contained themes about wanting to hear from her, how much he missed her, and how bored he was without her! He was a little annoyed and yet envious of her new adventures beyond South Branch without him. And Elmer was afraid Tilly would find his letters boring since there was nothing newsworthy in South Branch. At least his next letter had a bit of South Branch gossip for her; their high school friend Margery was pregnant and would be getting married on Labor Day!

Elmer assured Tilly he missed her and told her he was excited to be leaving South Branch even though he wasn't sure how he would do in college. Meanwhile Tilly had written back before she received this letter:

August 19

Golden Gate Park is a huge park right at the edge of San Francisco near the beach. Some people go there and smoke pot right out in public! No one smokes pot outside our apartment though so don't worry, I'm not going to become a drug addict!

We haven't been to the beach yet because it's been so cold! Can you believe that? It's supposed to be warm soon, and Carol promised to take me to a beach called Devil's Slide when it's warm enough. I was going to buy a new swimming suit, but she told me not to bother. Maybe the styles are the same in California as they are in Iowa.

Love,
Tilly
XXOO

Ten days later Elmer received her response to the gossip letter:

August 27

I can't believe Margery got PREGNANT! I didn't know her that well, but wasn't she awfully religious? I guess it could happen to just about anybody – you and I were mostly careful, but we forgot to use rubbers a few times! That could have screwed everything up, and I don't mean that to be funny!

Speaking of scandal, you would be shocked at how scandalous I was on Thursday! I'm not EVEN going to tell you what I did, but you would have loved being there! No it wasn't anything that could get me pregnant, silly!

Carol and I start nursing school next week! We can hardly wait, especially after we went to the beach Thursday and got a head start on studying anatomy! Oops, I wasn't going to tell you! When do your classes start? Are you excited? Write and tell me all about it. Have fun when school starts!

Love,
Tilly
XXOO

Elmer was happy to get her letter and he was glad she was having fun – although there would have been nothing wrong with finding out she was as miserable about their separation as he was. Of course, he was curious about what scandalous thing she had done on Thursday, but he assumed she was teasing him, and he resolved not to ask what it was. And to be honest, he was a little afraid to find out. Maybe she had gone outside without a bra. Apparently, from what he had heard, that was all the rage in San Francisco.

Elmer wrote back to Tilly on September 3, to let her know that he would be heading up to State College on the 14th. He chastised her for studying the anatomy of men at the beach and assured her he hadn't so much as looked at another girl since she left South Branch.

Elmer's mom helped him pack for college. Apart from a few pencils, his transistor radio, and a toothbrush, he couldn't think of anything he needed. But with his mother helping, it turned out there were several more necessities he would have forgotten otherwise. Everything seemed so complicated and on top of that, he was vaguely worried about Tilly. Finally, a couple of days before he was to leave, a letter from Tilly seemed encouraging about college:

September 7, 1963

Hi Elmer! Classes have started – and it's SO exciting.
This semester we aren't doing anything with patients,
but next semester we'll be going into the hospital and
actually learning from real sick people. As it is, we're

learning the basics and it's so interesting to be
learning how things work in the profession.
I'm meeting lots of new friends from all over and they
have really opened my eyes to lots of things I never
thought about back in Iowa!
Carol and I have a LOT of work to do though, so if I
don't write to you every week, don't worry, I still love
you!

Love,
Tilly
XXOO

September 14, 1963

Elmer's departure from South Branch was less exciting, and less airborne, than Tilly's. Freshmen were not allowed to have vehicles with them on campus the first semester, so with his truck at home for now, his mom, dad, and little brother delivered him to the State College of Iowa on Saturday, September 14th. Elmer was slightly relieved that he didn't begin his college career on Friday the 13th, but this didn't fully eliminate his nervousness. He didn't feel especially worldly at this moment and was understandably concerned about whether he would be able to fit in with hundreds of strangers and whether he could keep up with college work. Mostly, he missed Tilly. They had become best friends as well as lovers, and in the 41 days since she left South Branch for San Francisco, Elmer realized how much he had come to rely on her as someone he could confide in. He loved their letters, but it wasn't much of a substitute for making love in his pickup every night.

The drive from South Branch to Cedar Falls took two hours, plenty of time for everyone to give Elmer advice on venturing out on his own. This conversation in the car didn't make Elmer feel any more confident either. Elmer's dad admonished him to work hard but not to listen to any crazy ideas from his professors, by which he meant anything his dad didn't understand or agree with. Elmer's mom looked at him, nearly in tears, and reminded him that he could come home any time, especially if things didn't work out at college. It sounded like she almost hoped he would flunk out and have to move back. In the end, it was Elmer's 12-year-old brother Alex who gave him the best advice: "Make sure you get a girlfriend with gigantic knockers!"

Both parents reprimanded Alex, but Elmer thought his advice was hilarious even though he wouldn't be looking for a girlfriend since he had Tilly.

Elmer moved his stuff into the dorm, met his roommate who seemed to be somewhat shy and studious, then drove around the campus with his parents and brother. Elmer would have a few days to get used to the place and go through registration; then he would be an official college student. Elmer's family didn't stick around once they got Elmer moved in. Like most farmers they had chores to do that required them to be home before dark.

Elmer didn't have much of a chance to get acquainted with his new roommate Wes, who returned to their room late after having a tour of the campus and a late dinner with his parents.

In the meantime, Elmer hung up his clothes in the closet even though they would spend most of the semester on the floor. He distributed his school supplies in his desk and climbed onto the bed, leaned against the headboard, opened the letter he had received from Tilly a couple of days before, and reread it for the fourth time.

Elmer had hoped to get more letters from Tilly, but he understood she was busy, and if he wrote to tell her about his arrival, that should make her feel at least a little guilty about not writing. He moved to the desk, got out a sheet of paper, and wrote a short letter to let Tilly know he has arrived in Cedar Falls, that his roommate seemed nice, and that he was looking forward to seeing her at Christmas.

On Tuesday, Elmer found his way to his first class, English 101. He was rather proud of himself, having tested out of having to take English 100, "bonehead English" for no credit, which was for those needing to "brush up" before beginning a real English class. The class involved lots of reading and writing, not Elmer's favorite pastime, apart from writing letters to Tilly anyway. But he liked the reading and came up against some ways of thinking about things that had never occurred to him. His first reading assignment, from the chapter "College and Conscience", was "The Eighty-

Yard Run" by Irwin Shaw.[1] The story recounts the life of a college football player who, for a short time, is a star on the gridiron, marries his college sweetheart, and then his life gradually disintegrates.

"That will never happen to Tilly and me!" Elmer thought. *"I'm not a football player!"*

He hadn't heard from her for a week and a half, but decided she'd want to know how his classes were going and wrote to tease that he had had four days of classes and was already three days behind. He did reveal he was having a good time and enjoyed the bull sessions with his buddies.

At first, Elmer was too busy to fully venture into the college life, but once he had gotten his feet on the ground, and realized he could keep up, he began joining new friends from the dorm at football games, participating in "bull sessions" in one another's rooms, and checking out the fashionable girls on campus in their increasingly short skirts. This was a look Elmer definitely approved of, as long as Tilly didn't take it up out there in San Francisco.

Tilly's next letter came on Friday:

September 22. 1963

Dear Elmer,

I can't wait to hear about your classes! What are you

taking? I hope you like the college life as much as I do.
Are you meeting a lot of new people? There are people
here from everywhere. I've met people from India, New
Zealand, and even Jamaica so far. Everybody is so
interesting and it's very cool to learn how different
things are where they grew up.

Love,
Tilly
XO

The majority of Elmer's fellow students were male, especially in classes related to his major in "commerce", but there were plenty of girls around to admire, even if he wasn't looking for a romantic partner. He and his buddies were very observant of the charms and shortcomings of these girls. Of course, Elmer found most of them inferior to Tilly, but now and then, he noticed someone especially attractive and imagined having sex with her. He had no plans to try getting a date with any of these girls, or any clue how to accomplish that, but he was aware of the delights he was putting on hold until he and Tilly were together again. He wrote to her about how he had survived the first month at State and how he was reminiscing about their first few months together two years ago.

His dormitory, like all those on campus, housed only

members of the same sex. The discussions about girls, and the pointing out of the best-looking ones, was a ubiquitous pastime among the boys. No girls were allowed in the men's dorms under any circumstances, so these accommodations had a rather untidy and raucous quality. Each floor was overseen by a Resident Advisor, normally a graduate student, who didn't particularly care what went on as long as it didn't come to the attention of the school authorities and cause the RA to get into trouble. Risqué pictures from Playboy magazine adorned the walls, dirty jokes were told and retold, and soiled clothing haphazardly festooned the floors. Masturbation was known to take place under the covers once the lights were out. The untidiness of the accommodations was kept slightly at bay by a group of middle-aged female housekeepers who came through every Tuesday afternoon, changed the sheets on the boys' beds and rearranged the clutter slightly.

Tilly's teasing letter arrived the next day:

October 9, 1963

Dear Elmer,

I can't believe you forgot the name of the movie we went to on our first date. It was "Blue Hawaii". And you know I never grabbed any part of your genitalia (that's a medical term, you may not understand it!) that night. You can quit teasing me about it any time, although you seemed to like it when I actually DID grab that part of your body later on!

103

I hope you're keeping up with your classes. It's hard to catch up if you fall behind!

Love,
Tilly

Even though it was only mid-October, fall was in the air and Halloween was approaching. Naturally, this made Elmer nostalgic for the thrilling, confusing, and perilous days when they were first beginning their relationship. And their history gave them something in common as they found themselves in such different places. This nostalgia must have affected Tilly too, since a brief flurry of letters followed:

October 16
Dear Tilly,

I just saw my first Halloween decorations of the year here. It appears that Halloween is a big deal at State College of Iowa! I might go as a pirate – I probably still have my old Pirate costume – I don't think it was too badly damaged when you pushed me off the porch a couple of Halloweens ago.
Do you still have your fangs? You should wear them to dissuade any guys who might want to kiss you!
I hope you're still having fun but not overdoing it on

the Halloween parties!

Love,
Elmer

Tilly's short reply arrived a week later:

October 21, 1963
Dear Elmer,

I didn't push you off the porch on Halloween two years ago – that was a little Dutch Girl who was a vampire on the side! I would never do such a thing to a boy I was about to kiss!
No Halloween decorations here so far, although some people look like they celebrate Halloween all year round so I might have missed something. Are there going to be big parties at State? Will there be a Pirates vs Hobos touch football game? However they do Halloween in Cedar Falls, I hope you have fun.

Love,
Tilly

October 25

Dear Tilly,

Today was the first big mid-term in English. We had to write an in-class essay on the most exciting thing that happened to us in the last year! I had several ideas and you were the central character in all of them! But none of them were appropriate for an English class essay! So, I wrote about going to St. Louis to see the Christmas decorations last winter. I was a virgin then, remember? I really wanted to write about Christmas day when your family was in Chicago and you and I were in your bed! But I thought my hand might be shaking too much to write!

OK, now I'm really missing you. I hope you're behaving yourself and won't be doing anything too scary on Halloween!

Love,
Elmer

Halloween was comprised of Elmer and his buddies wandering around campus looking at their costumed colleagues partying in the frat houses and apartments around campus. By law, no bars could open within a mile of campus so that adventure was off limits although Elmer didn't have a fake ID card so his ability to buy a drink was questionable anyway. Any disappointment regarding the tedium of this Halloween was removed though, when he got Tilly's letter a few days later:

October 31, 1963
Hi There Wiggle Bear,

I just loved the letter I got from you yesterday, and now I'm especially missing you today. Do you remember 2 years ago? I know you do – our first kiss. The first of about a million. I could really go for a million more of them right now. Sorry I almost knocked you off the porch that first time, ha, ha. I guess that didn't deter you too much. I really miss you. I love you so much! And I remember your Christmas "Presence" too!

Halloween just seems weird in San Francisco. For one thing, everybody here looks like they're wearing Halloween costumes all the time. I thought people on Haight Street might show up for Halloween in business suits to look as scary as possible, but it's just the usual clown costumes they wear every day. There are no kids coming around to Trick or Treat either – I think their parents are scared for them to be out in this neighborhood after dark. It's perfectly safe, but it's pretty Bohemian. I must say, it's a lot different than

Iowa. Most of the differences are fine, but the biggest difference is that you're not here and that's a bad one. My roommates have gone off to a poetry reading so I'm going to get to bed early, snuggle with my pillow, and pretend it's you. I'd better take a towel with me just in case my imagination is too realistic, ha, ha!

Good night Wiggle Bear – I love you forever!
XXOO Flash

As delighted as Elmer was with Tilly's letter, he was aware that Thanksgiving was coming and that for the first time in two years, he wouldn't be spending it with Tilly. Still, she was planning to come home for Christmas, and this became the life preserver he held on to for the next month as their letters slowed to a trickle.

Even for those who were dating, the rules at State College were stifling. Female students were required to live in approved housing and all women students had to be in, and locked in, by 10:30. Elmer contrasted that in his mind with Tilly's San Francisco accommodations; living in her own apartment with her cousin and two men, able to go anywhere whenever she pleased. This was a long way from Cedar Falls, Iowa and, while Elmer thought State College was unnecessarily restrictive, he worried about Tilly's temptations out on the coast.

The few letters Elmer received seemed dashed off without much emotional content and only occasionally included items that gave Elmer pause. Now and then, Elmer would read a magazine article about hippies in San Francisco, but he was fairly sure Tilly wouldn't be doing anything too wild. He told himself she wasn't brought up to go to crazy, and he hoped he was right. They rarely talked on the phone since each was on the go, and Tilly's call while Elmer was home for Thanksgiving only made him miss her more.

Christmas 1963

When Christmas arrived and Tilly was unable to come home for the holiday, Elmer was heartbroken, but he enjoyed coming home as a newly minted grownup and successful college student. He was peeved when his parents failed to treat him with the deference he felt he deserved. They admonished him to take out the trash and required him to perform other tasks that, as a recognized scholar, were now beneath him. Elmer spent time with a few of his high school friends, mostly bragging up their scholarly achievements and their popularity among the co-eds.

He was confused about the Christmas gift he received from Tilly. It was a necklace with little disks hanging down with pictures on them. *"I don't know what she had in mind, but men don't wear necklaces. Maybe she got my present mixed up with her mom's or something,"* he thought. Just to avoid embarrassment to her though, he just thanked her for the gift and changed the subject.

109

After Christmas, Elmer's dad drove him back to Cedar Falls for the remaining days of his first semester. Elmer had enjoyed being at home for a while, but he was looking forward to getting back to school, in spite of the imminence of final exams. During the trip, his dad, Fred, grilled him about the details of his classes and the attractiveness of the girls he met on campus.

Both of Elmer's parents liked Tilly. His dad had been impressed when he had started dating her two years ago, but they suspected that a girl from South Branch would never come home once she had a taste of "Sin" Francisco. Fred had read about the beginnings of the hippie lifestyle in Look Magazine and feared that Tilly would be lost to the temptation so he was hopeful Elmer would take up with a nice Midwestern farm girl and settle down after college. Elmer was as in love with Tilly as ever, but he did miss her and was concerned about the gradual loosening of their distant connection. He looked forward to Tilly's return to South Branch for the summer, and he imagined that they would instantly take up where they had left off the day she left.

Things looked up during the spring semester. Elmer now had his truck on campus with him, and he found himself increasingly focused on his classes. He had done well the first semester and now was confident he wouldn't flunk out as happened to many students who didn't take to college life or who enjoyed partying too much. He and Tilly sent each other a brief flurry of letters, cards, and tiny but romantic gifts around

Valentine's day, but soon Tilly's letters had become rare again and Elmer feared that their connection was disconnecting.

One Friday afternoon in mid-March, Elmer found himself in the University Library. He should have been studying because his Economics 102 mid-term was the next day, and to assert that he wasn't 100% prepared would be 100% correct. It was a cool but sunny afternoon in Cedar Falls. Elmer was sitting at a table with an open Econ book and a binder full of college-ruled paper in front of him, but his mind wasn't on economics or the sunny afternoon. It wasn't even on the co-ed at the next table whose skirt he could look up if he tilted his head just right. His mind was on Tilly. A year ago, at this time of day, he and Tilly would have been waiting for the school day to end so they could spend the rest of the afternoon in Elmer's truck, teasing, kissing, and anticipating making love once it got dark as they were parked on the dirt road next to Old Man Smith's orchard.

Maybe Tilly was just too busy with nursing school to write, but the content of her letters, originally focused on how much she missed him (and his genitalia), now consisted primarily of how much fun she was having in California and how much she liked her cousin Carol and Carol's friends. He figured the majority of those friends were young men, and he could just imagine how tanned and muscular they probably were. He hadn't had a letter from Tilly for a month, and his mood was glum. Glum and worried. Glum and worried and a little pissed off.

He had been faithful to Tilly and she had assured him that their love could withstand any separation. He hadn't even had an innocent date with any of the girls on campus. He didn't have any evidence that Tilly had found a new boyfriend in San Francisco, but her letters implied that she and Carol liked to hang out with all manner of shady characters.

Even though he had been the last one to write, he decided to send her another letter; maybe it would get her attention enough to reply. He took a piece of lined paper from the binder and began a letter:

Friday, March 13, 1964

Dear Flash,

You must be having a lot of fun in San Francisco, you haven't written me a letter for a month at least! How is school? Is it hard? I'm very busy. I have an Econ test tomorrow, but I keep thinking about you and hoping you're doing OK. I miss you. It's sunny here, but still cold. Can you believe spring is only 8 days away? I can't wait. Mostly I can't wait because that will mean summer is just around the corner and we'll be back in South Branch together for 3 whole months. Did I mention I miss you? I had to get a new battery for my truck; the winter was really bad, and I didn't get to drive it much, so it didn't get charged up like it should have. How is Carol? Tell her "Hi" for me. I hope I get to meet her sometime. Is she showing you all the exciting parts of San Francisco? I hope they aren't TOO exciting, ha, ha. You and Carol are probably hanging out with all those Charles Atlas types at the beach.

I'm learning a lot in my classes! Maybe when we get out of college, I'll go back to South Branch and start a business as a contractor or something. You can be the bookkeeper, but it will be a hard job since I'm sure we'll be millionaires. Or at least thousandaires. We could build a fancy house down by the creek, maybe next to the spot where we always go skinny-dipping. We could just go out the back door and go skinny-dipping any old time – as long as the kids weren't watching! Well, I guess I have to get back to economics if I'm going to get rich. Please write! Even if it's just a short letter. I really want to know what you're doing out there! I miss you!

Love,

Wiggle Bear

To his momentary delight, a letter came back from Tilly a few days later:

Dear Elmer,

Sorry I haven't been good about writing to you lately, but I've been really busy. I started keeping a journal but it's mostly little drawings and things. No, you can't see it! It's private and the drawings are not very good anyway, but they express my inner feelings so that makes me happy. I'm finding out lots of cool things; it's so exciting but laid-back too. I mean in school and everything.

Last week we went out for a drive around the city. We stopped at Fisherman's Wharf and looked at the tourists. They are so funny! They think it's going to be warm in San Francisco and they are shivering in Hawaiian shirts and shorts when it's 50 degrees out. I just got the pictures back. Carol, Hub, and I are going to spend the summer driving down the coast to San Diego. We'll camp out and just go wherever we want; it will be so groovy! I think Big Sur is really going to be a blast. Carol has friends in San Diego, so we'll camp out in their backyard whenever we finally get there. I hope the three of us and all our camping gear can fit in Carol's VW Beetle. I'm sure we can squeeze in somehow! It doesn't look like I'll make it back to Iowa this summer, but I'll send you pictures if I can find a drug store to get them developed. I miss you too.

Love, Tilly

PS: Here's a picture of Hub, Carol, and Me out by the bay.

This was a blow to Elmer's expectations. He had been expecting to spend the summer with her in South

Branch and now she was going to be cavorting up and down the coast with her hippie friends. And who was in the part of the photo that she had torn off?

Elmer got a C- on the Econ test.

In contrast to Tilly's exciting life in San Francisco, Elmer's life was mostly work and worry. He was doing all right in school and by now, he was confident he wouldn't flunk out, but the work was difficult. Some of his classes were interesting and he enjoyed the reading and lectures, but others held little interest for him. Keeping focused in these subjects proved a struggle. He had many friends, but none of them were female, and he was increasingly depressed about Tilly. The physical distance between them was beginning to be matched by the romantic distance. Her letters were now all about the details of the concerts she had gone to, the beaches they had visited, the places they went to dinner, and how much she was enjoying her school. If he was mentioned in her increasingly rare letters at all it was just a "Hope you're having fun!" or something to that effect. He wrote back when he heard from her, but he didn't want to overdo it and appear needy, even though he was. When he did write back, his letters were mostly about things he was doing, and he nearly always exaggerated their importance in his telling.

Anticipating that he would be going back to South Branch and working in construction, as he had for several previous summers, Elmer joined a college fitness club and began working out with weights, partly to avoid the sore muscles he experienced every year at the beginning of his summer job, partly to have something to take his mind off Tilly, and partly to at least admire the girls who hung out at the rec center gym. This did build up his strength so as to be ready for the summer job, but it also allowed him to get acquainted with several young woman who seemed to find him agreeable enough to at least chat with. He didn't actually date any of these women, assuming they were hooked up already, but this did give him confidence that if and when he had to look beyond Tilly, candidates for his affections might be out there.

Summer 1964, Tiffany

Once the semester ended, Elmer came home to his old summer job and settled into the familiar routine. He worked during the day, hung out with his old friends who were in town, and thought about Tilly, although these days those thoughts were mostly nostalgia for things they had done together rather than anticipating their next adventure. He and his old friend Eddie made two or three weekend trips to St. Louis for Cardinals' games and spent time hanging out at the Burger Shack with nothing to do.

One of the waitresses at the Burger Shack, Tiffany, a new graduate of South Branch High, began to favor Eddie and Elmer with special attention during their idle hours there and, since she knew Elmer was a college boy, he seemed to attract most of her flirtation. Elmer had been thoroughly distracted by Tilly and hadn't paid

117

any attention to Tiffany when they were all at South Branch High. She seemed sweet enough, although Elmer's impression was that she was a bit ditzy. Tiffany had a soft, round figure which, while not pinup material, he found very cute. And her smile and hair style fit right into his built-in image of the sexy sweetheart. Elmer smiled at the thought of his little brother's year-old recommendation that he should find a girlfriend with large breasts, and Tiffany met that criteria.

He was flattered by, and especially susceptible to, her flirtation, since his relationship with Tilly seemed to be fading. Tiffany's attention was a sweet treatment for the vague worry about his ability to eventually attract another girlfriend. He found himself showing up at the Burger Shack without Eddie in the late evenings, and sometimes when business was slow and she wasn't busy, Tiffany would bring a couple of Cokes to his table and sit with him for a chat about college life. She also remembered he used to go with Tilly back in high school and seemed interested in their history and current relationship. Elmer was cautious about revealing too much, but she could tell things weren't going well between Elmer and Tilly and didn't go out of her way to defend her potential rival's imagined San Francisco lifestyle.

The Cokes evolved into meeting Tiffany on her dinner hour and, eventually, going to a movie together now and then. Elmer was hesitant to push her toward any physical relationship; she seemed innocent and inexperienced, and he didn't see their relationship becoming significant for many reasons. On the other hand, he hadn't had any physical female companionship for nearly a year and he was, shall we say, easily aroused.

Despite, or because of, her innocence, Tiffany seemed to need no great amount of pushing to want to jump into a hands-on relationship with Elmer. When she joined him for a Coke or dinner at the Burger Shack, she began sitting next to him in the booth. She became quite direct about putting her arm around him, touching his thigh, and eventually resting her head on his shoulder, especially when her co-workers were watching. Elmer found this curious since his relationship with Tilly had proceeded very slowly and carefully whereas Tiffany seemed to have few inhibitions about teasing him sexually. Perhaps she didn't know that, with many men, she would be risking a sad ending, or worse, an unfortunate pregnancy. Or perhaps she was desperately attracted to him for some reason he couldn't figure out. He resolved to enjoy her company, but to avoid unprotected sex with her at all costs.

In his darkest imagination, she could get herself pregnant by somebody else and point the finger at him. Even short of that, he didn't want Tilly getting word that he was fooling around with a South Branch girl just in case their relationship wasn't as damaged as it seemed. These thoughts weighed on Elmer's mind when he wasn't with Tiffany, but when they were together, he wasn't nearly so bothered by the risk.

By mid-summer, they were spending considerable time together and Elmer began to notice several curious features of their summer romance. For one thing, she went out of her way to avoid introducing him to her parents or even having him pick up at her house if they were going to a movie. She would walk around the corner to her friend's house where he would pick her up and drop her off after the movie. Apparently, her parents were opposed to their little girl dating – or dating HIM anyway. Elmer also noticed that Tiffany was especially affectionate with him when they were in public, but when they were alone, saying good night in the truck or driving around with nowhere to go, she was nervous about going beyond kissing and hugging. She seemed to like it when Elmer snuggled with her, and she was very enthusiastic when he fondled her breasts through her top. But when he put his hand on her knee, and began slowly sliding it northward, which had driven Tilly wild with delight, Tiffany always put her hand on his before he got too close to her sex. She didn't push his hand away but held it in check.

The most common way for young couples to spend private time together in the summer of 1964 was to just get into a car and drive around. This led to quite a lot of "distracted driving" but at least the speeds were kept low. Of course, the most romantic option was to find a private place to park and "make out" but this was something the driver had to do deliberately and there could be an objection if the partner, usually the girl, was hesitant about the implied activity. As an interim measure, the couples simply spent increasing amounts of time in the car saying goodnight when the boy brought her home at the end of the evening. This though had a limited shelf life since the girl's parents might be monitoring their private minutes. Elmer knew the perfect place to park and make out outside of town, but even if Tiffany was all for this idea, Elmer was hesitant until he got to know her a bit.

Tiffany usually got a ride home with one of her girlfriends after work, but Elmer began the custom of showing up at the Burger Shack at quitting time and giving her a ride home himself. He dropped her off at her house on these occasions, but they couldn't extend this sojourn too long because her parents stayed awake to monitor her arrival. Still, they could delay her arrival since she could always explain ten or fifteen minutes of lateness by explaining that the restaurant cleanup took longer than usual.

Their conversations in Elmer's truck had the tone of intimate interrogations.

"Is it fun being in college?" Tiffany asked.

"It's great, except for all the work. And of course, all the girls who want to spend time with me," Elmer teased.

Tiffany looked crestfallen. "You're so smart and handsome you probably have tons of girls after you," she said dejectedly.

"Tons would be an exaggeration. I haven't dated all

that much," Elmer admitted. The truth was that he hadn't dated at all since Tilly left for San Francisco.

"I've never been on a real date," Tiffany revealed, and then wished she hadn't.

"Why not?" Elmer asked. "You're very cute. Didn't every boy at South Branch High have a crush on you?"

"Well, my parents didn't allow me to date in high school, but now that I'm eighteen, they can't really stop me. Of course, they could kick me out of the house, so I have to be careful. I can't wait until I have enough money to move out and do whatever I want!"

"What do you want to do?" Elmer asked.

"Marry a nice boy and live happily ever after, I guess."

"Well, at least she doesn't keep her plans a secret," Elmer thought.

"Any thoughts of going to college?"

"I'd be scared to go to college," she said, "and I wouldn't know what to study."

"Well, you can go and figure out what interests you later," Elmer said.

"What are you studying, Elmer?" she asked.

"Commerce," he said.

"That sounds fascinating, what is it?"

"Buying and selling, the flow of money, profit and loss, things like that."

"I'd be good at the buying part!" Tiffany giggled.

"What do you tell your parents about me dropping

you off at midnight every night after the Burger Shack closes?"

"They wait up for me, but they don't look out the window unless it gets late. They think my girlfriend is still the one dropping me off every night. If they see your truck some night, I'm going to tell them you work at the Burger Shack."

"That could get you into trouble," Elmer pointed out.

"It would be worth it to get to hang out with you, Elmer," she said, sliding over next to him on the bench seat and laying her head on his shoulder.

Without a thought, Elmer put his arm around her. She gave a little shiver and put her hand on his thigh.

Elmer added this conversation to the part of the Tiffany puzzle labeled, "Don't get involved with this girl, and he added her hand on his thigh to the part of the Tiffany puzzle labeled "Get involved with this girl."

"I love you, Elmer!" she whispered into his ear.

This assertion was assigned to the "Don't get involved!" region of the puzzle.

Elmer didn't know what to make of this situation. Tiffany was clearly inexperienced, immature, and naïve. Leading her into a sexual relationship would be the work of a scoundrel. Elmer didn't want to picture himself a scoundrel, taking advantage of a young woman for his sexual pleasure. On the other hand, he didn't want to be stupid either. She had to get experience some way, and just about every guy he knew would have no qualms about having a roll in the hay with her.

Whenever he spent time with Tiffany, Elmer masturbated as soon as he got home, imagining Tiffany screaming with pleasure as he introduced her to the pleasures of sexual intercourse for the first time. This took care of his immediate urges but enhanced the appeal of introducing her to the pleasures of sex.

About the time he began taking her home after work, a goodnight kiss seemed innocent enough. This became many goodnight kisses. Elmer had to do something with his hands while they were kissing, and they naturally began to fall on her breasts. When Elmer thought he might be going too far and began to remove them, Tiffany, who was getting used to this, silently reassured him by putting her hands over his and pressing them firmly against her large breasts. If she was wearing a skirt, which was her usual outfit, she began the habit of placing her left leg over his as she sat next to him in front of her house. This had the effect of spreading her legs and when she placed her hand on his thigh, his hand naturally fit on her thigh and this became as likely as not to be under her skirt as the summer wore on. Tiffany's caution about becoming too physically intimate seemed to be fading away day by day.

Tiffany's friend from around the corner became her partner in crime, vouching for her whereabouts in exchange for being told all the titillating details of their sexual adventures. And this freed Tiffany to go out on weekend nights with Elmer under the ruse of spending time with her friend. Now she and Elmer had hours to play instead of a brief interlude after work, and once it got dark, Elmer began thinking about taking Tiffany to the little secret dirt path off the country road next to Old Man Smith's apple orchard. Tilly and Elmer had spent many glorious hours hidden in that location, and Elmer had many noteworthy memories from those days nearly two years ago, including the time Tilly gave Elmer the first hand-job he didn't have to provide for himself.

He and Tilly had been together for a year before they reached that point in their intimate relations; this time around, he had only known Tiffany for two months. Still, she seemed increasingly anxious to experience everything, and Elmer was willing to accommodate her up to a point. Where that point was, Elmer was still working on in his mind.

One Saturday night they went to a movie, stayed just long enough to see what it was about, and headed back to Elmer's truck.

"I know a place where we could park out in the country that would be very private. Would you like me to take you there?" Elmer asked as they left the theater.

"Are you going to "TAKE ME" there?" Tiffany giggled.

"Well, my plan was to take you "THERE," and see what kind of naughty things we can think of to do."

"I'll put myself in your hands," she said, not noticing the double entendre, "I'm sure you college boys have plenty of exciting ideas."

Elmer did have an exciting idea, which was to take off Tiffany's top and see how she would behave if he rubbed and perhaps kissed her bare breasts. When they arrived at Old Man Smith's, Tiffany was thrilled. She had never been in a place that seemed more perfect for a tryst. By now she was used to Elmer fondling her breasts, which made her feel a little frightened at how good it felt, and now, in their new secret place, she could let him take her blouse off and remove her bra and she could feel the warmth of his strong rough hands touching her sensitive nipples. These feelings were new to her; she had never been with a boy and, even though she masturbated from time to time, she always stopped short of reaching an orgasm because her parents had warned her against the practice when she first experimented with her hand between her legs. Now she feared she might become insane if she went too far. Now, even when Elmer touched her covered breasts, the word quickly got to that special spot between her legs, and she began shivering with excitement.

Tiffany was remarkably animated when Elmer stopped the truck behind the tall hedgerow that shielded the spot from any passing cars on the nearby road. She got onto her knees on the bench seat and danced around as well as she could, shaking her breasts.

"I feel so funny, Elmer!" she said. "I sometimes feel this way when I see boys on the basketball court or handsome men in movies, but I'm shaking with excitement being here with you!"

"I hope it's good funny," Elmer said with a smile.

"It's the most wonderful funny I've ever felt!" Tiffany said, climbing onto his lap facing him with her short, pleated skirt spread over his knees. She leaned back against the steering wheel, sounding the horn which made both of them jump with fright. It took Tiffany a second to realize she was the cause of the sound before she leaned forward, hugging Elmer tight and holding her breath until the danger of being discovered seemed to fade.

"I'm sorry Elmer," she said.

"Let's just move over to the passenger seat, okay?"

Once they had taken up the same position with Tiffany astride Elmer on the passenger side of the truck, Tiffany began wiggling again in a way that gave Elmer an impressive erection. Even though Elmer was fully clothed, Tiffany was startled to feel his manliness through her panties and slid back to give him room. Without making a conscious decision to do so, Tiffany's curiosity led her to place her hand on Elmer's erection, nearly making him come.

"Ouch!" Elmer said.

"Oh, no, did I hurt your thing?" Tiffany asked.

"No, but it's too cramped in my pants. I need to adjust it."

Tiffany slid farther back onto Elmer's knees while he unzipped his jeans and reached into his Y-fronts to straighten out his misbehaving member. Tiffany watched this process intently but couldn't see any detail because of the darkness.

"Did you get all excited because of me?" Tiffany asked.

"You're the only girl here, Tiffy!" Elmer said, perhaps leaving out part of her name due to overstimulation. Or perhaps his mind was mixed up with the time he had tried to take Tilly's bra off in this parking spot. Or maybe he was thinking about his "Stiffy" at the time he tried to say "Tiffany". In any case, "Tiffy" became his pet name for her even though he was aware of the danger of calling her "Tilly" or calling Tilly, "Tiffy" at a careless moment.

Once they had regained their composure a bit, Elmer began to gently touch Tiffany's breasts as she tipped her head back and spread her arms to give him as much access as possible.

"I didn't know anything could feel so good," Tiffy enthused.

"Shall I unbutton your blouse?" Elmer asked, rhetorically. He put his index finger from each hand on the sides of her neck and began slowly moving them down along her skin just inside her collar toward her cleavage.

"YES!" she said as though he couldn't finish that task soon enough.

Keeping her arms spread she looked down to watch him slowly unbutton her top in the dim light. Each button seemed to take him an hour, his fingers dallied with the newly revealed areas on their way down to the next button. The final button fastened the lowest part of her white cotton blouse and, to get to it, he had to untuck her top. Rather than pull it forcefully from the tight waistband of her skirt, which she might find unsettling or result in tearing her blouse, he gently unbuttoned the skirt at her side and unzipped the associated zipper to free up the blouse for removal. Tiffany closed her eyes as he gently pulled the bottom of her blouse upward and undid the final button. Her hips moved involuntarily, sliding the now soaking crotch of her panties against the ridge in the front of Elmer's jeans, creating a dark wet spot on the fly which he added to from inside with a dollop of pre-come.

Elmer watched her face as he opened her now unbuttoned blouse completely. He moved his hands to her waist, slowly squeezing and rubbing her sides just below her rib cage. Tiffany sucked in a long breath of air and wiggled her upper chest in an attempt to remind Elmer that her breasts were waiting for him to free them from the bondage of her brassiere. Elmer enjoyed her obvious pleasure and was in no hurry to bring it to a conclusion, especially since observing the power he had to please her was arousing his desire as much as hers.

Finally, Tiffany had enjoyed all the beating around the bush she could stand and took Elmer's hands in hers and moved them around to the hooks in the back of her bra.

"This silly bra is in the way, isn't it?" he said softly.

Fearing Elmer's plan was to engage in a conversation about whether her bra should remain on or come off, Tiffany wordlessly moved Elmer's hands away and unhooked it herself. This disappointed Elmer slightly since he had, a year ago, been quite adept at removing Tilly's bra with one hand and he wanted to test whether he was still a master at this gambit. Once the bra was loosely dangling from Tiffy's shoulders, Elmer slid his hands around to the front and began gently caressing her large, soft breasts and hardened nipples with the tips of his fingers.

This brought out a surprising reaction from Tiffany; she began to cry silently.

"I'm sorry," Elmer said, thinking he had gone too far with her.

"Oh, my god! Don't be sorry, Elmer! That was the nicest thing I've ever felt. I never thought any boy would do that to me."

"So, you're crying because it was so good?" Elmer asked.

"Yes, don't stop!" she said.

Elmer resumed his ministrations. Tiffy now began shaking and moaning softly. In spite of her troublesome fears about masturbation she thought perhaps she would be okay if a boy did it to her. Meanwhile, Elmer decided that since she seemed to be enjoying his efforts so much, he should move on to applying his lips to these sensitive areas. He gently bent forward and, placing his arms around her, began to kiss her nipples and suck them into his mouth. Elmer knew she was aroused by this since they became even more rigid as he softly licked them. Tiffy was breathing heavily and beginning to rhythmically squeeze his thighs with hers as she sat astride him. She was approaching her first orgasm, and, in spite of the almost unbearable pleasure,

Tiffany suddenly became irrationally frightened of the effect it might have on her if she let him continue.

"Elmer?" she said.

"Hmmm?" he responded without detaching his mouth from her mammaries.

"You have to stop now," she said.

Elmer leaned back. "You want me to stop?" he asked, confused.

"No, I don't want you to, but we have to stop before I go crazy."

Elmer stopped his romantic ministrations; he remembered feeling overwhelmed the first few times Tilly was about to make him come so he understood her reaction somewhat.

"What happened? You seemed very aroused just a minute ago," he asked.

"I don't know. It just seemed to feel so good I wasn't sure what might happen."

"We can call it a night for now. Let's try it another time and I think you'll like what happens," Elmer said reassuringly. "I think I should take you home now, it's getting late anyway. I'll see you at the Burger Shack tomorrow."

Elmer worked late the next day, and after going home and taking a shower, he was later than usual getting to the Burger Shack. When he arrived, Tiffany was working behind the counter and, when she saw him, she smiled and puffed out her chest a little as a subtle greeting. He ordered a Coke and sat down to wait for closing time. Elmer was curious at the behavior of some of Tiffany's female colleagues who seemed to be smiling at him as they had private conversations with each other. Maybe they had been informed about his previous misdemeanors. This possibility annoyed him until he realized they might have found the information enticing.

Tiffany made a quick trip to the ladies' room and they set off toward her house hoping to delay their arrival as long as possible. No sooner had they left the Burger Shack parking lot than Tiffany opened her purse, removed her bra from it, and hung it by a strap over the rear-view mirror in Elmer's truck.

Elmer gave her a quick look and noticed she was unbuttoning her top.

"Beautiful!" he said, turning onto a side street and parking under a streetlight so he could examine her offerings without risking an accident – at least an accident with his truck. "Do you think we have time to take another lick at those before I have to get you home?"

"Elmer, they have been begging me to get you to do that again all day. I could hardly concentrate on work! And my panties have been wet all day."

Before he could agree to her request, which took almost no time at all, two cars drove by them and beeped their horns. Elmer recognized them as vehicles belonging to her co-workers.

"Tiffany," he said. "Did you tell all the girls at work that I was sucking on your tits last night?"

"No!"

"What DID you tell them?"

"Just that you were a very nice boy who knew all about how to make a girl feel good."

"You told them I made you feel good?"

"Actually, I told them how good you were at making a girl feel 'BAD'!" Tiffany giggled.

"Tiffany, we both like fooling around that way, but it's really not a good idea to give all your friends the intimate details of things that I thought were private between us."

"Okay. But you made me feel so good I couldn't keep it inside."

"You need to from now on, Tiffany. If this gets all over town, your parents are going to hear about it and keep you far away from me!"

Okay," she pouted. "Can you just suck on them a little right now, so I know you're not mad at me?"

Elmer didn't want Tiffany to think he was mad at her.

Elmer usually worked on Saturdays, but now that Tiffy had recruited her friend around the corner to cover for her, she was able – using the ruse that she and her friend were going on an outing together – to spend some Sunday afternoons with Elmer. Tiffany was required to go to church with her parents and the rest of the day was sometimes taken up with church affairs. On the occasional free Sunday afternoons, she would tell her parents she and her friend were going out and instead meet Elmer for their own intimate outing. For the first of these adventures, Elmer supplied a picnic and took Tiffany to the little county park that ran along a creek for a quarter of a mile perpendicular to one of the county roads near South Branch. This was a wooded area a few hundred yards wide that cut through the surrounding cornfields and couples who walked along the creek to the far end would find a rather private picnic table where they could amuse each other as long as they maintained a small awareness of anyone approaching. Elmer and Tilly had spent many a pleasant afternoon here until their activities began to preclude being watchful for interlopers. At that point they found even more secluded venues for their delightful debauchery.

Elmer and Tiffany set out the picnic items on the table and then promptly forgot all about them. Elmer suggested that she would be more comfortable if she unbuttoned the top of her sundress and removed her bra, and she was happy that he had approved her plan even before she had suggested it. Up until now, Elmer had not enjoyed an opportunity to admire her breasts completely uncovered in sufficient light to examine them in detail, and Tiffany arranged herself astride the picnic bench a few feet away and treated Elmer to an amusing strip tease as she opened her dress, removed her bra, then leaned back alluringly, allowing him to fully admire her round, beautiful breasts. Tiffy's nipple area was topped by a lightly colored areola and large nipples that were erect as they usually were when Elmer had the opportunity to admire them. She had never had her top off outside and loved the daring quality of the experience and the bulge in Elmer's shorts that her exposure seemed to cause.

As a precaution, Elmer suggested she put her top back in place without buttoning it so that she could cover up in a hurry if necessary. Tiffy turned around and lay on her back on the picnic bench with her head in Elmer's lap. As he massaged and squeezed her breasts, she enjoyed the feeling of his erection throbbing and lurching under her head. After some time, as Tiffany appeared to be in a daze of desire, Elmer bent over her and began to kiss and gently suck on her nipples. This had the familiar effect of bringing her close to a climax and she didn't resist this time. Even so, as much as she loved his manipulation of her breasts, she began to realize, to her alarm, that her pussy was begging for attention and wouldn't take no for an answer.

In spite of her desire, Tiffany could not bring herself to be so forward as to suggest this to Elmer. Happily, after a few minutes he seemed to read her mind, as he reached down, gently slid the hem of her dress up, and began to stroke her inner thighs. Tiffany was desperate for him to touch her between her legs, and scared for him to do so, until she felt his finger softly settle into the wet valley in her panties between her labia. Elmer began rhythmically moving his finger along this slippery channel and Tiffy soon began moaning encouragement, raising and lowering her hips to suggest her preferred tempo, and squirming involuntarily. After a few delicious minutes she started flailing her arms and legs as they extended beyond the sides of the bench she was lying on, then reached around and hugged his head firmly against her breasts and held on for dear life as her body jerked uncontrollably with her first real orgasm.

It took some time for Tiffany to recover and, in spite of her delight at discovering how great sex could feel, this was diminished slightly by a tinge of guilt she had carried over from her imperfect upbringing.

"Are you okay?" Elmer asked when she had stopped shaking.

"Yes, I'm okay. I've never felt anything that good in my life."

She didn't sound fully convinced but she did seem to enjoy the process and her reaction made Elmer extremely aroused. They hugged and kissed for a while and Tiffany seemed to become reanimated, maybe her orgasm had just worn her out.

Tiffany became an unusually playful version of herself, perhaps because her first orgasm had not made her go insane. She sat facing Elmer astride the bench, put her hand on the bulge in his shorts, and began experimentally playing with the button at the top of his fly. Looking into his eyes she said, "You don't really need these shorts on right now, do you?"

"No!" Elmer whispered.

Tiffany unbuttoned and unzipped his fly, then wiggled his shorts down to his mid-thigh. For some time, she observed the bulge in his briefs, studying how animated this appendage was even without her touching it and she noticed an occasional spasm which resulted in a spreading region of wetness near the tip.

"Am I making you come, Elmer?" she asked.

"That's pre-come," he told her. "If you make me come, you won't have to ask!"

"I'm going to pull these down. I don't want you to get in trouble for wetting your pants," she informed him.

She slid his underwear down as Elmer lifted his butt up to make her work easier. Tiffany had never seen a man's genitals except in photographs, and she found his erect penis and tight scrotum fascinating, playing with them as a child might to discover the features of a new toy. She amused herself by seeing how far she could bend it, watching it spring back after pushing it to the side, checking out the action of twisting it, and grasping it near his body to wave it back and forth. All of these things felt nice to Elmer but didn't have the specific movement he was looking for, so he placed his hand over hers and began stroking his member as he wanted her to do. She caught on right away and Tiffany looked intently back and forth from Elmer's face to his manhood.

"Have you ever seen a man come?" Elmer asked

hoarsely.

"I've never even seen a man's penis before Elmer, but I have to say yours is fascinating!"

"Well, you're about to see a man ejaculate if you keep that up."

"Shall I stop?"

"OH GOD NO, DON'T STOP!" he said. "Just keep doing what you're doing."

This wasn't going to take long; no girl had done this to him for a year and he was ready to explode. Tiffany sat astride his legs as he was stretched out on his back along the bench, his hands gripping the edge of the bench tightly at his sides. She kept up her rhythm of stroking his cock, which was now oozing a steady stream of pre-come.

"Does that mean you're coming, Elmer?" she asked.

"You'll know!" he whispered.

She watched the changing expressions on Elmer's face, curious about what was going to happen. Elmer began breathing heavily and whispering sounds she couldn't make out and then unexpectedly, she felt his entire body stiffen and felt then a quick relaxation followed instantly by an expansion of his penis as though it became even more inflated than it already was. She looked down to see a long rope of liquid squirt from the opening up to Elmer's shoulder. This reminded her of when the girls at the Burger Shack would sometimes fill up a mayonnaise bottle and jump on it in the parking lot, squirting a stream of mayonnaise several feet. She never found this as funny as the other girls and now she realized why they were laughing.

Assuming Elmer's squirt was the event, she quit stroking him.

"DON'T STOP! He begged.

Tiffany restarted her stroking and was surprised that Elmer repeated this trick a half dozen or more times before his efforts gradually diminished to dribbling and oozing. Tiffy was amazed at the volume and vigor of his ejaculation, although she had nothing to compare it to apart from her expectations. Elmer's body jerked involuntarily as his breathing slowly returned to normal.

"Wow!" was all Tiffany had to say.

There was only a short time left before Elmer would be leaving for the fall semester at State College, and Tiffany's plan at this point was to lose her unwanted virginity to Elmer before that happened. She had, in her opinion, remained a virgin long enough and once she had seen what Elmer was capable of, she wanted to feel that event happen inside her. For Elmer's part, he wanted to be inside her, but not when THAT happened.

On the Sunday before Elmer would be driving up to State College, he and Tiffy went on another private picnic in Elmer's old favorite place near the creek where he and Tilly had first gone skinny dipping together. Again, they took a perfunctory picnic, and again most of the food went to waste. They hadn't talked explicitly about going all the way, but both understood, or at least hoped, that activity was on the program for the afternoon.

As though they were old hands at this, there were fewer preliminaries. After a replay of Elmer's nibbling of Tiffany's breasts and her preliminary manipulation of his manhood, Elmer removed Tiffany's panties and took his time admiring her vagina. He was ready to go, but he understood that this represented a memorable, and possibly scary moment for her and paid careful attention to touching her sufficiently to bring forth abundant lubrication. All that remained was any last-minute negotiation and the commencement of the copulation.

"Elmer," Tiffany said, "are you planning to fuck me?"

Saying this word, which Elmer didn't think she even knew, made her feel sinful. Wildly, beautifully, deliciously, delightfully, thrillingly, sinful. She couldn't wait another second to enter the grownup world of magnificent wickedness.

"Do you want me to fuck you?" Elmer whispered, hoping she wanted him to.

Something about saying this word, and hearing Elmer say it, made Tiffany tremble.

"I really want you to fuck me Elmer!"

Tiffany suddenly couldn't get enough of this talk.

"I want you to stick your hard cock into me and fuck me! Fuck me hard, goddamn it! Fuck me, Elmer! Fuck

141

me until I can't stand up!"

"It will be my pleasure!" he told her.

"Elmer?"

"What?"

"I want us to both be naked the first time!"

"Okay."

Elmer unhesitatingly removed his shirt and his shorts which were already around his ankles. Tiffany, either in an unnecessary attempt to make herself as sexy as possible, or not having had time to change out of her church costume, was overdressed for the occasion. In addition to her blouse, bra, and panties, which she had already tossed aside, she wore a pleated skirt, a garter belt, nylon stockings, and patent leather flats. Elmer helped her out of these, and the couple looked at each other's unclothed bodies admiringly. Elmer noted to himself that it had been in this same spot, just over two years ago, when he and Tilly had seen each other completely naked for the first time.

"There should be a little monument here," he thought.

"Fuck me, Elmer!" Tiffany insisted. She loved the feeling of forming that word with her mouth and listening as it traveled to a naked boy who stood ready to carry out her ultimatum. "I've been waiting all summer to feel your big hard penis fucking me."

As exciting as this moment should have been, Elmer had mixed feelings about what was about to happen. He knew this wouldn't be a long-term relationship and it seemed like he was just using Tiffany for a moment of personal pleasure. At the same time, he understood she was just using him to break her hymen, and more importantly, the rules her parents had laid down. In spite of these thoughts, he was quite ready to sample the charms of someone besides Tilly and prove to himself that he was a man of the world.

Tiffany had not given a thought to the possibility of pregnancy, but Elmer had come prepared; he had purchased several condoms from the vending machine in the men's room at Smitty's gas station. A package of three condoms cost a quarter, and he bought two packages just in case. He intended to use them to prevent pregnancy, in spite of the warning on the package that they could be legally used "For the prevention of disease only!"

Tiffany had never seen a condom and watched with curiosity as Elmer unrolled the device over his erection.

"I'm glad you thought of that, Elmer," Tiffany said. "I forgot all about the possibly that a strong man like you could get me pregnant! Now fuck me!"

She was a little disappointed that she wouldn't be feeling his bare skin inside her and wondered if it would really count as losing her virginity if his member was covered in rubber when he pushed it into her, but she kept this to herself. She had it on good authority from her friends at church that it was impossible to get pregnant the first time, but maybe Elmer didn't know this, and she didn't want to get into a discussion about it right then.

In spite of the passage of time since Elmer had last

had sexual intercourse, he hadn't forgotten what to do. Tiffany, who had listened to advice from her more worldly girlfriends positioned herself on her back atop the blanket they had brought along, spread her legs, and awaited her induction into adulthood. During his tenure with Tilly, Elmer had become fond of, and adept at, cunnilingus as a means of foreplay, and as a way of giving Tiffany the full measure of pleasure, dropped to his knees and began kissing his way up between her thighs. This was all new to Tiffany, and she liked the idea until he began to get near her pussy.

"What are you doing? Elmer?" she asked, somewhat breathlessly.

"You like it don't you?" he asked, rhetorically.

"Yes, but you're not going to kiss me THERE are you?"

"I was planning on licking your pussy to get you hot. I've never met a girl who didn't love that," Elmer said, implying wider experience than he had.

"It seems too weird!" Tiffy said.

"If it still seems too weird a minute from now, let me know'," Elmer said.

Tiffy soon found she had no objection at all to Elmer's clever, college boy, idea.

Elmer climbed on top of her in the missionary position, and gently pushed his manhood into her tight opening. Tiffany had feared this would be painful, but after Elmer's work with his tongue, she was so ready her mild discomfort with his initial penetration turned quickly into delight with how filled up, and grown up, she felt. She enjoyed the feeling of Elmer on top of her, his arms around her, and his rhythmic movements. But the strangeness, the importance of the moment, and the fact that his cock didn't quite hit her most sensitive area, interfered with her arousal and she was unable to have the kind of full orgasm that she had experienced with his fingers earlier. Elmer had no such problem, and soon, being extra cautious, he extracted his erection from her vagina, slipped off the condom, and masturbated for a few seconds before ejaculating across her thigh and into the grass.

"I liked the feeling of you inside me, Elmer," she said when things calmed down.

"I liked that feeling too," Elmer told her while mentally comparing the experience to having sex with Tilly. It was thrilling to do it with a new partner, yet the experience lost some of its passionate content since he didn't feel any special connection with Tiffany.

A few days later, they had to make do with too public a kiss at the Burger Shack as Elmer departed for his second year at State College of Iowa. Tiffany took a break from her duties to walk with Elmer to his truck.

"When are you coming home?" Tiffany asked, leaning onto the driver's window and resting her foot on the running board.

"I'll be pretty busy, Tiffy, so I probably won't be back in South Branch until Thanksgiving," he told her.

"I'll never forget you, Elmer," she said, as though the process might already be under way. She looked around to be sure they were alone. "Thanks for fucking me and making me a real woman!"

"It was fun helping out with step one!" Elmer said.

After a final kiss, Elmer departed, giving her a wave before gunning the truck out of the driveway. Of course, Elmer had loved having sex with Tiffany, but for some reason he couldn't figure out, he felt like he was making an escape from her. He felt a little guilty about any suggestion he might have given to her that they might have a future together, and he tried to remember whether he had ever told her he loved her. He thought of Tilly and had a moment of unease that she might find out about his summer fling.

PART II CRUISING ALTITUDE
CHAPTER 3 THE LEFT COAST LIFE

Tilly had no husband or wife
And these days no trouble or strife
Life filled up with joys
And with plenty of boys
This left coast is really the life.

Fall 1964

Carol and Tilly began their sophomore year in nursing school with confidence and stable love lives. Tilly, especially, was delighted to have a steady boy to tuck in and wake up with. She felt a bit of sadness and nostalgia about the fading away of her relationship with Elmer, but she was in a very different place than Elmer now in every way. She and Gary were having a fine time together, and Tilly was becoming more interested in politics and philosophy, subjects she had previously paid no attention to. Her roommates kept themselves current on political news and the upcoming election was the subject of lively discussions.

Now as sophomores, their classes increasingly involved hands-on patient care, and they were becoming more confident in their growing skills. Carol and Tilly sometimes "experimented" on Gary and Hub by removing the men's clothing and testing each other on naming various muscles and tendons as they pointed them out and sometimes massaged or tickled.

Fall was a delightful time in San Francisco. After their summer trip, their beach activities usually involved one couple or the other heading down the beach or up into the deserted dunes for an afternoon tryst.

When Tilly and Gary weren't at the beach or in bed together, Tilly studied while Gary focused on his poetry. Anything he thought was worthwhile he would read to Tilly, who loved them for the most part and offered constructive criticism. Now and then, the two would have little contests, usually after a few servings of wine, where they would try to outdo each other with funny poems or limericks. One weekend in mid-November, they had such a contest, writing limericks to amuse each other and had engaged in an 'argument' over whose were best. After a while, the argument evolved into a tickling and kissing contest and, after this had resulted in a session of silly, sensational sex, they realized that they had gotten distracted from deciding whose limericks were the best. After dinner, they agreed that Carol and Hub should listen to them read the limericks and decide on the winner. Each had written three limericks and a game of rock, paper, scissors determined that Gary would read first:

Gary:

An Iowa girl from South Branch,
Flew out West to Frisco by chance.

She met a hip poet
And wouldn't you know it
She caused quite a stir in his pants!

Tilly:

Haight Ashbury boys are a whirl.
Quite a thrill for an Iowa girl!
If he's having a smoke,
He'll give you a toke,
And at bedtime he'll make your toes curl!

Gary:

Not a person considers it rude
To go to the beach in the nude.
In fact – if you're dressed,
It's probably best
To just tell folks you're not in the mood.

Tilly:

Said the Iowa girl with alarm,
San Francisco is far from the farm.
The animals here,
Are especially queer,
But still I find SF a charm.

Gary:

The wine and the poetry flow,

But you Iowa girls should go slow.

That handsome young man

With the beautiful tan

Might turn out to be crazy you know.

Tilly:

We Iowa girls aren't so dumb.

Don't judge us by where we came from.

If you think we are clueless,

And that you can fool us,

We'll wrap you three times 'round our thumb.

All were received with good cheer and after a short confab the judges declared the contest a tie.

It's surprising how quickly things done once become traditional, and Tilly and Carol once again spent Thanksgiving in Berkeley with Aunt Bev, who cooked a traditional Thanksgiving turkey dinner and began the meal in the Berkeley tradition of rolling a joint and passing it around to her daughter and niece, who joined this part of the ritual this year. It was a fine time. Tilly smiled at the thought of the look on her mother's face, if she discovered her Berkeley sister was smoking dope with the two girls.

As they had done the previous Christmas, the roommates threw themselves a little Christmas party complete with a tiny tree, gag gifts, and plenty of marijuana and refreshments. This year, Carol instructed Tilly on the proper preparation of a Dungeness crab Christmas feast, and it would be fair to report that Tilly preferred crab to calamari, although even squid was fine with her these days as long as it was deep fried.

Winter 1965

After Christmas, Gary went to Los Angeles to visit his parents, and, Tilly suspected, Nama. Tilly and Gary had a lovely relationship, playful and sexy, but while it seemed they loved each other, it wasn't mentioned in so many words. Back in South Branch, boys were expected to be gentlemen and stick to one girlfriend at a time, especially if overt sex was involved. But here in San Francisco, she wondered if things were different. Maybe it was generally understood that a person could have a playdate with an old lover without disturbing another ongoing relationship. Maybe she was just being unnecessarily jealous or maybe nothing was going on between Gary and Nama. But what if they had been a couple all along and she was the momentary distraction? Tilly began to think of "Nama" as "Nema", short for nemesis!

Tilly brought this up with Carol while Gary was away, and Carol revealed that she and Hub didn't see anything wrong with an occasional lusty liaison with someone else. They had agreed it shouldn't be secret, and it should be limited to a short dalliance. Otherwise it would suggest that the peripatetic partner was more attracted to the new person and that was likely to cause a rift in their relationship. Carol made it clear these extracurricular escapades were rare, but sometimes spiced up their sex life by introducing a newly learned technique they hadn't thought of.

She advised Tilly to ask Gary whether he saw Nama while he was in LA without suggesting she was angry about it and try to get him to discuss the situation without making a federal case of it. If he saw her and it didn't seem serious, she might suggest he let her know that was his plan beforehand next time and then go with the flow and assess the situation as it developed.

Gary was away for two weeks, and when he returned, things resumed as they were between them. Tilly was hesitant to confront Gary about Nama and no doubt a little scared of what she might find out. Anyway, he had come back so that was a good sign. On the other hand, when he returned, he wasn't desperate to have sex at first, not as desperate as Tilly was anyway, and she suspected it wasn't just that he was tired from a day on the train from L.A.

"Did you wear your out your dick in L.A.?" she asked the afternoon after he got home, trying to make the question sound like a joke.

"No, I was just tired last night," he said. "I'll be ready to go tonight, and I want to try something new!"

"Now what? And where did he learn 'something new' down in L.A.?" Tilly thought.

"Well, all I learned while you were gone was that I can't last two weeks without a fuck!" Tilly said with a hint of affection and a hint of accusation.

After dinner and a couple of glasses of wine, Gary suggested to Tilly that they go for a walk and then head to bed early. Tilly was looking forward to whatever idea it was that Gary had come back from LA with, but she thought their sex life was already pretty good. She could only compare Gary to Elmer, and she realized that wasn't fair since both she and Elmer were completely inexperienced when they became intimate. Learning about sex with Elmer was rife with clumsiness and misunderstanding; it was also gloriously thrilling. Getting it on with Gary was less clumsy, but more predictable and therefore a little less electrifying.

Curiously, February often is unseasonably warm in San Francisco, and Tilly and Gary set out for a walk on a mild and moonlit night. They held hands and Tilly could tell Gary had something important to talk about but was not sure how it was going to go.

Not one to waste the whole evening on whatever he wanted to talk about, when they could be back in the apartment having sex, Tilly opened the door to the conversation.

"Okay Gary, something's on your mind, and I hope

it's about wild sex!"

"Well, it's about sex, that's for sure," Gary laughed. "Have you heard of tantric sex? It's wild, but not in the bouncing off the walls manner."

"I've heard of it. Isn't it some kind of 'new age', 'yoga' kind of thing?"

"In a way. It's kind of 'mindful sex' where you focus on each other and have sex very slowly and thoughtfully."

"I'm never thoughtless when we have sex, Gary. I'm always thinking all kinds of thoughts!" Tilly laughed. "But tantric sex sounds like fun. What do we do?"

"We begin by looking deeply into each other's eyes."

"And what do we do after that ten seconds is up?"

"Let's go home and I'll show you!" Gary said, continuing to walk.

"I thought we were going home?" Tilly noted.

"We'll walk home slowly and thoughtfully. Part of tantric sex is not to be in a hurry."

"Oh," Tilly said. "Where did you learn how to do this?"

"Los Angeles," Gary said, not really answering the question she was asking.

When they got back to the apartment, Gary lit three candles and a stick of incense. He then took a record album from his suitcase, put it on the turntable, and turned the volume low. The music was soft and sweet, but Tilly had never heard anything like it before and couldn't identify the instruments at all.

"What is that album?" she asked, "I've never heard any music like that before.

"It's an album of Indian Ragas," he told her.

"What kind of instrument is that?"

"It's a stringed instrument called a sitar, along with several instruments used in India."

Gary instructed Tilly to stand quietly while he undressed her. He spent quite a while on this task and stopped now and then to look into her eyes while holding her face in his hands. When she was completely naked, he invited her to do the same to him, which she did although she didn't quite see the point of going so slowly. Still, it was fun to undress Gary and watch him becoming increasingly aroused while trying to remain quiet and meditative. Once both were naked, they got into bed where Gary sat upright with his legs crossed and invited Tilly to sit on his lap facing him and wrap her legs around his waist. Each placed their hands on the other's buttocks and, in this position, sat quietly looking into one another's eyes in the dim flickering candlelight.

This did seem very sensual and loving to Tilly except that any meditative mood she might have managed was interrupted by her increasing certainty that he had learned this technique from Nama while he was down in L.A. He seemed to be in no hurry to get on with the excitement, suggesting to her that he and Nama, or some other slut, had practiced this method so often that he was still recovering from the loss of testosterone. Whatever was going on with Gary, either an overabundance of love for her or an underabundance of sexual desire, she was more than ready. After all, she hadn't been fucking around for the two weeks he was gone. As they looked into each other's eyes, Tilly began to massage his bottom, slowly moved around to his belly, and worked her way down to his scrotum which distracted Gary from whatever sacred trance he was in and turned his thoughts and the tip of his penis, to her waiting pussy.

By now Tilly was ravenously ready and she took charge, bending forward until he was flat on his back and she was on top. She didn't waste any time taking his member in hand, slipping it into her lubricated opening, and using his agreeable appendage to satisfy herself until she was completely pleased with the outcome. This was especially fun since Gary usually climaxed first when they were having sex, and, although he always felt it was his duty to bring her to orgasm when they were enjoying sex together, his heart often wasn't fully in the game after he was finished. At the moment, Tilly could see how this could happen. But to be fair, she wanted to please Gary the same way and she moved her face down to his midsection and gently began licking the tip of his manhood in the way she knew would drive him wild. This had the expected effect and within a few minutes, she gently took him into her mouth and teased him until he was shaking in the way that she knew indicated he was seconds away from ejaculating.

"Am I doing this tantric thing well enough, Gary?" she said, raising up on her elbows and disengaging from his glans.

"DON'T STOP!" Gary said, drowning out the music for a moment.

"I guess that means 'yes'!" she said teasingly before returning to her post and feeling his body shuddering as he ejaculated into her mouth.

"I was afraid you were out of ammunition but apparently I was wrong," she said matter-of-factly.

She mulled over their reunion in her mind the next day and decided she loved the connection a couple could enjoy together using that technique under the right circumstances. As to the question of whether Gary had been stepping out on her while he was in L.A., she decided that she didn't have the standing, or the confidence, to question Gary about where he had learned that technique. Still, until she found out for sure what his intentions were, she would try to give him the benefit of the doubt as much as possible and await further revelations. They hadn't made any commitment to each other, although she thought it was implied by their intimacy. But maybe things didn't work that way in San Francisco.

Eventually the rainy season grudgingly gave way to spring. The roommates began spending more weekend time in Golden Gate Park, certain parts of which, by now, were considered "tops optional" by a majority of the local young women, and Tilly came to enjoy the freedom and "not Iowa" nature of the custom. This part of the park, which became known as "Hippie Hill", was often the site of spontaneous music and the smoking of marijuana, and Hippie Hill became a favorite hangout of the roommates and their growing number of interesting friends.

As spring slowly came to resemble summer, it became common for perhaps eight or ten of these friends to gather in the roommates' apartment in the evenings, bringing with them intoxicants and musical instruments. None of their neighbors objected to these events since the neighbors were invited too. The gatherings took on all the qualities of parties. The attendees were a diverse group and conversations about life in their home countries or states became the focus of many of these get-togethers. Tilly became especially friendly with several of the newcomers and was happy to find that she wasn't the only Midwesterner in San Francisco.

Betsy had run away from her rural Indiana home as soon as she graduated from high school and hitchhiked to San Francisco. She was a smart girl who had been valedictorian of her small high school class but was working diligently on her degree in "street smarts", San Francisco style. She had arrived the previous fall and was interested in what Tilly had learned about "sex, drugs, and rock and roll" during her tenure in the city. Both had come from a somewhat similar upbringing, although Betsy had suffered through some "boyfriend trouble" back in Indiana that she was trying to forget.

Tilly, who had been in San Francisco a year longer, took Betsy under her wing but in truth, each had plenty to learn from the other.

Samuel and Martha were a couple from Brooklyn who just wanted to try a different coast and were delighted with what they saw as the provincial nature of life in San Francisco. Tilly had the feeling that they had plenty of money and were in San Francisco only because they wanted to try on the West Coast lifestyle briefly as though they were at an amusement park, and then return to New York with a supply of amusing stories to tell about their safari. Niko was a cute and shy Japanese girl who was interested in everything and who Tilly thought was the most likely to write a future best seller about the inner workings of the cohort of young people in San Francisco during the 1960's.

The strangest and yet somehow the most interesting character in Tilly's estimation, was ReX. He sought her out at one of the parties because he heard someone call her "Iowa", and since he was from Nebraska, he thought she would be fun to talk to. Being an old hand at "San Francisco" characters, she took his appearance in stride. ReX was, under his costume, a good-looking man, if a little thin for her taste. And while he was dressed for the most part as a regular guy in a paisley shirt, vest, Donald Duck socks and tennis shoes, he was wearing a short plaid skirt instead of pants and carried what could only be described as a purse. This, she discovered to her relief, was filled with his art supplies. Tilly was a little embarrassed at first when she began giggling after he told her he was from North Platt, Nebraska, and she blurted out, "I can see why you're not in Nebraska anymore!" This didn't disturb him in the least and they had a brief, friendly conversation about the shortcomings of the Midwest as a place to live. As part of the conversation, ReX paraphrased a quote from the Chicago columnist George Ade, *"A lot of smart young people have come out of Nebraska, and the smarter they were, the faster they came out!"*

Tilly also had enlightening conversations with "Jasper, the juggler from Juno", "Barbie", a young woman from Alabama who dressed the part and who had seemingly slept with most of the occupants of the room, and a delightfully lively, outgoing, and overweight woman named "Merry Queen of Scotch". Tilly found her cute and cuddly and thought that, should she ever began wanting to snuggle into bed with another woman, Merry would be at the top of her list. As Tilly sat on the sofa with Merry, she noticed that ReX was sitting on one of the bar stools next to the kitchen island staring intently at her. She found this unsettling until she realized he had a sketchbook in his lap and was drawing her. She knew he was an artist of some kind, so this solved her question of the moment, and as the assembly was disbanding, ReX thanked her for inviting him and providing a good subject for his drawing. Tilly was a little flattered that he would be interested in drawing her and suggested she would model for him again sometime, not really considering that he might expect all his models to be nude.

"Do you mostly draw people?" she asked.

"Well, people are endlessly interesting, aren't they?" he said.

ReX opened his sketchbook and showed Tilly his drawing.

"Did I really look like that?" Tilly asked.

"I don't know. I just draw people the way I see them in my mind. Other artists might see you differently," he said, as though any relationship between his drawing and what a photograph would record was immaterial to him.

"I like it," Tilly said.

"Good. That indicates you're a talented art critic!" ReX said with an endearing laugh.

The last to leave the party was Barbie, who was engaged in a philosophical discussion with Gary. This went on until after the others had tucked in and Tilly woke up when Gary finally got into bed.

"That must have been an interesting discussion," Tilly said.

"Yeah, she's a doll," Gary said with a laugh.

"Well, apparently you liked playing with her," Tilly said sarcastically.

"Never fear, Baby. I prefer cuddly dolls like you," Gary said, rolling over halfway on top of her and rubbing his erection against her thigh.

Tilly was tired and not really in the mood, but she didn't want to get into a fight at this hour, so she licked her fingers, lubricated her vulva with them, and pulled Gary on top. He reached a climax in record time, then gave her a perfunctory kiss and fell asleep. Tilly, in the mood by this time, took care of her own needs with her fingers and noticed that she was imagining what it would be like if ReX was her bed partner.

Spring 1965

As the spring wore on, the tantric sex idea reverted to rather routine romance. They had been a couple for nearly a year, and Tilly wondered if this was the usual shelf life of the passionate part of a relationship. Nothing was wrong especially, but neither of them found their sex life, or their affection in general, as thrilling as it had been at first. For Tilly, this was caused in part by Gary's continuing contact with Nama. He got a letter from her at least every week, and he was very secretive about their existence and content. Tilly became even more suspicious when Gary felt the need to spend a week in Los Angeles "with his parents" around Memorial Day. When he returned, Gary was curiously distant, and Tilly knew something was on his mind that didn't include her. She was technically wrong about this, but when he eventually revealed his proposition, it wasn't much better. It turned out that Nama had gotten involved with a group of young people in Los Angeles who planned to form a commune. Their plan was to buy land east of Los Angeles and build a free sex commune where everyone would be free, and everything would be perfect. Gary wanted to join Nama there and he proposed that Tilly join also.

As someone may have said, "You can take the girl out of Iowa, but you can't take Iowa out of the girl." This summed up Tilly's reaction. She loved San Francisco and all her new friends, but this was too big a stretch, and as lovely as it sounded to Gary, she was pretty sure it would come to a bad ending. More importantly, she was halfway through nursing school which she was determined to finish. Gary wasn't surprised at her reaction, but was disappointed, nevertheless. A week later, almost a year to the day from their first camp-out together, he packed his few possessions and caught a ride to Los Angeles, asserting to Tilly that they would always remain friends.

Summer 1965, ReX

Tilly was disappointed to lose her lover and bed partner, but she felt curiously free to open herself up to new friends and ideas. With the departure of Gary, Tilly became curious about her old boyfriend, Elmer. She hadn't written to him since the previous fall and, feeling a little nostalgic, decided to write him a friendly letter in hopes of finding out what he was up to and, perhaps, reestablishing at least an occasional contact since she was without a boyfriend for the summer. Elmer, who was at this moment, working in construction while still living in Cedar Falls, would have been quite receptive to more contact with Tilly, especially since his love life wasn't thriving at that moment. He still thought about Tilly often, even though he felt abandoned by her and his thoughts varied in the wide range of possibilities between disdain and desire. If Tilly's letter had reached him at the right moment, and if it had expressed any desire to reconnect, the future might have worked out quite differently in spite of his assumption that Tilly had become hopelessly heedless of decent demeanor after two years among the beatniks.

Tilly, unfortunately, assumed that Elmer still held to the thought-free lifestyle and the mindless form of patriotism she had remembered from her less "enlightened" days. The continued existence of this Midwestern idea was reinforced by news articles Tilly read in magazines and in conversations she had with her friends. Given her somewhat inaccurate assumptions about Elmer's attitude, her letter was mostly a recount of her strange friends and her year of exciting adventures. And she didn't want Elmer to know anything about Gary; especially that he had dumped her for a skinny, new age, girl gadabout.

Naturally, given their inaccurate assumptions about each other, Elmer interpreted her letter as an exercise in gratuitous one-upmanship and, not wanting to admit that he hadn't established any serious romantic relationship since she had left South Branch, tossed her letter in the trash and didn't respond. Everything he feared about her current lifestyle seemed to be confirmed in the letter and he was hurt and depressed for a week afterward. Naturally, his lack of response confirmed to Tilly in turn that it was finally over and that he had moved on, or more likely backward in her estimation.

In spite of Gary's absence, Tilly enjoyed a delightful summer of 1965. She had lots of friends in addition to Carol and Hub, and something was always afoot; trips to the beach, music concerts, picnics in Golden Gate park, and what amounted to a more or less ongoing party at the apartment with a curious and interesting collection of young people. With Gary gone and Elmer no longer in the back of her mind, Tilly was free to imagine the possibilities, to try new things, and to fly free as an experienced resident of San Francisco.

Halfway through their course of study she and Carol had begun to think very tentatively about the future. They would graduate in two years, and while this seemed far in the future, they began to have conversations about where they might settle and what kind of life they envisioned for themselves. Carol was focused on her career, assuming that her domestic life would take care of itself – perhaps with Hub but if that didn't work out, she was confident that something comfortable would develop. Tilly, on the other hand, pictured her future featuring a worthwhile career but with more emphasis on her family. Tilly had very little experience of women who didn't marry and have children and she had always assumed that that's what girls did when they grew up. She thought, without careful consideration, that her future path would follow that model. Her growing self-confidence and the influence of female friends who focused on their careers was a revelation to her and, for the moment, caused her to question, although not renounce, her ongoing assumptions.

She had been, to some extent, a little worried about a long-term relationship with Gary because, while he was fun to hang around with, she didn't feel he would turn out to be an equal contributor to the economics of keeping up a household. The new ideas that influenced her, however, gave her permission to enjoy whatever came along and trust her instincts to weed them out when the time came. She was going to want a man in her life and her bed and, at this moment, he didn't have to be a prime candidate for becoming her future husband, he could merely be a temporary dalliance.

This expansion of the field of carnal candidates bent her thoughts toward ReX. She knew he would be a strange, sometimes embarrassing, sometimes hilarious bedfellow, but why not have a tumble with someone out of your comfort zone for a while? She would definitely learn something, for better or worse, and have some good stories to avoid telling her future grandchildren.

ReX was a regular at Hippie Hill. He liked to take his sketch pad there on Saturday afternoons and draw the current cast of characters so Tilly knew where to find him. They often chatted in the park and he was frequently included in gatherings at the apartment, so Tilly knew he was a bit shy, in spite of his sometimes outrageous costumes, and he liked wine. How hard could it be to focus his attention her way? The answer was – not hard at all.

One Saturday afternoon, Tilly put on a low-cut top (she had given up wearing a bra a year ago), a pleated miniskirt, and boots. She grabbed a bottle of wine and went out to flirt with a fellow who could get them both excommunicated from South Branch if she were to bring him back home. She found ReX wearing men's clothing except for a skirt instead of pants, sitting on a folding stool drawing a young woman who was practicing doing headstands in a pair of tight shorts. Tilly knew he was an artist and cartoonist, that he originally came from North Platte, Nebraska, and that he was an iconoclast in his choice of clothing, but that was about it. She climbed the hill and waved to him.

"May I see?" she asked, gesturing toward his

sketchbook.

"Sure, why not?" he said.

His drawings were strange in that they exaggerated the parts of the figure that he was interested in, and minimized, or eliminated, other parts. As for the girl doing headstands, ReX had drawn her as though his viewpoint was a few inches in front of her intertwined fingers on the ground and looking up toward her feet which looked, in his drawing, to be hundreds of feet in the air. Also, he had drawn her in a skirt that cascaded sensuously downward from her upside-down position over her breasts, revealing bright red panties instead of the shorts that she was actually wearing.

"That's an interesting view," Tilly said cautiously. "But she's wearing shorts, not a skirt."

"Artistic license, my dear," ReX said.

In the ensuing conversation, Tilly learned that his

real name was Rockefeller E. Cox, and that he had decided to capitalize the final letter in each of his proper names rather than the first because it seemed too self-important to capitalize the beginning of one's name. He left out any punctuation as unnecessary. This made his name spelled rockefelleR e coX, hence, ReX was his initials rather than his proper name.

"Artistic license?" Tilly asked.

"No, poetic license," he laughed.

"So, ReX is your 'pen name' as it were?"

"I think of it as my pencil name."

"So, what do your friends call you other than ReX?" Tilly asked.

"They kind of invent names to suit the moment. The rest of the time my intimate friends call me 'Rocky'."

Tilly was in a playful mood. She slid her hand up under his skirt, squeezed his bare thigh, and said, "Rocky it is then!"

"And what do your intimate friends call you, Tilly?" he asked.

"Iowa."

"I've always wanted to spend more time in Iowa!" he told her. "I hear it's delightful this time of year."

"Is there anything your intimate friends understand about your manner of dress that I should know?" Tilly inquired.

"It's a protest against people judging one another by their clothing. Also, you must know yourself that sometimes it's more comfortable and freeing to wear a skirt, and other times pants are called for by the weather or situation. Women can do this without a problem; it should be the same for men." He said this matter-of-factly as though it should be obvious to everyone.

"I can't think of any counter argument. And anyway, I brought a bottle of wine," Tilly said, unscrewing the top of a bottle of Red Mountain.

Rocky put away his sketchbook and they passed the bottle back and forth. A 'getting to know you' discussion was held covering their childhoods in Iowa and Nebraska, how and why they came to San Francisco, what they were studying and where, and so on. Rocky was attending art school at the San Francisco Art Institute, although he wasn't fully convinced art was a subject that could be taught.

"Are you coming over to the gathering at our apartment tonight?" Tilly inquired.

"I figured I would," Rocky said.

"Bring your toothbrush," Tilly said, suggestively. She blushed at how brazen she was acting.

Rocky arrived in the evening with a change of underwear and a toothbrush in his bag, in case Tilly wasn't putting him on. They stayed up late talking about diverse subjects, including art and nursing, and Tilly found him interesting and funny in every sense of the word. He was definitely an iconoclast, just the opposite of the boys she had grown up with in Iowa.

She had reached a level of self-confidence that allowed her to enjoy exposing herself to strange ideas, and Rocky was just getting started. After several hours of sipping wine, punctuated now and then when a joint was being passed around, they unsteadily made their way to Tilly's bedroom.

"Just to be clear, Rocky," Tilly said, "I'm expecting you to sleep over."

"Good. By now, I might not be able to remember whose sofa I was otherwise planning to sleep on."

"Do you have everything you need?" Tilly asked.

"Everything but my nightgown," he said.

Tilly got out a pair of flannel pajamas Gary had left behind which she thought might be suitable if he actually needed nightwear for some reason.

"Those won't work," he said. "I believe if you spend the night in someone else's night clothes you begin to take on their characteristics. I'm sure Gary was a nice man, but I don't want to take the chance. It would be best if I slept in something YOU would normally sleep in. How about that pink baby doll there in your closet?"

"You want to take on MY characteristics?"

"It would bring us closer together if I become infused with your essence – and sleeping in your PJs would be the best way to do that."

Rocky said this convincingly and it did seem reasonable after several hours of wine consumption. Tilly typically wore panties and a nightshirt in bed, and she tucked in with a remarkably well-endowed man in a lacy pink baby doll outfit. Maybe it was the wine, but she thought he looked cute in it.

They got into Tilly's bed and Tilly expected to begin the assignation with kissing.

"There's something I have to tell you. Iowa, before we get too intimate," Rocky said.

"Oh, oh," Tilly thought, edging away from him. "He's got some kind of sexually transmitted disease! Just my luck."

"What?" Tilly said, expecting that one of them would be sleeping on the sofa.

"I don't indulge in mouth-to-mouth kissing."

"Why?" Tilly asked, surprised. Maybe he was just crazy instead of diseased.

"It's uninteresting and, more importantly, it's unsanitary. Kissing any of your other body parts is fine with me though."

"Okay. You can start with my cunt, then!" Tilly said, in a slightly drunk, slightly joking, and slightly annoyed tone.

"I'd love to," Rocky said, doubling his value as a boyfriend immediately.

Tilly started to giggle, imagining meeting him in the park and exchanging greetings that way. Rocky demonstrated his technique, which immediately doubled his boyfriend value once again. Tilly hadn't had sex for a while and twiddling her clitoris with his tongue hadn't been Gary's primary skill, so Rocky's fetish seemed especially welcome. Tilly's vocal climax woke up Carol and Hub, who commented on it in the morning once the new lovers had awakened and reprised their earlier performance, with a similar result.

"It sounds like the two of you got along all right together!" Hub noted when Tilly came into the kitchen.

Tilly blushed and just noted that he was correct. A minute later, Rocky came in, still dressed in her lacy pink pajama panties now speckled with wet spots.

"Do you guys have a phone?" he said. "I always call my mother back in Nebraska on Sundays after she gets home from church. Don't worry, I call her 'collect'." The phone hung on the wall at the end of the kitchen bar that was open to the living room/dining room and Rocky perched on a bar stool and dialed his mother in North Platt.

"Hi Mom!"

"I'm fine. What's the news in North Platt?"

"She DID! I'll bet that's the talk of the town."

"Right on the steps of City Hall? They must have been especially drunk last night. Is the sheriff going to get fired?

"I figured that, especially since you told me the mayor had his eyes on her already. Where did you hear this story?"

"I thought so. You learn a lot of important things in church, don't you?"

"Yes mom, of course I went to church early this morning."

"The sermon? It was about fully enjoying gifts from god! I'm going to be practicing that as much as I can!"

"Okay, Mom. Have a good week. Bye."

"She worries about me if I don't call every week. She's afraid I'll get involved with some strange characters; can you imagine ME doing that?" Rocky said, opening his eyes wide.

"I don't remember you going to church this morning!" Tilly said, remembering their morning sex from a few minutes before.

"I did go to church," Rocky retorted. "I just didn't mention the details of my new religion. Since last night I've become an ardent 'Iowaist'!"

In spite, or because of, Rocky's "peculiarities", the roommates found him friendly and funny. All in all, a very acceptable roommate, and without a formal discussion, Rocky moved into Tilly's room and became part of the family. He turned out to be a pretty good cook, taking over for Tilly when it was her turn in the kitchen and this further endeared Rocky to others. Over time, the housemates began to count on Rocky for coming up with the most unusual and interesting proposal on just about every subject that came up – what beach to go to (Lake Anza in Berkeley was much warmer than the Pacific Ocean), how to spend an entertaining evening (having too much wine, dressing in each other's clothes and drawing one another – even if you couldn't draw), non-boring foods (watermelon omelet with peanut butter), and, for Tilly, sexual venues and varieties.

Rocky's idea of sexual play was that every time should be a celebration. He wouldn't turn away from a routine roll in the sack, but he would prefer doing it while rolling down a sand dune wrapped around Tilly inside a sleeping bag. And while the missionary position could be all right for a quick twiddle, for serious erotic entanglements he preferred the downward-facing genuflection, or on special occasions, the pronated paddywankle. Tilly, who was hesitant at first when presented with some of the strangest of Rocky's cocky creations, eventually came to appreciate the supine slithertickle, or even, when she had consumed too great a volume of intoxicants, the Cockwomble's Gambit.

Tilly, who was still learning the ins and outs of sex, thought Rocky was crazy, but in a way that usually was enlightening and enjoyable. Her first experiences with Elmer were heart-poundingly thrilling, but awkward, imperfect, and unnecessarily serious. Gary had taught her to treat sex as play, and successfully helped her let go of any lingering feelings it might be dirty or immoral that were left over from her upbringing in South Branch. She thought of sex with Elmer as learning to ride a bicycle no handed; a little confusing, a little scary, and frowned on by your parents. She equated sex with Gary as learning to ride her pony, "Licorice" around the south forty, safe and fun. And unremarkable. Now that she was in bed with Rocky, she had her first experiences with sex that were more like riding a roller coaster.

Even though she was "in bed" with Rocky, his sexual inventions were not at all confined to the bedroom. Rocky's favorite locations for sex play were as varied as the clothing he might choose to wear on a particular day. He loved having surreptitious sex outdoors, and if their secret shenanigans were observed by a furtive observer, this made them even more to Rocky's liking. Tilly agreed with him about the pleasures of behaving naturally in nature, but the idea of being watched still took some getting used to for her, even though Gary was never especially opposed to doing a favor for the local voyeurs himself. Sometimes, Rocky would choose a location and position that would allow him to see any half-hidden observer without Tilly knowing about it. Tilly secretly found showing off her uninhibited side arousing since it would have been quite taboo in South Branch and began to see this "accidental" exhibitionism as adding an extra kick to their outings. Once this little kink became clear to Rocky, he would often give Tilly a running verbal commentary about someone who was secretly watching them, describing in detail the masturbatory misdemeanors of the voyeur. Most of the time, of course, they weren't being watched, but Rocky was fully capable of making up this commentary in his imagination if he felt they needed to supercharge their stimulation.

Even though Golden Gate Park is in the middle of a large city, it covers 1000 acres and there are many hidden places for lovers to canoodle under cover. During the Fall of 1965, Tilly and Rocky found quite a number of these places which they utilized for their own frolics. Naturally, many couples and voyeurs had discovered these same places so if Tilly and Rocky found their favorite place occupied, they became the voyeurs themselves until it was their turn. In this way, they learned several techniques from their fellow miscreants.

Most aficionados of outdoor sex lacked the imagination of rockefelleR e coX, and as a result these amateurs discontinued this part of their lovemaking during the winter months, which are sometimes, but not always, rainy and chilly in San Francisco. Rocky and Tilly solved this problem, except for the most disagreeable days, by adopting a costume that allowed their perversion to persevere. Rocky found, at a secondhand store, two outsized bright yellow hooded raincoats, and two pairs of clunky rain boots. These would keep them dry, but what if the chilly air began to cool their ardor? Tilly solved this problem in a very sexy way that Rocky completely approved of; they would each wear heavy women's stockings, held up by garter belts and, on the top, a heavy shirt left unbuttoned down the front. No underwear would be present to get in the way or need to be removed. The adventurers tried this in their usual places in the park, now free of waiting lines of voyeurs. The coats could be opened and wrapped around to hide their mostly naked fronts and they could fulfill their desires in a standing position as the sexy wetness of the rain enveloped them in what seemed like a protective hideaway. After a few tries at this technique, they realized they didn't really have to traipse into the wooded areas of the park. There were few visitors on rainy days and from a distance, even though they stood out in their yellow raingear, they appeared to be quite proper lovers enjoying a hug and a kiss on a rainy afternoon. Even if their movements were a bit suggestive, none of the few observers imagined that a couple would be so brazen as to have sexual intercourse in the rain under a tree at the edge of a meadow.

Although Tilly made gestures suggesting that she was embarrassed by Rocky's inventions, both knew this was just an insincere formality to preserve her now nearly abandoned veneer of womanly propriety. Tilly was vaguely aware that, in her mind, she had over-embraced the delightful silliness of San Francisco and exaggerated the disagreeable prudishness and provincial character of South Branch. This brashness, though, was the booster rocket she needed to escape the pull of her past, and Rocky, for now, had his finger on the launch button controlling her lift off toward escape velocity.

Rocky not only had a fun fetish about having sex outdoors, he was also jarringly iconoclastic about clothing, or anything that one might put on one's body as decoration, protection, or costuming. While he was, of course, aware of the customary differences between "men's clothing" and "women's clothing", he looked at clothing in quite a different way. That is, he was interested in whether it was fun to wear and fit the underlying requirements of the situation. He often, but not always, wore a skirt instead of trousers simply because he liked the feeling; it didn't cramp his scrotum, it was easier to free his penis to urinate, and the cool air reduced the unpleasantness of a sweaty crotch. He had no particular interest in whether others misinterpreted his intentions, and all manner of interesting and useful clothing was available for practically nothing in second-hand stores – why not live it up?

Rocky actually thought it silly there was some kind of requirement that people wore clothes at all. It wasn't required of animals, and there were instances when clothing was unnecessary or even in the way. The idea that there was a LAW against going naked in public annoyed him. Why should it be anyone else's business? He thought it was nuts for women to dress as animals by wearing fur coats, but he didn't see it as any of his business. And if he wanted to walk around as a hairless animal it shouldn't be any of their business either.

Rocky was also frustrated that people, looking at his drawings, sometimes were put off by their erotic content.

"They're lines on a sheet of paper. It's not as if I'm recommending they have sex with the spare tire in the trunk of their car just because I drew that!"

In spite of Rocky's iconoclastic attitude, he didn't make a big deal of any of this. Others' attitudes just seemed as strange to him as his did to them. His ideas seemed strange to Tilly as well, but she considered them "un-Iowa" which made them somewhat endearing to her. Not only that, once one gave up the somewhat random and indefensible attitudes, especially about clothing, they made perfect sense. Ironically, under Rocky's influence, Tilly began dressing in more "feminine" clothing. She had taken up the habit of dressing in T-shirts and jeans or shorts, but these were tight, hard to get off, awkward in the bathroom, and sometimes too hot, whereas a short, swishy skirt felt sexy, allowed one to keep cool, and gave a nice effect should one feel like spontaneously twirling.

Tilly knew when she took up with Rocky that he was an artist who specialized in erotic cartoons, and he had expressed a desire to draw her even before they became a couple. While being an artist's model sounded easy, Tilly found that it was strenuous to maintain a fixed position for twenty minutes at a time. But she was in good physical shape and learned to adjust her pose to minimize the stress. She had expected that Rocky would be primarily interested in drawing her nude, but she found that he usually liked her to pose in at least some clothing, or other covering, not necessarily worn in the usual way. She also had to get used to his drawings being created from odd viewpoints and that he took his "artistic license" seriously, exaggerating his favorite body parts which often made her unrecognizable, a fact that Tilly frequently appreciated. Since they enjoyed an intimate relationship, Rocky would sometimes arrange their bodies in a sexual position and draw her while they had sex. On these occasions, Tilly had to enjoy what she could until he finished drawing and got to work on her. These drawings, by their nature, were extreme close-ups, and her favorite of these were recognizable as erotic but the viewer was left to guess what body parts were being represented and what sex the participants were.

From time to time, Rocky attempted to sell his cartoons which usually featured erotic drawings of things that most people would find a turn off (there weren't that many spare tire fetishists out there). This didn't really bother Rocky because he had a monthly stipend from his mother to cover his schooling and take care of routine expenses and contributions to his church. The "contributions" portion of his income was used religiously for taking Tilly out for a fancy dinner once a month. The lack of a requirement for Rocky to earn any kind of living fit right in with his complete disinterest in and lack of attention when it came to money. He didn't have a checking account, but instead, kept cash in an envelope in the drawer of Tilly's desk. When the amount in the envelope got low, he cut down on his spending until it was refilled or borrowed money from people he had helped out when the envelope was full. Rocky was a devotee of Henry David Thoreau and, when Tilly questioned him about money, his response was always a quote from *Walden*:

"Through want of enterprise and faith men are where they are, buying and selling, and spending their lives like serfs."

As to his schooling, he increased his rate of attendance after moving in with Tilly since she was in class every day and he had no one to play with at home so he figured he might as well attend classes. These he enjoyed although he considered the attempted instruction a waste of time and often spent the time drawing his classmates at work on their assigned projects rather than working on his own.

Most of the time, Tilly was humorously bemused by

Rocky, a situation that she enjoyed. It kept her on her toes, required her to think carefully about life and the accuracy of her automatic reactions to new situations and ideas. His comfortable craziness was usually endearing and his bad habits easy to deal with. Like many of the young men in San Francisco, Rocky was casual about cleanliness. Tilly took care of this mild annoyance by sweetly inviting him to shower with her when necessary, and this had the added benefit of turning into a sweet sexual tryst. If his underwear needed laundering, she simply threw it in the wash with hers, or suggested he leave it on when they got into the shower together and washing it in situ before removing it to dry. This turned out to be so much fun that she often required him to wash her undies in the same way.

Her other ongoing annoyance with Rocky also related to his clothing. When he took her out to dinner, their choices were somewhat limited because many of the nicer restaurants required their customers to dress presentably. Of course, they wouldn't have been going to the Tadich Grill anyway, but even less formal restaurants were leery of "hippie types" and required unripped long pants and collared shirts for the men and dresses for the ladies. And shoes of course. This, to Rocky was painfully formal, but Tilly found that if she promised to rip these garments off him as soon as they got home, he could be persuaded.

Apart from these minor troubles, Rocky was a sweetheart in every way. He genuinely cared about her and he kept her laughing, either with or at him, every day. She had a vague feeling that his outlook would eventually get old but, for now, she chuckled every day that it took a nutcase from North Platt to impart the real San Francisco style into a formerly sensible girl from South Branch.

Summer 1966

By the summer of 1966, Tilly and Rocky had been together for a year. Tilly and Carol had finished three years of nursing school and were looking forward to graduating and beginning their "real lives" the next summer. Tilly still loved being with Rocky, but she couldn't really say she "loved" him. He was endless fun, and endlessly annoying, but it had always been clear, and was clearer now, that he would be hard pressed to take adult responsibility for anything when he grew up, and she wasn't at all sure that he would grow up at all. His mother would continue supporting him and would probably leave him enough to struggle along with eventually. But while he was very much rolling-around-in-bed material, he would probably never become husband material. As "San Francisco" as Tilly had become, she still had enough practical Iowa girl in her to perceive the potential perils and humble prospects of Mr. rockefelleR e coX. The result of this growing realization was not a breakup, but an increasing awareness of other candidates for her affection.

As part of their nursing studies, Tilly and Carol volunteered at the newly constructed French Hospital on Geary Street. They worked as assistants to interns at the hospital, and Tilly was assigned to work under Ira Gold, a young doctor who seemed to be the exact opposite of Rocky. Dr. Gold was serious, focused, responsible, and solvent. He was good-looking and had no problem with wearing a business suit. Tilly couldn't imagine him in any variety of work clothes other than scrubs. She considered it a virtue that he didn't joke around on the job and that she never had to parse his statements for hidden meanings or obscure references to Thoreau. Of course, he had no imagination, which was a shortcoming, but Tilly was gradually leaning toward becoming more serious in her choice of boyfriends. Future boyfriend or not, she wanted to develop a friendship with Dr. Gold in hopes he could help her in her career once she graduated next summer. It didn't take long for Tilly to discover he was susceptible to a bit of flattery and, over time, they developed a comfortable working relationship although there was no hint of a future romantic relationship from the young doctor.

Meanwhile, Tilly and Rocky had settled into an affectionate and routine relationship, inasmuch as Rocky ever could be counted on for routine. If anything, he was gradually becoming more unconventional. Now, if he was naked when the postman came, he no longer bothered to put on clothing before walking downstairs and retrieving the mail from the mailbox outside the front entry. He claimed this was no problem since he was on his front stoop rather than in public, but he did draw some stares from the passersby on occasion. He also developed a liking for talking Tilly into getting naked and going down the outside fire exit stairs to the backyard with him late at night. There was a picnic table in the small backyard that could be observed from five neighboring apartment buildings if anyone were awake. Having sex on this table was not terribly risky on a dark night, but there usually was light from the moon, the urban sky, or an exterior light nearby, and this could allow any nosy neighbors to secretly observe their activities. To be fair, Tilly loved the risk when they were in the middle of a semi-public frolic, but afterward, she often couldn't sleep due to the conversations she would have with herself about the propriety of such a performance. She wasn't ready to give up on Rocky, but so far, her attempts to ease him into taking more responsibility for his public persona had not succeeded. Carol and Tilly discussed the subject of their future careers and romantic associations often and, for now, Tilly decided to take Carol's advice and just let things play out as they happened.

Toward the end of summer, Rocky's mom was diagnosed with a serious illness and he had to return to Nebraska to take care of her for an undetermined amount of time. Tilly was sad to see him go, although it did take away her daily need to think about how it was going to play out between them.

In his absence, Tilly decided to go back to South Branch for a brief visit to her parents and friends before she and Carol began their senior year. She planned to let Elmer know she would be there, but after thinking about his failure to respond to her letter the year before, she decided he had written her off. This had infuriated her, and she assumed he would be spending the summer in Cedar Falls as usual anyway. To hell with him she thought, why subject herself to another disappointment?

Fall 1966, Dr. Gold

Not long after Tilly returned from South Branch, she and Carol were invited to a party celebrating the end of Dr. Ira Gold's internship. At the party, Tilly and Ira had a friendly conversation during which they discovered they were both fans of the San Francisco Giants. As it happened, the season was winding down, the Giants were in the running for the pennant, and Dr. Gold had tickets for the game the next Wednesday afternoon. On the spur of the moment, he invited her to join him. Of course, she accepted, not really expecting much apart from a pleasant afternoon at the ballpark, but, as Carol had said, "Just wait and see what happens".

The day was sunny, and the game was exciting. The score was 0-0 after six innings, but over the last three innings the Pirates scored 5, but the Giants scored six for the win. Ira was a baseball buff and recounted statistics from memory during the game, and since he was a doctor, he was also able to recite the detailed physical characteristics of the players, their height and weight, speed on the bases, previous injuries and so on.

In the excitement after the win, Ira gave Tilly a hug and invited her to dinner at Alioto's, a fancy seafood restaurant on Fisherman's Wharf. She had taken the bus to his house and he had driven them to Candlestick Park for the game, so he drove Tilly to the restaurant and home afterward. Tilly was not sure their gameday dress would be appropriate for a fancy restaurant, but he assured her that he ate there often and there would be no problem. He was right about this, and about his choice of restaurant. The dinner was fantastic and since they were celebrating, she enjoyed a cocktail before dinner and a glass of wine with her cioppino. Afterward, Ira dropped Tilly off in front of her apartment. She didn't want to invite him in due to the usual untidiness, but they both thanked each other for a good time and expressed a desire to repeat the rendezvous. There had been no romantic gestures or propositions, which Tilly took to indicate that Ira was a gentleman, a mark in his favor.

Meanwhile, Rocky kept her up to date about his mother's condition, which was not improving, as well as the annoyances of Nebraska. Tilly responded to his letters with the latest news from San Francisco although she didn't mention Dr. Gold since there was nothing significant to report. Once there WAS something significant to report, she didn't mention this either.

The Giants' final eight games were on the road. Tilly and Ira had attended the final home game of the season, so for the next game, on Saturday in Houston, Ira invited Tilly to come to his apartment and watch the game on television. She accepted with pleasure and dressed carefully for the afternoon. Tilly didn't want to be aggressively sexy, but she didn't want to express aggressive disinterest either. She wore a knee-length black skirt and an orange sweater, Giants' colors, and took a jacket and Giants hat with her in a large purse, into which she also tucked a change of panties and a toothbrush just in case. Carol drove her to Ira's apartment in Pacific Heights, an upscale part of town, so she would know where he lived in case Tilly might need to call her to come and rescue her from some difficulty or if she needed a ride home due to a late hour and an incapacitated boyfriend.

There was no need for a rescue. The pair had a fine time watching the game and a fine celebration once the Giants had won. The celebration included hugs, celebratory drinks and a bit of flirtation and concluded with another invitation to dinner at a local restaurant they could walk to. The setting was intimate this time and, as they walked back to Ira's apartment, he hinted that he'd like to see more of Tilly in the future. Neither wanted the evening to end early, so they watched a romantic movie on TV, holding hands and sitting close together on the sofa. In Tilly's experience, even this modest level of intimacy could be expected to conclude with an invitation to stay overnight, but Ira seemed too shy to bring up the idea, and Tilly couldn't bring it up without appearing too eager or promiscuous. Still, Ira seemed like a gentleman, not an unwelcome trait in a man that a young lady from Iowa might find herself interested in.

On Monday, Tilly received a phone call from Ira who seemed unusually nervous. He obviously had something he wanted to talk to her about, but the conversation took a while to get there. They discussed the weather, Saturday's game, and the Giants prognosis for the rest of the season. They talked about the upcoming schedule, a mildly interesting topic, but what Tilly really wanted to know was how soon they would be naked in bed together. Finally, Dr. Gold got around to the topic of the Giants vs. Pirates series in Pittsburgh the next weekend.

"Sure, I'll come over, those clean panties are still in my bag!" Tilly thought.

"What do you say we fly to Pittsburgh and take in a couple of games?" he asked.

Tilly was stunned and took the offer as a joke at first. "That sounds like fun, but my budget is too thin for a cross-country trip to see a ballgame," Tilly told him with a laugh.

"Well, I'd be picking up the tab for everything of course. It's customary for the gentleman to pay when he asks a girl for a date!"

"Do you really mean it? Wow. That sounds like great fun!" she said. "I think flying is so cool, and I've never been east of Chicago."

"You know we'd have to fly out early on Friday and hope to make it in time for the night game. Then see the Saturday game and come back on Sunday, right?" Ira said cautiously.

"Great!"

"And we'd have to stay over in a hotel," he said.

Tilly paused for a couple of seconds to picture him in bed naked.

"I could get us two rooms of course, if you'd rather," he added quickly.

"Oh, no. I wouldn't want you to have to spend that much money!" she said, as though minimizing his outlay was the most important thing on her mind. "We can stay in the same room. I'm sure nothing bad will happen!"

Tilly meant this as:

"I'm sure we'll be fucking like minks and it will be great!"

Ira heard it as:

"I'm sure you won't pressure me to have sex with you."

"I'll be on my best behavior," Ira promised.

"No need to overdo it!" Tilly said flirtatiously.

The trip was agreed to. Carol was thrilled for Tilly when she found out, and they went shopping to find just the right nightwear, sexy but not slutty. Carol also helped her pack for the trip, and they went over each item, imagining the events where it would be worn, if the sexiness coefficient matched the circumstances, and in particular situations, how easy it would be for a man to remove it. A great deal of giggling took place during this process.

On Friday, Ira picked Tilly up early, lowered the top on his recently purchased Pontiac GTO convertible, and they headed down the Peninsula toward San Francisco International. Tilly was so excited about the trip and the possibilities that she could hardly sit still. In her fantasies, she and Ira were already lovers, and she had to be careful to hold back her expressions of affection to match reality. This time, Tilly hardly felt any nervousness about the flight since she couldn't get over the idea that she would be spending two nights alone in a motel with a handsome, wealthy, man who always dressed properly in public, at least as far as she knew.

It was a long flight, with stops in Denver and Chicago on the way, and this gave them time to talk. Ira was from New York. His father was also a doctor, and he had traveled widely with his parents as he was growing up. He had a sister in Florida. Tilly got the idea that he was a shy, studious boy growing up, who spent much of his time playing baseball, which he was good at and still very interested in. Neither gave any details of their previous sex lives, but it was clear that Ira wasn't all that experienced with women. That was okay with Tilly; she could train him to her liking.

As it turned out, it was raining when they arrived in Pittsburgh and, when they landed, they discovered the game had been rescheduled as part of a double header on Saturday. This was fine with Tilly; she could begin Ira's training on Friday night, and have time to give him a quiz on Saturday morning.

They checked into a nice hotel in Pittsburgh and settled into an upper floor room with a spectacular view over the city and the Allegheny River. They were three hours ahead of East Coast time, so this allowed plenty of leisure for a flirtatious dinner and a memorable bedtime. Once back in their room, Ira turned on the TV and Tilly slipped into the bathroom where she took a quick shower, dried her hair, and put on her new baby doll pajamas with the ruffled bloomers and the low-cut neckline. She checked her look in the mirror, and, although imperfect, her body looked sufficiently tempting in her opinion. Tilly twirled once in front of the mirror, then slowly opened the door and slinked dramatically into the bedroom.

Dr. Gold was nowhere to be seen. There was nowhere he could be hiding, although Tilly looked under the bed anyway. Surely, he didn't find her so unacceptable that he just left town while she wasn't looking. His suitcase was still there so maybe he had just slipped out for some fresh air. Sprays of windblown rain pelted the window. Before she could get too worried, Tilly heard the key in the lock and Ira came in, carrying two bottles of champagne.

"I think we should celebrate now so we don't have to worry about how the games come out," he said. "That's quite a nightie, by the way."

"Thank you," Tilly said.

They turned off the TV and sat close together on the sofa, sipping champagne and disinterestedly talking about baseball. Each wondered if the other was going to make a romantic move or suggestion.

"I'm not too good at girls," Ira finally said by way of explanation of his hesitation.

"I haven't noticed any problems so far," Tilly said.

"I mean I don't have that much experience. I haven't dated that much. Mostly I was involved in baseball or school," he said.

Tilly wondered if this was a gambit to get her to show him how she liked it. He was in his twenties after all; nobody could be THAT shy.

"Shall I show you the ropes?" she asked with a champagne-assisted giggle.

"Did you bring ropes?" he asked, slightly too enthusiastically.

"That was a figure of speech, Ira."

Dr. Gold's shyness notwithstanding, Tilly was getting horny, and she began to encourage him by pulling out his shirt tail and rubbing his belly. Her ministrations and the champagne began to take effect and he was obviously enjoying her touch. This led to gradual removal of more clothing, enthusiastic kissing, and the enlargement of body parts. Ira stood up facing the seated Tilly, whose obvious next move was to remove his jeans and lower his white, Y-front briefs. She willingly accepted this implied invitation, quickly dispensing with his pants and pulling the waistband of his briefs toward her so as not to disturb his erection, then sliding the garment sensuously down his legs to reveal his manhood in close up detail for the first time. His cock, (this was the first word that came to her mind, in spite of her medical training) was remarkably large, fully erect, and three inches in front of her face. Tilly cradled this appendage in the palm of her hand and addressed it as though it was a new friend:

"Hello there, it's nice to meet you," she said softly. "I think we're going to be great friends."

She gave the tip a tentative lick, which caused a twitch and an exclamation of pleasure from Dr. Gold, who grasped her hair in both hands, gathered it behind her head and forcefully pushed his erection into her mouth. This was a little abrupt for Tilly's taste, but she understood some men behaved this way. It could just be his modus operandi, or the result of his inexperience with women.

A moment later, he reluctantly pulled back and took Tilly's hand, raising it so she stood up and turned her to face away from him, then took off her frilly nightgown and matching panties, and tossed them aside. Tilly anticipated that since he wasn't an expert at this, he would escort her to the bed and after a few preliminaries, climb on top of her. Apparently though, he had had his fill of preliminaries. Standing in front of the couch, he bent her over from the waist. Her hands rested on the back of the sofa. Ira placed his hand between her legs, pushed her thighs apart, and without fanfare, took his member in his hand and guided it into her vaginal opening. Tilly was well lubricated from anticipation, not foreplay, but at least there was enough lubrication to avoid discomfort. She looked out the rain-streaked window behind the sofa, admiring the lights draped over the landscape of Pittsburgh that seemed to be animated by the rainy veil as he held her hips and pounded his penis in and out of her. He was well-endowed, but apart from that, Tilly found little to excite her. He only touched her in a way that would increase his own gratification. He seemed quite uninterested in her pleasure, and after a few minutes of pushing himself in and out of her, pulled out and ejaculated a large volume of semen onto her back.

After a minute or two of rest, he straightened her up, turned her back to face him, gave her a kiss and complimented her skills at lovemaking. Tilly didn't feel she had been given time or inspiration to demonstrate any of her skills and, if Dr. Gold had any, he didn't demonstrate them either. Ira left it to Tilly to deal with his untidiness and got into bed. By the time she had ducked back into the shower for a minute to clean up, pulled on the panty portion of her PJs, and then climbed into bed, Ira was asleep.

Tilly remained awake for some time. She considered masturbating but her level of desire had dropped precipitously after her imperfect experience a few minutes before, and she involuntarily took up the task of reviewing in her mind both the praiseworthy and the irritating qualities exhibited by the four men she had been intimate with so far.

Elmer was a little hard for her to review since they

had both been so inexperienced when they were a couple. He was sweet and clearly loved her, to the extent either of them knew what that meant at the time. She tended to raise his ranking due to the fact that he was thrilling by virtue of being her first, but she marked him down because he had unceremoniously dumped her when she got to San Francisco, and because he was hopelessly dull and provincial. He was good-looking and well intentioned in bed, but clumsy and unimaginative as a lover. This could be chalked up to his inexperience, but she doubted he had learned much over the ensuing years because he only had Midwest girls to practice on. And anyway, she was a San Francisco girl now so any "farm boy", including Elmer, was out of the running as a long-term companion.

Gary was more experienced and wonderfully fun-loving. Although he wasn't the most well-endowed of her lovers, he was good in bed and taught her that sex was for fun and there wasn't a huge moral issue at stake as long as neither wanted to hurt the other. She would have even called him imaginative in bed if she hadn't spent time with Rocky later! Gary was smart and funny, and she loved his poetry. On the debit side of the ledger though, Gary was unrealistic about practical matters like figuring out how to earn a living or navigate any serious life issues that might arise. And, of course, his running off to live in a commune with Nama didn't raise his long-term value in her mind. She still considered Gary a good friend, but his standing as a potential partner in perpetuity was not promising.

Rocky was in a class by himself, although she wasn't completely sure what the subject matter of the class was. He certainly wasn't dull, that was for sure, but although riding a roller coaster is fun now and then, it can become tiring as an everyday adventure. His drawings were fun to look at, but he had no interest in turning them into a money-making venture; in fact, Tilly realized that if they were to become popular, Rocky would lose interest in doing them.

Rocky was hilarious and embarrassing, thought provoking and irrational, brilliant and stupid. She wasn't sure how long Rocky would have to remain in Nebraska to take care of his mother, and she was anxious to see him. But she wasn't sure what she wanted to happen when he got back. She wondered if there wasn't something out there between the continual chaos of rockefelleR e coX and what could become the daily dullness of the doctor who, having satisfied his personal urge, was now dreaming sweet dreams of fast Pontiacs and fat stock portfolios under the covers next to her.

Dr. Gold was certainly correct when he told her he wasn't good with girls, which she took to mean inexperienced. Tilly believed this could be remedied in time, and he did have many promising qualities one would desire in a man that, she hoped, might be more than a temporary dalliance. His performance wasn't promising, but Tilly expected that enlightening a wealthy man about her expectations in the bedroom would be easier than schooling a sexy man to be a standout in the boardroom. She drifted off to sleep, only to dream about a baseball stadium full of beautiful men desperate to please her but distracted by fighting over who got to go first.

On Saturday morning, Dr. Gold got up first, taking care not to awaken Tilly who had not gotten a full night's sleep. He took a shower, dressed in his Giants regalia, and ordered breakfast for the two of them from room service. Twenty minutes later, Tilly was awakened by the commotion of the room service delivery boy entering and setting up their breakfasts on the coffee table. She propped herself up on an elbow to see what was happening, forgetting she was topless. This caused an embarrassing but exciting moment for the young delivery boy, a puff of manly pride for Ira, and a little arousing moment for Tilly.

"You gave that boy a nice tip!" Ira noted after he left. "Two of them as a matter of fact."

"He was cute. Maybe he can bring us dinner too," Tilly said, imagining herself and the young man giving Dr. Gold a demonstration of how a tryst should transpire.

Ira could tell that Tilly was a little distant this morning and searched his mind for a cause. Perhaps she was tired from the flight and hadn't wanted him to take so long having sex the night before. Anyway, they had an important double header to look forward to and he wanted to be sure to get to the ballpark in time for batting practice. So much for Tilly's hoped for resumption of their game that, like the Giants/Pirates game the previous evening, had been a washout.

Any regrets about Ira's earlier shortcomings were gradually forgotten over the course of the two games as the Giants scored 2 runs in the eighth inning of Game 1 to win 5-4 and the same in Game 2 to win 2-0. They were in a tight race for the pennant, and this helped their pennant chances. After the game, they went back to the hotel and straight into the bar. As it turned out, there was a small collection of far-from-home Giants fans gathered there and apart from a break for some bar food, Tilly and Ira spent the evening overindulging in intoxicants with their new friends. There was a moment during the drinking spree when, had they gone upstairs to bed, Ira would have still been interested in sex, erect enough to carry it out, and slowed down enough to please Tilly with his longevity. By the time they staggered upstairs after the celebration however, Ira was too plastered to perform, and Tilly was wildly horny but too tired and fuzzy to make a successful attempt to get herself off.

The next morning, Ira proposed a morning quickie, but Tilly had a headache. Ira interpreted this to mean she just wasn't in the mood and dropped the subject, and by the time they got back to San Francisco that evening, there was a fog of misinterpretation between them. Tilly thought her opportunity for a continued romance between them was irreparably damaged, but a few days later, Ira called to invite her to dinner and bemoan the fact that even though the Giants had won eight out of their last nine games, they still fell 1½ games short of winning the pennant. They ended up at Ira's apartment, and a cautious conversation commenced about the future of their relationship. Tilly definitely wanted it to continue; she liked the doctor and thought she could improve his bedside manner with some personal instruction. Dr. Gold liked her too and knew he had a lot of catching up to do on his checklist of life experiences. Since they had spent two nights in bed together already, uneventful as they had been, Dr. Gold invited Tilly to sleep over in his apartment.

Thinking they wouldn't be needed, Tilly had not brought any bedtime necessities with her. She didn't have a toothbrush, a change of underwear, or sexy nightwear.

"Oh my. I didn't expect to be invited so I didn't bring anything with me," she said, hoping he would tell her that her delicious body would be all they needed.

"I can take care of that," Ira told her. "I have a few new toothbrushes laying around, and no nightwear is sexier than a man's shirt with nothing under it! I have plenty of shirts that would look sexy on you."

Tilly accepted his proposition before she considered how disheveled she would look in the morning with no hairbrush, hair dryer, or makeup. "You have to promise not to complain in the morning when I look like a wreck," she admonished, anticipating that Ira expected her to look slightly less like a hippie than she usually did in the morning.

"I've seen you first thing in the morning, remember?

And both the delivery boy and I thought you looked perfectly lovely. Let's go pick out some evening clothes for you."

They went into Ira's walk-in closet and Ira picked out a ratty old shirt for her to wear. It had paint stains on it and holes in the elbows. Tilly didn't find anything sexy about it, except that the front and back extended only an inch below her crotch. Dr. Gold however, loved it.

"I like imagining you as a farm girl," he said to her astonishment. Ira took a moment to fantasize about spending an afternoon plowing her furrow after she had spent her morning plowing the north forty.

"Well, I was a farm girl, so I guess you should like me just fine!" Tilly said.

"And should this shirt get torn or soiled in any way, we could just throw it away!" Ira noted.

This gave Tilly pause, but Ira was removing her clothes in a way that was fun, and she didn't pursue his thoughts about how the shirt might become damaged. She tried on the shirt which looked horrible to her, but she understood that to a man who had never seen a farm, a farm girl in an old shirt might stir up some fantasies, and that could work out well for her.

"Do I get to dress you up?" she asked.

"What would turn you on?"

Tilly went through the hanging clothes. "I like this tie," she said, then started on his dresser.

She pulled out a stretchy garment that, at first, she took for a swimming suit.

"What's this?"

"That's a wrestling singlet. I used to wrestle," he told her.

"Ok, that and the tie. Which drawer are your socks in?"

"The next one."

Tilly chose a pair of hideous socks with butts on them. "The tie, the wrestling singlet, and the butt socks. If you want to get silly, we might as well match," she said. "Where did you get these socks?"

"A fraternity brother gave them to me for my birthday a few years ago. He was quite the joker."

"It's fun poking around in your drawers," Tilly said, continuing to rifle through his belongings out of curiosity. That's when she found the small duffel bag containing a supply of ropes, handcuffs, clamps, other restraining devices. Tilly looked at Ira suspiciously.

"Were you planning to bring this out later?"

"Well, I was going to keep it under wraps until I had a sense of how you might respond to it," he said.

"That depends on who the victim would be," she said. "You're not an axe murderer, are you?" she said this as though it was a joke. Still, she began to feel a little vulnerable – she was dressed only in a shirt and wasn't sure where Ira had stashed her clothes.

"I can guarantee I'm not an axe murderer. Some people think it's fun to be tied up and played with. You might like it, or you might like tying me up. You're the one who found that. I wasn't going to bring it up for a while."

"I've never been tied up," Tilly said.

This was a lie. Rocky had tied her up a few times and she liked it because he had used the opportunity to drive her wild with desire before making her come. Still, jumping into this with someone she had only known for a short time was problematic.

"What do you do with girls when you tie them up?" Tilly asked.

"I've never tied up a girl so far," he said.

"What do you imagine doing to them?"

"Touching them until they get very aroused, and then having sex with them."

Ira was embarrassed about this. He hadn't intended for it to come out, and he had forgotten about the duffle bag or he would have steered her away from it.

"Forget about the idea," he said. "We can just do what we've done before."

Tilly was not thrilled with this idea since she had gotten the short end of the bargain the last time in Pittsburgh. "Let's bring this stuff out next time," she said, proposing that they just pretend to tie her up for now.

Before they began playing on the sofa, Ira brought out a knit cap and tucked her hair under it so it wouldn't get in the way. As a prelude to lesson one in pleasing her, Tilly took Ira's hand and slid it inside her shirt demonstrating how to arouse her nipples. Before long they were fondling each other quite effectually and they took the play to the floor where Ira showed her some delightful wrestling holds and taught her to reproduce them on him.

After they were both rather aroused, Tilly suggested they pretend she was restrained and see how it went. They got into bed and Ira arranged her to his liking. Her shirt was unbuttoned by now and he laid her face down on the bed, raised her arms over her head and demanded she grasp the vertical bars on the headboard and hold on. He spread her legs wide apart and laid down on top if her. She could feel his erection through the tight wrestling singlet.

"I'm going to have my way with you!" he announced quietly.

"Oh, Ira, please don't rub your fingers against my pussy. That would be torture!" she said.

He did and it wasn't – except in his fantasy world. Before long, Tilly, who hadn't had an overabundance of sex lately, was shivering involuntarily.

"Please don't take your singlet off and tie me up with it!" she begged.

Ira was confused by this – was she telling him what to really do, or did she want him to only imagine himself taking off his singlet.

"Um…" he said.

"When I tell you not to do something, you'd better do it, or I'll strangle you with that lovely tie!" she said sweetly.

"If I really don't want you to do something, I'll yell out 'Pirates Win' and you'll know what I don't want. Now, leave that singlet on and don't tie me up with it."

Fortunately, the doctor was a smart guy and had no trouble navigating the conversation once the rules had been sent down from the female-in-chief.

Ira took off his singlet and tied her wrists to the headboard, then reclaimed his place on top of her. Tilly wriggled her butt seductively against his erection as though trying to escape. Finally, she was getting a turn at being the 'victim' of receiving the pleasurable attention.

"You're so much stronger than I am. Please don't push that big penis into me," she pleaded. "And don't reach around and play with my vagina. That would be pure torture!"

"All right, whatever you say," he whispered.

"You'd better not, you bastard," she said, a little surprised. "And don't fuck me until I can't stand up for a week, damn it!"

Ira got up to his knees over her prone figure, and began admiring her ass, squeezing her butt cheeks with his hands. Tilly began to get a little desperate. She was ready for him and thought maybe he had gotten confused about the instructions. His finger gently slid down the crack of her ass and continued until it reached her labia which were now swollen and sopping wet. He barely touched her clit and observed her reaction which was wild movement of her body to try to increase the contact and random calls for him to do it more and quit doing it.

"Don't not stop playing with my cunt that way," she moaned, confusing herself and the Doctor.

Nevertheless, it was clear what she really wanted so Dr. Gold moistened his member with her juices and slipped inside her, then reached under her and gently fingered her as instructed. Or not instructed. This was gloriously perfect, and Tilly was seconds away from a magnificent orgasm, when Ira abruptly withdrew and, as he had before, ejaculated stream after stream of semen onto her back.

"Oh my god!" she shouted, frantically thrusting her hips against the pillow that was raising her midsection off the bed.

The doctor took his time recovering, then belatedly realized his work wasn't finished and reached between Tilly's legs, bringing about her desperately needed but imperfectly timed orgasm. Once both of them had stopped their involuntary twitching and regained their normal breathing rhythm, they were able to form words and a quiet conversation began again. Tilly had been furious when he had pulled out, but she now considered the risks if he had ejaculated inside her and forgave him for the awkward delay. And she had enjoyed a climax that, while imperfect, was pretty damn good.

"That was great," Ira said.

"Strange but nice," Tilly agreed. "Would you mind getting a towel and wiping your come off my back and helping me take off this shirt, it's soaking. I must say, doctor, you do know how to make a massive mess!"

"Sorry."

"Don't be sorry, it's flattering when that happens."

The pair were exhausted after their encounter and, following a hasty clean up, went right to sleep.

This experience encouraged Tilly, in that it seemed a little progress had been made toward getting Dr. Gold to think about her needs as well as his own, even though it didn't seem to come naturally to him.

Spring 1967

Tilly put the next eight months into an effort to turn Dr. Gold into an adequate lover. Her progress was hit-and-miss; sometimes he seemed to be interested in her pleasure, and other times it seemed his own needs were the only thing on his mind. Over the winter and spring, she learned his habits and peculiarities; he was uninterested in seeing her in fancy dress, couldn't look into her eyes when they made love, preferred to copulate "doggy style", and was careful to wear a condom when he was inside her unless he intended to withdraw before ejaculating. Many of these things indicated that he wanted to be cautious regarding pregnancy, but some seemed unusually careful. They spent nights together several times a week; always at his apartment. They ate at top-notch restaurants, always at his expense. It was clear he liked spending time with her, and in the spring, they took up their baseball game outings once again. Ira seemed fascinated by her rural upbringing and he admitted to fantasizing about her life on the farm.

One afternoon they attended a Giants game and, upon returning to his car, found that it had a flat tire. Ira told Tilly to wait for him as he walked back to the stadium to make a call for someone to come and put on the spare.

"Why don't YOU just do it? If you call someone, we'll be here until dinnertime."

Ira admitted he had never changed a tire and didn't know how. "It's easy, I'll show you," Tilly said. "Give me your keys."

She opened the trunk, located the jack and removed the spare tire. As though she had done this many times, which she had, she expertly loosened the lug nuts on the offending wheel, installed the jack and lifted the car, removed and replaced the flat tire with the spare, tightened the lug nuts working her way from one nut to the one opposite, lowered the car, gave the nuts a final tightening, replaced the hub cap and put everything away. This had taken her seven minutes, slow by her standards but miraculously fast in Ira's mind.

"I couldn't even have walked to the pay phone and back in the time it took you!" he marveled.

"You'll know how to do it next time, Baby," she told him, hoping he would have learned how to properly tickle her clit by next time too.

Their sex life did progress. She introduced him to the technique of performing oral sex on her. This was only fair since he expected that service from her every time, and he introduced her to anal sex, which she enjoyed once she got used to how strange it felt at first. And any "naughty" idea that Ira came up with seemed like a step in the right direction.

All in all, by now she was quite comfortable with Ira. He remained good-looking, gentlemanly, and rich. And he seemed to be very fond of her. But like all the men she had spent time with over the years, he didn't seem to share her yearning to eventually form a family unit. In spite of her mother's unrelenting inquiries on this topic, Tilly observed that women she knew weren't rushing to get married as was expected of girls in Iowa, and she was confident that she would either meet the perfect man, perhaps a future co-worker or friend of a friend, or something would suddenly bloom with one of her many San Francisco friends.

And anyway, she and Carol were about to graduate and they would have the entire summer to play, enjoy the city, and hang out at the beach if the weather cooperated.

CHAPTER 4   BIG MAN ON CAMPUS

Back on campus again for a go
Our Elmer was ready to show
All the girls at the gym,
Their dream guy could be him
Surely not ALL could say no.

Fall 1964, Betty

Elmer's thoughts turned from his summer tumble with Tiffany to his sophomore year ahead. He felt like this would be a great year at State College. He was confident he would do well, and he was anxious to reunite with his college friends. Plus, a whole new crop of freshmen girls would be arriving on campus; if nothing else, Tiffany had boosted his self-assurance that someone besides Tilly would find him boyfriend material.

Elmer was proud of his muscular physique and, when he returned to campus, he again began spending time at the Rec Center lifting weights and admiring the girls. He now had his truck with him and he and several of his friends occupied an apartment near campus. Elmer had reached the elevated status known as "sophomoric" and he embodied this designation with his unearned expertise on everything. This boosted his confidence and coolness at the gym and increased the number of girls he was friends with. However, most of the girls he met already had steady boyfriends, so this didn't immediately translate into a romantic relationship.

Elmer received a letter from Tilly shortly after he arrived back on campus, describing her summer trip, how much she loved her roommates, and the enchanting eccentricities of California. He responded with a one-paragraph summary of his summer, from which he left out any mention of Tiffany.

His twentieth birthday was a couple of weeks later and Tilly sent him a card wishing him a happy birthday and noting that her old friend Linda had let her know he had been seen publicly displaying his affection for a young waitress at the Burger Shack. "I hope that works out!" she had written. Elmer wasn't sure whether she was being sarcastic or congratulatory.

Elmer, exhibiting his new confidence, took a full load of courses. The most problematic of these was beginning calculus; Elmer was never a talented math whiz, and even the name "calculus" sounded more like a disease than a branch of mathematics, ("I'm sorry Mrs. Ruffintumble, but I'm afraid your husband has terminal calculus!"). Now that Elmer was a sophomore however, he felt ready for anything. And besides, it was a required course.

Elmer was lost within the first fifteen minutes of the opening lecture and turned his attention to a young lady sitting to his right. He first noticed her geometric shape and thought a hands-on study of her curvilinear geometry might be educational. She was attractively voluptuous and delightfully cute. Her countenance gave him the impression she was both studious and fun loving and her focus on following the lecture and taking notes might make her suitable as a tutor during those moments when they were resting between sexual romps. Elmer studied her in detail.

She had dark brown hair, stylishly styled in a "flip" which swished like a skirt when she moved her head. He couldn't see her eyes from his point of view, but she had a turned-up nose which he found to his liking. She was attired in a tight red sweater that showed off her rounded and attractively oversized breasts. Her knee-length poodle skirt and saddle shoes suggested she was a freshman who hadn't had time to catch up on the latest college fashions. Her lower legs were shapely and had only a hint of the unattractively large ankle circumference common to midwestern farm girls. Her hands didn't display any of the roughness that might have suggested she was used to working on a farm. His new friend's lack of obvious makeup gave Elmer the idea that she was a normal girl and not excessively flirtatious, and he found these qualities enticing. The young woman was dutifully writing in her new notebook and Elmer observed that she was left-handed, noting that this would be advantageous. When she snuggled next to him in the truck, she could comfortably use the hand with the most developed motor skills to tickle his inner thigh.

Before he knew it, the class was over, and Elmer

maneuvered his way next to her as they were leaving class. As they walked down the hall, he casually asked if she had understood everything.

"I think so," she said, a little shyly Elmer thought. "I had some of this in high school."

"I noticed you were taking a lot of notes."

"Well, I don't want to get behind the first day. This is my first college class ever and I want to do well," she told him.

"You mean this is your first class on your first day of your first year?"

"Yes. I'm SO excited. I suppose you're an old hand at all this," she said, smiling at Elmer like he was an expert at this college stuff.

"I'm a sophomore this year so it's very familiar," he told her.

"I don't even know my way around campus yet, but I suppose I'll learn eventually. It's all just very confusing right now."

"Don't worry, I can teach you everything you need to know," Elmer said with a laugh. "First, never talk to strange boys you run into on campus!"

"Oh, oh," she grinned. "I've messed up the first day."

"My name's Elmer," he said. "So, you're fine now!"

"Thank you, Elmer. I wouldn't want to fall in with the 'nameless' crowd. My name is Betty."

"Glad to meet you, Betty," Elmer said. "I'm not very functional when it comes to mathematical functions.

Maybe you can clue me in one of these days."

"Maybe I can. You could show me where the best coffee shop is sometime, and I could enlighten you on the details of differential calculus if you get stuck."

"That sounds fair!" Elmer laughed. "Do you have the next period free? I could take you over and introduce you to the State College of Iowa by buying you a coffee. It's a traditional welcome here."

"Is it safe for a girl to let a strange boy buy her coffee on her first day on campus?"

"No," Elmer said, steering her in the direction of the 'Campus Coffee Cup Café', "Unless his name is 'Elmer'. How about if I take you over to the 'Straight C's'?"

"The Straight C's? That doesn't seem like the most scholarly gathering spot in town!"

"It isn't, but the 'Straight A's' has lousy coffee."

They had a friendly and funny conversation in which Betty didn't seem as shy as he first thought. During their impromptu coffee date, Elmer learned that Betty lived with her parents in Cedar Falls, that she was an only child, and that her old boyfriend had gone off to college in Southern California. Having a former lover who left for college in California gave them something in common.

"The same thing happened to me last year. We spent the whole semester writing to each other, but she got so caught up in California craziness that I don't even hear from her anymore."

"Well, you were ahead of me," Betty said. "My boyfriend dumped me before he left town so he wouldn't have to waste time writing. It's okay though, I have new people to meet and lots of studying to do."

"It must be hard to meet people when you don't live on Campus."

"Well, Elmer, I met you and that's a start!"

Elmer noticed how blue her eyes were and how the corners of her mouth turned up just so when she said something that could be either flirtatious or a casual joke. He removed her outer clothing and approvingly admired her underclothing in his imagination.

She tilted her head. "Has your mind wandered off, Elmer?" she asked.

"Oh, no! Sorry!" he said, focusing on the conversation again. "What were you saying?"

"I asked what you like to do for fun."

"I work out at the gym, tinker with cars, hang out with friends, that sort of thing."

"And you live on campus?"

"I have an apartment with a couple of other guys," he told her.

"Lucky you! I don't mind living at home though. It's cheap and I never have to cook or do my own laundry."

"So, you get along with your parents all right?"

"Pretty well. My dad drives a truck so he's on the road a lot, and my mom and I get along all right most of the time. And we're both busy so we don't have time to get on each other's nerves."

"What are you busy doing?"

"I work at the library and my mom's a fifth-grade teacher."

"I'll have to be on my best behavior if I get to meet her sometime!"

After a pleasant half-hour or so of pre-flirtatious conversation, the romantic hopefuls said goodbye and dashed off to the next item on their schedule, then spent the remainder of the day fantasizing about each other. Thus began that always-too-brief period when everything is potential and the kinetic has not yet had an opportunity to cause trouble.

Elmer was suddenly anxious to get to class on calculus days, although Betty's presence and their increasingly friendly flirtation didn't improve his focus on functions. On the other hand, if a 'function' is a binary relationship between two sets of numbers, Elmer did spend plenty of time considering the binary relationship between himself and the cute little number named Betty. An after-class visit to the Straight C's became a little tradition and, mixed in with revelations and inuendo, Betty did her best to enlighten Elmer on the ins and outs of calculus. She was only mildly successful at this effort, but her assistance did raise Elmer's calculus comprehension to the barely acceptable.

Without any complicated plotting on either of their parts, they began to see each other more often, sometimes for a movie in the evening or at a college football game. Unlike the initial clumsiness in his pursuit of Tilly, his interaction with Betty seemed to fall into place with little effort or strategy. Since Elmer had a vehicle on campus this year, their dates came with a built-in venue for private conversations, tentative touches, and exploratory, then expected kissing. Over some weeks, Elmer and Betty each built up an imaginary caricature of the other, a model of perfection that was pure delight while it lasted, even though each was now experienced enough to know that this image of perfection was temporary.

For Elmer, the first tiny prick in the aura of perfection surrounding Betty came when they were talking after enjoying a nice dinner and a movie together. They snuggled together in the truck, which Elmer had parked in a private location on his way to take Betty home. After fondling Betty's glorious breasts through her underwear, Elmer casually took the expected next step in their progressing intimacy by softly placing his hand on the inside of her knee. This didn't bring about any objection, but as he began to slide his fingers up her stocking-covered legs under her skirt, she shifted her position to make this a little more difficult. Elmer was undaunted; the first time he had done this to Tilly, the day after the prom, she nearly had an orgasm. As Elmer's index finger reached the bare skin of her inner thigh above the top of her nylons however, Betty wordlessly placed her hand over his through her skirt and stopped his upward progress. This didn't seem like a temporary signal, and after a time, Elmer retracted his hand a bit and rubbed the inside of her thigh well below her most interesting body part. Nothing was said by way of explanation or admonishment, so Elmer assumed this was due to a momentary situation. Maybe Betty was having her period or was becoming so aroused that she might do something she needed more time to build up to. Or perhaps she felt there wouldn't be enough time on this occasion to complete his obvious plan no matter how delightful.

Over time however, this pattern continued in a way that Elmer found a little curious. Betty seemed to be fine with intimate touching, more than fine in fact, as long as he steered clear of her vaginal area. She seemed to be careful to avoid his manhood and associated accessories during their intimate times as well, but above the waist, it was full steam ahead! One evening, when this behavior began to seem quite permanent, Elmer cautiously brought up the subject, commenting that other girls he had been with enjoyed that kind of below-the-waist intimacy and didn't find it objectionable.

Betty assured him that she knew that activity was pleasurable, and that she had enjoyed it in the past, but that she had found it too pleasurable for her own good and had endured a pregnancy scare that lasted a month. She had never been sure whether she had just skipped a period for some reason or had been momentarily pregnant, but it wasn't a situation she wanted to risk. In addition, she felt she could become addicted to his skills at arousing her this way and neglect her studies which she was determined not to do. Elmer found this flattering, but not really satisfactory as a long-term policy. Nevertheless, he was very fond of Betty and continued to enjoy her company since he wasn't flooded with prospective girlfriends. This limitation on their sex life also had the benefit of leaving more time for tutoring, and Elmer was able to finally pass the calculus class with a surprising C.

Winter 1965

By the time the semester was over, Elmer and Betty had a close but complicated romantic friendship. They went to movies, romantic dinners, and sporting events together. And they enjoyed intimate but limited "foreplay" that was delicious but frustrating. Of course, Elmer could take care of his own sexual frustration, but it wasn't ideal. He understood her situation, and admired her willpower, but he couldn't figure out whether this affair might evolve into an unsatisfying future or, at some future point, a lifetime tsunami of sensational sex.

Despite the problem of Betty's program, Elmer noticed that he was a little in love with her, as she was with him. At a different time and place he would have found her an ideal partner; as it was, the two were tethered such that their needs couldn't completely overlap. The result of this imperfection was that their relationship gradually became more and more platonic. Elmer resumed his search for the perfect girlfriend, not that he had ever completely abandoned it, and Betty relaxed into a great friendship with Elmer that didn't involve daily self-doubt about her decision to set aside her desires. Gradually the sexual component of their activities together lessened but their affection for each other remained.

Elmer enjoyed a snowy Christmas at home, hanging out with his friend Eddie, but avoiding the Burger Shack since he didn't really want to encounter Tiffany, about whom he felt a touch of guilt in case he had led her, over the previous summer, into a situation she now regretted.

Spring 1965

By springtime, any worry that Tiffany would want to take up where they had left off the previous summer was eliminated when she wrote him that, over the winter, she had acquired a new boyfriend, had become pregnant, and would be getting married on the fourth of July. Elmer sent her a card wishing her the best. He was happy for her. And even happier for himself.

The school year continued as normal, but in the spring, Elmer's gym schedule began overlapping with that of a young freshman, Patti. She seemed to take a liking to Elmer and they often talked while waiting between sets or after their workouts. Elmer found her a little intimidating at first; she was stunningly beautiful and bristled with self-confidence and worldly knowledge. Patti was always fashionably dressed and drove a new convertible, even though freshmen were officially forbidden to have a car on campus. He found out she was from Detroit so maybe that explained it. Like most of the other girls he had met at the gym, she had a boyfriend, so Elmer didn't feel any particular pressure to impress her and, as a result, he was unusually relaxed around her in spite of her stunning looks.

Patti's boyfriend was not on campus. She knew him from an elite high school in Detroit and he was now a freshman at Yale. This settled in Elmer's mind the idea that she wasn't a serious candidate for his affections, but they would often have coffee together after their workouts and became good friends. When Patti left Cedar Falls to go back to Detroit for the summer after her freshman year, she gave Elmer a hug and a peck on the cheek and told him she would be thinking about him while she was gone. Elmer wasn't too sure exactly WHAT she would be thinking about him, but he did notice that Patti began to regularly occupy a place in the rotation of girls he fantasized about.

Elmer stayed on campus in Cedar Falls for the summer and found a job with a local construction company. This allowed him to stay in his apartment with a few friends and enjoy the amenities of being near campus as well as to continue his association with Betty.

Fall 1965, Patti

Elmer, now beginning his junior year, turned twenty-one, a milestone that made him officially an adult in every way except personal maturity, and he was working on this as well. Classes were under way again and Patti was back on campus. Their friendship resumed as before and he noticed that Patti had by now become the central character in his sexual fantasies, even though there had been no overt romantic sparks between them the previous spring. They did become more intimate in the sense that they began to share their troubles and successes with each other. Elmer told Patti about his romance with Tilly and how it had slowly diminished until nothing was left, a situation that he blamed on her and her wanton West Coast lifestyle. Patti revealed that she and her former boyfriend had broken up over the summer. Apparently, he had been cheating on her for quite some time and, at least in his mind, his status as a Yale student put him in a higher echelon of elitists than she occupied. Elmer and Patti consoled each other over these setbacks and, gradually, their interactions became more frequent and flirtatious. Over a month or two, the flirtations became teasing, which became touching, which became fondling, which became foreplay for a full-blown romance that both knew was going to burst into full bloom before long. Both were looking forward to this development but were slightly afraid that a wild romance would overwhelm the things they enjoyed about the platonic aspects of their friendship.

Each planned to go home for Thanksgiving, although Patti's overprotective parents were hesitant about her driving to Detroit by herself. She revealed to Elmer that her parents were very protective of her, which she found infuriating, and that she had no desire to spend Thanksgiving in Detroit with her parents and their wealthy and inebriated friends. She planned to go only because it was expected. Elmer had intended to go home to South Branch for the holiday as well, but the apartment would be empty and if, for some reason, both he and Patti had to stay in Cedar Falls, they could hide away in his apartment and minister to each other's sexual needs. Patti agreed this would be something to give thanks for, but each of them would need an excuse to stay on campus and neither had a good idea.

Fortunately, Mother Nature took care of this problem by conveniently staging a blizzard two days before Thanksgiving that made the roads impassable across much of the Midwest. Bingo! Now they could spend the holiday together and give thanks as often as possible!

Elmer was thrilled by the prospect of spending several days alone with Patti. He had been in intimate relationships with two different girls so far, but except for the night he and Tilly spent together at the Sleeptite Motel in St. Louis, he had never awakened to find a naked girl in his bed. He pictured nonstop sex, only pausing to eat now and then. He savored the idea of watching her getting dressed in the morning, just so he could undress her five minutes later. Elmer expected it would be like being married for a few days. He wondered if this might perhaps be the optimum duration for a marriage.

Everything would be so cool! He could show her his erotic moves and take a shower with her. They could slip morsels of food into each other's mouths at their candlelight dinners. He and Patti would be the perfect picture of affectionate domesticity. He could admire the

231

way she brushed her hair and applied her makeup, perhaps even watch her pee as he shaved. Elmer was sure she wasn't a virgin, but being older, he would naturally be able to teach her a few new sexual delights she had yet to discover.

They began their rendezvous on the day before Thanksgiving. Once his roommates had left Cedar Falls, they went grocery shopping just like an old married couple. It would be fair to say that neither knew much about cooking although Elmer knew how to make spaghetti and Patty could whip up a simple omelet so they wouldn't starve. And Elmer was an expert on ordering pizza so they would be fine.

Elmer's grocery list included Kraft macaroni and cheese, spaghetti, peanut butter, six meatloaf and, as a nod to the holiday, two turkey TV dinners. And two weeks' worth of desserts. Patti was especially excited about the TV dinners since she had never tried one. The only items on her list were a large bottle of chocolate syrup and a quart of extra virgin olive oil and her intended use for these items had nothing to do with cooking.

Their next stop was the liquor store where Patti directed the purchases; these had to be made by Elmer since he was officially an adult. Her shopping list consisted of four bottles of champagne, two bottles each of cabernet sauvignon and gewürztraminer (or a pedestrian chardonnay if gewürztraminer was unavailable in Iowa). A bottle of Highland Park Scotch completed her list; quite impressive for a girl of nineteen. This part of their shopping added up to approximately five times the cost of the food, but Patti handed Elmer the cash out of sight of the cashier before they checked out. They climbed into Elmer's truck for the drive to his apartment, and turned to each other, anticipating with pleasure the delights to come. Patti began the delights by sliding over and giving Elmer a toe-curling kiss and putting her hand in his lap.

"I've got a feeling you're anticipating more than a good dinner when we get to your apartment!" Patti said with a big smile.

"I'm looking forward to several days of frisky domesticity!" Elmer told her.

Once they got the supplies into the house and Patti brought in her suitcase, the cohabitation commenced. Both knew what to do, they just didn't know what to do first.

"Pour us a glass of champagne, Elmer. I'll be right back," Patti said, picking up her suitcase and disappearing into the bedroom.

Elmer didn't have a better idea than to do what he was told, so he opened one of the bottles of champagne, found two ordinary drinking glasses, and filled them three-quarters full of bubbly champagne.

After a few minutes, Patti, dressed in silky, transparent pink baby doll pajamas, rejoined him in the kitchen.

"I'll pick up some champagne flutes for you the next time I'm in the liquor store," she said, clinking glasses and taking a sip. "Here's to the daring and delightful days we have ahead of us."

Elmer had never heard champagne glasses called flutes, but if Patti was going to supply them, they must be the "in" thing.

"Let's go in on the sofa and enjoy our champagne and each other!" she said, taking Elmer by the hand.

Patti's outfit didn't leave anything to the imagination and Elmer couldn't take his eyes off her.

"Let's play a game, Elmer," Patti said.

"Do you have a game in mind?" Elmer asked.

"You know that kids' game, 'Simon Says'?" she asked.

"Sure. The leader gives a command and if he or she doesn't say 'Simon Says' first, there's some kind of punishment if the others follow the command."

"Right. This is just like that except you always have to follow the instructions whether I say 'Simon Says' or not."

"What's the punishment then?"

"If you don't do what I tell you, you get a little spanking. But you'll want to do what I tell you."

"Okay."

"Take your shoes off," she said, leaning back on the sofa like Manet's Olympia.

Elmer took his shoes off.

"Now stand over there on the other side of the coffee table," she said, taking another sip of champagne.

"Okay, you may entertain me by taking off your shirt."

Done.

"Simon Says, 'Now your undershirt'."

Elmer dutifully followed her instructions, glad not have to think up every move and then make sure it was okay with her.

"Unbuckle and unzip your jeans and let them slide down your legs naturally, don't push them down until Simon tells you."

Elmer did this, although his jeans only dropped a couple of inches before they caught on his erection.

"Extend your arms out to the sides and twirl around."

"Okay, take your pants all the way off and toss them aside."

Elmer did all these things and then, clad only in his white Y-fronts and socks, awaited his next instruction. There didn't seem to be that many possibilities left. Patti took her time admiring his muscular body and his endearing confused look.

"Come over here, Elmer, and sit with me on the sofa," she said.

Elmer sat next to Patti, facing her and they entangled their bare legs and sipped champaign.

"Did you like following my instructions, Elmer?" she asked.

"Sure."

"Good," Patti said. "Sometimes I like being in control of my men."

This was a little confusing to Elmer, beginning with the question of how many men she had been in control of and what they were required to do, but he wasn't going to start questioning her about that right now!

"Shall we play a game of 'Patti-CAKE'?"

"Clapping our hands together like kids?" Elmer asked.

"Oh no. 'Patti — Cuddle And Kiss Everywhere'!"

"Oh! That sounds like fun," Elmer said enthusiastically.

They began a slow-motion game in which they attempted to kiss every square inch of one another. Of course, this was impossible, and some regions received more attention than others. During the flow of the game, Elmer's underwear and Patti's pajamas were discarded as one delight led to another. Patti produced a condom and applied it to Elmer as though she had done it a million times. The game ended with the two of them on the floor as Patti wiggled seductively and purposefully, astride Elmer's midsection. This ultimately caused both to express their pleasure vocally, yet incoherently.

Once the excitement diminished into the normal range, Elmer retrieved a towel from the bathroom and dried their midsections and the carpet as well as he could.

"I loved the 'Opening Ceremony' of our personal

Winter Olympics, Elmer!" Patti declared, raising her glass

"I think we tied for Gold in the 'Patti-CAKE' event!" Elmer said. "And I can't wait to team up with you in 'Doubles Luge' over at the single-bed venue!"

"I'm especially looking forward to the 'toe-CURLING' match," Patti asserted.

Elmer was already reconsidering his assumption that his experience in the erotic arts would require him to tutor Patti a little.

"Patti, where did you learn all these great games?" he asked.

"You didn't think I was a virgin, did you Elmer?" she asked with a giggle.

"No. Neither am I, but I never learned THOSE games!"

"I'll tell you, but you have to promise not to think I'm a slut!"

At this moment, if her cleverness in bed made her a slut, Elmer was well on his way toward developing a special fondness for sluts!

"I promise," he said.

They sat facing each other at opposite ends of the sofa, legs intertwined.

"I may not have told you that I went to a fancy boarding school in Detroit. My parents have lots of money and they were too busy to put up with a teenager. It was an all-girls school, but there was an all-boys school across the street so there was a secret sex club that met in a storeroom the boys had turned into a sex den. They had keys and all the staff just thought it was off limits to them and that only some higher-ups had the keys. Girls who met the criteria, being nice-looking and horny, were invited to join and I lost my virginity, which I was happy to get rid of, at my first meeting."

"So, you must have had sex with lots of men?" Elmer asked, rather taken aback.

"I was counting at first but after a couple of dozen I couldn't remember whether I had already counted my latest partner or not, so I gave up."

"And you never got any STDs or pregnant or anything?"

"Everyone had to use rubbers, that was a strict rule, and several of the members had parents who were doctors so they could supply the girls with birth control pills, which were only available to married couples otherwise. I have a connection, so we don't have to worry about pregnancy. I've been tested for STDs, although we never broke the rules, and I'm pretty sure you're clean, but we should get in the habit of using condoms until you get tested. I don't want to have to explain a penicillin prescription to my folks."

"Wow," Elmer said. "What else did you learn at this sex school?" Elmer was pretty sure he wanted to know but was a little nervous about the details.

"Come with me, Cowboy, and I'll show you," she

said, spontaneously making up a nickname for him. She led him into the bedroom.

Patti opened her suitcase and displayed a selection of devices only a few of which Elmer could identify. He had seen plastic dildos in a porn shop in Des Moines once, so he understood the general theme of the contents, but the exact use of many of the devices in her possession was not apparent to Elmer.

"Are you going to demonstrate all these to me?" Elmer asked hesitantly.

"Yes. By the time we've used all of these on each other, neither of us will be able to get out of bed for a week!"

He hoped she was joking.

"Ready to get started?" she asked.

"Sure, I haven't gotten laid for twenty minutes!" Elmer reminded her.

Patti gave Elmer a tour of the contents of her suitcase. There were very few articles of clothing, especially outer clothing, which Elmer took as a good sign. On the other hand, there was considerably more makeup than seemed necessary for a woman who didn't intend to leave the house. Patti was beautiful without make-up and Elmer thought any time she spent applying makeup would be better spent making out. Among the powders, creams, and sprays; hair curlers, blow dryers, and rollers, Elmer did notice a box of "body paint" that tickled his curiosity.

Patti's collection of sex toys was contained in a large,

padded container, similar to a jewelry box. Elmer recognized several plastic dildos of various shapes, sizes, and anatomical accuracy, in both black and pink colors. Some were powered and one was a gigantic, plug-in model that would clearly not fit inside her, but would shake the entire house when she used it! These didn't seem to have any erotic application to Elmer's needs, apart from the amusement of watching Patti use them on herself, possibly aided by the three different types of "personal lubricant". Other items did make him wonder. A package of various sized short, fat, dildos labeled "Butt Plugs" drew Elmer's curiosity although he didn't contemplate the idea that he might have one in HIS butt within the hour.

Patti's collection contained various masks, two or three kinds of short whips, an array of ropes and straps, a package of "French Ticklers", as well as curiosities whose use Elmer could not ascertain by a visual inspection alone: pairs of brass balls, sets of small clamps connected by a short chain, and a series of beads connected in series on a string.

"Are you going to explain all these thingamajigs?" Elmer asked.

"It will be better if I just show you how they work," she said. "If I explain them first you might be hesitant."

"What if I'm hesitant after you try them out on me?"

"We're going to try them out on each other. You know I'm not going to hurt you, Elmer. If you don't like something, I'll stop doing it. And anyway, you'll be using most of these gizmos on me. Now lie down on your back and spread your arms and legs out wide!"

Elmer gave her a suspicious look, but her grin looked sufficiently enticing that he followed her orders.

"I think I'll leave your socks on," she said. "You look sexy in socks. Socks and a blindfold."

Patti chose a blindfold from her collection and fastened it in place. He could feel Patti sitting cross-legged between his outstretched legs and felt her observing every detail of his nearly naked body. This caused him to feel a twinge of embarrassment, modified by a surge of arousal.

Patti leaned forward and placed her hands on his chest.

"Elmer," she began softly, "I'm going to restrain you and tease you until you can't stand it. And then, once I've decided you've gone crazy enough, I'm going to cause you to ejaculate all over us. Won't that be fun? And don't worry, next time you can tease me the same way. Now, reach up to the headboard of the bed. It's so convenient that you got a bed with these attachment points. You must have known I'd be coming over sometime."

Elmer was naked and blindfolded, and even though he thought this sounded a little kinky for his taste, he was not going to try to talk her out of her plan. He felt her get up and heard her rummaging around in her collection of toys. A moment later his wrists were handcuffed to the head of the bed.

Patti took up her position sitting between his spread

legs and began very softly touching his thighs, the front of his hips, and his belly but carefully avoiding his genitalia for now. During this time, she kept up a sexy patter letting him know how attractive she found him, how sexy he was, how she enjoyed watching his erection trembling, and assuring him it would just be a little longer before she began massaging his more sensitive parts. After he began gasping for air and shivering, Patti gave him a short rest while she retrieved two lengths of rope from her kit of kink. These she tied expertly around his ankles and pulled his legs up and over his supine body and attached the other end of each to a bedpost at the head of the bed next to his wrists. Resuming her cross-legged position behind him, she now had full access to all of his most vulnerable regions including his genitals, belly, thighs, and spread buttocks.

Elmer didn't care what she did next as long as it involved touching his privates. He didn't know that she had brought back more toys than just the ropes and that she would definitely be touching him. No sooner had his shivering and gasping moderated than he felt Patti's fingers caressing the backs of his raised thighs and in their circumnavigation of this part of his anatomy, he noticed they were slowly zeroing in on his anus. Elmer had never considered the erotic possibilities of his region, but suddenly these possibilities became very apparent. Elmer was embarrassed to realize this girl he was trying to impress was now rubbing him in a shockingly intimate way. He felt drops of a cold liquid drip onto the area just below his scrotum and dribble down his butt crack, followed by the feeling of the tip of Patti's index finger just resting in the dimple of his anus.

"Oh my god, Patti!" he said. "I thought only men did that to each other!"

"I'm sure they do, but why should they have all the fun?" she asked.

Elmer couldn't think of a reason. She slipped her finger into him up to her first knuckle.

"I know it's strange the first time, but just relax and enjoy it. There's more to come!" she said, with what Elmer could hear was a big smile.

Elmer didn't have any choice in the matter at this point.

"Okay. This part is going to feel VERY weird, and you'll feel like it will make an embarrassing mess, but trust me, everything will be fine!"

"How could it get any weirder than this?" Elmer wondered.

Patti rubbed more slippery lube around his opening, and he felt an object being slowly inserted.

"Just relax your bottom, Elmer," Patti cooed. "Just give yourself to me completely, I won't hurt you. Well maybe a little as it gets closer to the big end, but it will feel good by the time I'm finished." Patti laughed out loud.

"Closer to the 'BIG END'?" Elmer thought, hovering between ecstasy and panic. The slow insertion

continued inexorably, and Elmer had no idea how much progress Patti had made toward the 'BIG END'!"

"Don't forget to relax your ass sweetheart," she said, caressing his buns with her free hand.

Elmer realized he was being penetrated with one of the 'Butt Plugs' he had seen in her gear, and surely the biggest one. Finally, he could feel the diameter of the object getting smaller, leaving him feeling filled but strangely stretched.

Surely Patti would make him come now. Pre-come was already oozing from him and dripping on his belly; he was shaking with desire.

"Are you ready to come yet, you beautiful man?" Patti asked. "You look so hot tied up that way with a little plug up your ass!" she giggled.

Elmer made sounds that she couldn't understand.

Patti stood up on the bed, turned around facing Elmer's bottom, and carefully stepped astride him with her feet next to his armpits, then lowered herself down to her knees with her sex a few inches above Elmer's face, removed his blindfold, and began to masturbate. He was, by now, crazy with lust.

"Ready Cowboy?" she asked, touching the tip of his already dribbling member with one finger as her copious vaginal lubrication dripped onto his face. Patti continued to masturbate with her other hand and soon reached her vocal and wiggly climax. Elmer followed suit even though Patti never stroked him; the gentle contact between her finger and the tip of his penis was enough to launch his outrageous outpouring of ejaculate.

After a minute or so of fluid chaos, she collapsed onto his front as his body became limp with release. The lovers panted, twitched, praised one another's performance, kissed their partner's nearest body part, and gradually regained their wits.

A significant cleanup was required once they returned to reality.

Needless to say, these five days constituted the sexiest and most delightfully exhausting Thanksgiving holiday Elmer had ever spent, in spite of the TV dinners. He hadn't had any female companionship for a year, except in his imagination, but even his imagination couldn't match the real-life Patti.

As it turned out, Patti's little scene of dominating Elmer was a means of introducing him to one of her favorite amusements; being dominated herself by a good-looking man who could clearly overpower her if he wanted to. Of course, this required a man that Patti could trust to stick to the practices that thrilled her rather than actually abusing her. She was attracted to Elmer in part because she trusted him to be a good and safe partner in this game. Elmer, having next to no knowledge of this practice, had to be trained in pleasing her this way. Although it seemed curious to him, he was quite interested in pleasing her, and his small introduction as the subservient partner gave him an appreciation of her liking for this game.

Over the course of the Thanksgiving holiday, Patti introduced Elmer to most of her collection of sex toys, told him tales of the boarding school sex club that he didn't really believe, and introduced him to a playful side of sex that his earlier experiences hadn't emphasized. Naturally he loved her delightful notions, but he found himself worrying from time to time whether he could keep up with her, and, if they were to have a long-term relationship, whether she would get tired of him and look for more variety elsewhere. For now, however, Elmer was a willing student at Patti's Playschool.

Thus, began Elmer's two-year tumble with a girl who seemed perfect in just about every way as long as they were in bed together, which they were at every opportunity. As the year progressed, Patti and Elmer learned how to please each other, and how not to, and pursued advanced research in the ins and outs of sex play. For the most part, Patti was the one who took the lead in trying new things and she encouraged Elmer to join her, often including things that had never crossed his mind. Patti didn't know everything however, and when spring came, Elmer searched the fields and woodlands around Cedar Falls and identified a number of spots that would be interesting places for outdoor sex. Patti had little experience with this since she had grown up in an urban area and fucking outdoors appealed to her sense of adventure and risk. It didn't, however, appeal to her dislike of bugs so this venue didn't become a focus of their research.

Summer 1966

By summer, their relationship had settled into a comfortable routine. Patti wasn't a fan of anything routine of course, so their routine was a bit less routine than one would expect. For some reason, which Elmer only later discovered, Patti wanted him to visit her in Detroit while school was out for the summer. He was agreeable to the idea and was curious about her wealthy background although he was somewhat nervous about what he might encounter in an enclave of wealthy city folk. The plan was for Elmer to drive to Detroit for the Fourth of July holiday, two weeks after school was out. Elmer was rehired for his summer construction job in Cedar Falls but arranged to start work after the Fourth which would give him time to prepare before visiting Detroit.

Elmer's uneasiness about the upcoming trip was heightened by Patti's insistence that he acquire a new suit before the visit in order to be admitted to some of the likely dining establishments they would be going to. Patti proposed to take him shopping before she left Iowa for the summer. She resolved to buy him a new summer suit as a belated birthday present since she had missed his twenty-first birthday, which had occurred before they had become an item the previous fall. Elmer supposed that was a good idea because he owned a total of one suit that fit him when he was eight years old. Even the idea of shopping for a suit was foreign to Elmer, but Patti took him to a men's store in downtown

Cedar Falls, and handled everything including, and especially, picking out just the right garment and accessories. Elmer felt stupid in the suit, but he did agree he looked sharp. Before leaving campus, Patti introduced Elmer to her hair stylist and the two of them "improved" his hair style. By now, Elmer felt like a new piece of artwork Patti was taking home to show off to everyone, although Elmer didn't feel like he was that big a prize, so he just took all this as an amusing escapade.

When it was time to head for Detroit, Elmer packed his suit, casual clothes, and swimming trunks and set off as though he was heading for an exotic adventure. When he arrived at Patti's address, he found a grand house with a circular driveway guarded by iron gates. A party was under way, and the young men at the valet parking station directed Elmer around to the kitchen entrance, assuming, since he arrived in an old pickup truck, that he had come to deliver party supplies of some type. He wandered in, dressed in his blue jeans and Iowa State T-shirt, and inquired where he might find Patti. He was directed to the living room, where he found a crowd of impeccably dressed, but impossibly old, people sipping drinks, smoking cigarettes, and chatting about the stock market. His entry caused a bit of quizzical conversation among the party goers. In a moment, Patti came running up to him, looking gorgeous in a slinky dress and high heels, and gave him a kiss that was deliberately too passionate for the situation. Elmer hadn't expected to arrive in the middle of a party and suddenly had been involved in two breaches of etiquette, neither of which was his fault. Nevertheless, Patti's kiss focused his mind on a desire to get her alone in her no doubt lavish bedroom and remove that dress as soon as possible. Unfortunately, it wasn't possible. Patti took Elmer by the hand and together they worked the crowd where Patty introduced him as her "Iowa Cowboy". The fact that Elmer didn't live on a farm or have anything to do with cattle didn't really matter in Detroit. What did matter was that it made Elmer seem exotic to the assembled old folks and dangerously unsuitable as a potential son-in-law to Patti's parents.

Patti overdid the demonstration of her affection for Elmer when she introduced him to her parents. In the process, Elmer experienced a feeling of being out of place which competed for his attention with an awareness of how Patti's parents were struggling to be gracious hosts while contemplating the possibility that their only daughter might marry a ne'er-do-well nobody. Elmer would come to find this conundrum quite amusing, but this was in the future as he stood, clad in his T-shirt and jeans, in the middle of a flock of old people who looked like inebriated penguins.

Once Patti felt she had created enough of a disturbance in the social whirl, she took Elmer outside where he retrieved his suitcase, and then took him upstairs by the back stairs.

"You were magnificent, Elmer!" she said when they

got to her bedroom.

Elmer felt the opposite of magnificent.

"Unfortunately, they won't let you stay in my bedroom overnight. They sleep next door and would hear us screaming with delight if we were to try it. You'll be sleeping in a room downstairs originally meant for servants. But don't worry, I'll sneak down once they're asleep and allow you to serve me to your heart's content! For now, I'm getting out of this dress and we're going over to my friend Heather's house so I can show you off!"

Elmer thought this sounded good, beginning with her plan to get out of her dress. She didn't hurry with this process, giving Elmer sufficient time to remind himself what he had been missing for the few days they hadn't been together. On her way out of the house, she sent Elmer ahead to start up the truck as though she was going to rob a bank and he was to drive the getaway car, located her parents, and told them she would be at her friend's house, and dashed off before they could question her.

Elmer liked Heather and her boyfriend, students at Colombia, and the foursome discussed the differences in college life on their disparate campuses. Elmer was interested in the deliberations that he couldn't imagine having with his friends at home: the latest fashions, the relative status that would be conveyed by owning different makes of cars, and the importance of belonging to the right country club. Elmer had no knowledge of any of these topics, although he had completely random opinions about each. He asked about the country club question and was informed that Silver Lake Country Club topped the elitist heap. Patti let him know that they would be spending the day there tomorrow.

"This should be interesting!" Elmer thought.

The pair returned to her parents' house, sneaked in through the kitchen, and had enthusiastic sex in Elmer's room. Patti then went up to bed so her parents would find her in the proper place when they called her to breakfast the next morning.

During breakfast, Patti's parents grilled Elmer about his background, parentage, scholastic achievements, and future prospects. It would be fair to say that Elmer didn't score one hundred percent with Patti's parents in any of these categories. Elmer had very few of the qualifications they were looking for in a future son-in-law, and they had been worried about this eventuality when Patti couldn't get into an Ivy League school and chose to go to the unimposing State College of Iowa.

"I'm going to take Elmer to the club and introduce him to everybody!" Tilly told her parents when breakfast was over, knowing this would drive them crazy.

"You should take your car, Patti," her dad told her, not wanting his daughter arriving at the Silver Lake Country Club in an old rattletrap pickup truck. Especially a Chevy! And don't forget we're going to "Joey's" for dinner at 8! Make sure your friend is wearing a suit or they won't let him in."

"Don't worry, I'll dress him up like a Hollywood star, Daddy!" she said, giving Elmer an overly affectionate squeeze and looking up at him like he was Marlon Brando.

"We'll come back here and change for dinner," Patti told Elmer as they collected their swimming suits for sitting by the pool. "And I may need you to zip up the back of my dress after you've fucked me until I can't stand up."

This comment added a nice glow to Elmer's afternoon thoughts. They arrived in style at the country club in Patti's Mustang convertible, where she was waved through the gate by a young man who gave her a smile that suggested they knew each other very well. Elmer wondered if he was one of her former lovers from the high school sex club.

They changed in fancy locker rooms, and when they arrived poolside, another young man gave Patti the same familiar look as he took their drink orders. He regarded Elmer as though he was sizing up his suitability as a proper companion for Patti.

"Two Manhattans please, Reggie," Patti said. "You do like Manhattans don't you Elmer? They make wonderful ones here!"

"Sure," he said, wondering what a Manhattan was.

Elmer sipped his drink, which he found very agreeable, and looked at Patti who was reading a magazine while artfully displaying her body on the chaise lounge next to him. She was clad in a remarkably skimpy bikini, which the older members of the club would probably report to her parents, a large floppy hat, and expensive sunglasses. Elmer didn't have anything to do but sip his Manhattan and admire the beautiful young people gathered by the pool. He wondered if they were just there to make him feel inadequate. On the other hand, he was, for now at least, with the cutest and sexiest girl there, and his cock would be inside her later in the afternoon, so he really didn't need anything else to think about. Everyone seemed to know Patti and she introduced Elmer to several of her friends, who promptly ignored him and began innuendo-filled conversations about the "old days" with his girlfriend.

Between conversations, Patti teased Elmer with whispered hints about how she couldn't wait to have sex with him and secretive "accidental" touching of his body. This behavior caused Elmer to spend considerable time lying on his stomach to hide his nearly constant erection, a situation which obviously pleased Patti a great deal. Elmer couldn't decide whether he was Patti's favorite lover or her favorite fashion accessory.

Patti never entered the pool for fear of dislodging what there was of her "swimming" attire, but Elmer swam a lap or two now and then to cool off and get in a little exercise. Elmer was an adequate swimmer, but he hadn't learned in any professional way, so he wasn't fast or graceful in the water, unlike nearly everyone else in the pool, so he didn't spend a lot of time showing off his technique. He was having a fine time, though, and would have liked to stay until evening if Patti hadn't mentioned an activity they would enjoy before going to dinner. She and Elmer headed for the dressing rooms to get into their casual clothes for the drive to her house where they would dress for dinner. As Elmer was about to go into the men's dressing room, Patti told him to get his street clothes out of his locker and meet her in the hallway in a minute or two. She then took his hand and led him down a side hallway to a private dressing room, accessed by a key she had been given at the desk, where they could dress, eventually, in private.

"Not everyone knows about this room, Elmer," she said. "But before we get dressed, I want you to enjoy what it has to offer in the way of comfort and privacy."

The room was a large dressing room, equipped with fresh towels, and soft chairs as well as a sofa in case any users wanted to take a "rest" before leaving.

"My idea is that we should have a couple of appetizers before we go out to Joey's if that suits you," she said, licking her lips and locking the door.

Elmer was pretty sure her idea would be quite suitable. They began to kiss and each spontaneously slipped their fingers down the back of one another's swimming costume.

"I want us to walk into Chateau Joey's still savoring the taste of each other's genital juices on our tongues," she informed him as she slid his swimming trunks off. Patti placed a towel on the sofa, sat Elmer on the edge, removed her top, and got down on her knees in front of him. Elmer knew what was coming, boy did he, and he closed his eyes and grasped her hair to make minor corrections in her pace and position if necessary. Even after eight months of practice, he usually found Patti moving faster than he liked with this process, but her efforts always led to a satisfying outcome, so he didn't interfere with her old habits. He wondered if some of the boys he had met during the afternoon were responsible for her assumption that faster was better.

In spite of this slight imperfection in her technique, the fact that he had been anticipating a tête-à-tête all afternoon, as well as the sexy and semi-secret venue they occupied, caused him to ejaculate into her warm mouth as though he been saving up for weeks. While Elmer rested for a few minutes, Patti walked over to the water cooler, took a cone-shaped cup from the dispenser and, Elmer assumed, took a drink of water. *"So much for tasting me all evening!"* he thought.

They traded positions and Elmer treated Patti to a similar oral extravaganza. Of all the varied and imaginative skills Patti had taught Elmer, his ability to tease her with his tongue was her favorite, and she had carefully instructed him on the functions and erotic sensitivities each part of her vulva; how forcibly and at what rhythm she liked these parts attended to with his tongue, as well as how to adjust his force and rhythm in keeping with her positioning of his head, the sounds she made, and the angle and thrusting tempo of her hips. She had taught him the trick, which worked on Elmer too, of inserting a lubricated finger into her bottom at just the optimum moment, and this always accelerated her orgasm to orbital velocity. He had become, through diligent practice, an expert on pleasing her in this fashion and as expected, she came to an equally tasty climax at the perfect moment in her arc of arousal.

They snuggled naked on the sofa, quietly praising one another's skills at providing oral pleasure. Elmer would have been quite happy to stay hidden there all evening. He wasn't looking forward to a fancy dinner with Patti's parents, but that was the plan, and it wasn't up to him. The lovers donned their street clothes and returned to Patti's house where they dressed in their fancy evening clothes.

Patti dressed upstairs, then came down to Elmer's room to be sure he looked just right in his new suit. She was wearing a short dark dress with a pattern of small light flowers, stockings, and high heels. Her jewelry consisted of a tasteful silver bracelet and a heart-shaped pendant on a chain around her neck which hung low enough to make a nice contrast with the dark color of her dress. She approved of Elmer's attire, with a few minor adjustments, and he approved of her attire with no adjustments at all, especially after she casually lifted her dress as though to straighten her slip and revealed that she was wearing a garter belt but no panties underneath.

"You look spectacular!" he told her.

"Thank you, Elmer. We make a cute couple, don't you think? I just need your help with one more detail of my outfit."

She produced a paper cone-shaped cup, folded over

at the top.

"I saved a supply of your come from my mouth in this cup. I want you to locate on my dress the spot where the pendant falls, and mark it with your finger, then pour a little of your come on that spot when I lie down. No one will notice it, it will fit in with the pattern, and it's somewhat hidden behind the pendant, but you'll know what it is and how it got there. If the dinner gets boring or awkward, just let that remind you of this afternoon's pleasure. I'll be doing the same."

Elmer was stunned and thrilled at her imagination and her understanding of what would drive him wild. He followed her instructions and created a barely visible stain right on the front of her dress where he couldn't take his eyes off it.

"Oh my god, Patti. What if your parents ask about it?"

"I'll tell them exactly what it is and who put it there!" Patti smiled and gave him a luscious kiss.

"Maybe you should tell them it's gravy or something," Elmer suggested.

"Oh, all right!" Patti said with a sexy pout as she rubbed his manhood through his trousers. "You're SO strait-laced, Elmer."

Dinner was good, but the conversation was more of the job interview-like grilling that had started at breakfast. Patti's parents wanted to know what Elmer grew on his farm (he had to tell them once again that he lived in town, not on a farm), what his dad did for a living (train dispatcher), what he was studying in college (commerce), what he liked to do for fun (have sheet-ripping sex with their only daughter until she couldn't stand up for a week). These didn't especially give him top marks for the position of son-in-law, and when it was revealed that Elmer was a fan of the St. Louis Cardinals rather than the Detroit Tigers, they mentally shredded his resume.

Patti's concerned parents turned the conversation to the topic of Patti's dad's many accomplishments and financial successes and Elmer turned his attention to the little spot of his semen that decorated Patti's dress. Patti surreptitiously moved her hand under the linen tablecloth and placed it gently on the bulge in his lap, which caused him to produce a dime-sized wet spot near the top of his fly.

The visit continued in this manner until July fifth when Elmer had to be heading back to Cedar Falls to begin his summer construction job. The visit with Patti and her parents had brought forward a theory that he had been pondering, that Patti's main interest in him was to piss off her parents. Not that she didn't love his company and his increasing knowledge of how to please her in bed, but he realized he would never find her or her parents' lifestyle a comfortable fit. Still, he wasn't ready to cast Patti aside and before he left Detroit, they arranged for her to visit him in South Branch before school started in the fall.

August 1966

Not surprisingly, Patti was no better fit for South Branch than Elmer was for the wealthy side of Detroit. When Elmer took Patti to his favorite secret swimming hole at "Skeeter Crick" she was afraid to get into the water because it hadn't been treated with chlorine. She found the music at the Thursday night band concert in the town square too old-fashioned for her taste, and the burgers at the Burger Shack didn't meet her standards. He did cautiously introduce Patti to Tiffany, who was still working as a waitress at the Burger Shack. It was obvious Tiffany was soon to be a mother for the second time. Neither woman could picture what Elmer ever saw in the other.

Elmer had enjoyed sexual intercourse with three women in his life so far, and he was silently celebrating to himself that a potentially awkward meeting between two of the three had not caused a dust-up of any kind. He felt he had somehow dodged a bullet even though Tiffany was married, very pregnant, and presumably not in competition with Patti for his affections.

Just as Elmer breathed a big sigh of relief, he turned to confront, three feet away, a shocking presence!

"TILLY?"

"Oh, hello Elmer," she said indifferently, not yet aware of any details regarding the two women he was with.

"Tilly! What are YOU doing here?"

Elmer said this in a tone of voice that an amateur criminal might use when confronted by the Chief of Police in a flashlight-lit bank vault late at night.

"I used to live here," Tilly said as though Elmer was a halfwit.

Tilly had come in with her friend Linda who tried

unsuccessfully to hide a smile she couldn't resist.

"I know," Elmer said as his face turned red. He wasn't sure what he was feeling guilty of, time moves on and things change, but he definitely felt guilty of some dreadful felony.

Normally, Elmer would have greeted Tilly, whom he hadn't seen for three years, with an affectionate hug, but his arms hung by his sides as though immobilized. A self-conscious silence hung over the group as the participants sized each other up. Elmer, under Patti's tutelage, was dressed in stylish trousers and a patterned shirt with proper leather shoes. Tilly had not recognized him at first without his traditional faded jeans. He had obviously been working out, but otherwise looked much like he had when she last saw him.

Patti looked gorgeously out-of-place in a short, tight, cocktail dress made from a black and white stretchy material. A pearl necklace gleamed against the perfect tan above her low-cut neckline. Her hair and makeup looked professionally done. Her legs were perfectly shaped with the help of those new-fangled pantyhose and go-go boots protected her feet from the bare concrete floor of the Burger Shack, possibly the first pair of such footwear ever to come in contact with that sticky surface. Tilly at first thought she might be a prostitute until she realized Elmer could never afford such a flashy specimen.

Tilly, in contrast, wore a patterned skirt, held tentatively in place with an elastic waistband. She wore a silky turquoise top that just managed to cover her breasts. This was thin enough to reveal that she was braless. She wore no makeup; her facial decoration consisted of rose-colored glasses in round frames. She had long, straight brown hair, that was kept clear of her face with a tie-dyed headband. Her footwear consisted of leather sandals.

Linda wore a halter top and shorts, while Tiffany was dressed in black shorts with an expanding panel in front and black maternity top with a pinned-on name tag: "Tiffy".

By now, several diners had turned to see what this curious crew were up to, wondering if they were about to shoot a scene from a movie right there in South Branch.

"Linda, do you remember Elmer?" Tilly said to her old friend who had accompanied her to the Burger Shack for a nostalgic hamburger.

Elmer's face turned, if possible, a deeper shade of red. Linda and her boyfriend Bob had been the couple who Elmer and Tilly had conspired with to cover up the fact that the two couples had, three years ago, secretly spent the night in adjacent rooms at the Sleeptite Motel in St. Louis. Linda not only knew Elmer, but a few of his secrets as well.

The four women studied each other to determine one another's position in polite, or boorish, society and internally speculated about how each of them happened to know Elmer Talbot. Before Elmer thought to begin the tricky introductions, he stopped to consider how much trouble he was in if it was revealed that he had slept with three of the four women in front of him. His first thought though, was to question himself as to why he had never tried to chat up Linda, the one unfortunate attendee who had not enjoyed a taste of his talents under the covers! Well, in spite of this failure to entertain Linda between the sheets, he was still the greatest stud west of the Mississippi! His biggest problem now, in his mind, was to decide on an escape route if the four, once they realized what they had in common, were to begin fighting over him!

"Are you going to introduce us, Elmer?" Patti asked pointedly.

Elmer swallowed hard. "Sure," he said, trying to regain his wits.

He began with what he hoped would be the least problematic. "Tiffany, Patti, this is Linda, an old friend from high school, and her friend, Tilly." Of course, this was greeted with a raised eyebrow from Tilly.

"Oh, YOU'RE Tilly?" Patti said. "Elmer has told me everything about you!"

"Probably not everything since we haven't seen each other for three years," Tilly said coldly. "And how do you know Elmer?"

Elmer realized he had lost control of the narrative, and that if there were a melee, he might be on the losing end.

"Elmer is currently my favorite lover. My name's Patti. I'm delighted to meet you, Tilly." This was said with exaggerated politeness as an important person might address an underling.

"Good luck!" Tilly said.

Seconds ticked by with the situation at a simmer.

"And this is Tiffany," Elmer said indicating the very pregnant fourth woman at the table.

The others nodded but didn't speak, and Elmer unfortunately felt he needed to add something to the introduction.

"Tiffany is going to have a baby one of these days," he said, stating the extraordinarily obvious.

"Oh, I heard you two were an item. So, you're going to be a father then, Elmer! How wonderful," Tilly said, having heard from Linda, two years before, that Elmer and Tiffany were carrying on together.

"Oh, Elmer isn't the father!" Tiffany said. "I'm certain it's Buff!"

"Buff Stevens?" Tilly asked.

"Yes. Do you remember him? He used to be the quarterback for South Branch High!" Tiffany asserted proudly. She didn't know that Tilly and Buff had dated briefly before Tilly and Elmer got together.

"How nice for you," Tilly said.

No one thought it a good idea to say more, and gradually the tension dissipated. Elmer and Patti said hasty goodbyes and left Linda, Tilly, and Tiffany to chat about topics of mutual interest while Elmer tried not to think about what those topics might be.

Elmer's senior year began in the fall of 1966. By now, he and Patti were an item. Their relationship had become comfortable even though neither had great expectations that it would become permanent. Elmer continued to be enthralled with Patti's experience and imagination when it came to sex play, and Patti enjoyed his body and his acquiescence to whatever she wanted to try next. And Elmer still provided Patti with the benefit of keeping her parents worried about the possibility he might turn out to be their son-in-law and, heaven forbid, the father of their grandchildren!

CHAPTER 5   AN ABUNDANCE OF ADMIRERS

Again, Tilly's ready to fly
And give independence a try
• get new digs in San Fran
• find a wonderful man
And finally wave South Branch goodbye.

Summer 1967

"We did it, Carol!" Tilly said.

"We did it a lot!" Carol giggled. "But which thing we did are you referring to?"

"Graduating of course!"

"Yeah, that's pretty cool," Carol said. "I'm so glad you were here to go through it with me – you were a big help in keeping me focused."

"I think we helped each other that way," Tilly said.

The roommates threw a graduation party with several friends and several bottles of Champagne. Everyone had a fine time, apart from moving slowly the next morning, and facing a troubling clean-up project ahead.

Now that she had graduated, Tilly turned her full attention to her immediate plans. First, she was going to enjoy the amenities, and the men, of San Francisco.

She planned a trip of a couple of weeks to South Branch in August to reconnect with her parents and brother, after which she would return to San Francisco and look for a nursing job. Nurses were in high demand and she didn't expect this would be a problem.

She and Carol considered moving in together, but Carol expected that she and Hub would find their own apartment so Tilly would have to find other accommodations. She had an ongoing relationship with Dr. Gold, but he had never suggested they live together and there was an unexpressed but mutual hesitancy about their relationship. So Tilly wasn't confident her future was going to involve Dr. Ira Gold, regardless of his likely financial success. Nevertheless, she was quite confident about the outlook, although she was a little curious why most of the men she had met in San Francisco were unconcerned about how they were going to make a living in the future. She chalked this up to the fact that she was mostly in the company of devil-may-care college students or hangers-on and once she entered the business world as a nurse, she would meet a more responsible class of men.

Tilly saw the end of summer as the end of her youth in some sense. Rather than rely on money from home as she did while she was in school, she would have to become a grownup, at least in the sense of making her own way in the world, earning a living, and living on her own. She felt quite capable of this, and was looking forward to it, but to celebrate the end of her days of "leisure" she planned a summer of parties and overindulgence in all things San Francisco. Then, in August, she would fly to Iowa, spend a couple of weeks saying a goodbye forever to South Branch, and fly back to tackle her new responsibilities. She was excited and delighted at the prospect but meanwhile, a fun and fabulous summer stretched out before her and she planned to enjoy every moment.

It was her custom to spend three or four nights each week at Ira's apartment, still trying to perfect his understanding that he wasn't to be the only recipient of sexual gratification when they spent the night together. This still didn't come naturally to him, but with enough reminders, he was getting there. His favorite ways of "doing it" didn't perfectly align with her preferences either, but she thought it best to focus on one topic at a time. Ira seemed to dislike the missionary position, preferring "doggy style", which Tilly feared was because he felt it was excessively intimate to be looking into each other's eyes as they were having intercourse. Similarly, while Ira was not the first to introduce her to anal sex, which she liked now and then, he was very fond of this activity, especially when he was the recipient. In spite of these minor mismatches, they had a comfortable relationship. Tilly liked to tease Ira about being too strait-laced, and often invited him to join her, Carol, and Hub at Devil's Slide beach on his days off. He never rejected the invitation outright, but always had an excuse to avoid going along.

Despite both being layabouts, Tilly missed Rocky and Gary. They were creative, imaginative, and fun; if either had shown any signs of mixing those qualities with a bit of ambition, she would have contemplated how they might fit into her future. Until then, it appeared she would have to keep working on Dr. Gold. Even if their sex life wasn't completely satisfactory, they still had a great time attending Giants' games and enjoying upscale dinners at the best restaurants in San Francisco. Dating Dr. Ira Gold did have its advantages, even if he didn't know how to change a flat tire!

Toward midsummer, two letters arrived the same day. To Tilly's surprise, one came from Gary and the other from Rocky. Even more unexpected, the letters brought news that both men were returning to San Francisco! Sadly, Rocky's mother in Nebraska had died and he was returning to settle down in San Francisco. He had received a small inheritance, enough to tide him over for a year or two – and, true to form, he planned to live it up for a few months and then take his chances. He noted how happy he would be to see Tilly and how all the girls in Nebraska avoided him once they saw him in a skirt.

Gary was returning as well, due to a failure of the commune idea that had sounded so promising to him the year before. Not long after they had settled into their new lifestyle, Nama had begun spending most of her days, and nights, with a former football player who struck her fancy. The compound had been founded on the idea of free love, but Gary hadn't realized that Nama might actually sleep with other men and find them more interesting. Meanwhile the women in the community were free to love anyone who pleased them, but very few had found him pleasing enough. To his surprise, the person who pleased him the most was another man in the group, and Gary, having tried both sexes, concluded that, all things considered, he often preferred the intimate company of other men.

Tilly wasn't aware of this latest wrinkle in Gary's sexual preferences and was hoping to enjoy his company in bed after he arrived to provide a welcome contrast to the cautious Dr. Gold. Tilly hadn't let Gary (or Rocky) in on any shenanigans she had engaged in with Ira, but she had never known Gary to be the jealous type. This brought an outrageous thought to her mind, and if she could bring it about, would provide a highpoint to her summer and perhaps mark the apogee of her wild youth.

She spent a delightfully wakeful night plotting a sensationally sinful event that she could keep in the double-locked "shocking secrets" file in her memory of youthful misdemeanors. This particular idea took a while to sketch out in her mind since she had to pause to masturbate three times during the planning phase. In the morning however, just after breakfast, came a curve ball in the form of a phone call from her mother. Edith had a proposal regarding her visit to South Branch that Tilly couldn't turn down, even though she desperately wanted to. This would definitely complicate her summer, but Tilly expected her mother's plan would only cause a temporary interruption in her busy summer dance card.

Tilly would have to move out of the Haight Street digs before leaving for South Branch, and to this end, one of her tasks for the summer was to sort through her collected possessions and dispose of most of them, perhaps asking if her aunt in Berkeley could find room for two or three boxes in her garage until she returned. None of the furniture in the apartment belonged to her and would probably be left for the next tenants. She did have a modest wardrobe of clothing, a few books, and assorted papers and memorabilia to hold onto, but she had been reading Thoreau's *Walden* and was convinced that owning too many things was more of a burden than a convenience.

Tilly decided she would only keep the amount of clothing that would fit in a suitcase, the number of books that would fit in a box she could easily lift, and only those pictures, papers, and other assorted mementos that would fit in a backpack. She had a couple of months to work on this and enjoyed what she called her "Weight-Loss Plan".

By the end of July, her possessions consisted of a suitcase containing:

Clothing she would need for attending job interviews; beachwear, which was almost nothing; casual clothes for trips to the park, shopping, etc.; a nice dress for parties and romantic dinners; a sexy nightie; flannel PJs; and a selection of underwear including only one bra which she might need for formal occasions.

The suitcase had an interior pocket into which she dumped the meagre contents of her jewelry box along with useless memorabilia she didn't want to part with just yet. In the category of footwear, she selected a pair of nice-looking flats, two pairs of sneakers, and two pairs of sandals. She hated high heels and threw away the one pair she had foolishly acquired when she first met Dr. Gold.

In her box of books, Tilly placed six selected textbooks from nursing school, and a few other favorites: *Franny and Zooey, One Flew Over the Cuckoo's Nest, Catch 22,* and *The Feminine Mystique,* as well as four books by Alan Watts: *The Way of Zen, The Book, The Wisdom of Insecurity,* and *Beat Zen, Square Zen, and Zen.* She topped off this collection with her well-worn copy of *Walden.*

In the backpack she put a couple of notebooks of Gary's poems, a folio of drawings Rocky had given her, and various photos, letters, and other odds and ends. She had saved Elmer's letters – it seemed important at first – and she now half-heartedly threw them into the backpack as "Ancient History".

CHAPTER 6   ELMER'S DILEMMA

The world is coming for you
Even if you haven't a clue
Just find the right girl
Let her know you're a pearl
You two might just make it through.

June 2, 1967

"Elmer — Franklin — Talbot!"

Elmer walked self-consciously across the stage. He knew this was an important moment, but he felt like he was watching a movie of himself as he shook hands with the Dean of the Commerce Department, who was already looking past him at the next graduate in line. Elmer took possession of a rolled-up sheet of plain paper tied with a ribbon. This symbolized his college diploma; the real one would be forthcoming by mail at a later date, as long as he paid the required fee. But the blank paper in his hand also symbolized the blank page of his future plans. Apart from having dinner with his parents and his girlfriend Patti, then attending a party with her and his roommates later in the evening, his future was a complete blank. Elmer didn't find this unusual, but he was vaguely aware he would now be required to give it considerable thought.

The ceremony concluded with the customary hugs, congratulations, and a period of polite but uncomfortable conversation on the quad. Once this was out of the way, his parents and little brother, along with Patti, withdrew to a ritzy supper club at the edge of Cedar Falls. The marquee sign outside the Red Barn Steakhouse exhibited the temporary message, "Congratulations — State College of Iowa — Class of 1967!" During dinner, Elmer tried to avoid the expected questions about his future plans; his parents were subtly trying to pump him for information regarding the future of his relationship with Patti, whom they weren't fond of. In fact, Elmer himself was anticipating the end of their relationship, mostly with pleasure, although he would miss the enthusiasm Patti exhibited whenever they spent the night together in his single bed.

He and Patti had been an item for over two years, and it was clear to Elmer that her interest in him was due primarily to her knowledge that her parents were frightened by their daughter's possible future as the wife of a ne'er-do-well Iowa farm boy. He also understood that, if they remained together, he would eventually be the one she expected to fund her taste for the high life.

After dinner, Elmer's family dropped the couple off at Elmer's apartment, then headed home to South Branch. The graduation party was raucous, and Elmer was quite generous with his personal ration of Hamm's Beer; generous enough that when Patti draped herself over him on the sofa as the party was winding down, he spent no time at all considering her long-range shortcomings as she demonstrated her enthusiasm for his affections.

The next morning, after another round of enthusiasm, Elmer got up, took a couple of aspirin, stepped into the shower, and began to plan out the next few days. Sunday morning, he would load up his wired-together 1952 Chevy pickup and make the two-hour trip home to South Branch. In the meantime, there wasn't much to do apart from getting rid of a lot of junk he wouldn't need any more and trying to resolve whatever was going to happen with Patti. Elmer wasn't sure how she would react to any official breakup; judging from last night and this morning her affection for him had not diminished, but she never seemed particularly committed to the idea of them staying together for the long term.

Involuntarily, Elmer's thoughts turned to Tilly and his mood turned gloomy. Despite his admonitions to himself to get Tilly out of his mind, he began to picture what Tilly might be doing at that moment. She was probably high on marijuana and having sex with two or three longhaired and unwashed San Francisco boys in her sleazy apartment. He tried unsuccessfully to avoid filling in all the imagined details; the way she sensuously danced for them while they removed her dress, probably the only garment she was accustomed to wearing. Now she was naked except for a wreath of flowers in her hair as they —

"Hi!" Patti said, pulling aside the shower curtain and stepping in with him. She noticed the condition of his midsection. "I thought I had taken care of that already, but I'm delighted with your idea!"

"I'm afraid that's false advertising right now, Babe. you've handled everything that needed handling already this morning!"

She gave him a kiss on the cheek. "I love how funny you are," she giggled.

That small exchange cheered Elmer up but didn't resolve anything about their future. The cheering up didn't last long. Patti had things to do before she left for the summer, so she was off to get started on her 'to do' list. Elmer knew she would be spending most of the summer sitting around the pool at the Silver Lake Country Club before coming back in the fall for her senior year.

When she had gone, Elmer contemplated the uncertain future of their relationship. Last summer's visit to Patti in Detroit had been a disaster that wasn't going to happen again. The fairest thing would be to agree that their romance was ending, celebrate the good times with a night of wild sex, and say goodbye. On the other hand, Elmer would be going home to South Branch. He didn't have any other ideas, and the prospects of finding a girlfriend as enthusiastic as Patti were slim in his old hometown. The interesting girls had left South Branch after high school and probably had no intention of returning, and the ones who had stayed were, well, not likely to be as enthusiastic as he wanted them to be. He could stay on in Cedar Falls, but he had no prospects there and he didn't feel he and Patti were likely to suddenly develop a long-term commitment for each other in the fall if it hadn't happened already.

Setting aside his many uncertainties about the future, Elmer began half-heartedly sorting through his belongings, trying to decide what he would take home and what could be disposed of. He decided to tackle the heavy stuff first – textbooks. Elmer's major was in the rather vague subject of "Commerce". Even though he now had a college degree in the subject, it was still a bit vague to him. He decided to hold on to a textbook on economics, three on business administration, and one on sociology. During his college career, he had accidently signed up for a philosophy class and found it fascinating. He had subsequently chosen philosophy for several electives and decided to retain three books from those classes. The others he took to the bookstore, sold back what they would take, and left the remainder in the apartment for the enlightenment of his successors.

Apparently, Elmer had actually done some work in college, judging from the loose papers that were spilling over the tops of his desk drawers. Once he began to look through them, though, most were mimeographed handouts rather than examples of his own writing. Most of those could go but he felt he should sift through them a bit in case there was something he might need later. The sifting did not involve a fine-grained sieve. His method was to dig out a two-inch stack of papers, riffle through it, and then toss the pile in the wastebasket. After 45 minutes of this, Elmer was near the bottom of the lower drawer when a smaller sheet of paper happened to fall from the handful of papers he was about to finish off.

Elmer recognized Tilly's handwriting.

October 31, 1963

Hi There, Wiggle Bear,

I just loved the letter I got from you yesterday, and now I'm especially missing you today. Do you remember 2 years ago? I know you do – our first kiss. The first of about a million. I could really go for a million more of them right now. Sorry I almost knocked you off the porch that first time, ha, ha. I guess that didn't deter you too much. I really miss you. I love you so much! And I remember your Christmas "Presence" too!

Halloween just seems weird in San Francisco. For one thing, everybody here looks like they're wearing Halloween costumes all the time. I thought people on Haight Street might show up for Halloween in business suits to look as scary as possible, but it's just the usual clown costumes they wear every day. There are no kids coming around to Trick or Treat either – I think their parents are scared for them to be out in this neighborhood after dark. It's perfectly safe, but it's pretty Bohemian. I must say, it's a lot different than Iowa. Most of the differences are fine, but the biggest difference is that you're not here and that's a bad one.

My roommates have gone off to a poetry reading so I'm going to get to bed early, snuggle with my pillow, and pretend it's you. I'd better take a towel with me just in case my imagination is too realistic, ha, ha!

Good night Wiggle Bear – I love you forever!
XXOO Flash

Elmer looked at the letter and thought back to the night he kissed Tilly for the first time, after the Halloween dance their junior year in high school. Tilly had worn an elaborate costume, which involved Dracula fangs, and this, along with his nervousness, had caused a little problem with the kiss. He smiled at the memory. The misunderstanding now seemed funny, but it hadn't at the time.

Elmer remembered that he had, at first, carefully placed each letter from Tilly in his drawer intending to collect them together in a large envelope or something at a later time. He had continued to toss her letters into his drawer on top of the latest printed material as they became less and less frequent, eventually forgetting where they were. Now he realized there were probably dozens of letters hidden in the early years of material he had intended to dispose of. His first reaction was to retrieve the entire mound of paper from the trash and go through it again.

He read the letter once more. Those were such good

days. It would be time-consuming, but those letters would be fun to read again in a few years. The next pulse of thought, though, took him in the opposite direction. The gradual and painful death of their "undying" love would be miserable to relive through the letters and would just remind him of how much he hated her by now. He wadded the letter up and angrily launched it into the wastebasket. All his thoughts about Tilly, which once had been thrilling, sexy, and delightful, were now ugly and unbearable. She had, as he feared, become part of the San Francisco scene after leaving South Branch for nursing school, and had become a wild-eyed hippie as far as he could tell. Even though they had a brief encounter in South Branch last summer, he didn't have much detail about her behavior in the hippie scene, but he could imagine it. And she seemed to have forgotten him pretty fast for someone who vowed to "love him forever". By this time his mood was dismal. He retrieved the letter and reread it, then tossed it back in the wastebasket. Those letters were toxic to him now.

Patti's parents would be arriving Sunday afternoon, so she and Elmer arranged to have a wild Saturday night before they left Cedar Falls, and perhaps each other, although that possibility was never mentioned. By the time Elmer drove over to pick up Patti at her apartment, he was in a foul mood regarding girls in general. Tilly's letter had rekindled the hurt, anger, and confusion he felt toward her. This attitude had brought Patti's deficiencies to the foreground as well. As usual, she greeted him in full makeup, a look that fit her personality but, in Elmer's mind, made her look superficial and slutty. Elmer knew that later in the evening, he would find superficial and slutty very attractive qualities; that knowledge didn't make him feel any better about himself either. Patti was dressed in a fashionable tight white dress; short, with a low-cut top. The dress showed off her thin form in a way that Elmer thought she should have saved for him rather than displaying to the world at large. With the makeup and perfect shoes, she looked like a Hollywood starlet, as she intended. Elmer loved the outfit on one level of course, but he felt a little intimidated by someone who would wear such a thing. Whenever they went out together, Elmer had the vague impression that she was trying to attract someone better looking, richer, and with more prospects than he had.

For their last night together before leaving town they had planned a fancy dinner. Patti had insisted on paying, as a graduation present for Elmer. There were no specific plans for after dinner, but they both knew it involved retiring to Elmer's apartment (his roommates had left for the summer that afternoon), drinking until they were wobbly, then having sexual relations as often as possible. No doubt they would end up in Elmer's bed, but Patti, in the right mood, liked to try out every item of furniture and patch of floor on the way!

Patti directed Elmer to a nice restaurant downtown; she had instructed him to wear his suit and tie for the occasion. Patti had thoughtfully brought along a bottle of expensive Scotch and two glasses, which she produced from her purse. This they sampled in the car before they went inside as a little pre-celebration celebration. Elmer had never tasted this brand of Scotch, it being too expensive, and he thought it was a bit too much like cough medicine, but Patti seemed to be very familiar with the product. Inside they were seated at a quiet, romantic table in the corner. Elmer had the impression that the host knew Patti even though they had never been there together.

The Scotch, disagreeable as it was, had brightened Elmer's mood a bit. Patti seemed completely at home in this kind of ritzy place and he decided to play along, pretending to be a sophisticated gentleman out on the town with his swanky girlfriend. Patti, who had apparently been there many times, recommended the lobster. He couldn't reveal to her that he had never tasted this delicacy, so he went along with her recommendation as though it was his favorite. He also noticed it was the most expensive item on the menu so it might be his only chance to give it a try. In the spirit of going all out, Patti instructed Elmer to order a specific, and similarly expensive, bottle of wine. In spite of finding lobster something of a challenge to consume, especially without causing a fragment of the creature to go flying across the table due to lack of skill on the diner's part, he loved it. He assured Patti it was the best he had ever tasted. When she complained that, in her experience, it was a mediocre example, he responded that perhaps he liked it so well due to the pleasure of having it with her. He left out the rest of his hypothesis, that the Scotch and wine had played a more significant part in his gratification. Patti leaned forward and reached across the table, taking both of his hands in hers.

"I love you," she reported, as though commenting on the weather.

"I love you too," Elmer said, not wanting to go into any detail about exactly what that entailed. He didn't want to get into an intimate discussion of their future together right at that moment. He didn't feel they had a future together over the long-term, but he looked forward to the future he expected they would have together the rest of the night.

When they arrived at Elmer's apartment, Patti brought the partially filled bottle of Scotch inside and they drank a toast, or two, to the conclusion of another year together and to Elmer's graduation. He tried to remember what he thought was imperfect about Patti and found himself unable to do so. Her heavy makeup now appeared to convey her desire to make herself attractive to him; and it was working. They sank into the sofa together and began an evening of sexual delight.

Even after two years together, Elmer always felt slightly unsettled when they were in these situations. For one thing, his ability to predict what Patti would be in the mood for was limited. Whenever they spent intimate time together, she seemed to have a secret plan for the entertainment, which Elmer only became aware of as Patti directed the performance. Her stage directions never failed to please him, but he preferred a more even split in the management of the business at hand, to coin a phrase. At this point in their relationship, he knew the elements she liked to use to weave together the production and by the time the work of art reached its climax, Elmer's needs were almost always resolved so he rarely went away disappointed. Still the action usually struck him as a little bit more of an exercise in pleasing her than mutual lovemaking by a devoted couple.

Patti had two main themes for her intimate games; one in which she demanded that Elmer behave exactly as she directed from moment to moment; the other in which she commanded him to dominate her while still giving him explicit instructions for that role, too. The intensity of these themes varied with her mood; usually they were carried out with sweetness and good humor although sometimes Patti was in the mood for a more extreme variation as she was tonight. After a few minutes of kissing, Patti got up and lay on her back on the living room floor, stretching her arms over her head and looking at Elmer as though she were helpless. Elmer knew from this the basic procedure he would be following. This theme was Patti's favorite, the innocent girl overwhelmed and seduced by the strong, irresistible man. Elmer had learned to manage this, but it didn't come naturally to him since his experience of falling in love with Tilly back in high school had resulted in an inner desire to be the protector rather than the seducer, and the idea of forcing himself on a woman was not something he was comfortable with. Still, he could play this role, and the better he played it the more he would be rewarded before they finished. Elmer stood over the supine Patti.

"You aren't going to strip me naked, are you?" Patti asked softly. He assured her that was exactly what he was going to do.

By morning, Elmer had forgotten any thought of suggesting to Patti that their love affair, if that was the correct term, was about to end. As usual, Patti gave no indication their future was on her mind at all. From time to time, each would profess his or her love for the other, but Patti never suggested that she expected it to go on forever, as Tilly had. And anyway, Elmer had personal and painful experience with the lack of veracity in that kind of declaration from a girl.

After breakfast, Elmer took Patti back to her apartment to await her parents; he didn't want to be around when they got there. They hugged and kissed goodbye without fanfare or discussion and Elmer headed back to load up his gear and head for South Branch.

June 4, 1967

On the trip home, Elmer's attention turned to contemplating his future. He had been procrastinating about this, but he couldn't put off giving his situation some serious thought – or time would make all the upcoming decisions for him. Among his various dilemmas, the problem of the military draft was the most urgent. Elmer had grown up a patriotic young man because that was the way everyone felt during his boyhood. He couldn't picture refusing or even trying to slip out of military service; doing so would make him a pariah to his family and the good citizens of South Branch. During normal times, he would have volunteered for one of the services to "get it out of the way". The usual attitude in South Branch, indeed in most of the country, was that a couple of years in the military would "make a man of him".

At this point though, the Vietnam war didn't seem to make sense as a threat to the country; it seemed like a mistake that none of the old men sitting behind big desks could get out of without unacceptable damage to their macho self-images. The fact that young men who had better things to do were the ones being killed did not sit well with Elmer, or with thousands of other men his age as could be seen in the increasingly frequent protest demonstrations. Elmer's options, apart from entering the service by enlisting or waiting to be drafted, were to claim to be a conscientious objector, leave the country, go to jail, or figure a way to get a deferment. He decided that the deferment option, if it would work, would be the best way to go and resolved to look into this possibility as soon as he got home.

Elmer let his eyes focus on the sunny, undulating

Iowa landscape. Newly planted corn was already ankle high, giving a light green geometric tint to the rows hatched across the brown farmlands. He rarely noticed how beautiful Iowa was, but he smiled at the moment. Iowa was beautiful, at least in springtime. He felt an unexpected rush of freedom; from now on he would be on his own. No more assignments coming down from on high, no more girlfriend choreographing their lovemaking to her specifications, no more routine of class schedules and vacations. In spite of the decisions ahead, he was free to march to his own drummer for once. The future was totally up to him; he could play it any way he decided to play it. Elmer noticed that he was happy and made a mental note of it.

Next, Elmer turned to consideration of his living situation. He could live at home for a while when he got back to South Branch but, having been on his own for four years, the idea of living under his parents' roof, not to mention their thumb, would get old pretty fast. Before he would be able to afford a place of his own, though, he would need a job of some kind and here he was without an idea. He had studied business but had no idea who might hire him, what he could do in the business world, or even how to look for a job. On top of this, he knew he would begin to miss female companionship before long. That would have to take care of itself; for now, he would have to rely on "Rosy Palm" and perhaps an occasional visit with Patti to tide him over on that score.

Once the subject of female companionship had entered his mind that was the end of serious thought and the beginning of serious fantasy. Tilly, who had once been real, was now the fantasy, as she often was. Involuntarily, he began to review his coming-of-age with Tilly back at South Branch High. Every detail of their two-year love affair stood out in stereo and Technicolor: the night he first called her for a date, their first kiss, the step-by-step progress of their do-it-yourself sexual education, culminating with their secret, sleepless, and sensational night at the Sleeptite Motel in St. Louis. Mostly though, he remembered the exact time when he fell completely, overwhelmingly, astonishingly, in love with her. Before he had kissed Tilly for the first time, Elmer had had no idea what the concept of "love" was all about; fifteen minutes later, by the time he had arrived back in South Branch from Tilly's house outside of town, he understood everything he needed to know. By now, though, he knew something more; how painful it could be when love disappears.

When Tilly left for nursing school in San Francisco, she vowed that a love as strong as theirs would last forever. Before long though, she had become fully engaged in the life of San Francisco and seemed to feel the 2000-mile physical separation between San Francisco and South Branch was just about the right distance. And, it seemed to Elmer, she felt the same way about their romantic connection as well. Elmer had expected Tilly to come back to South Branch every summer, but he had only seen her once since she left, when she spent a few days in South Branch a year ago. And she hadn't even told him she was going to be there!

The void created by a lack of actual information about Tilly was filled with information about hippies in general, and San Francisco hippies in particular, that Elmer found in alarmist newspaper and magazine articles. He couldn't imagine Tilly engaging in some of the things he read about, but there they were in black and white and Tilly was sharing an apartment right in the middle of the hippie universe so what else could he think? Elmer took each of the qualities that the magazines used to define the hippie "lifestyle" and applied them to his image of the new Tilly to see how they fit. The magazines seemed to be particularly interested in writing about the hippies' propensity for "drugs, sex, and rock and roll". Apart from rock and roll, which Tilly loved, Elmer had a hard time at first picturing Tilly engaging in promiscuous sex or illegal drugs. Of course, neither of them had been particularly hesitant about alcohol, even though it was illegal; what would prevent her from slipping into smoking marijuana or worse? And, she had liked sex with him; maybe she liked it even better with other guys. Maybe those wild hippie boys knew all kinds of tricks he had never thought of; new tricks that drove Tilly wild with desire?

Elmer imagined Tilly's cousin Carol and their roommates and ragtag band of friends, sitting on the mattress-covered floor of their apartment, smoking reefers and encouraging Tilly to join them. He could see it clearly – the room was lit by candles, aided by a bit of moonlight coming in through the open windows. Rock and roll music issued from a portable record player. They had been drinking, lowering Tilly's resistance. Not wanting to be called a square, she thought, "Why not, it doesn't seem to be doing them any harm!" Almost aloud, he begged her to stop, and then watched her, in his imagination, take a small puff, then begin coughing and gasping for breath. Tilly had never smoked tobacco; surely this would dissuade her from continuing.

He saw the encouragement from the others, maybe one of the men in the room comforting her, patting her on the back, and telling her it would be wonderful once she got used to it; the idea that it was harmful was just one of the deceits of old people. The same old people who had no problem getting drunk and killing people on the road but who were scared to death that young people would discover they could get high gently and harmlessly with an ordinary plant that grew wild all across the country. Elmer tried not to watch the scene play out in his imagination, but now he could see Tilly take another puff, inhaling a little with less coughing this time, then smiling and saying softly, "Wow!" After two more puffs, he watched her lazily roll over and press her face into the tie-dyed T-shirt worn by the nearest man. He watched her put her arms around him and rub her cheek against his belly. She began to laugh as he stroked her hair.

Elmer felt a little queasy.

He had played out this scenario in his imagination

many times since Tilly's letters became less frequent and less affectionate. She had never told him anything explicit about her sex life in San Francisco, but she didn't have to, he could see everything in his mind's eye!

To put off the continuation of the scene he couldn't resist replaying, Elmer stopped for gas. He put a dime in the Coke machine while the attendant pumped $2.75 worth of gas into the truck and washed the bugs off the windshield. In truth, although he was hurt by the thought of Tilly having sex with other men, Elmer found this imaginary scene of Tilly and several other men and women in an apartment in San Francisco thrillingly erotic. He had even been known to boost his arousal during sexual intercourse with Patti by replaying this scene in his mind, substituting himself for the anonymous man Tilly was cuddling up with.

Like a song you can't get out of your head, Elmer continued his internal movie: *Before long, Tilly and her stranger were half sitting, half lying on a mattress with their backs against the wall of the apartment, passing a marijuana cigarette back and forth. Tilly's eyes began to glaze over, and she smiled, moving in slow motion to the music. The ten people in the room had grouped themselves into couples and foursomes and began touching each other affectionately.*

When Tilly, with a faraway look in her eyes, began lightly tapping her man's thigh in time to the music, Elmer, and Tilly's San Francisco friend, both began to get erections.

Elmer turned left from route 218 onto the Lincoln Highway.

Tilly's companion moved the arm that was around her shoulder to position his fingers against the bare skin above her low-cut top. She took another drag on the marijuana cigarette when it came around and closed her eyes. The man carefully put out the cigarette in an ashtray and slipped his fingers under the fabric of her blouse, slowly working them down toward her breasts in time to the music. The alcohol and marijuana had wiped out her earlier inhibitions and she gradually became submerged in sensual pleasure. Tilly wasn't wearing a bra to get in the way and soon the delicious touching of her nipples infused her with the understanding that sex was not immoral but beautiful.

Elmer knew it had been beautiful with him; hippies believed that it should be that way with anyone you're attracted to at the moment, according to the magazines.

As usual, when he got to this point in the fantasy, Elmer was torn in half by the thought of Tilly giving herself so casually to another man, and the extreme sexual arousal that imagining that situation brought on.

Elmer was fully engaged in his fantasy now; he might as well carry it through. And anyway, the drive was boring, and this made it much more interesting. Elmer knew how this fantasy was going to affect him before it ended so he turned onto a side road in search of a

private spot where he could take matters into his own
hands.

*Tilly and her hippie friend now felt a tie-dyed T-shirt land on
them, tossed at random by one of the other couples or foursomes.
This led to a giggling, slow motion, battle among the ten
participants, the weapons being articles of clothing. Fortresses
consisting of pillows were hastily constructed and blankets were
held up as shields to fend off the flying garments. Before long the
now-naked combatants had deployed all their weaponry and
began crawling around on their hands and knees back and forth
across the mattress-covered floor in search of articles of clothing
they could use to rejoin the fray.*

Elmer turned onto a seldom-used gravel road and
parked the truck on the shoulder near a small bridge
over a tree-lined creek, manipulated his erection to
allow him to stand up, and got out of the truck. He
walked along the creek until he was hidden from the
road, then leaned against a tree and unzipped his jeans.

*The room was dimly lit, and the action seemed hilarious to
the unclothed, giggling participants who ended the battle in a
jumbled pile of human forms, wiggling weirdly as each began
fondling whatever body part they found at hand, unaware of the
identity, or in many cases even the gender, of their partners.
Nevertheless, the undulating mass adjusted itself until the
various genitalia each found an appropriate connection. The
orgy continued, with laughter, exclamations of sudden pleasure,*

and changes of partners, until everyone was exhausted. Gradually the writhing of the participants ceased, and everyone fell asleep wherever they happened to run out of vitality.

Elmer exhausted his supply of vitality into the vegetation at the same time.

The sexual arousal he had enjoyed when contemplating this imaginary scene was now gone; all that was left were his hurt feelings and anger at Tilly for her infidelity. Ironically, Elmer also felt guilty for imagining such unkind things about her. Elmer noted that his feelings about Tilly were far from resolved, but anger was the feeling that always bubbled to the top so that's what he talked about with himself the rest of the way home.

Elmer arrived in South Branch with a degree in commerce but without an idea. Having nowhere else to go, he moved back into his parents' house and began looking for a job and a draft deferment. He was opposed to the Vietnam war, but was clueless about the possibilities of getting a deferment. He knew that if he were to get into graduate school that might work. When he looked into that option however, he learned that graduate study had been eliminated as a deferment a few months before.

As he was contemplating his options for a job, avoiding the draft, and getting his own place to live, Elmer happened to find himself in the local Piggly

Wiggly grocery store one afternoon, trying to remember what brand of canned baked beans his mother had asked him to pick up on his way home.

"Elmer? Is that you?"

He turned around to find Tilly's mother calling to him. He hadn't seen Edith for nearly four years, and Elmer didn't know where he stood with her since he and Tilly were now the opposite of an item. Elmer had been fond of Tilly's mom since the first time he spent Christmas at her house six years ago, when Edith sent the young couple on an errand to protect them from harassment by Tilly's inebriated uncles. His liking for her mom was about the only thing Tilly had going for her in Elmer's mind these days, and he didn't have the heart to tell Edith that their romance had been dead for three years.

"Hi, Mrs. Williams, how are you?" he asked cautiously.

"I'm fine Elmer. We haven't seen you for quite some time, how's school going?"

"I just graduated a couple of weeks ago. So, here I am, back in South Branch."

"What do you hear from Tilly?" Edith asked.

"I haven't heard from Tilly for quite a while," Elmer said. "She seems to be having a fine time out there in California."

"Fucking every suntanned son-of-a-bitch in San Francisco!" he thought but didn't say.

"We don't hear a lot either, but she does seem to like California. How are you going to spend the summer, Elmer?"

"I'll be looking for a job and a place to live," Elmer said.

"I hope you don't have to join the military. I think that war in Vietnam is stupid, and a lot of boys are getting killed for nothing!"

Edith's opinion was definitely not the majority view in South Branch, but Elmer agreed with her.

"I'm with you on that, Mrs. Williams. What's going on over there doesn't seem like any of our business. I hope I can figure out some way to get a deferment, but I don't know what that could be."

"What about getting a 2-C?" she asked.

"A 2-C?"

"It's an agriculture deferment. You can get a 2-C if you work on a farm."

"That sounds good, apart from the fact that I don't know anything about farming, and I don't know anybody who would hire me," Elmer laughed.

"Well, you know Frank and I are getting older, and we could probably find plenty of useful work for a young strapping boy like you, Elmer," she said. "I'll have to talk to Frank about it, but I'm sure he'd be all for it since it would give him more time to fool around in his wood shop. You could even move into Tilly's old room since she's not going to be using it. Let me give you a call tomorrow. Maybe we could work something out that would help all of us."

"Thank you, Mrs. Williams, that does sound like it might be a good deal for me right now. And I'd be happy to learn what I can about farming since I've grown up with lots of farmers."

So, just like that, Elmer's prospects began looking up, as long as Edith and Frank didn't find out that he and Tilly hated each other by now. And the idea of moving into Tilly's old bedroom seemed astonishingly weird since he and Tilly had lost their virginity together in her bed four-and-a-half years ago. Elmer didn't yet realize how the search for a can of baked beans would change his life for the decades to come. When he got home however, he discovered his life had changed for the next few minutes because he had to drive back to the store and pick up the can of beans he had forgotten after his conversation with Tilly's mother.

Edith called Elmer the next morning and told him that Frank agreed it would be a good move for them to hire Elmer, and if he wanted to move into Tilly's old room, that would be convenient and save him from having to pay rent somewhere else.

"I know you might have secret memories of excitement in that room that would tend to keep you awake at night Elmer, but I'm sure you'll sleep well after all the work you'll have to do," Edith said with a smile in her voice.

"Um, how ..." Elmer said before he thought to deny

what Edith was implying.

"I had to wash the sheets I found wadded up in the back of Tilly's closet!" she laughed. "And when my mom, who Tilly was staying with while we were in Chicago that Christmas, mentioned the condom wrapper that fell out of Tilly's pocket later, it was pretty obvious the two of you had a good time while we were out of town!"

"I'm sorry ...!" Elmer stammered.

"No, you're not, Elmer. And neither am I. And Frank would have recovered by now if I had mentioned it to him."

"You're right, I'm not the least bit sorry. Tilly and I were quite fond of each other back then," Elmer said, blushing. "I am sorry about the sheets, though."

"Why don't you move out to our house on the weekend and you can start work on Monday?"

"All right. I don't have much stuff so moving should be easy."

Elmer had reconnected with his old pal Eddie when he got back to South Branch, and the two of them went out to celebrate Elmer's new job with supper at the Burger Shack. To Elmer's surprise, they were waited on by Tiffany, Elmer's summer girlfriend three years ago. She joined the two men for a few minutes and Elmer asked about how things were going.

"Your little boy must be two by now?" Elmer asked.

"Well, my little boy is almost two and cute as a

button," she said. "And the baby I was pregnant with last summer is nine months already! But Buff and I got divorced last winter."

"That must be hard," Elmer said.

"Yes. The famous quarterback turned out to be rather infamous instead," she said, giving Elmer's thigh a squeeze. "So, I'm available again!"

Elmer's mind teed up a flashback of an afternoon with Tiffy down by the creek, but he thought it best not to pursue this topic any further.

"I hope things work out better next time," Elmer said.

Elmer moved a few things into Tilly's room on the farm a few days later and began work. It turned out to be somewhat more interesting than construction because it was more varied and less familiar. Once he learned what was required for the various kinds of work in the fields, he was able to work by himself which pleased him. As long as he kept the cultivator aligned with the corn rows so he was getting rid of the weeds rather than the corn, he could turn his attention to his private thoughts and plans. Elmer also cultivated a good working relationship with Tilly's dad, and often teased him about his mention, as Elmer and Tilly were about to leave for their first date nearly six years before, that Elmer shouldn't get fresh with Tilly because had a shotgun in the closet. Frank insisted he had been joking but at the time, Elmer had been none too sure of that.

There wasn't much talk of Tilly these days. Her parents knew she was all right in San Francisco, but it seemed she was deliberately withholding any details regarding her daily affairs from them. Like Elmer, they had read magazine articles about young people in San Francisco and were concerned she had left her Iowa upbringing too far behind after she got out to the coast. At least Edith and Frank received occasional letters or phone calls from Tilly, unlike Elmer who hadn't heard from her for a year or more. He wasn't hearing anything from Patti either and his prospects regarding romance with any woman seemed bleak. There were not many young women in South Branch that would interest him, and he feared he would go crazy without some kind of female companionship now and then.

His thoughts drifted to Tiffany. She had never seemed like a good long-term possibility, but it would be fun, he thought, to explore how far she had come in the three years since her first experience with him down by the creek. And, she had already suggested, when they met at the Burger Shack, that she would have no problem recommencing their relationship. Elmer chuckled to himself at the idea that he and Tilly first began dating as she was on the rebound from Buff and thought it would be ironic if that happened again six years later with Tiffany. What could it hurt if the two of them had a little reunion for the summer? Of course, she now had a toddler and a baby, which would complicate things, and Elmer was wise enough to understand that she was looking to recruit a new father for her kids more than she was looking for a playful roll in the hay now and then.

Armed with the questionable assumption that he could control what happened between them, he decided to take himself out for supper at the Burger Shack and assess the possibilities. He remembered that she had a half hour off at 9PM, after the supper rush, and thought it might be interesting to show up at that time just in case her schedule remained the same. Elmer had very mixed feelings about his motivations as he drove into South Branch from the farm. Like a sign from the heavens, he now heard from the radio, the beginning lyrics of the Jefferson Airplane hit "Somebody to Love":

"When the truth is found to be lies
And all the joy within you dies
Don't you want somebody to love, don't you
Need somebody to love, wouldn't you
Love somebody to love, you better
Find somebody to love"

Sure enough, Tiffany joined him for a burger and fries, and they caught each other up on the latest news. She was a little rounder, just as cute, but no less ditzy than she had been earlier. On the other hand, she seemed more serious and worldly than she had been at 18. Tiffy seemed to have no hesitation about telling Elmer that she had started dating Buff shortly after

Elmer had left for State College, and she was pregnant a couple of months later. They had gotten married that summer. Her son, Buck, was born that August. By last summer, she was pregnant again, and her husband had a new girlfriend. Three months ago, they were divorced. Tiffany was sharing an apartment with her sister, trying to make ends meet, and recruit a new father for Buck and the baby. Elmer realized he was three years more serious as well, and it soon became clear that whatever summer fun he might have with Tiffany, it could result in a lifetime of trouble. Elmer told himself not to get involved with Tiffany again, but chemistry being what it is, he might have gone ahead if another possible crisis hadn't diverted his attention.

The day after his dinner with Tiffany, Edith had what she considered good news; Tilly, who had just graduated, was coming to South Branch to see everyone before going back to settle down permanently in San Francisco. Her plan was to fly home, stay for a couple of weeks, then fly back, find a nursing job, and move into a new apartment. Tilly's mom however, had what she thought was a simple and ingenious idea. Her sister, Bev, Tilly's aunt, lived in Berkeley just across the bay from San Francisco, and Bev was in possession of a dining room table and chairs that had been in the family since the two sisters had been little girls. Bev was looking to get rid of them and was happy to keep it in the family by passing them on to Edith if there were a way to move these items to South Branch from Berkeley safely and at a reasonable cost.

Edith's idea was to send Elmer and his pickup truck out to California to pick up both Tilly and the family heirloom and bring them back to Iowa. Of course, Edith didn't mention to Elmer that her grand plan was partly based on the idea that if he and Tilly had to spend several days traveling across the country together, they might rekindle their affection for each other, and that Tilly might thereby be convinced to remain close to home and find a nursing job in South Branch or somewhere nearby. She had never mentioned to either Tilly or Elmer that she had been picturing them as the parents of her future grandchildren since their first prom night when she took their picture together in front of the fireplace in her living room.

Elmer, of course, had no idea about Edith's secondary motivation for wanting him to go to California. Even after all these years he was furious with Tilly for abandoning him once she got to San Francisco. With the scarcity of letters from her over the last three of those years, Elmer had no trouble imagining what kind of disreputable dalliances and nefarious felonies she had become involved in. In truth, he was a little frightened to find out in person how far Tilly had fallen. And even if she wasn't a drug addict or a guttersnipe, he just wanted to forget her and get on with his life, as unsettled as it was. Elmer was a little annoyed with himself that he continued to think about Tilly and wonder about her, even worry about her a little. He had had other girlfriends, and Tilly was just one that hadn't worked out. So what? Of course, Elmer would have found this internal dialog more convincing if either of the other three had worked out. But still, his relationship with Tilly was odious after all that had gone wrong between them, and the very idea of spending time with her, especially alone in his truck where they had had such delightful adventures, was distasteful.

At first, Elmer tried his best to talk Edith out of the idea: It would take too long to get back to South Branch and this would cut into her time with her daughter. His truck was old and might break down on such a long trip, perhaps stranding them somewhere in the desert without water. Where would they stay on the way back? Wouldn't there be work he should be doing on the farm that would preclude him from being away for two weeks? And, what if Tilly refused to come back with him, which he saw as a real possibility, although he didn't present this possibility to Edith.

Tilly's mom dispensed with each of his objections and offered her own arguments: It would be a great opportunity for Elmer to "See the USA in his Chevrolet", to quote an old advertising jingle. It would cut Tilly's risk of flying in half if she only had to fly one way. He could do the cultivation in the north forty before he left and finish when he got back. They would get Elmer's truck inspected and maintained before he left. And he would get to spend some "quality time!" alone with Tilly on the way back.

Except for this last idea, which Elmer knew would have the "quality" of nonstop hostilities, he did see that she could be right on some of her arguments. Elmer had never been west of Iowa, and it did seem that a long solo trip west, alone with his thoughts and the scenic vistas, could be just what he needed to clear his mind. And, as he thought about Tilly, perhaps he would actually be rescuing her from a bleak future among drug addicts and clueless philosophers.

Finally, Elmer agreed to Edith's proposal. She had already written to tell Tilly that Elmer would be coming to pick her up but was still working on convincing Tilly that it wouldn't be so awful to spend some time with Elmer for old time's sake and, anyway, that was the only sensible way to get the dining table back to South Branch. Tilly had to agree finally, even though she was grumpy about the idea and equally grumpy that she still had to listen to her parents because she was living on an allowance from them. Well, she would just have to put up with it for a few more weeks and then she would have a nursing job in San Francisco and plenty of her own money to spend any way she chose.

PART III LANDING
CHAPTER 7 TRYING TRAVEL

Elmer's turn now to head for the coast
he'll find people there who will boast
that the West is so cool
If you leave you're a fool
But South Branch has better pot roast

Thursday, July 27, 1967

Edith wanted to give Elmer a sendoff as he left to bring Tilly home from San Francisco, and of course, she served him a huge breakfast of bacon, eggs, fried potatoes, and toast, after which he doubted, he'd need to eat for the next couple of days. Elmer was admonished to drive safely, pull over when he got tired, not to pick up any hitchhikers, and jokingly, not to become a hippie while he was out in California!

When it was time to go, Tilly's dad gave him $50 for expenses on the trip, slowly counting out the cash like he was peeling off pieces of his own skin. After Frank left the room, Tilly's mom handed Elmer another $20. "Take Tilly out for a nice supper when you get to San Francisco!" she whispered, giving him a hug. Elmer couldn't imagine how any two people could spend $20 for a single meal, but he figured it wouldn't go to waste. "Thanks," he said. "I'm sure she'll like that."

"And these are for you, I don't want you starving on the trip!" she said, handing him a large tin pail filled with homemade chocolate chip cookies. Elmer regretted for a moment that she would never be his mother-in law.

Edith watched him go until he gave her a final wave as he pulled out of the driveway and turned left onto the two-lane road heading west toward Route 34. He wasn't looking forward with any enthusiasm to the trip as a whole, spending time in San Francisco and being alone with Tilly in the truck for five days would be trying. Nevertheless, he was excited to be on the road with his thoughts and the seemingly unending highway ahead to keep him company.

At first, the landscape was familiar. He had been on Route 34 many times on his way to Ottumwa and even, once, as far west as Council Bluffs, so he paid little attention to the fields now covered in shoulder-high corn as far as he could see. A few unfamiliar landmarks, such as a tiny chapel someone had built in a corner of a cornfield, attracted his attention momentarily. It looked lonely and Elmer imagined he and Patti could have livened it up in a way that the builders never intended if he had only known about it during her visit last summer. Elmer looked forward to reaching the mountains. He had never experienced these in person, and momentarily wondered if the truck would have any trouble climbing the steep inclines.

His thoughts, naturally, turned to Tilly. He assumed

she had a boyfriend, or a dozen of them. He pictured the awkwardness of seeing her in whatever form she now occupied. He had been watching the news on television lately and reading articles about the craziness out in San Francisco; 60,000 people marching in the streets to protest the Vietnam war just a few months ago, the "Summer of Love" and all the rest. He was opposed to the war himself and was very impressed that so many marchers would take to the streets, but he wasn't anxious to go marching. And he was all in favor of love, just not watching your girlfriend engaging in it with 60,000 people!

After enjoying a lunch of five chocolate chip cookies, Elmer crossed the Missouri River below Council Bluffs and entered a new state for him – Nebraska. Disappointingly, it looked just like Iowa, but before long he reached the recently completed Interstate 80 "freeway" and this felt like the real beginning of his adventure. The miles flowed behind him in the rearview mirror on the smooth four-lane concrete and Elmer left his thoughts of Tilly aside as he admired the landscape that gradually began to feel bigger than it had seemed on his passage through southern Iowa.

Toward evening, Elmer exited the freeway at Grand Island and was surprised to find the actual town was ten miles north of the interstate. *"Who thought this up?"* he wondered. On the way into town, he pulled into a gas station where his tires ran over the hose activating the bell to alert the attendant. An older man emerged from the garage, wiping his hands on a towel, and studying

Elmer's Iowa plates.

"Regular or Ethyl?" he asked.

"Regular."

"Fill 'er up and check yer oil?"

"Yes, sir," Elmer said. He consulted the map while the older fellow washed the layer of bugs off Elmer's windshield.

"How far ya goin'?" the older man asked, making conversation.

"California!" Elmer said, feeling a little proud that he was such an adventurer.

"Not gonna to turn inta one a them hippies, are ya?" he asked.

"No, sir," Elmer said. The older man continued to make eye contact.

"I'm going out to meet an old girlfriend."

"I seen pictures a them California girls. Lots of 'em don't wear no clothes I guess!"

"I imagine she'll have a few clothes on – at least until I can talk her out of them!" Elmer said this as though there was any possibility of that happening.

The old man laughed, no doubt remembering his ill-spent youth. "Good fer you!"

"Where's a good place to eat around here?" Elmer asked his new friend.

"Bub's Grub, about a quarter mile up the road toward town. It's fine as long as you stay clear of the potato salad!"

"Thanks!" Elmer said. "By the way, I need a free place to camp tonight. Any ideas?"

"Take a right up here on Husker," he said, pointing. "There's a little lake down there. Pitch yer tent or unroll your sleeping bag out on the grass. If the cops bother you, tell them Rufus said it would be okay."

"Thanks Rufus!"

"Yer welcome, but I'm not Rufus. He's the mayor! Don't worry, you'll be fine there."

Elmer enjoyed an adequate hamburger at Bub's and spent the night fully enclosed in his sleeping bag, preferring to be annoyed by the heat rather than the mosquitos. He woke up with the sun, threw his sleeping bag into a box in the back of the truck, had a quick breakfast at Bub's, and headed west.

The scenery provided a nice distraction from Tilly, and Elmer was surprised at how quickly the landscape of Nebraska changed from gently rolling farmland green with corn to drier ranchland dotted with cattle. The next time he stopped for gas, everyone seemed to be wearing cowboy hats! He had made it to the Wild West!

Out here you could see for miles. Rainstorms were visible in the distance and since he was racing toward them, they arrived quickly. Elmer pulled off the road briefly and brought his suitcase, pup tent, and sleeping bag inside the cab. At first the rain was just a few drops on the windshield, but within a minute or so, a deluge of water was falling. Elmer leaned forward and squinted in a futile attempt to see more than a few feet ahead of him. The rain kept up and before long, Elmer came up behind a slower-moving semi-truck, its taillights appearing alternately bright and then nearly invisibly blurry in time to his unenthusiastic windshield wipers. Despite its slow speed, Elmer decided to stay behind the truck and let the driver ahead figure out the exact location of the road surface. After twenty minutes, the rain stopped as quickly as it had started. Elmer picked up speed, and for the first time, could see misty-appearing mountains in the distance. The sight was thrilling and beautiful and he caught himself looking forward to showing it to Tilly on the way back before he realized that they probably would not be speaking to each other since they no longer had anything in common.

His plan was to make it to Cheyenne by nightfall, mainly because he remembered seeing a movie by that name when he was a 10-year-old. As it was, Interstate 80 was incomplete for the 16 miles east of Cheyenne. He had to squeeze into a heavy line of slow-moving trucks for the final leg of the day's trip, so he was tired and hungry as he rode his horseless carriage into town. Elmer had pictured Cheyenne as looking a lot like Dodge City from the TV series "Gunsmoke"; he was surprised to find the city larger and more modern than he expected. There were plenty of saloons, but no hitching posts out front. As he had earlier, Elmer grabbed a bite to eat and looked for a local park to camp out overnight. This was quite pleasant until 2:30 AM. Elmer was working his way through a dream where he was wading across a raging creek to rescue Tilly who was trapped on a small island in the midst of the flood. He awoke to find himself on the verge of being drenched by another heavy rainstorm. He quickly crawled out of his now-sopping sleeping bag, climbed into the truck, spread the gear across the steering wheel and dashboard, and curled up on the seat. He had been sleeping in his clothes, which were also wet, and since it was a warm night, he stripped down to his Y-fronts. He finally went back to sleep but was interrupted again at 5AM when a city policeman knocked on his fogged-up window to inquire about his reason for being there. Elmer explained about the rain and the sleeping bag and that he was leaving shortly for points west. The policeman mentioned laws about vagrancy, public indecency, parking restrictions, and trespassing on public property and suggested that Elmer put his clothes on and be on the road before he returned. The place didn't seem that public to Elmer at 5AM, but he followed the officer's instructions.

Heading west, he stopped at a truck stop outside Laramie for gas and breakfast and then pressed on. Just beyond Laramie, the route detoured around a long unfinished portion of I 80, shifting traffic to Route 130, and Elmer tackled the Medicine Bow mountain via a twisty two-lane road. The scenery was spectacular, and he didn't mind the slow going which delayed the awkward moment when he would be face-to-face with Tilly once again. Just before leaving Wyoming, Elmer grabbed a takeout burger, found a state park on the banks of the Bear River, and paid fifty cents for a proper campsite where he could make up for an interrupted night and a hard day's driving. Given that he was a visitor to the BEAR River campground, he thought putting up the pup tent would be a good idea; maybe the bears would eat the campers in open sleeping bags first. No campers were eaten during the night and Elmer awoke refreshed and excited about the day ahead. According to the map, serious mountains were coming up and now that he had successfully traversed yesterday's offerings, he felt ready for more of the same.

Now came Utah. Here, the mountains were even more dramatic, the roads more twisty, and the certainty of death if one drove too close to the cliff at the edge of the road even greater. After winding through a long valley, the road made a sharp descent and, around a turn, Salt Lake City with the Great Salt Lake beyond was revealed from above. Elmer had a momentary thought that this would be similar to arriving by air as he looked down on the city. He confronted troublesome traffic on his way through the city and only stopped to resupply his stash of snacks once he was past the most populated area.

The road west of Salt Lake City wound through relatively flat terrain before vaulting a range of hills and then reaching the famous Bonneville Salt Flats, forty miles of straight, flat highway. Elmer, as usual, turned his attention to Tilly, first telling himself that he was thinking about her all the time only because he was on his way to retrieve her, not because she meant anything to him now. She had abandoned him for a bunch of California guys and a lifestyle that he didn't understand. He hadn't heard from her for a year or more, only having heard snippets of information about her accomplishments from her mother. Edith apparently didn't know much about San Francisco, her daughter's hippie lifestyle, and the sex, drugs, and rock and roll she was awash in out on the coast.

He pictured their upcoming reunion – their first face-to-face meeting in a year:

Tilly, opening the door to a filthy apartment, braless in a too large, torn, tie-dyed man's T-shirt extending just a few inches below her crotch, and smoking a marijuana cigarette. Her hair askew with a few wilted flowers entangled in it. A glazed look in her eyes. Two or three tanned, shirtless surfer types, high on drugs, sitting on the floor reciting incomprehensible "poetry". The tick, sssk, tick, sssk, of the record player, which no one noticed had finished playing the current hit song. He imagined her disdain as she recognized him, saying nothing, just leaving the door open as the extent of her welcome, then stumbling back to her boyfriends, laying her head in one's lap, and grooving to the poetry that Elmer was too dull to understand. He imagined one of the tanned men, wearing sunglasses inside the house, asking Elmer who he was, then waving him inside before Elmer could think up an acceptable answer. Elmer pictured himself standing forlornly inside the door hopelessly watching the proceedings.

Elmer hadn't enjoyed any intimate female companionship since he and Patti had gone their separate ways. And so, in spite of his anger at Tilly for abandoning everything they had together in favor of a bunch of lazy, self-important, pseudo intellectuals, Elmer's manhood was not displeased with her at all.

Tilly, in her stupefaction, turned over to kiss the bare belly of the man she was cuddling with and, in doing so, positioned herself on her hands and knees, unconsciously spreading her legs to reveal the crotch of her unwashed panties.

Elmer adjusted his position to relieve the now-painful angle of his erection. *"Damn it!"* he thought.

He took a moment to admire the scenery, the vast area of salt with mountains all around, dozens of miles away. He knew that somewhere near the road was the place where land speed records were set every summer, and he could see why – there was nothing out here to run into for forty miles! Elmer checked the gas gauge and resolved to fill up in Wendover just across the Nevada state line.

"How could Tilly change from a sweet, loving, kind, Iowa girl into a raving, drug-taking, immoral sex fiend?" he wondered.

Could he have been such an inspiring lover that she now craved it all the time? That wasn't likely since she was the one who was leading him on as often as not. Maybe she had always been a nymphomaniac and he was just her first conquest. Or maybe it was the drugs that had ruined her. Part of him felt that he was on his way to rescue her from a life of debauchery, but on the other hand, she didn't deserve rescue after the way she had treated him. What could cause love to disappear like that? It was a mystery.

As much as he now hated her for throwing away their future together, he couldn't help but dwell on the good times they had enjoyed, no matter how painful they now were. He remembered their first kiss, which, to his complete surprise, changed his whole life. He chuckled to himself as he remembered the time he had gotten his hand stuck in her bra trying to take it off without her noticing. And the first time she had jerked him off in this very truck, when he had ejaculated all over both of them and how relieved he was when she not only didn't find his performance disgusting, she had shown her delight by kissing the tip of his penis. When they got caught in his basement by his father, who had distracted Elmer's mom so they wouldn't get in trouble. And then their first time going "all the way", that Christmas in her bed while her folks were out of town. He had been so crazy in love with her back then. He had nicknamed her "Flash" because she had given him a flashlight for Christmas and they had used it to enjoy each other's nakedness under the covers, and she had nicknamed him "Wiggle Bear" in celebration of how involuntarily wiggly his bare body became after his first ejaculation inside her. It was pure luck that she hadn't become pregnant since he had forgotten to use the rubber he had procured in anticipation of this event. Elmer realized they could have a four-year-old child together if things had gone differently, and when he remembered they had both lost their virginity that Christmas afternoon, he began to tear up. The bitch.

July 30, 1967, Wendover

Once the mountains took over for the salt flats, Elmer turned off on the "business route" leading into Wendover in search of a gas station. As he reached the edge of town, he couldn't fail to notice a young woman with her thumb out and a cardboard sign saying, "San Francisco or bust!" The message was adorned with two peace symbols. Elmer didn't need any company, that was for sure, but her attire was just like the hippie clothing he had seen in Life magazine, and it did look, um, interesting. She was thin, with long hair dyed a magenta color, kept out of her eyes with a braided headband. The girl wore a skimpy halter top that was tied in a knot between her breasts and a long skirt with a complicated pattern. Her midsection was bare, and she wore leather sandals on her feet. Elmer slowed down to take it all in, anticipating that she was a foreshadowing of what he would find in San Francisco. As he drove by, she smiled, flashed him a peace sign, and called out, "Take me with you!" in a voice that suggested she would make an interesting companion for a couple of days. Elmer waved to her and then kept going. *"That's the last thing I need,"* he thought.

Elmer filled the truck up with gas and went next door

to a burger joint. As he sat at the counter, he began to wonder about the young hitchhiker; how she had gotten there, where she slept, if she was hungry. Should he give her a ride? It could be annoying, and he probably wouldn't have the nerve to kick her out. On the other hand, this WAS an adventure wasn't it? Why not do something adventurous? He began to feel a little sorry for her – a young girl out on the road by herself. Any kind of unsavory character could pick her up and cause her harm. He began to feel maybe he would be saving her from danger if he picked her up.

He bought a hamburger to go and resolved to go back — if she were there, he'd offer her a ride, if not, he could leave her to her fate and eat the hamburger later. Elmer drove back three blocks to her location, but she was nowhere to be seen. *"Oh well,"* he thought, noticing that he was a little disappointed. He turned around and drove back through Wendover to rejoin the interstate west of town.

To his surprise, he saw his anticipated companion again just before the main street led onto the freeway. Elmer took a deep breath and stopped the truck.

"I thought it was all over between us!" she said with a giggle.

"How did you get HERE?" Elmer asked through the open window.

"I got a ride," she said, "but the guy was so creepy I told him I was only going to this side of town for now!"

"So, you're headed for San Francisco?" Elmer asked.

"YES!" she said. "Are you going that far?"

"I'm going that direction," he said, wanting to be as non-committal as possible.

"Groovy!" she said. "Can I come with you?"

Elmer thought she used the word "come" in a way could have had a more sexual interpretation, but perhaps that was just the way his thoughts were trending.

"Sure, throw your bag in the back and climb in," he said, reaching across and opening the passenger door for her. Her duffel bag seemed too small to contain everything a traveler might need for a trip to San Francisco.

"Oh WOW! I love your truck. My dad used to have one like it until he drove it off the side of a mountain one time. My name's Prudence," she said, extending her hand.

"Elmer," he said. "Glad to meet you, Prudence."

They shook hands. "Was your dad okay?"

"He was NEVER okay, but that little drunken adventure killed him, thank goodness!"

"I was hoping this would be interesting," Elmer thought, but perhaps it would be best not to follow up on this topic right away.

"Want a hamburger?" he said as they got under way.

"Oh my god, yes!" Prudence said. "I'm fucking STARVING!"

Elmer had never heard Tilly use this word as far as

he remembered, and even Patti, who wasn't a saint, used it rarely. Prudence's use of the word within a minute of their first meeting was shocking. And gave him a little thrill.

"You're a real sweetheart! What did you say your name was?"

"Elmer!"

She reached over and casually gave his thigh a squeeze. "You're a real sweetheart Elmer. Thank you!"

Elmer surreptitiously watched her while she ate. She looked, for better or worse, very much like Suziebelle, the girl he had had a crush on in high school before Tilly came along. He reminded himself to be a gentleman with her, not that this wasn't his normal behavior.

Nothing was said as she worked on the hamburger.

"Where do you come from?" Elmer asked when she finished.

"Provo. It took me four days to get to Wendover, but the first two were with a girlfriend in Salt Lake City. I left home Wednesday morning at 5 o'clock, just like the Beatles song!"

To Elmer's surprise, Prudence began to sing:

Wednesday morning at five o'clock
As the day begins,
Silently closing her bedroom door
Leaving the note that she hoped would say more

"Why did you leave?" Elmer asked.

"I couldn't stand my mom and her new boyfriend. I couldn't stand Provo. And I couldn't stand Utah," Prudence said matter-of-factly.

"Why are you headed for San Francisco?" he asked.

"It's where everything is happening! Free love, warm weather, plenty of pot, I can go topless wherever I want to, nude beaches, music, war protests, psychedelics! Where else would you want to be?"

Elmer felt it would have sounded stupid to say "Iowa", so he didn't respond.

He considered her assertion and found it attractive but naive. If everybody sat around everyday having sex and doing whatever they wanted to, who would do the work? And how would they survive when the money from home or the government dried up?

"What part of Iowa do you come from?" Prudence asked. She must have seen his license plates.

"South Branch," he told her.

"Where's THAT?"

"The southern part."

"Is it nice there?"

This stumped Elmer a little. Of course, he thought it was nice, but in truth he had never really compared it to anywhere else since he hadn't been anywhere else to speak of. St. Louis and over into Illinois, but those weren't that different from Iowa.

"I guess so," he said.

"Did you go to college?" Prudence wanted to know.

"Yes. State College of Iowa."

"What did you learn?"

She had him there! Not an easy question to be sure.

"Not to trust that girls will be faithful to you!" he said before he gave his answer sufficient thought.

"Oooh! And you're still mad at her, I can tell!" Prudence said. "Is she why you're going to San Francisco?"

"I don't really want to go into it," Elmer said. He didn't remember telling her that he was going all the way to San Francisco.

"So, you're going to San Francisco to look for this girl who 'done you wrong' and you're going to kill her. That would make a good story!"

"I'm NOT going to kill her, Prudence. Just drop it, okay?"

Elmer had never considered murder, but it WAS an idea.

Prudence continued. "I can picture myself on the evening news, saying in a somber voice 'But he seemed like such a nice boy, a perfect gentleman. I can't BELIEVE what he did that to that poor girl!'."

This stopped the conversation for a few minutes. Prudence took off her shoes and put her feet up on the dashboard, hiking her long skirt up to mid-thigh in the process. Elmer glanced at her and the 20-mile-long basin they were about to cross on a dead straight road. The scenery was spectacular both inside and outside the truck.

"What did you study at college?" she asked.

"Commerce."

"Like buying and selling stuff?"

"Well, there's more to it than that, but that's the general idea."

"So, you're going to be a capitalist pig, then?"

Elmer considered several possible responses but couldn't choose one. He looked at her and smiled.

"Want to fuck me?" she asked, as though she was asking what time it was.

Elmer looked at her, almost driving off the road. He was speechless! No girl had ever put that question to him directly. Tilly and Patti had made flirtatious suggestions once their relationships had been established, but he had only met Prudence twenty minutes before. Of course he wanted to fuck her, who wouldn't? But in his experience, it took weeks or months to become close enough to make that a possibility. Maybe this was what "free love" was all about.

"No!" he lied.

"Why not? Don't boys in Iowa like to fuck?"

"Sure we do, but I'm driving right now!"

"Okay," she said – turning her attention to the

mountain scenery. Elmer made sure her attention was elsewhere and manipulated his erection to forestall permanent damage to his confined manhood.

Elmer was not really a "laid back" person, and this development added several worries to the top of his list of concerns. First, what if she was underage? For that matter, even if he didn't do anything, wasn't there a law against taking underage girls across state lines? Thankfully she had moved to the Nevada side of Wendover before he picked her up. And if they had some kind of casual sex, what if she got pregnant? And there were a bunch of venereal diseases that Elmer couldn't even remember the names of. And crabs, tiny genital lice which he had heard weren't as funny as they sounded. He looked at Prudence for signs of an infestation. And, to his annoyance, he found himself feeling guilty for imagining having sex with a stranger behind Tilly's back. He and Tilly didn't even have a relationship anymore.

As tempting as a roll in the hay sounded, Elmer couldn't really believe that any girl would be THAT fast and decided his worry and anticipation were premature at best.

"Are you a college student?" Elmer inquired as a means of judging her age.

"Oh no. I just got out of high school!"

"You mean you just graduated?"

"I would have, but I got kicked out a month before."

"Why did they kick you out?" Elmer asked as calmly

as he could.

"None of your business!" she said, in a way that appeared to close that door for good.

"Is that why you're hightailing it to San Francisco?"

"Well, it didn't endear me to the old home place," she said.

Elmer now began to wonder if the police might be on the lookout for Prudence. He imagined them chasing him down and a gunfight at a corral out in the desert somewhere.

"The cops aren't after you, are they?" Elmer tried to make this seem like a joke.

"Fuck the pigs!" Prudence said. "They'll never take me alive!"

Elmer looked at her like she was an undiscovered species.

"Oh, Elmer! You are so funny!" Prudence said. She removed her bare feet from the dash and extended them out the side window then positioned herself on her back with her head against Elmer's thigh. She looked up at him, laughing.

"Have you been taking drugs or something?" Elmer asked incredulously.

"No Elmer, not today anyway. But I'm high on leaving Utah. I'm so happy you picked me up and you're so cute and worried. Don't worry about anything. We're going to California, and everything is going to be so cool!"

"Right," Elmer said.

"As soon as I find my old boyfriend and kill him!"

"Come on, Prudence. Knock it off."

"Okay. I'll lay off for now, but you ARE fun to tease!"

The road across Nevada alternated between curvy climbs into mountain passes and descents into basins that were flat and straight for miles with the next mountain range slowly approaching. It was a hot afternoon, and Elmer pulled off on an exit that just led to an underpass and a gravel road going perpendicular to the freeway in each direction serving a few local ranches. He stopped the truck under the overpass in the only shady place for miles.

"You aren't kicking me out are you!" Prudence asked with a smile.

"Nope. I'm going to put on some shorts and take a leak. Don't look!"

"Awww," she whined. "Okay, I'll do the same."

Prudence went in front of the truck and Elmer stepped behind the back and took care of their tasks.

Once back in the truck, they resumed their positions with Prudence lying on the seat.

"Elmer, is it okay if I take a nap? I didn't get much sleep last night?"

"Sure."

You won't take advantage of me if I take my top off, will you?"

"No."

Prudence untied and slipped out of her halter top, shaking her chest a little to tease him.

"Wake me up when it's bedtime, okay?"

As she slept, Elmer attempted to come to grips with what he had gotten himself into. He tried to assess the various issues that Prudence had stirred up although it was difficult to focus on these issues because she was lying on her back with her long hair tickling his lower leg and her top tucked under her head as a makeshift pillow. The narrow width of the truck cab required her to bend her knees up to fit on the available portion of the bench seat, and this caused the hem of her long skirt to gradually descend from her raised knees down toward her upper thighs like an unintentional, slow motion, striptease. He decided to begin his assessment of the situation by assessing the attractiveness of her breasts. These were nicely round and sized just pleasantly too large for her thin build, with somewhat puffy, dark nipples. He resisted the temptation to touch them.

She seemed clever, fun-loving, flirtatious, and devil-may-care. She was not a person for planning ahead; Prudence seemed unconcerned about how she would survive in San Francisco or, for that matter, with how she would have gotten there if he hadn't happened by. Mostly she was a mystery.

They had only spent a couple of hours together so

far, and already Prudence had told him about her father, asked if he wanted to fuck her, teased him unmercifully, and exposed her breasts within easy reach. She was either dangerously naïve or completely in control. Was she about to become the most playful lover he had ever encountered or an evil temptress who would cause endless trouble? Was she about to teach him all about a wonderful world of pleasure that neither of his previous two girlfriends had known about, or was she counting on him to teach her about the wide world? Should he embrace everything that he could suddenly imagine, or should he run like hell?

Elmer looked down at Prudence. She was sleeping like a baby. Either she intuitively knew he was trustworthy, was unaware of the possible danger of being alone in the middle of nowhere with a perfect stranger or was confident that she could take care of herself whatever happened. Her small duffel bag was in the back of the truck, but she had brought a shoulder bag into the truck with her which now rested in the space on the seat under her knees. It crossed his mind that she might have a gun in her bag, just in case. Elmer imagined that she planned to murder him and bury his body in the desert as soon as he had bought another tank of gas, but that seemed illogical because if she did him in, she could just take his billfold and buy gas when needed. He involuntarily put his hand against his back pocket to be sure the billfold was still there. In doing so his hand brushed against her hair which interrupted her sleep just enough for her to turn onto her side and bend her right arm over his leg. Her hand was now against his inner thigh and she sleepily held on like she was dreaming of drowning and his thigh was a life preserver.

Elmer couldn't remember being with a girl who he felt needed protection. He had felt protective toward Tilly when they had first fallen madly in love, but he didn't feel she really needed his protection as they were learning about love together. Patti had always been in charge and this relieved him from being responsible for all the ideas, but he always felt a little insecure in this role. But Prudence seemed fragile, like a small bird leaving the nest and entering a threatening world, delighted yet filled with false bravado.

Now that Prudence was on her side facing the front of the truck, Elmer felt it would be safe to place his hand gently on her bare shoulder in a caring gesture. This resulted in Prudence sliding her hand further up his leg and squeezing him tighter.

"Arm-on," Prudence said indistinctly in her sleep. "Pleesh, Are-ron."

Elmer dared not move his hand from her shoulder lest this movement wake her up. He tried to figure out what she was trying to say. Was it about her arm on his leg, or perhaps a boy named Ron? And what was she hoping for?

The truck began to descend a hill and Elmer had to shift down to second gear to slow the descent while avoiding unnecessary wear on the brakes. He removed his hand from Prudence's shoulder and pushed the floor shift up into second.

Prudence woke up with a start. "WHAT?" she said.

"Nothing, I just had to shift gears."

"Oh," she said, waking up and rolling onto her back to look up at him. "Where are we?"

"We just passed Battle Mountain, according to the sign," Elmer told her.

"How long was I asleep?" she asked.

"Maybe an hour and a half."

"Thanks for not raping me," she said.

"You thought I was going to rape you?" Elmer asked, stunned.

"It wouldn't be the first time."

"You were hitchhiking, and someone raped you?" Elmer almost shouted.

"No, at home. I don't want to talk about it. But thanks."

The conversation paused while Elmer considered this news. How could she let herself go to sleep if she was worried about THAT?

"Prudence," Elmer said. "Let's get one thing straight. I'm not going to rape you under any circumstances. You're a beautiful young woman and obviously you are 'adventurous' but whatever happens between us the next two days is not going to involve me harming you. You can relax about that."

"I know. Did I mention that you're a sweetheart, Elmer? Don't worry, I feel very safe with you, especially now."

333

"What about when we get to San Francisco? You know I'm just going there for a couple of days, don't you? I'm not going to be keeping you safe once we get there."

"That's too bad!" she smiled. "Are you going on the lam once you've killed her?"

"Damn it, Prudence! I'm NOT going to kill her. I'm going to take her back to South Branch."

"WHY?"

"That's a good question. I don't imagine she wants to go, and I don't want to take her!"

"So, you're kidnapping her!"

"No, I'm just giving her a ride back to South Branch to see her family."

"I know why you're kidnapping her," Prudence said with an unreadable facial expression. "You're still in love with her!"

"Okay. I'm NOT in love with her. I hate her if you have to know. It's none of your business, but her mother asked me to bring her back and I agreed."

"So, you're in love with her mother then?"

"I AM NOT IN LOVE WITH HER MOTHER!"

"I'm in love with your thigh though," Prudence giggled, as she reached up and playfully tickled Elmer's thigh below his shorts.

Ahead, the western sky was darkening in a way that, in Iowa at least, would indicate a thunderstorm was coming. Elmer wondered if it was a warning about the tempest he might be in the middle of by the time they got to San Francisco.

"Are you taking me to a luxury motel where we can cool off in the pool, have a few drinks in the bar, and then have sex in a soft bed all night?"

Elmer just gave her a bemused look. "I applaud your imagination, Pru, but the reality is going to be much more pedestrian."

"Don't call me Pru! That's what he used to call me."

"Who's 'he'?" Elmer asked before thinking. "Oh, I'm sorry. What about 'Prudy' then?"

"That's nice. No one has ever called me that before. It's usually 'Prude' or 'Dense'."

"Pretty Prudy," Elmer said, falling for her a little.

Prudence, still on her back, stretched her legs up and put her bare feet on the headliner above, causing her skirt to drop down to her hips, exposing a tantalizing triangle of her pink panties. Elmer had forgotten that Prudence was topless and when he looked down, he involuntarily said "Wow!" in a soft voice. Prudy reached over her head and gently put the palm of her hand in Elmer's lap.

"It feels like you're a panty fancier!" she said looking up at him with a big smile.

"I'm an equal opportunity fancier of female underwear, especially when it's hung over the back of a chair," Elmer said. He was loony with lust and was completely at sea about what was going to happen between them and how he felt about it.

Without taking her eyes off Elmer, Prudy bent her knees back down and placed her feet on the seat once more. She now raised her bottom and slid the garment in question up to her knees. Elmer took a deep breath.

"I'm sorry, but these have to come off, Elmer," she grinned. "They're getting wet."

"Of course," Elmer said, nearly out of breath. He glanced at the road and quickly turned his attention back to Prudence.

She extended her arm to hold the panties against her right knee, then slid her other leg up through the leg opening until she grasped the waistband between her toes. After engaging in a bit of teasing exercise involving stretching the waistband in several directions with her toes, she moved her foot back to the seat, taking the panties down to her ankle. Elmer awaited her next move. Still holding the waistband with her toe, Prudy freed her right foot from the garment, then placed her feet back on the ceiling of the truck, spreading them wide apart with the scanty pink panties dangling just inside the windshield from her left toe. Elmer squirmed in his seat.

"Oh my god, Tilly!" he said.

"Who's 'Tilly'?" she asked.

"Um...," Elmer stammered.

"It's HER isn't it?"

Suddenly Elmer's attention was captured by a vibration caused by the truck's tires encountering the rumble strips at the side of the highway. He quickly steered the truck back onto the road, just as he noticed a Highway Patrol Officer waiting in his car in the median.

"Great!" he thought.

In the mirror, he could see the red light begin to flash as the officer prepared to pull out behind him. Before he could warn Prudence to put her things back on, however, a Corvette flew past him at 95 with the cop in pursuit.

Elmer took a minute to collect his wits. Prudence was unaware of the police presence, but she did suggest that Elmer pay visual attention to the road ahead, adding that he could admire her manually if he wished.

Elmer couldn't believe that a girl, especially one who had experienced unpleasant attention at the hands of men could behave this way.

"Are you sure you're not high on drugs?" he asked again.

"I told you, I'm high on leaving Utah. And on teasing you, of course!"

She lowered her legs and sat up, removed her dangling panties, and stashed them under the seat.

"I'm sorry if I was distracting you too much," she said. "I'm just so happy to be on my way to California with a nice guy who's cute and funny! I won't distract you ever again."

"That's okay," Elmer said, in the understatement of the day.

Prudence got up on the seat and sat on her haunches, looking at Elmer with her knees against his thighs. The sky ahead was very dark by now and lightning flashed in the distance.

"Do you think my titties are pretty?" she asked.

"They're lovely," Elmer said. "But I thought you were going to quit distracting me."

"Do you need something to nibble on?" she asked.

"PRUDENCE!"

"WHAT? I meant what are we going to have for dinner? You have a dirty mind Elmer!"

Elmer's mind was pulling him in several directions at once, but they WERE going to have to consider how to get something to eat.

"I'll fill up with gas in Winnemucca and we'll find a grocery store and get something," he said.

"Are we going to stop somewhere and 'sleep' tonight?"

"The map says there's a rest stop the other side of Winnemucca. We'll stop there and see if we can find time to sleep," Elmer said, feeling himself gradually giving in to the idea that having a tumble with this curious girl might not be inexcusably ungentlemanly.

By the time they got to Winnemucca, it was starting to rain. They found a grocery and, before going in, Elmer brought his suitcase, a small cooler, and Prudy's duffel bag into the passenger compartment while Prudy put her top back on. They looked bedraggled by the time they got inside, and apparently this part of the country wasn't fond of hippie types. They were treated rudely, but they did manage to get a loaf of bread, a jar of peanut butter, some candy bars, and a bottle of orange juice.

"You know, Elmer, orange juice is pretty uninteresting without vodka," Prudence noted once they got back in the truck.

Elmer wondered what she would be like after a few screwdrivers if she was this crazy sober, but at this point, he was game to find out.

"Hold on a second," he said, heading back inside.

They headed west again through what had now become a steady rainstorm. The truck cab seemed to be a tiny romantic hideaway in spite of Elmer's attempt to keep his romantic thoughts at bay. It was dusk when they pulled into the Cosgrove rest area. Apparently, it was a popular place to spend a rainy night, but they found a parking space next to a big rig and began their evening's adventures by taking turns running to the rest room to avoid getting soaked. When Elmer returned to the truck, Prudy had their first screwdrivers ready. They were delicious, even served lukewarm in paper cups, and Elmer began to relax and entertain the idea that one shouldn't stress out on the way to the most laid-back town in the country.

With the luggage inside, there was no room for Prudy's feet, so she sat with her back against the passenger door and Elmer sat against the driver's door, each with their feet extended toward the other. It was a warm night. Both were barefoot. Prudy's top hung from the rearview mirror to dry and Elmer's T-shirt was draped over the steering wheel for the same reason. Prudence, as a means of showing off her domestic skills, fixed two peanut butter sandwiches; Elmer couldn't remember a meal with more expectations for the dessert course. Each was anticipating a sexual romp. It was a romantic location, they were on their way to the join the "Summer of Love", after all, and each found the other intriguing as a potential sexual partner.

Elmer was unaware that Prudence, although she had experienced troublesome sex, had never had any kind of pleasurable experience with a man, although she had fantasized about this for a half-dozen years. The prospect that tonight might be the beginning of her anticipated awakening excited and scared her in equal measure. Facing her across the darkening truck cab, Elmer, who hadn't had any significant sexual excitement for two months, except through his own efforts, was similarly torn between anticipating some novel nookie and fearing that everything could go terribly wrong in a multitude of ways.

They finished the sandwiches and Prudy filled up their cups again as she slid her toe into the leg opening of Elmer's shorts.

"Tell me about this 'Tilly' person," she said, although she was a little afraid to find out about her. "Are you in love with her?"

"I told you I hate her, didn't I? Why else would I be going all the way to San Francisco to kill her?" Elmer laughed and raised his foot – moving his toe across in front of Prudy's neck as though slitting her throat.

"What did she do to make you so mad?"

This girl had a way of asking difficult questions. "I don't remember," Elmer said without thinking. "She just abandoned me I guess, once she went to San Francisco."

Prudy didn't find this a capital offence, but she didn't want to talk Elmer into falling back in love with her. "That must have made you feel awful," she said.

"And she got into this hippie thing, you know? Running around naked, smoking marijuana, having sex with every man that came along. I was totally in love with her and it was devastating."

Prudence resisted the temptation to defend Tilly, but if Tilly was guilty of that, she wanted to follow in her footsteps!

"No wonder you want to kill her!" she said, causing both of them to crack up with laughter.

Elmer gently slid his bare foot between Prudence's thighs. "Pour us another drink, Baby!" he said, still giggling about the idea that he was going to do Tilly in.

"Okay, tell me about your boyfriends," Elmer said as they started on round three. "Turnabout is fair play."

Prudence turned serious for the first time. "I've never really had an official boyfriend. My folks wouldn't allow it. But apparently when my mom's boyfriend would get drunk and get into my bed, they were fine with that."

"That's shocking. I can't believe they would do that to you!"

"They did," she said.

As they talked, a police car pulled up alongside the truck. Elmer grabbed his T-shirt from the steering wheel and threw it to Prudy. "Put this on, quick!" he said.

A minute later a Highway Patrol Officer knocked his flashlight against the window and shined it into Elmer and Prudence's hideaway. Elmer rolled the window down a few inches.

"Good efening ossifer," he said.

"There's been a report of underage drinking in this location. I'll need to see your ID," the officer said humorlessly.

"Yesch sir!" Elmer said, hoping he wouldn't ask Prudence for the same. He handed his driver's license to the officer who studied it and Elmer's face.

"How old are you son?" he said.

"Tweny-two, sir," Elmer said.

"All right," said the officer, handing Elmer his driver's license.

"And yours, young lady," he said to Prudence.

Elmer pictured landing in jail since he was sure Prudence was under twenty-one.

"Of course, officer," she said without a hint of concern. Prudence rummaged through her bag and handed him a document.

"You don't look twenty-three!" he said, taking a long look at her.

"Thank you," she said.

He checked her license again and handed the card back. Make sure you sober up before you get back on the road.

"Yes sir, we will," Elmer assured him.

"Have a nice night," the officer said with a leer.

"Are you really twenty-three?" Elmer asked when the officer had gone.

"No."

"Then what happened?"

"I showed him my fake ID of course, what do you think?"

"How old are you, really?"

"Eighteen," Prudy said with a big smile, conveying no information that Elmer could count on.

"Okay. Final, final," Prudy said, pouring another drink.

It was dark now and the talking was replaced by laughter and blatant manipulation of one another's genitalia with their toes. The rain began again and Elmer and Prudence, setting aside their half-finished drinks, rearranged themselves on the seat with Elmer on his back and Prudence half on top of him. They hugged and kissed each other, and sleepy but unsuccessful attempts were made to slide their hands into one another's clothing. This activity, delightful as it was, gradually slowed down and, with the rain for a lullaby, the pair slipped into a sound sleep.

Elmer woke up groggy, with a heavyweight headache and a full bladder. The sun was bright, and most of the cars and trucks nearby had already departed. He was entangled with Prudy and was sorry to wake her, but he had to head for the head. She was asleep with her head on his chest and her arms around him as though she was afraid he would disappear.

"Prudence! Wake up, Baby. I have to go take a leak."

Prudence stirred then opened her eyes, jumping back when she saw him. She looked at him for a minute as though trying to discern whether he was friend or foe.

"Oh god, Elmer. I feel like shit."

"Welcome to the club, but I have to pee."

They untangled their bodies and Elmer stepped outside to a beautiful day and walked across the parking lot, trying to work out the stiffness in his legs.

When he got back, Prudence was sitting cross-legged, bent over, and trying not to move. Elmer put the luggage back into the truck bed and got her a drink of water from a jug in the cooler.

"Did we do it last night?" she asked.

"Not that I can remember," he said. "So, it wouldn't count even if we did."

"Well, something's wet down there," Prudy said, sliding her hand up her skirt. Her fingers were bloody when she examined them.

"Oh, oh! Either you took my virginity last night, or I'm getting my period!"

It was clear that Prudy had no virginity for him to "take" and he was pretty sure he would have remembered if they had had sex. On the other hand, he had never known a girl who wasn't rather secretive at first about when she was having her period, although once they had become intimate, they had to work around it somehow.

"Are you okay?" he asked.

"I have a splitting headache, I can hardly move without feeling like I'm going to puke, and I have abdominal cramps. Other than that, I've never felt better," she said. "I'm sorry, Elmer. No wonder I was so horny yesterday!"

"Darn. I thought it was because I was so charming. Can I do anything to help?" he asked.

"Carry me over to the bathroom," she said, managing a tiny giggle. "I'll get better, but I'm not going to be the playful nymphomaniac you were hoping for today."

Prudence procured a fresh pair of panties from her duffel bag and headed across to the ladies' room. While she was there, Elmer checked the oil in the truck and washed the windshield. He was clueless about female menstrual cycles, but he did know that none of his previous girlfriends would have anything to do with sex while they were having their period. If Prudence was the same, they wouldn't be having sexual intercourse any time soon. This would relieve him of any worries about pregnancy or of having taken advantage of her. On the other hand, it would eliminate, for now at least, his anticipated enjoyment of serendipitous debauchery.

"Is there a town anywhere up ahead?" she asked when she returned.

"Lovelock is about forty-five minutes from here."

"Can we stop there? I have to get some Tampax. The stupid machine in the bathroom was empty. And some aspirin would be helpful."

"Sure."

"And we're out of vodka!" she said, in a failed attempt at humor.

They stopped for supplies in Lovelock, filled the tank, and bought two hamburgers in case either of them ever felt like eating again. Back on the road, the conversation restarted.

"Were you kidding about your boyfriend in San Francisco?" Elmer asked.

"What boyfriend?"

"The one you were going to murder! Rod or Armond or something?"

"Oh, Aaron! Did I tell you about him?"

"You said something in your sleep yesterday."

"Oops! Okay, Aaron is a friend from school. He sends me letters from San Francisco sometimes. He has to send them to my girlfriend because my parents would have thrown them away if he sent them to my house. He's a nice boy, but he's not my boyfriend," Prudy said. "I wish he was though. I think about him all the time."

"Is he expecting you to show up?"

"No. He tells me how nice San Francisco is and says I should look him up if I ever get there, but he's not expecting me. He probably has a girlfriend."

"So, what are you going to do if he doesn't take you in?"

"I'll figure something out."

"Not to be nosy Prudence, but do you have any money?"

"I saved up $30. That should hold me for a while."

"Prudence..." Elmer said.

"What?"

"...Nothing."

Early in the afternoon they passed through Reno and not long afterward they came to a parking area by the side of the road that featured a sign saying, "Welcome to California". They got out of the truck, took each other's picture with Elmer's camera, and ate what they could manage of their lunch.

"We made it, Elmer!" Prudence said. Suddenly, her enthusiasm for life returned, and she grabbed Elmer and kissed him like a lover she had been waiting for. "Thank you for bringing me here, Elmer! Whatever happens now is going to be okay, I'm sure of it!"

"Okay, I'll see you later!" Elmer said laughing as he got into the car and started it up.

"You're not leaving me out here with the bears, Elmer, no matter how anxious you are to get on with your murderous machinations!"

The closer they got to San Francisco, the more excited Prudy got, pointing out every unusual feature of the scenery and citizenry like a toddler just discovering the delights of the world and wanting to share them. Elmer appreciated this; it distracted him from tomorrow's awkward meeting with Tilly.

Near evening they found themselves at a roadside area called the 'Nut Tree' with a restaurant and shops. They were hungry by this time and some of Prudence's optimism and enthusiasm had rubbed off on Elmer.

"I'm going to buy you dinner to celebrate our first night in California, Baby," he told her.

"You are SUCH a sweetheart," she said, shamelessly giving his penis a gentle squeeze through his shorts.

"Ok, I'll throw in dessert just for that!"

They enjoyed a fancier-than-usual hamburger and a fancier-than-usual slice of pecan pie for dinner and then spent some time in the other shops nearby. Neither Elmer nor Prudence knew anything about wine, but after visiting the California Wine exhibit, Elmer decided they should give it a try since they were going to be Californians. At least for a few days. He selected an inexpensive rosé and bought a bottle to celebrate their arrival in California.

By the time the pair had explored the miniature railroad and the airport attached to the property, it was getting late and they set off in search of a safe spot to park the truck and continue with the unplanned events of the evening. Behind a nearby gas station, they came across a group of camper-type vehicles, some painted in psychedelic colors. Several young people were sitting outside, drinking wine and smoking. Elmer and Prudence learned the gas station attendant would not bother anyone out back if they slipped him a "camping fee" of fifty cents, which also let them use the rest rooms without hassle. Done. The wine bottles were passed around and, in this way, the newcomers were able to sample several varieties and get tips on road conditions, how to avoid the cops, and groovy amusements to be found in San Francisco. The party broke up early. It was clear that most of the couples were anxious to begin the sexual play portion of the evening, and once again Elmer and Prudy retired to the darkened intimacy of their truck cab.

As Elmer expected, Prudence expressed a disinterest in having sexual intercourse due to her period. Even though she was remarkably horny, it would be messy, and she assumed without evidence that any boy would find it a turn-off. Elmer in turn assumed that her disinterest reflected a lack of desire. This self-imposed limitation didn't foreclose on all romantic play, however. Before long, Prudy was sitting astride Elmer, tapping their paper cups of wine together, talking intimately, and sipping a vintage that they didn't yet know was too watery and sweet. It was a warm night, no one was outside, and the combination of the wine, Elmer's repressed stress about seeing Tilly the next day, and the inopportune timing of Prudence's period, led to a bit of craziness.

Inasmuch as they would be in San Francisco the next day, at the height of the Summer of Love, they began teasing each other about how wild the scene might be and daring each other to behave in ways they expected to find commonplace once they arrived.

"Life magazine had a picture of thousands of people, who looked like they were high on drugs, swaying around like zombies in the park. And all the women were topless!" Elmer reported.

"I'll be out there with them, tomorrow, Elmer. You've already seen my titties so that won't be anything new for you, though."

Elmer started to laugh.

"My tits aren't THAT funny," Prudy said with a pout.

"No, I was thinking of something that happened in college."

"You saw a girl with funny tits, or what?"

"No. Well yes, but that's another story."

Prudence gave him a playful slap on the arm.

"We had pictures from Playboy on the wall of our room in the dorm and the janitor came in one day for something and said, 'Man, I'd like to have forty acres of tits just to walk around on barefoot.'!"

"You can't walk around barefoot on my tits, Elmer," Prudy decreed. "But you can kiss them if you want to."

Elmer wanted to. He lifted Prudence's loose-fitting

top over her head and tossed it aside. A full moon illuminated the interior of the truck sufficiently for him to admire her attributes, and Elmer leaned her back, fortunately just missing bringing her back into contact with the truck's horn button. In Elmer's experience, girls wanted him to work up to manipulating their most sensitive regions, but Prudence was not in the mood to wait around. She put her hands behind his head and directed his mouth to the precise spot where she wanted him to begin. Even Patti, who had had plenty of experience before Elmer came along, was not this forward. He loved this discovery of course, and yet he vaguely worried that he would have to be the responsible one to avoid trouble down the road.

Prudence was experienced with sex, but not with loving, desired sex, and Elmer's touch thrilled her. Before long, both were simmering with arousal.

"Let's take all of our clothes off!" Prudence giggled.

In Elmer's testosterone-tainted thoughts, this seemed safe enough; after all, nobody wore any clothes in San Francisco so they might as well get used to the idea. They took turns awkwardly removing items of each other's clothing in the cramped quarters until everything was on the floor of the truck. Naturally, they expected to enjoy one another's nakedness, but suddenly the feeling of contact with the warm bare skin of a near stranger, in a semipublic location, bathed in wine and moonlight, and looking forward to the prospect of San Francisco, was nearly overwhelming.

Prudence was shivering with arousal, affection for

Elmer, the crazy karma of this gas station parking lot, and optimism for the future.

"Come outside with me!" she said, opening the door of the truck and stepping bare-assed out into the moonlight.

"Get back in the truck, Prudence. Anybody can see you out there," Elmer said, concerned that their tête-à-tête might be interrupted.

"I don't care who sees me, Elmer," she said, tilting her head back and spreading her arms up and out. "I'm in California now. I'm free of Utah forever. My knight in shining armor and I are naked out here where anybody could be watching us. Come out and feel me up in the moonlight. I dare you!"

"A knight isn't naked if he's wearing shining armor Prudence, but how could I resist a dare like that?"

Elmer climbed out of the truck, shutting the door as carefully as he could to keep the dome light from running down the battery while they were outside. They hugged in the moonlight and Prudence commented a little too loudly on the prominence of Elmer's erection. Elmer thought to chastise her but demurred. In truth, he felt excited by the naughtiness of being naked outside. No one would do this in Iowa, he thought, but everything seemed possible and permitted in California.

"I have an idea," he said.

Elmer retrieved his sleeping bag, which he unzipped to make a large comforter, and laid it out in the bed of the truck, filling the space.

"Come to 'bed' with me," he said, lowering the tailgate and helping Prudence climb in.

They laid on their backs, arms and legs spread wide and partially entangled, and looked toward the heavens, gently touching each other. The sides of the truck bed provided a slight amount of privacy from any observers who were not close by anyway, and that seemed sufficient.

They held hands and studied the moon.

"People are trying to go there," Prudence said. "Do you think they'll make it?"

"Yes," Elmer opined.

"I don't think it will be so romantic after that if they do," Prudy mused. "It won't seem so far away or so magical."

She rolled over on top of Elmer. "Kiss me some more while the moon is still a virgin!"

This happened of course, and before long the moon was forgotten in favor of manually studying one another's genitalia. Without discussion, they were soon softly encouraging one another in their explorations, and purposefully manipulating each other's most sensitive spots in full view of the moon and anyone else who might be watching.

Their entertaining touching escalated without any specific invitation. Before long, this became electrifying mutual masturbation, with each of them using their fingers to stimulate the other's favorite locations. Inexperience with each other's particular preferences caused the interaction to be imperfect, but perfection was unnecessary in view of the situation and, as Elmer tickled her, Prudence soon began flailing with pleasure and expressing her delight vocally in a way that Elmer attempted to quiet by kissing her forcefully.

Given his obviously successful efforts to please Prudence, his recent lack of female companionship, the unexpected thrill of the last two days, and Prudence's amateurish but more than adequate abilities at accelerating his arousal, Elmer knew he couldn't hold out long and, as it turned out, he barely had time to warn Prudence of the upcoming outpouring before her stroking of his manhood caused him to launch uncounted attempts to put his emissions into orbit.

Eventually they reentered the earth's atmosphere and discovered it was starting to get a little chilly. Elmer folded the sleeping bag back into its normal form and zipped it up, squeezing the two of them, and the liquids they had anointed each other with, into a loving bundle where they kissed and smiled each other to sleep under the California sky.

The morning began awkwardly. The sun was up by the time they awoke, and Elmer and Prudence experienced a period of uncertainty as they replayed in their minds the activities that seemed so natural and beautiful last night, and which now seemed perhaps a little crazier than either was used to. As if to exaggerate this uneasiness, their neighbors were awake and cooking breakfast over a small grill a few feet away from their bedchamber. Elmer planned to mitigate their nakedness by opening his suitcase and gathering enough clothes to cover himself enough to drive to a more private location until he realized that he had moved his suitcase and Tilly's duffel bag into the truck cab to make room for their sleeping accommodations. Plan 'B' was to wait until their neighbors were looking the other way and quietly climb out of the truck bed, then get somewhat dressed in the truck. This would be embarrassing, but in any case, they would never see these neighbors again anyway. Elmer quietly told Prudence of his plan and began to put it into practice.

The trouble started right away. As he began to move his body away from this suddenly unfamiliar woman, he discovered they were glued together with several regions of dried semen adorning the front of their bodies. To make matters worse, Prudence squealed as he tried to peel himself off her, alerting the young hippie couple nearby to their proximity. This moved them to come over to lend a hand if needed.

"Hey guys! Need any help under there?" the young man asked pointedly. Prudence put her arm over her face and tried not to giggle.

"Would you mind getting in the truck and handing me a shirt or something from the suitcase on the floor?"

"Sure man," he said, trying the door. "Do you have the keys?"

Suddenly, Elmer realized he must have locked the doors by habit with the key still in the pocket of his shorts inside.

"Oh shit."

The passenger window was lowered two or three inches and the neighbor attempted to insert his arm in a way that he could reach the unlock button. The fellow was rather rotund and couldn't manage this.

"I can't get my arm in there, but you probably could. Nobody cares if you're naked, but I'll stand between you and the road so anybody pulling in won't get excited."

Elmer painfully peeled himself apart from Prudence and climbed out to make the attempt. In order to get his arm into the window in a way that he could reach the button, he had to stand with one foot on the running board and his knee on the hood, an odd position, especially naked. Prudence had quit giggling by this time and had climbed out of the truck, completely naked, to watch the follies. The young woman next door offered her a cup of coffee and the two women sipped their java while they watched Elmer trying to contort his naked body to pull up on the lock button. No one offered any comments on Prudy or Elmer's lack of attire, and once the suitcases were retrieved and the pair was properly clothed, their benefactors invited them over for breakfast. Marijuana was brought out for dessert and Prudence joined in while Elmer declined with the explanation that he wanted to be on his toes when he got to San Francisco.

While Prudence was getting high, Elmer filled the truck up with gas and dealt with the issue of calling Tilly. This had to be done. Her mother had told her approximately when he would be there, but he was to call her when he got to California. He was not looking forward to talking to her. He knew she didn't want to go back to South Branch even for only a few weeks before moving to California permanently, and she especially didn't want to spend days in the truck with him. Beyond that, even though he no longer considered them an "item," it would hurt to see her showing her affection for other guys. It had to be done though, so he walked over to a phone booth at the edge of the property and went inside.

Elmer tried not to think of what could go wrong with this phone call. She might have forgotten him completely. She might yell at him and hang up. She might have a new baby. She might be so spaced out that a conversation was impossible. Her weight-lifter boyfriend might tell him to get out of town. He thought back to the awkwardness of the first time he had called Tilly to ask her out, nearly six years ago.

Finally, Elmer knew he just had to do it no matter how nervous he was. He looked at the black phone hanging on the wall of the phone booth. He reached for the receiver, slowly picked it up, and put it to his ear. He was instructed to insert ten cents. There was a dial tone. The big round dial on the front curled its lip into a sneer and dared him to call. Elmer put his index finger in the hole corresponding to the first digit of Tilly's number. He turned the dial until it reached the stop, released it, and watched it rotate back to its original position with an ominous whirr. When he finished dialing, a disembodied woman's voice asked for an additional thirty cents for the first three minutes. Elmer fumbled through his pocket and fished out a quarter and a nickel.

Elmer was startled when he heard the distant ring of the phone on the other end of the line. He imagined Tilly lounging around naked, her arms around a large man in his underwear, and he was anticipating the disapproval in her voice when she discovered who was calling.

Meanwhile, Tilly was sitting up in bed naked, evaluating the contents of her room, while Ira snored next to her with his morning erection brushing her leg. She unhappily contemplated packing. She had planned to fly home and stay in South Branch as briefly as possible, then come back to San Francisco, find a job, move into a cozy apartment, and live happily-ever-after. The happily ever after part was contingent on her relationship with Ira improving, which seemed uncertain for now, but Tilly was confident everything would work out.

Now, however, after her mother's phone call a few weeks ago, she had agreed to drive back with Elmer and her Aunt Bev's dining room table. She liked the table, but she anticipated that spending several days with Elmer, with whom she no longer had anything in common, to say the least, would be somewhere between boring and excruciating. This unwanted road trip would extend the time she would be away from "The City," and Ira would probably wait out her absence in some way that she wouldn't be happy about. Her agreement to her mother's plan had her feeling more and more stupid, and more and more annoyed, with every passing minute.

As the phone rang a second time, Elmer imagined Tilly and her musclebound boyfriend, laughing so hysterically at some in-joke that was only funny if they were stoned, that they couldn't hear the ringing phone.

When he heard the phone ring for a third time, Elmer began to hope no one was home and that he could just pick up the dining table and head back to South Branch by himself. Or perhaps deliver Prudence back to Salt Lake City when her San Francisco contact flaked out.

"Lo?"

Elmer was expecting Tilly to answer the phone, but this seemed to be the voice of a recently awakened male.

"Is Tilly there please?" Elmer asked, sounding to himself like a schoolboy.

Elmer could hear the voice shout out away from the phone, *"IS THERE A MILLY HERE?"*

"Not Milly, Tilly!"

"What?"

"TILLY!"

"IS THERE A TILLY HERE?"

Elmer heard a conversation in the background.

"Ira and Iowa are sleeping in. Tell whoever it is to call back later."

"It might be important; I'll go get her."

"Make sure you knock them up first before you barge in!"

Laughter.

"Just a minute, I'll see if she's able to come to the phone."

Elmer heard a sound like the phone receiver hitting the floor.

There was a long wait.

"Thirty cents for the next three minutes please!" his new disembodied friend demanded.

Elmer looked across to where the truck had been parked to see Prudence walking on tiptoe and doing pirouettes as she approached his position. She had attempted to get dressed and mostly succeeded except for the one breast that hadn't been tucked into her top. Elmer gave her a B+ in his mind on the attempt.

He heard a sleepy female voice on the phone.

"Hello?"

"I thought you'd abandoned me!" Prudence said, stepping into the phone booth.

"What?" Elmer heard from the phone.

"Tilly?"

"Yes. Who IS this?" This was said suspiciously.

"It's Elmer."

Prudence slipped her hand under his T-shirt. "Is it HER?" she whispered.

"Already?" Tilly said unenthusiastically. *"Where are you?"*

"In California."

"Can you be more specific?" Tilly asked.

"Someplace called the Nut House."

"Where?"

"No, wait, the Nut Tree!"

"I wondered," Tilly said.

Prudence slid her hand down the front of his shorts.

"Don't DO that!" Elmer said.

"Don't do what?" Tilly asked.

"Don't stick your hand down the front of my pants!" Elmer said.

"Shit," He thought.

"Oh, don't worry, Elmer. You can be sure I don't intend to do anything like that!" Tilly assured him.

"I wasn't talking to you, Tilly."

"Are you high on something, Elmer?" Tilly asked.

"No, why?"

"You're not making any sense."

"I'm coming to San Fran' to pick you up."

"And he's going to KILL you!" Prudence warned in a giggly voice.

"Prudence! I'm NOT going to kill her, okay? I'm sorry about that Tilly."

"Who's PRUDENCE?"

"Nobody. Just a girl I picked up."

"Did you try to kill HER when you picked her up?" Tilly

asked.

"Of course not! We'll be there this afternoon sometime!"

"WE?"

"Well, Prudence doesn't have anywhere else to go until she hunts down an old boyfriend."

"Oh, I see," Tilly said. *"Is she armed?"*

"Nobody is armed; she just likes to play around," Elmer explained.

"I'll BET she does!" Tilly said.

"Are you ready to head back to Iowa?" Elmer asked.

"Oh, HELL no!"

"You're NOT? You ARE coming with me, right?" Elmer asked, thinking the trip would be smoother if she was staying.

"I have to come with you, Elmer, but it will take me a few days to get ready."

"A few days? What am I going to do in the meantime?"

"Maybe you and 'Prudence' can go hunting!"

"I guess I can sleep in the truck or something," Elmer said, clearly annoyed.

"You can sleep here on the floor if you want to; everybody else does."

"Okay."

"Oh, and Elmer!"

"What?"

"Ring the bell three times so we know it isn't the cops."

"Three times? Okay. Anything else?"

"Don't leave anything in your truck. San Francisco is a big city. Got to go. I'll see you."

Tilly hung up the phone without saying goodbye.

"That wasn't nice, Prudence, telling her I was going to kill her and everything."

Prudence manipulated his manhood under his shorts a bit and said with a pout, "I'm sure she knew I was kidding!"

"I hope so. You didn't bring any of that marijuana along, did you? I don't want any of it in the truck."

"Just this roach is all."

"Roach?"

"How straight ARE you Elmer? It's the unsmoked end of a joint."

"And a 'joint' is a marijuana cigarette?"

"Of course."

"Give it to me, Prudence."

She handed it over to Elmer and he tossed it in a trash can.

"ELMER!"

"No pot in the truck. I don't want to end up in San Quentin!"

"You're no fun," Prudy whined.

As they were about to get back on the road, Prudence needed to make a trip to the gas station ladies' room. It took her a while, and Elmer began to wonder if she was having a problem – or taking more drugs. As it turned out, she was buying snacks.

"I had to get some potato chips, candy bars, and Cheetos, Elmer. I'm starving for some reason."

"Didn't you just have some breakfast with the neighbors along with smoking pot?" Elmer inquired.

"Yes! I don't know why I'm so hungry," she said, unwrapping the first candy bar.

Once they got back on the road to San Francisco, Prudence regained her excited anticipation of their arrival. She opened the map and began pointing out landmarks and reciting how far they were from their destination. Suddenly, as Elmer navigated a tangle of traffic, Prudence cried out "There it is, Elmer! Mecca!" Elmer glanced out across the Bay. It seemed like trouble to him, but he had to admit it was beautiful! A few minutes later they drove through the toll booth on the Bay Bridge, paid the 25-cent toll, and prepared to make their grand entrance into San Francisco.

CHAPTER 8   TROUBLESOME REUNION

At last, our protagonists meet
But the meeting itself isn't sweet
They fight, not discuss
They tussle and fuss
But their history's not yet complete

August 1, 1967

It was Tuesday about mid-morning, and Tilly and Ira were snuggling together in her bed, alternately dozing and teasing each other about the pleasures of last night's sexual monkeyshines and considering whether they had time for a quickie before they had to get up and begin helping with the party that was planned for that evening. Tilly felt a little guilty for "sleeping in" since Rocky and Gary had arrived last night to help Hub, Carol, and Tilly (if she ever got out of bed) get ready for the festivities. As she absent-mindedly played with Ira's attentive appendage, she heard the phone ring in the living room; a minute later there was a knock at her bedroom door.

"Hey Iowa! Push Ira off you and come answer the phone."

Tilly stumbled into the living room, clad in panties that were ready for the laundry hamper. "Hello?" she said sleepily into the phone.

A conversation ensued; the others heard Tilly's

contribution but couldn't make sense of anything.

"Shit!" Tilly said, summarizing the conversation, after she hung up.

"Trouble?"

"My old boyfriend from high school, Elmer, is arriving this afternoon with some slut he picked up out of the gutter. I didn't think he would get here until Saturday."

"You can never have too many sluts at a party, I always say," Rocky proclaimed.

"I told them they could sleep here so I guess we'll have two more at the party. Welcome to San Francisco!"

Tilly was slightly worried that Elmer's arrival would somehow interfere with her plan to entice Gary and Ira into her bed after the party. This plan was to be a surprise to the two them. She had no worries about Gary who she expected to be all for it, but Dr. Ira Gold, as cautious as he was, might take some convincing. Tilly had plenty of Scotch on hand, Ira's favorite tipple, and there was a stash of marijuana for those who preferred that way of dispensing with their inhibitions for a while. If she could convince Gary and Ira to join her in bed when the party was winding down, she could enjoy making love to two men at once for the first time, and quite possibly the last time, in her life. She would be away for two weeks after the party and then would be moving to another San Francisco location, so she thought of this as the culmination of her Haight-Ashbury days.

Unbidden, an evil thought flashed through her mind although she dismissed it immediately. Since Elmer was to arrive before nightfall, maybe she could tie him up in her bedroom and make him watch her getting it on with two horny guys in her bed. She would just give him a sexy smile and let him imagine what he was missing. He had been out there in Iowa screwing around with every farm girl west of the Mississippi while she had been behaving herself in San Francisco!

Since she had heard herself tell Elmer that he could sleep on the floor of the apartment that night, presumably with this curious "Prudence" person, she wondered how this would play out. But she decided the sleeping arrangements among those who were unable to get home safely after the party would work themselves out when the time came. Not that she cared; she would be snuggled in, screaming with pleasure due to the ministrations of Ira and Gary, and possibly Rocky, too, if things went well, so the others could take care of themselves. There were plenty of mattresses in the living room for them to make use of.

Tilly turned her attention to the food and decided to add a bowl of marinated calamari to the offerings, just to creep Elmer out. The gathering was a going-away party of sorts because everyone would be leaving the apartment in the fall, although they would still be in San Francisco and would no doubt remain lifelong friends. Still, their four years together of sharing these Haight-Ashbury digs would be coming to an end.

The party would be complete with lighting effects (a blacklight and assorted lava lamps), soft drugs (marijuana and varieties of alcohol), and music (Hub's band would be there for a while, and records after that), food (chips, cheese, Cheetos, Tilly's calamari, and various other people's unidentifiable specialties). There would be incense and dancing as well as readings of Gary's poetry, and, as the night went on, increasingly perplexing portraits courtesy of ReX! The usual crowd was invited, it was going to be a great night, especially for Tilly and two or three of her sexiest friends.

By about 4 o'clock, all was ready. The work crew dressed for the party in their hippest outfits and sat down to rest for a few minutes and test whether the wine was poisoned. Tilly had momentarily forgotten the awkward imminence of Elmer's arrival.

Elmer and Prudence had, after mistakenly taking a circuitous route to Tilly's location, driven by the house to identify it and found a parking place three blocks away. Before they got out, Elmer gave Prudence a lecture:

"Okay, Prudence. I'm willing to look after you until I leave town, but I want you to promise not to act crazy. Don't tell Tilly I was going to kill her or talk about anything I've said about her. She invited us to sleep on her floor and we don't have any other options, so just try to act like a nice, normal girl for a while."

Prudence didn't feel like she needed any looking after and mentioned that to Elmer. On the other hand, this could be an opportunity to make some new friends, get an introduction to San Francisco, and find a place where she might be able to crash now and then if need be, so she promised to behave herself.

As they walked to Tilly's apartment, Prudence became more and more excited at being in the presence of the characters they passed; strange clothing, long hair, occasional marijuana smoking, she felt like she had come home. Elmer felt the opposite. This seemed to him like he had stepped into the "Twilight Zone".

The façade of Tilly's four-unit building featured a short stairway that penetrated the center of the building, topped with a landing and a pair of locked doors. Doorbells and their associated mailboxes adorned a sidewall, and two young men, seemingly engaged in a business deal of some kind, sprawled on the steps, requiring Emer and Prudence to detour around them; Elmer gave them a wide birth while Prudence greeted them as though they were already new friends.

Elmer scanned the mailboxes, found Tilly's, and took a deep breath.

"Here goes," he said out loud, and pushed the button three times. After a moment, a loud buzzing noise came from the area of the front door. Elmer was startled and quickly stepped back, in turn startling the two "businessmen" on the steps.

"Aren't you going to open the door?" Prudence said, stepping around him and opening the door to the dim stairway inside.

"Oh, it's one of those things," Elmer said, trying not to let on that he had no idea such systems existed. They walked upstairs as Elmer tried to figure out which apartment was Tilly's. At the top of the stairs a door was open on the right side of the hallway and several people were inside. Elmer didn't see anyone he recognized, but as they were about to look further, a woman came to the open door and looked Elmer and Prudence up and down. The woman looked nothing like Tilly, but before Elmer could apologize for the intrusion, she said, "Are you Elmer?"

"Yes," he said. "Does Tilly Williams live here?"

"This is Iowa's pad all right. Nice to meet you Elmer, I'm Carol!"

"Carol? As in Tilly's cousin, Carol?"

"Right on! Come on in and join the party!"

Elmer and Prudence stepped into the room. Ten or twelve beatnik-type characters were standing around chatting or sitting on mattresses on the floor. A distinct smell of marijuana mixed with incense flavored the air in the room. The shades were drawn, and the dim room was lit by filtered sunlight, candles, a fluorescent light in the open kitchen, and the glowing ends of what Elmer assumed were reefers. The tick tick of the record player waited for someone to turn over the stack of records that had finished playing earlier. Carol addressed the gathering although no one was listening:

"Everyone, this is Elmer from Iowa!"

A few nods or mumbled greetings came their way.

Elmer didn't see any sign of Tilly. Elmer realized that Carol's invitation to join the party was literal, there was an actual party going on but, apparently, he and Prudence weren't the guests of honor.

"There's food and booze in the kitchen. Help yourself to whatever looks good. There should be a joint going around if you want to slip into the rotation. Rocky, give these weary travelers a toke when it comes around," Carol said, motioning to a thin young man dressed in a vest and short pleated skirt.

"Hi, I'm Rocky, otherwise known as rockefelleR e coX. Or ReX if you're looking for my artwork," He looked at Prudence approvingly. "What's your name, my dear?"

"Prudence," she said, throwing her arms around Rocky and giving him a hug.

"That was imprudent, but I loved it!" Rocky told her. He looked over at Elmer. "Is this your old man?"

"Goodness no," Prudence replied.

The two of them drifted off in the direction of the lighted tip of the traveling joint, leaving Elmer adrift. In search of an out-of-the-way corner, Elmer eased his way toward the kitchen. As he entered the hall that led to the kitchen and the rest of the apartment, Tilly suddenly appeared out of a bedroom door, being carried horizontally by her hands and feet. Her captors or servants were two men; the three of them were obviously enjoying this mode of transport. Elmer flattened himself against the wall of the hall.

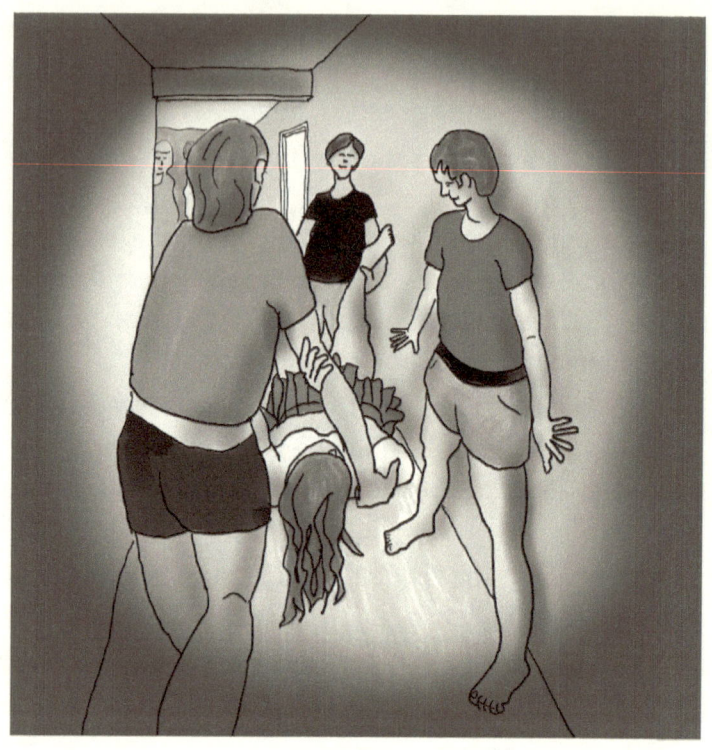

"Hello Elmer," Tilly said coolly on her way by. She was ceremoniously placed on one of the mattresses and it became clear that her departure for Iowa was the reason for the timing of the party.

Elmer helped himself to a plate of chips and one or two other items, avoiding the bowl of something that looked like large spiders covered in oil and bits of greenery. He sat down on a stool on the living room side of the kitchen counter to observe what appeared to be a planned reading by one of Tilly's followers.

Gary sat nearby on the edge of the counter facing the living room, opened his sketchbook, and addressed the partygoers:

"As you know, our little family here in 2A will be going our separate ways before long, and this evening is to say a very temporary goodbye to our delightful "Iowa" who will shortly be visiting her old hometown. When she comes back, we'll be inhabiting other digs, but we'll be friends forever and so here are a few poems to send Iowa off until she boomerangs back in a few weeks."

Our midwestern girl from I.A.
Is about to go far far away
But we know she'll be back
For more fun in the sack
And this time she's going to stay.

Our Iowa girl is such fun
On the beach in the buff in the sun
We head home to bed
With thoughts in our head
That will leave us completely undone.

Iowa's leaving is making us glum
She makes this small domicile hum.
What she makes in the kitchen
Is totally bitchin'
What she cooks up in bed makes us come.

These offerings were greeted with whistles and shouts of glee, and some of the partygoers appeared to have had intimate knowledge of the activities Gary was referring to, which didn't delight Elmer although he had such knowledge himself.

As the evening wore on, groups formed and reformed, conversations commenced and concluded, propositions were proposed and pursued. Now and then, Elmer caught sight of Prudence who had become quite attached, including physically, to Rocky. Maybe he wouldn't have to take care of her after all, but he hoped Rocky was a nice guy. Eventually, Barbie, the girl from Alabama, who was a regular at parties in the apartment, took Elmer under her wing. They had a friendly conversation about small towns and after a few drinks, Barbie began touching Elmer's thigh in a way that suggested she wouldn't mind ending up under the covers with him at the end of the party. Elmer wasn't completely sober himself, and was tempted, but wasn't sure about her health record, and didn't think being found getting it on with Tilly's friend on his first night in San Francisco would make the trip back to South Branch with her any smoother.

Meanwhile, Tilly and her two "boys" seemed to be three sheets to the wind and appeared to be having trouble figuring out which of their partners they preferred to play with. Eventually, the partygoers departed or began to find places to sleep in anticipation of a naughty night or sleeping off whatever they had damaged their insides with.

Elmer had forgotten to bring the suitcases with him from the truck but, hoping they would still be there in the morning, decided to sleep in his underwear. While he waited his turn for the bathroom, Tilly and her two boyfriends came out of the facility and all three ducked into her bedroom. The light in the hallway was dim, but when the three went by it didn't appear that Tilly was wearing any clothing. This was none of his business of course, but for some reason he felt unnecessarily nostalgic for her former virtue. He found a vacant corner on one of the mattresses, and leaving his outer clothing in a pile, tucked in to find Barbie waiting for him quite naked. Unfortunately, or fortunately, Barbie was too drunk to initiate anything, and Elmer was too much of a gentleman to do so.

Morning came late for the sleepyheads. Elmer was perhaps the liveliest, or the most clearheaded, and got up at nine – early compared to the others. He had the bathroom to himself and went into the kitchen to rustle up some breakfast where he found a box of cereal. He stopped in his search for milk to read some "poetry" and little messages that had collected there, fixed on the door of the refrigerator with magnets:

Hi Iowa,
You're asleep with your foot extending out from under the blanket. It looks like an invitation!
♡ Gary

We ran down the beach, waving our arms like excited children. The waves nipped at our feet like puppies. Our clothes waited for us on a blanket somewhere, like anxious parents. ♡ Gary—

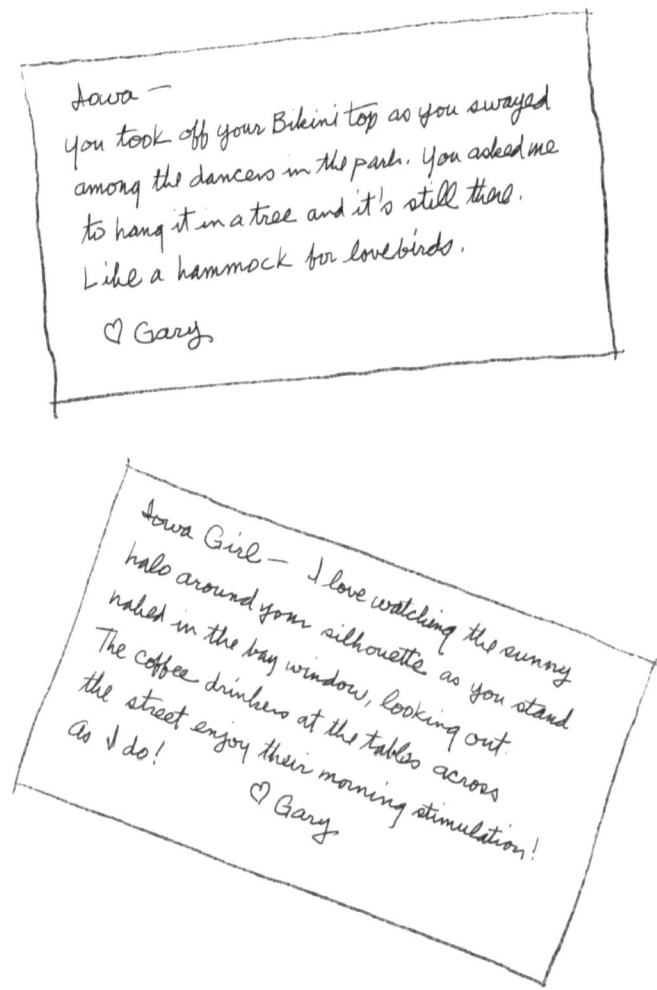

Iowa —
You took off your Bikini top as you swayed among the dancers in the park. You asked me to hang it in a tree and it's still there. Like a hammock for lovebirds.

♡ Gary

Iowa Girl — I love watching the sunny halo around your silhouette as you stand naked in the bay window, looking out. The coffee drinkers at the tables across the street enjoy their morning stimulation! As I do!

♡ Gary

Elmer shivered. *"If Tilly was going to sleep with a poet, couldn't she at least find one who knew what a rhyme was?"*

After eating, Elmer washed his bowl and surveyed the remaining devastation from the previous evening.

There was the expected wreckage from the party: empty bottles, assorted glasses and broken plates, forgotten articles of clothing, plates of cold food now warm, random spills and fallen food, the usual. There was no sign of Carol or her boyfriend, or Tilly and the two men who had accompanied her into the bedroom the previous evening. Enough body parts extended from under an old bedspread covering a mattress in the bay window to identify Rocky and Prudence, wrapped around each other and both snoring loudly, but not loudly enough to wake each other up.

Barbie was sitting up with her back against the wall, trying to remember if she had been ravished or rejected by last night's bed partner, whoever it was. She squinted at Elmer, but he didn't look that familiar. Her long blond hair looked wonderfully tangled and she had no concern that she was topless. Elmer remembered a little fetish he had for women who looked like they had enjoyed a wild night, possibly because he always wished he had been the man who caused them to cast aside their most closely held inhibitions and lose their last shreds of dignity. Elmer picked up her undamaged panties and handed them to her, suffering a moment of regret that he hadn't treated her to a little more excitement. He brought her a cup of black coffee and she agreed to buzz him back in when he went down to the truck and hopefully retrieved his and Prudence's suitcases.

When he returned with the suitcases, Prudence and Rocky were engaged in a giggling and energetic wrestling match on the mattress, in which each competitor was wearing only a skirt. In spite of a tiny bit of regret that his opportunity with Prudence had come at an inopportune time, he thought she and Rocky made a very cute couple and hoped things worked out between them.

It didn't appear to Elmer that anyone in attendance was ready to go exploring the city. Rocky reported that he was going to introduce Prudence to the pleasure of nude beaches, and invited Elmer to go along, although the invitation seemed to be offered halfheartedly. Elmer was too shy to accept anyway, and when Tilly stumbled out of the bedroom and told him she would have to spend the day packing and cleaning up, and that they couldn't possibly leave for South Branch before the next day, he decided to wander on his own in the direction of Golden Gate Park.

Elmer returned in time for dinner and was "treated" to a meal of fried calamari, which he pretended to like so as not to become the butt of yet more West Coast humor. The sleeping arrangements were similar to the previous night except that Gary went home with Ira, leaving poor Tilly alone to her own devices, and Barbie had departed, probably in search of a man who wouldn't be so gentlemanly. There wasn't the slightest possibility that Tilly would invite Elmer to her bed, and he had no intention of joining her if she had, so he was left to share the living room with Rocky and Prudence who were awake half the night giggling over their adventures at some nude beach out on the coast. It was a miserable night, and he didn't see the prospects improving anytime in the near future.

Elmer was ready to get started early the next day, but Tilly dragged her feet and by the time they got started for South Branch, it was midafternoon. By now, they would probably end up staying overnight at her Aunt Bev's house in Berkeley because they would have to load the dining table into Elmer's pickup and leave Tilly's few boxes of books and so on at Aunt Bev's until Tilly found a new apartment in San Francisco when she got back.

August 3, 1967

Tilly directed Elmer to her aunt's house in Berkeley, and Aunt Bev, along with Tilly and Elmer, and under the guidance of Tilly's uncle Elliott, got Tilly's items into the garage and the dining table and chairs secured in the truck and covered against bad weather. Of course, they had to stay for dinner, and after that there would be no point in starting for Iowa late in the evening so Bev insisted they stay overnight in the guest room. This presented a problem. Nowhere but in Berkeley would a young girl's aunt assume her niece would expect to sleep with her young man in the home of an older relative, but this being Berkeley, it was taken for granted. Tilly had to explain to her that while she and Elmer had formerly been a couple, she was now going with a young, handsome doctor who would object to that arrangement. This was not completely true, but she wasn't sharing a bed with the bastard who had dumped her for a flock of farm girls and then, as a last straw, showed up at her house with a skank.

Elmer slept in Bev's art studio instead.

After a healthy breakfast, Aunt Bev made sandwiches for their lunch, supplied a thermos of coffee, hugged both of them, and instructed Tilly to give her mom a hug from her. Tilly and Elmer got in the truck, slammed the doors, waved goodbye to Aunt Bev, and started East.

The first fifteen minutes consisted of Tilly telling Elmer how to get onto the freeway heading in the right direction. And then silence. Neither was happy with the situation; each dreaded the idea of starting a conversation which would surely devolve into accusations and misunderstandings, destroying the fragile truce that at least kept them from speaking to each other, the best idea under the circumstances.

To be honest, neither was completely sure why they were so mad at the other, but their anger was real anyway. Elmer, of course, saw Tilly as having left him and, just as he had feared, she became sexually involved with possibly dozens of strange men, she took drugs, she dressed promiscuously, and behaved in ways that he couldn't square with the nice ladylike girl he had known. In the process she had treated him badly, and then had the temerity to suggest he was a jerk because he had a little, mostly innocent, fling with a young woman A YEAR LATER!

Even her letters were all about herself and all the fun

she was having without him. And her high-and-mighty attitude because she was in California while he was freezing in Iowa didn't endear him to the idea of getting back with her. Elmer was annoyed with himself that he couldn't just forget about her and let it go. It was none of his business if she wanted to throw her life away with a bunch of pseudo-intellectual jerks. Still, he was pissed off at her. And he was pissed off at himself for caring that he was pissed off at her.

Meanwhile, Tilly stared straight ahead out the window. The hills east of San Francisco were turning a golden shade of brown; there had been no rain since May, and they reminded her of a young woman with sensuous curves and golden-brown skin draped over the landscape. She realized she would be on her own for any sensuous play for the next three weeks. She glanced at Elmer, who now looked better than he had when they were a couple, and this annoyed her too. If he weren't so dull and unenlightened, and such a jerk, she could have a lot of fun with him.

Elmer, meanwhile, began counting off the miles. He figured it was about 2000 miles from San Francisco to South Branch and they had gone about fifty miles so far. He wondered if they could maintain total silence for 1950 more miles. He was going to point out the Nut Tree as they passed by, since that's where he had called her from three days ago. It seemed like three months ago. Elmer decided Tilly probably knew everything about California and it would seem stupid to point out the obvious to her. He started to miss Prudence a little.

Problematic as she was, Prudence was lively and entertaining as a traveling companion.

Finally, Elmer decided to try something completely non-controversial just to see if Tilly was really mad at him or just tired or distracted or something.

"Your Aunt Bev seemed very nice," he said out of the blue.

"What?" Tilly's mind had been elsewhere.

"Your Aunt Bev seemed very nice."

"Yes."

Two words from her, a good start. More silence.

"Did you and Carol visit her a lot while you were in California?"

"No. But I'll have plenty more chances when I get back."

"Right."

Elmer ticked off another 25 miles. This was going to be a long trip; maybe he could pick up another young girl hitchhiker and install her on the bench seat between them.

Elmer stopped for gas in Sacramento and Tilly started for the lady's room.

"You are coming back, aren't you?" Elmer asked, hoping to add a little humor to the misery of their interaction so far.

"No, you go on. I'll walk from here," she said.

Elmer was pretty sure she was joking. He poured a lid full of coffee and chastised himself for admiring her braless breasts, but he still enjoyed the view of her prominent nipples bouncing inside her thin top as she walked back to the truck. What a shame that she turned out to be such a bitch, he thought.

"Don't even think about it," she said as she got back in the truck.

The trip continued.

They stopped in Auburn and bought a couple of sodas, then went to the town park for a quick lunch.

"Did you and your friends come up here to the mountains very often?" he asked.

"We came up here skiing one winter. But it was too cold for me, so Rocky and I just stayed in by the fire while the rest of them went to the slopes."

"Did I meet Rocky at the party?"

"He was the one who took up with your girlfriend."

"Prudence wasn't my girlfriend."

"Okay. Not that I care whether she was or wasn't," Tilly told him.

"Right. And anyway, I'm sure you were so busy entertaining those two guys in your bedroom, you didn't have time to worry about my girlfriend."

"Listen Elmer. It's none of your business who I choose to entertain in my bedroom, or how I choose to entertain them."

"I wasn't making it my business, I was just making an observation," Elmer said.

"I don't think you have any standing to make

observations after you were entertaining your two girlfriends in South Branch the last time I saw you."

Elmer decided to let this go and not turn it into an afternoon's battle, but if anyone had a right to be pissed off about the other one's sexual promiscuity with everyone in town, Elmer thought he should have the high moral ground on that one.

The silence lasted for a half hour or so, but in hopes of breaking the monotony Elmer turned on the radio. The news carried a story about an event from the previous week in Vietnam when a fire aboard the USS Forrestal killed 134 American sailors, bringing the death toll for that day to nearly 200 GI's.

"More cannon fodder!" Tilly commented.

"Patriotic Americans, don't you mean?" Elmer said.

"They died for nothing Elmer. A bunch of old men in Washington, sitting on their fat asses and parading their fat egos behind fat desks sent them to die so they could brag about how we won the war against a bunch of guys in pajamas. It's criminal. Those poor boys. At least you figured out how to get a deferment, even if it was by working for my parents."

Elmer was no fan of the war, but this landed like a mortar and was no more welcome, in the midst of his confusion about the situation. In truth, Elmer had given the Vietnam "conflict" very little thought. Politics was something that went on far away and had nothing to do with him. It was assumed that everyone was a patriot, especially when it came to flag-waving on the Fourth of

July, although not so much on Tax Day. If the powers that be thought that communism in Asia was a threat to us, they must be right, and we should all do our part.

The State College of Iowa had a few war protesters, but they were looked on as a splinter group of possible traitors and were ignored for the most part. As for Elmer, it was true he did jump at the chance to get a job which would lead to a draft deferment, but after all, if the Selective Service thought spending his afternoons atop a John Deere instead of a troop carrier was a vital service to the country, who was he to complain? He thought the idea that farming should be worth a deferment was silly, but he wasn't going to question it under the circumstances.

Usually, Elmer would have revealed that he was largely in agreement with his companion's assessment of the situation, but Tilly had gotten this information from a bunch of hippie, pinko, commies and he wasn't going to let it go so easily.

"Maybe those old men know something your pinko friends don't!" Elmer asserted. "The people you hang out with are just afraid to go in the army."

"Anybody in their right mind is afraid to go in the army, Elmer. Including you apparently. Especially for a worthless cause."

Elmer didn't want to pursue this point which was obviously correct. The people he knew from South Branch who had enlisted were macho guys who probably glorified the war and had no idea how ugly it could get. He wasn't sure about the ones who got drafted.

"Did you go to the big march against the war in April?" Elmer asked.

"Yes, along with 60,000 other smart people."

Elmer wasn't sure if he would have used the word "smart", but he did somewhat admire her for joining in. Of course, he wasn't about to mention that, so he tried to let the conversation drop.

"You should have been there. The energy and good vibes were so cool. You couldn't have been in favor of the war if you had been there."

"I didn't say I was FOR the war," Elmer said. "I just trust the people in charge to know what should be done."

"Then you're stupid," she said, ending the conversation on a downward trajectory.

Another sixty miles of silence. A stop in Nevada for a hamburger to go. And finally, near dark, a campsite in a small park near a lake in the middle of Nevada. "You brought a sleeping bag, didn't you?" Elmer asked.

"Yes."

"Okay, I'll go out and sleep on the picnic table. You can sleep here in the truck if you want to."

Elmer got up early, used the outhouse, and checked the truck. Tilly was asleep across the seat and, even though he wanted to get going, he decided not to interrupt her sleep if he didn't have to. He walked down to the lake where a couple of early morning fishermen avoided him because of his appearance but became friendly when he began asking them about the fishing. He clearly had engaged in that practice himself.

"What brings you all the way out here?" one of the men asked.

"Heading home to Iowa," he said.

"An easterner then!" the man laughed.

At that moment, the men looked up the hill to see Tilly, who thought they were alone out here in the wilderness, exit the truck and amble over to the nearby outhouse clad in nothing but her panties.

"Nice!" one of the men said.

"I wouldn't kick her out of bed, "the other man said. "Is that your girlfriend?"

"She used to be."

"Boy, if was you, I'd try to get that fixed!"

When Tilly came out of the facility, all three men were staring at her. Elmer expected to somehow get in trouble for this, but Tilly just waved to the voyeurs and got back in the truck without hurrying or trying to hide anything.

"Okay, see you guys later!" Elmer said.

"Have fun!" they said in unison wearing lecherous grins.

This interchange depressed Elmer a little.

When he got back in the truck, Tilly was dressed and seemed to be in a somewhat friendly mood.

"Were those fishermen having any luck?" she asked.

"No. You were the only thing giving their poles any action this morning."

Tilly giggled in spite of herself, and for a time, the conversation in the truck turned to small talk; the weather, the long, flat stretches of highway in Nevada, the occasional musing about what some large bit of construction with belching smokestacks was doing out in the middle of the desert. Now and then the boredom was momentarily diminished by a passing freight train, or an interesting view of the mountains.

Tilly had left her sleeping bag bunched up on the seat between them, and in a tiny burst of domesticity, decided to roll it back up and stash it under her seat. As she bent over to look under the seat to be sure there was room, something pink caught her eye and she pulled out a pair of silky feminine panties.

"Are these yours, Elmer?" she asked waving them in front of him.

"Of course not!" he said. "Where did those come from?"

"I just found them under the seat," she said suspiciously. "Which of your slutty girlfriends do they belong to?"

Of course, it was none of Tilly's business who they belonged to, but Elmer didn't want to be quite so direct in his answer for fear it would set off another argument. They had to be Prudence's although Elmer had no recollection of when she had put them there. Even a straightforward admission of this, delivered without reluctance would have been better than his chosen response:

"How would I know?"

"How would you KNOW"? Do you have so many girls leaving panties under the seat of your truck you can't even remember them all?"

"No."

"Do you have a big collection of panties as trophies from all the girls you've fucked since you dumped me?"

"Right. I have a huge warehouse of soiled panties back in Cedar Falls. I like to get naked and dive into them now and then when I'm not getting laid."

"You're crazy, Elmer!"

"I'm crazy? You're the one who thinks I dumped YOU! You're the one who didn't come back to South Branch the first Christmas, you're the one who couldn't stop rubbing my face in how much fun you were having fucking your muscle-bound California surfer dudes, you're the one who was showing off your cunt to everybody on all those sex beaches! And you think I was the one who dumped you?"

"I was just excited, you jerk. I wasn't fucking anybody back then. I thought you'd be excited for me. But I guess you were always jealous of what I was learning. You just had that provincial, boring Iowa life and you never wanted to learn anything new or meet anybody new. And then you were fucking that high school dropout from the Burger Shack. Jesus Elmer!

You're lucky you didn't get her knocked up like that asshole Buff Stevens did! Don't tell me I dumped YOU!"

"Meanwhile you took a trip down the coast and probably fucked every guy you met. Don't act like I was the culprit. How do you think I felt when you told me you weren't coming back to South Branch for the summer because you were going to fuck your way down the Pacific Coast with your beatnik friends?"

Tilly wadded up the panties and threw them at Elmer. This would have been cute if she had playfully thrown her own panties at him, but she wasn't being cute or playful. Elmer threw them back at her whereupon she angrily pitched them out the open window.

"That will be one pair that won't end up in your fucking collection!"

Both combatants took a few minutes to rest, but it was only to resupply their ammunition.

"Don't forget I wrote you a nice friendly letter last summer to tell you I was coming to South Branch and you didn't even answer me? And then you showed up with two girls who you were fucking and threw them in my face."

"You didn't send me any letter last summer at all, let alone one mentioning you were coming to South Branch, or I would have steered clear of that Podunk town. And I wasn't having sex with both of them, unfortunately. I wasn't as lucky as you were a couple of days ago!"

Tilly realized Elmer was right. She had actually decided not to send the letter, but she kept this to herself.

"Well, you could hardly expect a tearful and affectionate reunion when you show up in San Francisco with a scruffy guttersnipe in tow!"

"Come on Tilly. She had a hard time at home and was running away in search of a better life. I was just helping her out."

"By fucking her brains out and then pilfering her panties no doubt."

"I hope your skirt-wearing friend is good to her," Elmer said, seriously.

"Oh, Rocky will show her the time of her life!"

"I'm sure you'd know."

"Oh YES!" Tilly said.

This ended the skirmish for the moment, but it didn't do anything to endear the two opponents to each other, who now were even less fond of each other, if that was possible. On the other hand, it did represent the first time they had actually had a conversation in years, and, after a period of silent fury, they at least could see the outlines of that region of the battlefield.

They stopped in Wendover, Nevada/Utah and got takeout hamburgers for their evening meal once they found a campsite. Elmer didn't mention to Tilly that he had stopped at the same hamburger joint where he got a hamburger for himself and Prudence about ten days before. The vast space between them continued across the Bonneville Salt Flats, and over the mountains, and to a parking area just beside the Great Salt Lake. As before, Elmer rolled out his sleeping bag next to the truck and Tilly slept inside. In spite of the warm day, it was chilly at night and Elmer didn't sleep well. In the morning, they stopped at a donut shop and got coffee and donuts for breakfast, which Elmer hoped would get the day off on the right foot.

The scenery east of Salt Lake City was spectacular and they confined their conversation to an occasional sentence or two, with maybe a brief response, about the beauty of particular vistas or the picturesque quality of rail travel in the valley below. After the interpersonal military campaign of the previous day's interaction, this offered a momentary respite and the reminder of train travel gave Elmer the idea that he could, if things didn't improve, detour through Denver and put Tilly on a train for the remainder of her trip to South Branch. This seemed unlikely but gave him a "plan B" should the continued confinement become unbearable.

Tilly told herself that a discussion of their college experiences might form the basis of a noncontroversial conversation, but she actually was looking for a way to evaluate whether Elmer was really as unenlightened as she now imagined all Midwesterners to be.

"Did you take any interesting courses at Iowa?" she asked.

"State College of Iowa," he said.

Tilly didn't know there was a difference but decided to humor him. "Okay. Did you take any interesting courses at 'State College of Iowa'?"

Elmer had the presence of mind not to go with his first answer, "calculus". This was correct, but calculus class was only interesting because of Betty's breasts. He paused for a second to mentally fondle them.

"I took a class in 'negotiation and conflict management' that was pretty interesting."

Elmer realized he should have paid more attention in that class because he was in the middle of a conflict right now.

"What did you learn?" Tilly asked.

"Well, it's important to understand where your adversary is coming from, for one thing."

"I'm sure that's a good starting point," Tilly said.

"If you don't learn anything about the other person but just assume stuff about them, you won't get anywhere."

"I'll bet that problem is ubiquitous," Tilly said.

Elmer didn't know what ubiquitous meant but agreed with her anyway because he thought she was just showing off.

"What was your most interesting class in nursing school?"

"My most interesting class was 'Pat Psych'. But the most interesting I learned was who I am."

"What's 'Pat Psych'?"

"Patient Psychology. Like you get well slower if you think your sickness is a punishment for something you did wrong. Like maybe you deserved to get sick."

"Interesting. And who ARE you?"

"Creative. Brilliant. Sexy. Playful. Spiritual."

"Don't tell me you became religious," Elmer chuckled.

"Not religious in the traditional sense, heaven forbid!" Tilly said. "Spiritual. Did you ever read Alan Watts?"

"Never heard of him. Is he one of your professors?"

"You should look him up, Elmer. You could learn a lot. He's a Zen Master."

"Oh."

"I've learned a lot from Thoreau too. Have you read *Walden*?"

"I've heard of it, but I've never read it," Elmer admitted.

It dawned on him that Tilly had brought up this whole conversation just to demonstrate her skills at one upmanship.

"What have you learned from these geniuses?"

Tilly began to quote Thoreau from memory:

"Rise free from care before the dawn and seek adventures. Let the noon find thee by other lakes and

*the night overtake thee everywhere at home. There are
no larger fields than these, no worthier games than
may here be played. Grow wild according to thy
nature, like these sedges and brakes, which will never
become English hay. Let the thunder rumble; what if it
threaten ruin to farmers' crops? That is not its errand
to thee. Take shelter under the cloud while they flee to
carts and sheds. Let not to get a living be thy trade but
thy sport. Enjoy the land but own it not. Through
want of enterprise and faith, men are where they are,
buying and selling and spending their lives like serfs."*[2]

"So, your plan is to marry a rich man who will spend his life like a serf so you can arise free from care and seek adventures? Good luck with that plan, Baby!"

"I didn't mean THAT Elmer," Tilly said, annoyed that Elmer had effortlessly filleted, grilled, and served up Thoreau's profound thoughts on a paper plate.

As if on cue, it began to rain outside.

"Do you want me to let you out so you can take shelter under the cloud?" Elmer asked.

"Of course not. Don't be stupid."

Elmer smiled at her as a means of lessening the tension and sealing his verbal victory, at least this time.

"You just don't get it, Elmer!" Tilly said with a cute pout that reminded him of the old days.

"Maybe I don't get it, but we'd better stop up here in

Rawlins and get something for supper. Route 80 isn't finished up ahead and we'll have to take a detour on Route 130 over to Laramie.

"I'll run in and get a pizza and a six-pack, and you can stay here under the cloud and grow wild according to your nature," Elmer said when they got to Rawlins.

"Fuck you, Elmer!"

"Sorry Tilly, no time for that now. I'll be too busy buying and selling!"

It was still pouring rain when they turned south on Route 130 and Elmer was looking forward to dinner and a good night's sleep. He had hoped to make it to Laramie but that was looking doubtful and shortly after the road turned east, the truck began gradually losing power, as though it was in need of a good night's sleep itself. Elmer hoped it was some kind of problem related to the rain that would solve itself once everything dried out, but for now the problem was getting worse. Finally, they were moving so slowly that Elmer decided to find a place to park by the road and attempt to figure it out in the morning. A few minutes later he slowly steered the truck into an abandoned gas station on the edge of a small town. A sign up ahead said:

Centennial
Pop. 56

"I guess this is our camping spot. Want some pizza?"

"Yes, but I'm a little worried about whether we'll be

stuck here in the morning," Tilly said.

Elmer tried starting the truck, but it wouldn't catch.

"Don't worry, I'll arise free from care before the dawn tomorrow morning and fix it," Elmer said.

Tilly wasn't convinced and imagined being stuck there for days. After the afternoon's brawl, being stuck in a broken-down truck in the rain with Elmer seemed especially unpleasant.

Sullenly, they devoured the pizza, drank four of the beers, then negotiated the sleeping arrangements. Both had to sleep in the cab due to the rain, and being a gentleman, Elmer agreed to sleep sitting up while Tilly curled up as well as she could on what was left of the seat. Elmer got out, took a piss behind the truck, retrieved his suitcase from the back, and made sure the tarp keeping everything dry in the bed was still securely fastened while Tilly took shelter under what remained of the station canopy to relieve herself. Back in the truck, she removed her tight jeans and put on a comfortable long skirt for sleeping, ordering him to look away as she did so. He was reminded of other times they had been half-naked together in the truck, but he didn't bring this up. Elmer awkwardly removed his wet outer clothes, wrapped himself in his sleeping bag, said an unromantic good night to Tilly, and was asleep in five minutes.

Tilly was awake for quite some time, her thoughts alternating among annoyance at Elmer's response to her attempts to enlighten him, displeasure at his philandering, worry about the condition of the truck, and her efforts to avoid thinking about the nights they had spent playing with one another's genitalia in this very truck, an amusement they particularly enjoyed when it was raining outside. Elmer was, if anything, even better-looking than when they were in high school, and in spite of his clumsiness and lack of imagination when it came to sex, not to mention his mental mediocrity, she felt, once or twice, a tingle between her legs and almost wished he'd wake up and force himself on her. Thankfully he was too dull for that!

CHAPTER 9   ROAD TRIP TO SOMEWHERE

Sometimes you just never know
Which direction a road trip will go
It could all go to hell
Or cast its own spell
Thumbs up or thumbs down, yes or no?

August 8, 1967

Early the next morning, Elmer slowly awoke from a dream in which a young female detective was interrogating him under the merciless intensity of an accusatory spotlight. The detective seemed convinced he was guilty of something, and whatever it was, Elmer had an unsettling feeling she was right. He cautiously opened his eyes and was nearly blinded by the early morning sun shining through the windshield. Shielding his eyes, it took him a minute to remember where he was.

He remembered that late last night the truck had begun to lose power and that he and Tilly had pulled off Route 130 into an abandoned gas station at the edge of a small town called Centennial, Wyoming. Centennial didn't look promising, a few shabby dwellings and a dusty bar that didn't look welcoming.

Elmer looked down at Tilly, curled up asleep on the seat beside him, her bare feet against his thigh. She looked beautiful and innocent; the sleeping bag she had used as a blanket had fallen on the floor, revealing her bare legs below her long skirt that was pulled up and tucked between her knees. Her disheveled long hair was sweetly entangled with her left arm, which covered her face. He thought back to their long-ago love affair and the delicious and lusciously licentious things they had learned to do in this very truck, the seat of which still had traces of the fluids their two years of do-it-yourself sex education had produced. Those had been good days all right.

Now they were alone together again in the truck, but a solid wall of confusion, anger, and strangeness separated them as much as the 2,000 miles between San Francisco and South Branch, Iowa. Elmer looked at the sleeping girl for a long time. Four years ago, they were as intimately linked as it seemed possible to be. Now she seemed like a different person entirely. Back then, Elmer believed he knew everything there was to know about Tilly; now he couldn't be sure of anything about her. He tried to decipher his feelings toward this strange and familiar woman; was he in love with her or did he hate her? He was sure of one thing; he couldn't find a way to ignore her.

Trying not to wake her, Elmer got out of the truck as quietly as he could, partly because he was used to being as thoughtful as possible and partly because, whatever conversation was going to take place between them today, he wasn't ready. He left the door of the truck ajar and walked behind the boarded-up gas station to take a leak out of sight of the road. When he came back, Tilly was sitting up.

"Elmer, where are we?" she asked, rubbing her eyes.

"Somewhere in Wyoming. The sign says we're in Centennial."

"Do you think the car will start or are we stuck here in the middle of the desert?"

Four years ago, everything Tilly said to him seemed endearing and cute; now, her reference to his pickup truck, his pride and joy, as a "car" seemed surprisingly annoying to him. For some reason he couldn't figure out, this slight slip of the tongue infuriated him. Maybe none of the self-important hippie jerks she was used to hanging out with in San Francisco had ever heard of a truck. None of those guys would need a truck to carry around their incomprehensible "poetry" or their "lids" of marijuana. They were all a bunch of drugged-up perverts as far as he was concerned, Tilly included.

"I don't know, Tilly. I'll just have to figure it out," he said, tersely.

Elmer slipped into the driver's seat, pulled out the choke, pumped the accelerator a couple of times, pushed the clutch pedal to the floor, and stepped on the floor-mounted starter switch with his right foot. The engine turned over, sputtered a few times, but wouldn't start.

"Oh, oh," said Tilly.

Elmer silently got out of the truck, took a small toolbox from under the driver's seat, slammed the door, and raised the hood, propping it open with the hinged support rod, then removed the air cleaner from the top of the engine. He took a rubber tube from the toolbox, placed one end in the gas tank then sucked a quantity of gas into the tube. From behind the hood, he asked Tilly to start the engine. As she pressed the starter, he released a dribble of gas into the carburetor. The engine started and ran fine for a minute.

"Hooray," said Tilly, leaning out the window. "Is it fixed?"

The engine died.

"Not yet," Elmer said. "Give me your panties."

"Look Elmer, just because we —"

"Goddamn it, Tilly, I need them to fix the fucking truck!"

"Oh, sure you do, Elmer! Do you think I'm stupid, or what?"

"Tilly, there has not been a moment in the last six years when I was less interested in fucking you than I am right now," he said. He usually avoided using off color language around Tilly, but he was in no mood for niceties right now.

Tilly looked at him, trying to figure out if he was joking.

"How are you going to fix the motor with my panties?"

"I'm going to use them to replace the clogged fuel filter, unless you want to walk seventy miles to the nearest auto parts store."

An image of Tilly with her skirt up under her armpits as she bent over out of public view behind the vacant gas station crossed his mind; the fact that this was not going to happen turned his mood even glummer than it already was.

After taking a minute to consider the veracity of Elmer's assertion, Tilly slipped off the garment, taking care that he couldn't watch. She stepped out of the truck and handed him a pair of white undies printed with small blue flowers. Elmer wondered how many men had admired them before now. He tried using anger to rip them, but the fabric was too tough to tear, so he had to use his pocketknife to cut a circular piece out of the back.

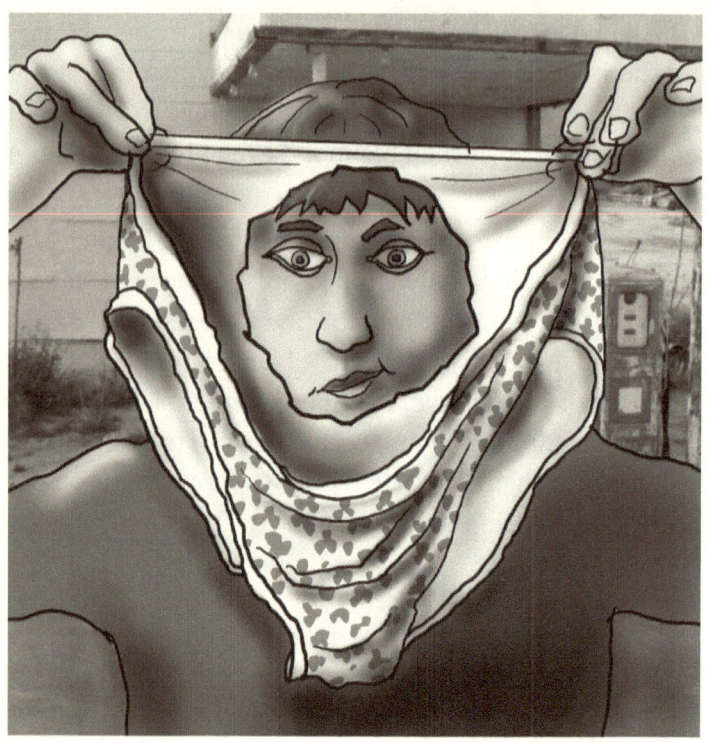

Taking care not to be in the way, Tilly watched as he disassembled the fuel filter housing, removed the clogged filter, and replaced it with the soft cotton fabric he had folded into the proper shape. Elmer reinstalled the mechanism, wiped his hands on a towel, climbed into the driver's seat, and started the truck. It ran perfectly.

"Okay, let's get the fuck out of here," he said.

Tilly got in and they rejoined the sparse traffic on Route 130 heading east.

Nothing was said for quite some time, but a lot was happening. Tilly was thinking about the human qualities one should admire. Knowing how to fix a truck for example, and Elmer's predictable ability at these things. For all their "worldly" and "spiritual" philosophy, none of the men she had found so exciting and impressive in San Francisco would have had any idea how to do what Elmer had just done. And Elmer had simply fixed the truck with no oratory or showboating, as though it was the most common skill in the world. He had not written a poem about fixing a truck or tried to find a metaphor between a clogged fuel filter and a foreign war. He hadn't even launched into a long, self-congratulating lecture on how this complicated task was accomplished.

Tilly noticed that he still looked cute when he was mad. He HAD been cute when he was mad years ago, but back then he was never VERY mad at her, and she knew he would get over it as soon as she smiled at him and touched his thigh. Now she didn't know any such thing, and she was surprised and slightly peeved when she felt a cool wetness between her legs. Was it the memory of "back then" that was arousing her, or the possibilities of "today"? Tilly told herself not to think about that question.

An hour later they reached Laramie, a town large enough to have a parts store where Elmer bought what was needed and fixed the truck with the correct filter. Without giving the matter any conscious thought, Elmer retrieved the circular piece of fabric and took it with him when he went into the men's room to wash his hands. He washed the gasoline out of the fabric and put it in his back pocket with the damaged undies, vaguely thinking she might want to sew them back together or perhaps he might keep the articles as a souvenir of the ongoing disaster the trip had been so far.

Next door to the parts store, a diner beckoned, and Tilly and Elmer decided to splurge on a sit-down breakfast. In spite of being angry with Tilly about, well, about everything that had happened during the last four years, Elmer held the door open for her as they entered. It never occurred to him not to do so. Tilly had gotten used to being annoyed when men treated her as a fragile creature who needed a man to take care of her, but this seemed to be just a gesture of kindness rather than an insult.

"Thank you," she said.

"Yeah."

Tilly had a bowl of oatmeal and Elmer ordered bacon and eggs; each silently disapproved of the other's selection. Their breakfast conversation was minimal. Elmer fixated on the knowledge that Tilly wasn't wearing any panties under her skirt, and Tilly chastised herself for becoming aroused by Elmer's physical appearance and handyman skills. Still, the successful repair of the truck and the consumption of a proper breakfast brightened up the morning's outlook and each was hoping the day would be less contentious than their previous travel days.

"That was very clever the way you fixed the truck, Elmer," Tilly said when they got back under way.

"Just a clogged fuel filter. That happens sometimes."

"Well, it seemed like a miracle to me. I wouldn't have known how to do that."

"Maybe I'll break my leg before we get back to South Branch and you'll have to fix me up. That would seem like a miracle to me."

"Are you saying you want me to play 'doctor' with you?" Tilly asked, then realized that was probably way out of line and certain to give Elmer the wrong impression. Or was it the right impression?

Before she could attempt to take that question back, Elmer looked at her like she was a creature from another planet, then unexpectedly began to giggle.

"I imagine it wouldn't be the first time for us," he said. Then added with insufficient thought, "But that would be a REAL miracle at this point."

She saw him smile for perhaps the first time since he arrived in San Francisco.

His smile was contagious.

"I don't remember us ever playing 'doctor', but I believe you did play the part of an amateur gynecologist quite a few times when we were parked out by Old Man Smith's apple orchard."

"I just wanted to make sure you didn't suffer from any 'female problems' or anything. It was only about my

411

concern for your health, Tilly."

"Well, your treatment did seem to cure whatever was wrong with me when you did that!"

"How are you feeling right NOW?" Elmer asked.

Tilly considered several possible responses and decided not to let the trajectory of this conversation get ahead of itself. If they weren't careful, she and Elmer could get into something that might turn even uglier than things had already gotten between them. On the other hand, her vagina was urgently advocating against completely foreclosing on the implication.

"I'm feeling fine right now, Elmer," she said. Then in a small adjustment to the nuance, she smiled and added, "Thanks for your concern."

Of course, neither Tilly nor Elmer had had sex, or even had an opportunity to take care of themselves, for several days and both would have been horny as hell if they hadn't been so angry at each other and the situation in general. This little back-and-forth had allowed a tiny bit of light to shine through the small crack around the nudged open door but, as had been true when they were first dating nearly six years ago, neither had a clear idea what the other was thinking or whether they were anywhere close to being on the same wavelength. For that matter, neither knew what wavelength THEY were on themselves. Still, the atmosphere in the truck had become friendlier, and this in itself seemed like a miracle.

They set this conversation aside for the time being,

but although they were silent, each was busy inwardly revising the recent history of their disdain for the other:

"How could Tilly have been expected to forgo the fun of new friends on the West Coast for four years when the two of us had never made any serious commitment to each other before she left South Branch?" Elmer thought.

"Of course Elmer would have girlfriends at college. He was good looking and clever, what did I expect?" Tilly wondered.

"So WHAT if Tilly went to the beach naked? I'm sure everybody in San Francisco was doing that, and I probably would have done the same thing if I had been there. What was so bad about it? And maybe she didn't actually get in bed with ALL of them."

"Just because Elmer took up with a sexy, beautiful, rich girl from Detroit, who could blame him? And maybe he got those kinds of girls out of his system! Or WAS she out of his system?" She looked over at Elmer who was looking at her right at that moment. *"No, surely Elmer would realize that a girl like that wouldn't be good for him!"*

"She probably took a few of the most well-hung beach boys up into the bushes!" Elmer figured, but when he saw her smiling at him, he decided to give her the benefit of the doubt.

These internal interrogations and revisions of history occupied them for most of the next fifty miles. Elmer stopped for gas in Cheyenne and Tilly went into a grocery store next door for sandwich makings. While he waited for her, Elmer visited the men's room and, even though it seemed wildly unnecessary, bought a package of three condoms for fifty cents from the vending machine. Better to be safe than sorry.

When they got back on the road, Elmer noticed that Tilly, who had positioned herself on the seat as close to the passenger door as she could comfortably sit for the entirety of the previous three days, now occupied a more normal seating position, perhaps six inches closer to him than before. He remembered that when they were in high school, Tilly had seated herself almost in his lap and with her legs straddling the floor-mounted gearshift, giving him an opportunity to treat her to a loving tickle whenever he needed to shift gears. In the heyday of their romance, he wore out the clutch by changing gears more frequently than necessary.

They crossed into Nebraska at lunchtime and found a roadside park where they made sandwiches and began a normal, mostly friendly, conversation.

"So, I guess you really loved California?" Elmer asked uneasily.

"I love California, yes." Tilly said. "Not 'loved' as in the past tense. The weather is nice although not as perfect as I expected. There are lots of interesting things to do there and lots of different people who are sometimes crazy, but overall, they're very interesting."

"I've read a lot of magazine articles about San Francisco over the last four years. It sounds like 'interesting' might be an understatement."

"Those writers love to make California sound crazy so people will buy the magazines. San Francisco is a big city. There are plenty of crazy people in South Branch too, Elmer."

"I can't disagree with that. And having an ocean right down the block from your apartment is definitely a plus."

"I wish I could take you to all the beaches someday, Elmer. They're so beautiful even if they are too cold sometimes."

Elmer decided to wade out a little farther into what could be a treacherous undertow:

"Did you ever go to a nude beach?"

Tilly didn't find this subject off limits or even controversial by now. "Sure! Nude beaches are great," she said matter-of-factly.

"Is everybody having sex all over the place?"

"Nobody's having sex in public, Elmer. You've been reading too many salacious articles. There are all kinds of people there – old people, kids, college students, fat people, skinny people, homosexuals, schoolteachers, and probably even preachers. It's completely ordinary."

"That doesn't sound completely ordinary, if they're

all naked."

"Not everybody is naked. Some people wear swimsuits, some women just wear the bottoms. Some people are in street clothes. True, most people are nude, but honestly it becomes completely ordinary after the first five minutes."

"I can't believe nobody is having sex out there on the beach!"

"Well, sometimes people go up into the dunes where they're out of sight, but nobody does it right out in the open."

"I assume you know this because you were up in the dunes yourself?"

"It's none of your business, Elmer. But I'm not ashamed of anything I did or expect to do again. If you really want to know, I'm not too shy to tell you, but you have to promise not to pump me for the information and then get all pushed out of shape because of what you hear!"

"Is it something that will push me out of shape?"

"I don't know. It shouldn't. It's what people do and it's gloriously beautiful, but you may be a prude, or jealous, or inexperienced, or a Jesus freak or something."

"I don't think I'm any of those things," he said, flashing her an adorable smile.

Tilly took a deep breath. *"What the hell,"* she thought. *"We'll either be good friends, or we won't say another word to each other for the rest of the trip; either option is better than a constant argument."*

"So, you want to hear all about my adventures up in the dunes?"

"Every scandalous detail!" Elmer said, even though he was pretty sure he didn't really want to hear EVERY scandalous detail.

"Gary and I did it in the dunes," she said.

"And?"

"There isn't much to add. We went up into the dunes, fucked like minks, and then came down and ate dinner with Carol and Hub."

"Was this in broad daylight? Were there other people around watching, were you afraid of getting arrested, did the Coast Guard do a flyover?"

"Yes. No. No. Of course they did!" she said.

"When was this?"

"It was the same summer Linda told me about you and Fanny, that high school girl from the Burger Shack YOU were shacking up with. Do you want to give me all the juicy details of THAT affair?"

"Tiffany," Elmer corrected.

"Right, Tiffany. The one that got knocked up by Buff Stevens, your predecessor on my list of conquests!" Tilly said.

"Look Tilly, let's be honest. I don't know about you, but it creeps me out to hear about all your 'conquests' as you so colorfully put it. And I doubt if I could match your accomplishments in that regard, but I could probably creep you out a little if we got into the intimate details of our adventures between the sheets these last four years. I wasn't just hanging out jerking off all that time, you know. What do you say we stipulate that each of us had some adventures that were enchanting and some that were unseemly and leave it at that? I'm not afraid to tell you everything either, but it might be excruciating to put everything out there right now, and it would probably take us all the way to South Branch to finish the recitation."

"Okay Elmer, but I first want to know if the girl I met in South Branch last summer is still your girlfriend."

"Oh god, no!" Elmer said. "I've had a dozen girlfriends since then!"

Tilly looked at Elmer warily. He was grinning from ear to ear.

"You asshole," she said and laughed so hard, tears began streaming down her face.

"Well, at least I didn't have them all in bed with me at the same time the other night."

"If it makes you feel better Elmer, all I got to do was watch Ira and Gary suck each other off. That was very interesting but, since we're being honest, it wasn't my plan when I lured them into my bed. And, as if that weren't annoying enough, my darling Rocky made off with your imprudent girlfriend, Prudence. You should have left her in the gutter where you found her in my opinion."

"Well, once we recover from the shock of all these

revelations, I suppose we could try to think of a way to comfort each other," Elmer said.

Each of them was grateful for at least a temporary thaw in their relationship, and, in the back of their minds, wondered if it would last out the trip, or maybe beyond. Since Tilly was going back to California in a few weeks, and Elmer was stuck in South Branch dodging the draft, the likelihood of a permanent thaw seemed unlikely, but maybe they would come out of this on friendly terms at least.

After lunch, they started the long voyage across wildest Nebraska. Tilly, who had been sitting upright with her feet on the floor for the entire trip, had now shifted her position so that she was sitting facing him with her legs tucked up on the seat under her. To combat the heat of the afternoon, Tilly was barefoot, and her skirt was pulled up to mid-thigh. Elmer couldn't see anything too scandalous, but he knew she wasn't wearing panties and the flow of outside air from the side vent windows and the cowl vent in front of the windshield animated the hem of her skirt in a way that made it difficult for Elmer to keep his eyes on the road. On top of that, Tilly's silky top and lack of a bra made her nipples poke small bumps in the thin fabric and, as the truck moved, these slid around under the material in a way that made Elmer's mouth water. By now he had a pronounced bulge in his shorts that he had no way to hide.

Tilly started to laugh.

"What?" Elmer said.

"I remember when I went to my first nude beach about two or three weeks after I arrived in San Francisco. There were dozens of naked men there, in all shapes, sizes, and colors, and not one of them had an erection, even though there were an equal number of naked women on display. I wondered what was wrong with them, because every time I saw YOU naked back then, I never saw you WITHOUT an erection."

"It's possible you have magic powers that don't work if you're close to the ocean."

"I don't think they're all that magical, Wiggle Bear."

Elmer had not heard Tilly's pet name for him in four years, and if he had been the type to get choked up over some romantic allusion, he would have gotten choked up. Apparently, he WAS the type, but he tried not to show it. He felt all the old feelings coming back and understood that it would be a tsunami before long if he didn't keep his thoughts in check somehow. This was easier said than done.

"Nobody has called me 'Wiggle Bear' for four years," Elmer told her. "It made me feel a little wiggly."

Tilly understood that this little back-and-forth flirtation was leading to a potential milestone in their history together. If she was not going to be willing to experiment with this reconnection, now was the time to try turning the discussion away from the reunion they were jogging toward. She tried to exert some logic into her deliberations; this was too significant a potential development to leave to emotion alone. Of course, she wanted to let this proceed to what she knew would be an interesting, and probably delightful sexual romp. It could go badly, but so what? She would be back in California before long and if Elmer turned out not to have learned anything since they were together, or if it led to a fight of some kind, she could just chalk it up to experience and forget it.

More problematically, what if it was perfect? That could totally screw up her plans. Elmer would probably feel out of place in San Francisco, and she had no intention of moving back to South Branch. Her careful scientific analysis of the situation only lasted about five seconds however, before she got a call from her vagina telling her to knock off the fooling around and start fooling around. Her vagina had given her bad advice before, but maybe this time would be different.

Tilly readjusted the position of her legs slightly and lifted the hem of her skirt straight up to direct the breeze from the vent in front of the windshield to her hottest body part. This caused her skirt to flutter wildly which was like waving a red cloth in front of a bull.

"It's hot here in – whatever state this is – this time of year," she said with a cute smile.

"I just crossed into the state of Arousal," Elmer said. "You might be a few miles back in Hesitation, I'm not sure."

"We're in the same truck, so I'm pretty sure we're in the same state," Tilly said, waving the hem of her skirt back and forth like a seated can-can dancer.

The town of 'Fervent' is just up ahead," Elmer pointed out.

"Fervent, Arousal?" Tilly said. "Always a popular place to take a break from driving."

She slid over next to Elmer and put her arm around his shoulder. "How far are we from Old Man Smith's Apple orchard?"

"Way too far, Flash, but there must be apple trees here in the State of Arousal!"

"Oh my god, Elmer. Remember the first time you ever took me to Old Man Smith's apple orchard late at night?"

"When my dad's old Ford got stuck in the mud, but we didn't care? That time?"

"Yes. When you drove in there and you told me we were going to go apple picking like Adam and Eve?"

Elmer gave her thigh a squeeze. "And then we had to find something to do while we waited for the apples to get ripe six months later?"

"And we did find lots of things to do during those six months, didn't we?"

"I remember getting my hand stuck in your bra that night. Bras have scared me ever since, but since you don't seem to be wearing one, I guess that wouldn't be an impediment this time."

Tilly's arm was across Elmer's shoulder, and she was flirtatiously tickling his neck.

"I don't remember you coming across any

impediments you couldn't overcome four years ago, Elmer!" she said softly.

"Over-coming was my specialty back then," he agreed.

She slid her hand down his neck and squeezed his earlobe meaningfully. After they had begun having sexual relations back in high school, this gesture used to be a little secret signal that the perpetrator wanted to make love as soon as they could get to a private place.

"Did I ever tell you that, through an accident of anatomy, my earlobe is wired directly to my genitalia?" he asked.

"I want to check if that works both ways!" Tilly said, moving her hand into his lap and giving the bulge in his shorts a gentle squeeze.

"Apparently the message just goes one way, Elmer. Your earlobe isn't getting any bigger or harder."

"There's a map in the glove box. Can you get it and see how close we are to an apple orchard? Or even a bush we can hide under?"

"There's something called Sutherland Reservoir about twenty miles ahead," Tilly reported. "There should be a bush around there somewhere."

"There's a bush closer than that, Flash!" Elmer said, sliding his hand under her skirt and wiggling his fingers in her maidenhair.

Tilly's midsection responded with an involuntary quiver.

"Oh my god, Elmer. I'm going to be squirming all

over this truck if you keep that up!"

"Okay, I propose we let go of each other's privates for twenty miles, so I don't forget to drive," Elmer said. His motion was voted down unanimously, but they did refrain from overtly masturbating each other until they could find a safer place. Instead, their conversation turned to naughty nostalgia.

"Do you ever think about that first time we did it?" Tilly asked.

"Sure, but it's kind of a blur for me. It seems like I was so desperate and so worried that I wouldn't get it right or you wouldn't like it or something, that I just remember it in general as the best afternoon of my life. And that the bedsheets were wrecked by the time we finished, however many times we did it. By the way, your mom knows all about that because she found the sheets in your closet and had to wash them!"

"We did it three times Elmer. And I just wanted to get that virginity thing out of the way and get on to a regular diet of being a grown up with you. Not that it wasn't fun, but neither of us had a clue about anatomy or pacing or what the other wanted."

"We learned a lot from each other though, didn't we?" Elmer said. "Have we agreed that we're going to review those lessons when we get to this lake you found?"

"We sure are, Elmer. And we may start on the advanced class. Speaking of learning, we'd better stop at a drugstore and pick up some condoms. I don't want to learn that the hard way. Well, I do, but you know what I mean."

"This isn't California, Tilly, they won't sell condoms to us unless we're married."

"Oh, NO! So we'll have to stick to oral sex? I love that, but I was hoping for something more old-fashioned."

"Don't worry, I picked up some from the vending machine in the men's room when we got gas this morning."

Tilly looked up at him. "My Renaissance man! In the morning he can fix a truck, and in the afternoon he's ready to fuck!"

"You've been hanging out with too many hippie poets, Tilly," Elmer said.

"Who ME? I never say anything clever, but you should know the next exit is our turn-off to turn-on."

They turned off Route 80 and followed a paved road south for a mile or so, then turned onto a gravel road that seemed to skirt the lake. Tilly was on her knees on the seat, bouncing up and down with excitement as she looked at the landscape. The lake was a couple of miles across and there were a few boats, all clustered close to the dock near where they had turned off the main road. Tilly was ready to stop behind the first tree, and kidded Elmer for wanting to get a little farther from the more populated end of the lake.

"Who cares if anybody sees us, Elmer. Remember what you used to say? 'If they haven't seen it before they won't know what it is anyway.' Let's get naked and do it in the middle of the road!"

"I'd hate to get squashed at an inopportune moment. We'll find a perfect place in a couple of minutes. I don't mind if someone sees us from a distance, but I don't want people crowding around critiquing our technique."

The gravel road was separated from the lake now and then by small copses of trees, and they parked in a somewhat hidden spot behind one of these on the grassy shore. The desperados spread out their sleeping bags within a shady nook in the trees a few yards in front of the truck where their debauchery was somewhat concealed from the road and where they had a lovely view of the lake.

Tilly and Elmer simultaneously removed each other's scant clothing, a clumsy process since they were in a hurry, and in a slight nod to the delicious improbability of what was about to take place, held each other at arm's length and admired the artful way each had physically matured. Even though they hadn't done this together in four years, and each had done it hundreds of times with others since then, they had developed a habit back then of positioning themselves for making love together, and without negotiation or confusion, this custom was revived. Tilly lay on her back, Elmer knelt on his knees between her open legs and bent over to kiss her belly, quickly working his way up her body, briefly sucking each nipple, then kissing her as she reached between their bodies to align his penis with the target. Each had learned to silently negotiate and engage in perfect foreplay since those days, and they would learn to apply this skill with each other. But this time, their fucking was as ingrained and involuntary as it had been when they last saw each other. And it worked just as well. This time was not about exploration, negotiation, or updating their skills to match their restructured notions; it was just about their now impassioned reconnection. The pattern played out as it had before. Surprisingly, there were no contemporaneous mental comparisons being made with other lovers, except that both felt a mysteriously intense connection to the other beyond the physical linkage.

A few things were different though. Neither was in any way hesitant. Neither was overly concerned with being caught. Each, unbeknownst to the other, had developed a whiff of affection for exhibitionism. And both knew that, when discretion would permit, everyone's pleasure would be enhanced by the unrestrained vocal and athletic expression of their feelings.

Under the circumstances, it didn't take long for these feelings to be expressed. Tilly squirmed and screamed in the most unexpected and uninhibited way and this enhanced Elmer's release which was equally vocal, not to mention remarkably abundant. Elmer couldn't remember a more unremitting succession of emissions and when he softly collapsed, exhausted, on top of Tilly, she held him and rubbed his back, praising his talent.

Abandoned channels of thought were reanimated as both attempted to make sense of how quickly all those old feelings returned.

After some time, they had recovered sufficiently to attempt to rise and as they did, they noticed a small boat, occupied by two older fishermen about fifty yards offshore. They seemed insincerely focused on their fishing lines, and it was clear they had been studying Tilly and Elmer's mating habits and hoping not to be distracted by any need to reel in a fish. Tilly and Elmer sat up, waved to them, and kissed, whereupon the fishermen applauded and waved back.

"They'll have a story to tell at the saloon tonight, won't they," Tilly said.

Tilly and Elmer weren't in any hurry to resume normal life and they sat next to each other exchanging affectionate thoughts and admiring the degree to which Elmer had gotten the maximum use of the condom, until the fishermen moved on, apparently assuming the excitement was over.

The heat of the day, the exertion, and the fact that neither had had an opportunity to shower now for four days, not to mention the desire to remove a few traces of bodily fluids, moved Tilly to suggest that Elmer retrieve a bar of soap from her suitcase and join her in the water. They sensually scrubbed each other, in between bouts of kissing, and rinsed each other with a splashy and energetic water fight, not knowing they were being watched by the fishermen's wives – a pair of grandmotherly birdwatchers – from further along the shore. The grandmothers expressed their shock to each other at the young couple's antics, but neither put down her binoculars or failed to wish that they themselves were participating in an equally disgusting water ballet with an attractive man. And, although there was no discussion of their voyeuristic interludes, both couples enjoyed an unexpected arousal of affection once they got home.

It was too early to stop for the night, so Tilly and Elmer set out east again. Large portions of highway 80 were under construction and Elmer was required to pay more attention to the road than to Tilly's acrobatic striptease, a situation that was delightfully stressful, and occasionally amusing to construction workers who happened to be observing from just the right spot as they passed by.

Tilly tired of this performance after a while, and the conversation in the truck became by turns teasing flirtation, and silent seriousness. When they had awakened that morning, the idea that the day would evolve as it did was the farthest possibility from either of their minds. Their unexpected afternoon tryst now required either a complete reversal of their preceding thoughts about each other, or a conclusion that they were just momentarily insane due to free-range arousal and that their frolic was simply a momentary misadventure. Their carefully cultivated dislike of each other over the previous three years had worn pathways in their thinking, but if anything would flood these channels and redirect their thinking into a new paradigm, or cause a return to even earlier practices, an afternoon of unexpected and jubilant sex might do it.

The mood turned serious.

"Elmer?"

"Yes?"

"What just happened?" Tilly asked.

Elmer couldn't read whether she was serious or joking.

"You just saw the previews of coming attractions and you're thinking you'd like me to take you to the full-length feature?"

"I'm serious, Elmer."

"Oh. In that case, you'll have to ask me again in twenty-five years. What do you think just happened? You seemed to like it."

"I really don't know. Of course I liked it. More than 'liked'. WAY more than 'liked'. But it could be nostalgia. It could be that my bevy of San Francisco boyfriends just took up with other people, maybe momentarily or maybe forever. It could be the strangeness of doing it outside by the lake. It could be that we … I don't know what to think about our little roll in the hay."

"I doubt either of us knows how this mischief will play out. Four years ago, I took for granted that we'd be together forever. I loved you so much I couldn't think of anything else. Then you left and what I had expected to be permanent became unbearably impermanent. I don't imagine that could reappear in the same form after an afternoon, no matter how much fun we had. On the other hand, I didn't anticipate ever speaking to you again, and apparently that idea got changed pretty fast. I propose that we enjoy each other's company and see what happens."

"Are we going to keep having sex?" Tilly asked.

"What do you say we let my dick and your pussy negotiate the answer to that question?"

Tilly started to giggle. "You know what THOSE two will want to do!"

"Right. We can't let them out of our sight for a second!"

"Did you used to be this funny, Elmer?" Tilly asked.

"No," he said.

It was getting dark when they got to North Platt and they splurged on a pizza at another actual sit-down joint. Before beginning their search for a place to sleep for the night, they stopped at a convenience store and bought, at Tilly's suggestion, two ice cream cones, a gallon jug of decent red wine, and some snacks for the next day. The clerk was about Elmer's age, and Elmer asked for a package of a dozen condoms that were in a locked case behind the counter.

"I wish I could man, but you have to be married," the clerk said, smiling in the direction of Tilly, "It's against the law to sell condoms to unmarried couples in this state. My boss would bust my ass if I did it. He's a stickler, and a prude on top of it."

"What makes you think we aren't married?" Elmer asked.

"Your girl isn't wearing a wedding ring."

"She IS my girl, but I have a wife at home!" Elmer said, trying to keep a straight face.

"Bring HER in next time," the kid said.

"How about if I buy a six-pack and leave it in your car on my way out?" Elmer asked. "That should be proof we're married!"

"Okay. That makes sense to me," the clerk said. "The guys who check up on us would never think up that one. It's the '57 Chevy. The trunk's unlocked."

"Nice car," Elmer said, sealing the deal. "Is there a place to camp free around here? We'll just be 'sleeping' in the truck."

"Just about any place that looks quiet would be okay. Don't go out by the lake just south of here. The cops love to go out there and roust couples who are making out. It's their nightly entertainment."

"Thanks."

Tilly and Elmer found a nearby truck stop that offered restrooms and had a large parking area where they wouldn't be noticed among a collection of vehicles including large trucks that would be there overnight. Apart from the awkward sleeping arrangements they had endured the previous night, this would be their first night actually sleeping together since the Sleeptite Motel four years earlier.

Elmer backed his pickup truck into the last row of

spaces, between two eighteen-wheelers backed into adjacent spaces, and moved far enough back that the drivers of these, if they were coming or going, wouldn't be climbing into their cabs right next to his and Tilly's cozy love nest. Behind his truck was a large field of soybeans; frighteningly bright halogen lights illuminated the entire parking area. Most of the interior of his and Tilly's "bedroom" was shaded by the adjacent trucks, but a narrow shaft of light from a distant light stanchion illuminated a corner of the dashboard.

They snuggled together under the unzipped sleeping bag, sipped wine from paper cups, and reminisced about their clumsy but thrilling high school romance.

"Remember when I made you come for the first time?" Tilly asked.

"Not to get mushy, Tilly, but that was probably the most exciting night of my life. I've had less clumsy and more exotic nights since then, but back then I never expected an actual live girl would ever do that to me, and I was scared you'd hate it. Thanks for not hating it!"

Both were a little drunk by now and were being less guarded than they might have been otherwise.

"My god, you drenched both of us and the truck. Your come is probably still dried on the ceiling. I had no idea! I thought you must be the most virile man in the world."

"Did I turn out to be the most virile man in the world?"

"I don't usually find myself in a position to scientifically measure distance and volume accurately in those situations, but I will say it was a very impressive performance to an inexperienced high school girl."

"Want to try reprising the finale?" Elmer proposed.

"Sure, but the dénouement has to be a duet this time."

"That would improve the plot, for sure," Elmer agreed. "And I remember you used to love it when I went down on you back then."

"I haven't changed my mind about loving that," Tilly assured him.

Unlike their first experiences treating each other to oral sex, when it seemed fun but weird and quite naughty, both were used to the idea and practiced at the practice by now. Elmer settled himself cross-legged on the floor of the truck; Tilly lifted her thin cotton skirt, draped it over Elmer's head just for fun, and placed her bare feet wide apart on the dashboard.

To her surprise and pleasure, Elmer had become adept at this activity since his younger days. Back then, he couldn't name the individual geographic features of her genitalia, or more importantly, locate them and understand their function. Now, she didn't care whether he could name them, but he certainly could tastefully tickle them with his tongue! Tilly held his head, still encased in her skirt, with both hands directing his attention to the proper locations, and Elmer, who in his inexperienced days didn't have a clue about taking his time, now realized it wasn't a race and slowly teased her until he reached the apogee of her arousal, then slipped his lubricated finger into her bottom as a final fillip. Tilly was already ready for a lovely climax, and this boosted it into a candidate for the highlight reel. Sounds were sounded, wiggles were wiggled, Elmer's head was momentarily clamped tightly between Tilly's thighs. Tilly released and uncovered Elmer's head and looked at him lovingly.

"WHERE did you learn to be an expert at THAT?" Tilly asked.

"Patti liked that trick a lot," Elmer said. He immediately regretted that he had not immediately recognized that it was a rhetorical question.

"I didn't REALLY want to know where you learned that Elmer, but holy shit. I'm glad you learned it somewhere."

"Okay, let's see what YOU learned from all those muscle men out west!" Elmer teased.

They traded places; Tilly removed Elmer's shorts and briefs, leaving his T-shirt in place for modesty should anyone walk by. She slowly and affectionately demonstrated her current level of expertise at this tradition and in between gasps and twitches of pleasure, Elmer assessed her level of advancement. This activity was something they had engaged in rarely when they were high school lovers, in part because intercourse seemed like the most grown-up thing to do and oral sex was problematic in various ways, not the least of which was Elmer's expectation that Tilly wouldn't enjoy administering it. By now Tilly understood the pleasures accruing to both participants no matter the outcome.

Elmer enjoyed the climax however it happened, but in the meantime, Tilly had perfected the gentle lick in just the right places and the sweet words of encouragement when her mouth was free. As a result, she only needed more experience with the details of Elmer's response to become the world's greatest expert in pleasing him. The only one of Elmer's previous girlfriends who made a habit of treating him to this delight was Patti, who usually seemed to rush the process. Tilly recreated their first time as well as she could, and the effect was similar although Elmer had expended a good portion of his ammunition a few hours earlier so the effect was just as pleasurable but not quite as dramatic as their first effort. It did however, douse Tilly's top and Elmer's T-shirt, the only clothing they were wearing, and these had to be hung over the seatback to dry.

They agreed the events of the day had been a surprise to both of them, and they stretched out as much as possible in the not-quite-long-enough seat, with Tilly on her back and Elmer half on top of her, both covered by the sleeping bag used as a blanket. They talked softly for quite some time, neither wanting the day to end even though they were ready for sleep.

"Do you think we're going to wake up tomorrow and realize it's still yesterday and we dreamed all of today?" Tilly asked.

Elmer playfully pinched her bottom. "Ouch'" she

squealed. "I guess it's not a dream, Flash!" Elmer assured her.

Camping in a truck stop parking lot isn't the quietest place in the world, and they were required to sleep through the noise of running engines, the starting up of diesels, the movement of large vehicles, and middle of the night conversations among their neighbors about road conditions. Once or twice, one of the ladies who made a living providing necessary nighttime services to lonely drivers could be heard negotiating a business contract near enough to interrupt the sleep of any light sleeper, but Tilly and Elmer slept through most of this. By 4 AM though, Elmer woke up from a sexy dream and realized he hadn't had sexual relations for nearly five hours.

"Tilly?" he whispered.

"Hmmm? What?"

"We haven't done it for five hours!"

"Rocky?"

"It's Elmer."

"Oh! I'm sorry Elmer, I must have been dreaming. What's wrong?"

"We haven't fucked for five hours!"

"Oh my god! You're right! What's wrong with us, Elmer?" she said, gradually waking up.

"Come over on top of me and I'll take care of that oversight," Elmer said.

"I have to pee first," she said, looking around. "I'm

not getting dressed and walking all the way over to the gas station. I'll just pee behind the truck."

"I'll go with you to protect you from soybean spirits."

"There's no such thing as soybean spirits, Elmer, but I guess it's better to be safe than sorry."

They strolled a few feet to the edge of the pavement behind the truck where Tilly squatted and took care of her necessary bodily function while Elmer stepped into the soybean field and did the same. In the two years they had spent together, Elmer didn't remember having watched Tilly relieve herself. This was less a turn-on for Elmer than it was an indication of how close they had become, practically overnight. He wondered if this was such a common practice for Tilly, peeing in front of her boyfriends, that it didn't represent anything especially unusual for her, or if the bond they had enjoyed in the past was being restored before his eyes in an even more intimate form.

It was a warm and beautiful night, strangely illuminated by a full moon and the garish lighting surrounding the parking area, and punctuated by the smell of warm, moist earth.

"I'd forgotten the smell of the Midwest fields on a warm night," Tilly said, thinking back to their evenings together, behind Old Man Smith's apple orchard, delighting and frightening each other by the strength of their urge to have sex together. "Of course, I'm not sure the added bonus of diesel exhaust and artificial lighting improves the romantic effect."

"I know how to improve the romantic effect!" Elmer said, taking Tilly's hand and leading her across a few rows of soybeans which they could just step over at this stage of the season. They had not brought any covering with them, but this didn't seriously deter their plan. Lying between the rows of crops, they were mostly hidden from anyone at large in the parking area, and Elmer, always the gentleman, took the bottom position so that Tilly wouldn't get dirty. At least in the sense of having her backside dappled with dirt.

Elmer, having failed to anticipate that they would be having sex outside, had left the condoms in the truck so it was agreed that at the last second, he would push her off so as not to ejaculate into her, and after a sweet session of slow lovemaking, during which he used his fingers to be sure Tilly got to her climax first, he withdrew just in time; They were going to need a bath before long at this rate.

They snuggled into the truck once again.

"See you for sex at seven?"

"If you're ready again in two hours, I'll be waiting," she said.

When they awoke at 9, all the surrounding trucks were gone, and they wondered whether word had gotten around among the truckers that they should casually walk by the old pickup in the lot for a little visual entertainment before they started their day on the road.

While Tilly dressed and tried to make herself

presentable, Elmer surveyed the truck stop's facilities, and found that showers were available for twenty-five cents. That would be a reasonable price if they could sneak in together, and that worked, except that the allotted time required another quarter for them to get finished, and even then, they used more time than absolutely necessary applying soap to each other, resulting in inadequate water for rinsing.

They went into the associated store, purchased coffee and a box of sugary doughnuts, and were ready to set out once more. It had been an interesting twenty-four hours, to say the least, and neither knew quite what to make of the situation. The conversation on the way to Grand Island cycled by turns from Elmer, expressing inwardly a total capitulation to the idea of falling in love with Tilly again, and vocalizing this in the most guarded and tentative terms. Simultaneously, Tilly, inwardly having serious doubts, left the understated suggestion open for future debate. This short conversation would, after a pause to talk about the weather, the Nebraska landscape, or the health of their parents, be repeated again. This time, it would be Tilly who was talking to herself about Elmer's attractive qualities and thinking South Branch would not be such a bad place to raise children, while Elmer wrestled with doubts regarding Tilly's ability to confine herself to the routine of rural life. There was little likelihood in Elmer's mind that he could adapt to San Francisco, and besides, he was more or less imprisoned in South Branch due to his draft-deferred job which he couldn't imagine finding in San Francisco. Neither was willing to let the other in on their doubts, or, for that matter, their equally frequent illusions that they would ultimately get married and live happily ever after.

Between these reciprocating positions, they both could agree that the trip itself had turned into a fun adventure and that they should make the most of it. And by making the most of it, they both meant: *"Have as much sex as we can manage in the craziest places we can find because whatever happens, we aren't going to be in this situation again."*

They had to keep reminding themselves of this, not only because the future looked too difficult and unsettled, but the present should be fun, if for no other reason than to offset the three days of misery they had spent arguing at the beginning of the trip.

Elmer noticed once again that Tilly's position on the bench seat next to him was a visual indication of how fond of him she was feeling at that moment. She was apparently feeling very fond of him at this moment since she had moved all the way against him with her skirt pulled up and her legs surrounding the gearshift lever. He began massaging her inner thigh, as though it was accidental, as she slid her left hand up the leg of his shorts and began the same treatment on him.

"Be careful," Elmer said.

"What do you mean? I'm not going to squeeze anything too hard down there."

"The last time you did that, on our first date, you

were stuck with me for two years!" Elmer reminded her.

"We actually enjoyed three pretty nice years together, Elmer," she laughed. "And then there were the other three."

"Are we ready to joke about the last three yet?" Elmer inquired, partly in jest.

"I propose we refrain from joking about them or rehashing them," she said. "Let's just forget them for right now."

"It's a deal."

If they were to forego a conversation about the recent past, that left the future as an equally perilous candidate for a conversation. Nevertheless, the immediate future was going to be upon them in a couple of days so they felt it would be prudent to discuss their next two days at large in the world together without any adult supervision they couldn't provide for themselves. It began to sink in that they had never had any extended period when they were alone together as a couple with no outside influences from parents, friends, or roommates. They hadn't even looked at a newspaper, watched a minute of TV, or had a conversation with anyone except each other now for several days, and now that they were thinking of themselves as a twosome again, for however long that might last, they should take advantage of it. Whereas earlier in the trip, they regarded the small cab of Elmer's truck as a prison cell, they now regarded it as a cozy retreat where they could focus on each other, fondling each other with words and fingers, jokes and memories, outrageous ideas and scandalous but impossible plans. Whatever had happened in the past or might happen in the future, they realized these next two, too-short, days, were a gift they had better get at unwrapping.

Elmer could see, in the rear-view mirror, a storm percolating in the west, and if it were like the storms he had been through on the way to San Francisco, it could be a gully washer.

"How much time do I have left to tickle your tallywhacker before we get back to South Branch?" Tilly asked.

"If we still hated each other we could get there tonight."

"I don't want to get there tonight, Elmer. Why don't we drive back to Berkeley, start the trip over, and see how it feels to cross the country in your truck when we like each other the whole way."

"Your mother would worry, Tilly."

"Nonsense. She'd just figure I was off having sex with some boy. And frankly, she'd probably prefer it was you rather than any of the boys I haven't told her about!"

"I'm not anxious to get back either, Flash, but I don't want to get fired by my authoritarian employers. And honestly, sleeping in your bed is more comfortable than here in the truck."

"So, you think they're going to let you sleep in my bed when we get there?" Tilly laughed.

"I've been sleeping in it all summer, but I don't know if they are going to let you sleep in it when we get there because I might be too tired to do any work the next day."

"You've been SLEEPING IN MY BED all summer?"

"Not so much sleeping as staying awake tossing and turning."

"Oh my god, Elmer. You've spent the summer sleeping in the bed where we lost our virginity together?"

"I've never successfully fallen asleep in your bed, but yeah."

"Why didn't you tell me?"

"Because any time before twenty-four hours ago, you would have jumped out of the truck and hitched a ride back to San Francisco."

"So how long can we put off getting back?" Tilly asked.

"If we take the long way, we could only get to Lincoln tonight, and get to South Branch late tomorrow."

"Could we stop in Chicago for a couple of days first?" Tilly asked.

"Not really. But let's get off Route 80 and find some more scenic back roads for a while."

"Good idea."

Elmer took the next exit south onto a two-lane pavement just as it was starting to rain.

"Do you know where you're going?" Tilly asked.

"Vaguely. We'll turn east after a while and that should take us in the general direction of Lincoln. Meanwhile, I don't really care where we're going as long as you're rubbing my leg that way."

The rain and lack of traffic made their small movable hideaway seem even more private and Tilly put her head on Elmer's shoulder and slid her hand further up his shorts. "I wish we were in my bed right now!" she said.

After a few minutes. Elmer turned east on one of the mile roads that divide the Midwest into mile square sections. The rain was coming down heavily now and they were in a long, mostly straight but mildly hilly landscape consisting of a packed gravel road flanked by drainage ditches and waist-high wheat as far as they could see.

Now and then, a culvert bridged over these ditches to give access for farm equipment and, without warning, Elmer guided the truck onto one of these flat areas next to the road. Without comment or negotiation, both Elmer and Tilly got out of the truck and after a glance up and down the road, ran headlong into the wheatfield in the pouring rain. Once they were a few yards into the field, they tumbled onto the ground in each other's arms and like obsessed creatures, clumsily pulled up Tilly's skirt, pushed her panties off one leg, and lowered Elmer's shorts just enough to free his equipment. Elmer positioned himself on top of her and kissed her so as not to waste time as he was manipulating his manhood in a position to enter her.

"Damn it, Tilly, he said at the last minute. "I forgot the rubbers in the glove box!"

"Don't worry big boy," Tilly told him. "I put some in my pocket this morning just in case."

"How did you happen to think of that?" Elmer asked, expecting her to tell him she expected they might need such a thing at any moment.

"It's happened to me before, Wiggle Bear."

Elmer put the condom on, taking longer than necessary because his hands were shaking with urgency. "You're a good girl you bad girl!"

Both had suddenly become so crazy with desire that the simplest actions were slowed because both were trying to do everything at once. But once Elmer had entered her, things calmed down a little. Elmer positioned his face over Tilly's and placed his hands on each side to look intensely at her as she tumbled toward her climax and to protect her from the rain that was now coming down hard. Their tiny enclosure made of flattened wheat stalks contained them and cushioned their bodies. Thunder rumbled above enhancing the feeling that they were hidden in a world occupied only by them and their desire to drive each other wild with delight. Everything about the place and the activity contributed to its perfection. The rain had saturated their clothing by now, and the runoff trickled down Elmer's butt, tickling his scrotum on its way to caress Tilly's labia and amuse her ass before it watered the field. Both Tilly and Elmer, who found all of this a turn-on, loved the sight of the other drenched and disheveled by the driving rain. The intensity of their connection disallowed a lengthy dalliance and Tilly squeezed Elmer as tightly as she was able as she shivered in anticipation of her climax.

Elmer watched her carefully as she closed her eyes tightly, frowned feverishly, opened her mouth wide to facilitate her rapid breathing, screamed barely intelligible encouragement above the sound of thunder and rain, then twisted her neck back and to the side, and began chaotically flailing and tightening her arms and legs. She gasped for breath as her body involuntarily jerked and shivered under Elmer as though she might fly into the air if he weren't holding her down.

This performance was wildly thrilling to Elmer, who found the idea that he could elicit such a response from a woman astonishing and flattering and no sooner had Tilly begun to calm down than she had the opportunity to enjoy a similarly out-of-control response from Elmer, defined by rapid rhythmic thrusting punctuated by random contractions of his entire body accompanied by sharp yelps that signaled his repeated ejaculatory outpourings.

Tilly held Elmer tight as she felt his body seem to deflate, as though every muscle was tightened to its limit and had suddenly gotten word to stand-down. They spoke quietly to each other, inadequately but enthusiastically attempting to vocalize how much they had enjoyed each other's ministrations. Elmer lay on top of Tilly and he began to giggle uncontrollably.

"What's funny?" Tilly mumbled.

"I don't know," Elmer said between heavy breaths. "Nothing and everything!"

Rain pelted them, soaked every shred of their clothing, matted their hair, entangled Tilly's long hair with the bent-over wheat stalks, mixed with Tilly's copious vaginal lubrication, and squished under their fingers as they held each other. They had no conscious awareness for quite some time that they were in the middle of a wheatfield somewhere in Nebraska, that their clothing was soaked by the constant rain, where they had come from, or where they were going. They were entirely consumed with the delightful unlikelihood of the tightly wrapped package, perhaps called "Tellymer" they had become.

Gradually, they considered the idea of beginning an actual conversation. Their intercourse had been so intense both felt just slightly self-conscious about having revealed so much of their passion to each other. And each of them feared the other, while they had obviously enjoyed the event, might not have seen it as earth-shattering as they themselves had. Elmer's natural tendency in this situation would be to joke about it:

"We might make the cover of a Wheaties Box after that one, Flash!"

"Sorry I couldn't have found us a sand dune by the ocean, my dear."

"I hope you brought a couple more of those condoms in your pocket!"

What the impressionable, critical-thinking free part of his brain wanted to say was more like:

"Let's get married as soon as we get to Lincoln and surprise your folks."

"Let's do it just like that every day from now on."

"I'm so crazy in love with you I can't even imagine not being with you every day."

Tilly was having approximately the same feelings about Elmer, and, like him, she was shy about going overboard. They had only been on speaking terms for a day and a half, even though it seemed like a year since yesterday. She rejected her first several ideas:

"Nobody has ever made me feel that good before, Elmer."

"Shall we have FIVE or SIX kids?"

"I'll stay in South Branch if you promise to do me that way every day!"

Her practical side wanted to say something more like:

"Do you have any prospects for earning an honest living, Elmer?"

"If we get married, would you promise not to wear a skirt in public. I'd be okay with it in the house?"

"Do you have any idea how to change a child's diaper."

None of these gambits met the standard of caution required at the moment so Tilly began the conversation with:

"Why didn't we try that out four years ago, Elmer. I might never have left South Branch!"

"We did do it in the snow if you remember," Elmer reminded her.

"And we didn't feel cold at all did we?" she said, giving him an affectionate kiss. "Just so you know, you're the only boy I've ever fucked in the snow!"

"Apparently you've only been with intelligent boys since then."

Tilly began to tear up a little, hoping that Elmer couldn't tell because of the rain. Elmer was still inside her and still somewhat firm, and he began to tease her a little with his movements. After a while these became more pronounced and enthusiastic.

"Are you getting serious about that squirming, Elmer?"

"I might be."

"Don't desist on my account," she instructed.

With this permission, Elmer found himself getting more interested in the idea and increased his activity and this in turn increased the firmness of his reinvigorated member.

"Oh my god," Tilly said, using her hands on his butt to suggest her preferred pace. "Are you going to come again, big boy?"

"Let me inquire … the captain says he thinks you're so hot it's a distinct possibility."

"Let's change the overflow protection," Tilly proposed.

"Did you bring more with you?"

"Yes."

"How many?"

"Three."

"That should last us until dinnertime."

Elmer withdrew and replaced the impressively filled condom that dangled humorously in front of him, then took up residence again. It was still raining steadily and to protect Tilly's face Elmer pulled the back of his T-shirt over his head and stretched it forward, holding it with his hands to provide a little umbrella-like tent over their heads. They made love more calmly but just as enthusiastically as before, instinctively paying attention to each other's movements, sounds, and touches. Elmer found that he could, to some extent, predict Tilly's level of urgency and, by adjusting his position and pace, affect the imminence of her upcoming orgasm. Elmer played with this knowledge a bit, and when she slipped her finger in between their bodies to supercharge her arousal, he took careful note. He made a mental note to extend this study to the effect certain words or admonitions might have on her timing. Because they had just finished round one a few minutes before, they now relied on harder and faster motion and this worked for both of them, causing a nearly simultaneous finale.

This time the conclusion was followed by a staring contest under Elmer's shirt umbrella which started out as individual emotional enquiries and ended up with them rolling over and over tickling each other and laughing crazily until they were worn out.

Eventually they haphazardly replaced their dislodged clothing and, looking like they had been swimming fully clothed, returned to the truck.

"Are we going to tell our grandchildren about this afternoon?" Elmer asked.

Tilly laughed and gave him a playful punch on the arm.

No traffic was in sight on the road, and before getting in the truck, they awkwardly helped each other remove the sopping garments now stuck to their skin. They wrung these out and arranged them inside to dry as well as they could. Tilly's panties hung from the rear-view mirror, Elmer's shorts dangled from the door handle, one sock descended from the window crank, and the other fit over the top of the gear shift lever. Once they got going again, Elmer turned on the heater to speed the drying, but this quickly fogged up the windshield, so the side vent windows had to be opened to offset this problem. Tilly's long skirt was stretched across their laps in a modest attempt at modesty, and her top occupied the passenger seat where she could raise it if necessary when a car passed them. No wetter but more sexually fulfilled couple ever occupied the confines of the cab of a 52 Chevy pickup than Tilly and Elmer at that moment and, as they snuggled together holding hands, both of them silently remembered New Year's Eve of 1961 when each had considered whether to say, "I love you!" to the other but were afraid to do so.

Since this might be their last night of intimate isolation, they decided to stay overnight in a motel in Lincoln. Elmer still had the $20 that Tilly's mom had given him to treat her to a nice dinner in San Francisco; spending the money on a soft, warm bed seemed like an even better treat. In 1967, renting a motel room for the night in the Midwest was a dicey proposition for a young unmarried couple; it was technically against the law to provide such accommodations because the state or local authorities anticipated that the "travelers" might have plans to engage in immoral activities, a major misdemeanor! Of course, motel clerks were motivated to interpret this rule loosely since they were in the business of renting motel rooms, not policing morality. Signing in as Mr. and Mrs. was required, lest the records be checked, but just about any other suggestion of marriage was usually enough to pass the investigation.

"You'll need a wedding ring," Elmer reminded Tilly, who had forgotten this bluenose nonsense after four years in California.

"Unfortunately, I don't have a wedding ring Elmer!" she said, hoping Elmer didn't take that as a premature proposal of marriage.

"Trust me," he said.

"What? Do you keep a spare wedding ring in the glove box to loan out to all the girls you shack up with in shady motels?" Tilly hoped she was joking.

"You're the only 'unmarried' woman I've ever spent time in a motel with," Elmer said, leaving Tilly halfway between flattered and flustered.

They stopped for gas at the edge of Lincoln and, while the attendant was filling the tank, checking the oil, and admiring Tilly's breasts through her damp blouse, Elmer took out his toolbox and rummaged through it for a three-quarter inch lock washer. He found what he was looking for and while wiping the oil off, noticed another item that would come in handy later.

"Try this on," he told Tilly, slipping the washer around her ring finger.

He adjusted the dimeter slightly to fit using a pair of pliers. "Perfect! How does that feel, Mrs. Elmer Talbot?"

"Strange," she said.

"You'll get used to it," he laughed.

The highway was lined with motels as they entered Lincoln, and, since it wasn't yet football season, there were plenty of rooms available. Tilly and Elmer surveyed the accommodations on offer: "Cozy Comfy Cottages", "Sunset View Motel", the "Quiet Rest".

"I'm not sleeping in a motel that sounds like a cemetery!" Elmer asserted. "Isn't there a 'Fuck the Night Away' motel around here somewhere?"

"Watch your language, Elmer. Your wife might not like to hear such talk," Tilly scolded.

"Yes, my dear. Sorry, my dear," Elmer said.

"That's more like it. You know I don't like a man who uses off-color language."

"Until you're in bed with him."

"Well, fuck yeah!"

How about the "Cornhusker C unt?"

"The WHAT?"

Elmer pointed out a motel named to attract fans of Nebraska Cornhusker Football. Its official name appeared to be "Cornhusker Court", but the neon "o" had fallen off. The "n" had begun its life as an "r". This was accomplished through the use of black paint applied to the lower leg of an "n" shaped neon tube leaving the "r" portion visible. This camouflage had worn away however, uncovering the remaining neon and revealing its underlying "n" shape. The sign appeared to have been deliberately left that way, no doubt because it was better for business.

"I don't think so, Elmer. The word "Cornhusker" doesn't sound nice to me. How about the one up ahead, "Dream-On Motel"?

"What appeals to you about that one, Flash?"

"If you wake me up to have sex tomorrow morning at 4 AM, that's what I'm going to tell you."

Elmer didn't like the prudish tone to this explanation, but he supposed he could wait until 4:30.

Tilly donned her new jewelry, keeping the split side of the washer hidden, and didn't call attention to her new "Wedding Ring", just letting it be seen briefly now and then. Both guests were required to sign the register and Tilly remembered to use Elmer's name at the last minute after she had written the first letter of her last name. She quickly used this as an initial and wrote "Mrs. Tilly W. Talbot". Except for the "W", she wondered if it was an omen.

They showered together, changed to dry clothes, and hung up their rain dampened duds to finally dry, then walked next door to the "Dream-On Diner". The meal was adequate, if not quite up to the "Dreamy" level, but anticipating the remainder of the evening made up for any culinary shortcomings.

"As long as the room has 'Magic Fingers' we'll be okay," Elmer said, remembering the bed-vibrating device they had tried in the "Sleeptite Motel" four years ago.

"I scared you to death when I turned that on, didn't I Elmer?"

"Everything about that night scared me to death Tilly!" he said, adding cheerlessly, "Especially knowing you were going to San Francisco a couple of weeks later."

The understanding that this was about to reoccur settled over them, interfering with a resumption of the conversation.

"Let's go. I'll load up on quarters and we can shake ourselves to sleep later," Elmer finally proposed.

"I'd better call home, so they know we'll be there tomorrow," Tilly said, gesturing toward a phone booth outside the diner.

"Why don't you tell your mom we'll be there the day after tomorrow? That way if we're still friends after tonight, we can have another night together and, if not, she'll be happily surprised to see us early."

"I think she'd be happier if we were still friends."

"So would I," Elmer assured her.

Elmer paid the bill, got some quarters in change, and joined Tilly at the phone booth where he could hear her half of the conversation:

"… on us around midday on Friday."

"So, mom, I hear Elmer has been sleeping in my bed!"

"Mom, he's NOT sleeping with Carl! He could give Carl all kinds of ideas a high school kid shouldn't be thinking about." Tilly turned away from the phone, put her hand over the mouthpiece, and said to Elmer: "She wanted to make you sleep with my little brother!"

"Okay, that sounds better. We could put a 'bundling board' down the middle between us if that would make you feel better. Elmer is a good climber though!"

"Tell dad I'm a grown-up now and Elmer is NOT sleeping in the barn."

"Just tell him Elmer is very responsible and we won't do anything that would be thought scandalous in San Francisco. And if I'm screaming with delight too loudly, DAD can go sleep in the barn." Tilly turned to Elmer again and covered the mouthpiece. "She's laughing and telling that to dad."

"Okay, I'm out of dimes. Love you guys – we'll see you in a couple of days."

"Well?"

"She finally agreed it's your room now and if it won't bother you to have me sleeping there, it's up to you."

"Good, but I'll have to charge you rent."

"I can sleep in the barn for free, Elmer."

They brought the wine in from the truck and settled

in. Even though it was getting dark, it was still hot, and they stripped down to their underwear and opened the windows. The curtains undulated open and closed in the breeze, giving anyone passing by brief glimpses of their dishabille as they sipped the wine and avoided talking about the future.

"What's the slowest route through Iowa, Elmer," Tilly asked.

"We could hang out here until check out time, then go slowly."

"So, we stay in bed until 10, Get out of here at 11, have breakfast, and drive the speed limit out into the wilds of Iowa, then stay overnight, then mosey in the next day?" Tilly confirmed.

"Right. So, we can stay up late!"

"And wake up early, Wiggle Bear!"

After their crazy frolic in the wheat field, neither was desperate for wild sex, but soft, snuggly coupling in a cozy bed seemed like fun. After they overindulged in wine and affectionate teasing, they snuggled in and made love slowly and luxuriously. Unlike their earlier adventures on this trip, which were athletic, energetic, and explosive affairs, this night was slow, languorous, and luscious. They took turns pleasing one another until the recipient was about to climax, and then switched roles. Eventually they went to sleep in each other's arms, not remembering in the morning how many gentle orgasms or near climaxes they had had. They slept soundly except when Elmer woke Tilly up at

4:30 for a short sleepy snuggle, after which they went back to sleep for five more hours. They woke up at 9:30 full of energy and urgency and had gotten themselves into a complicated variation on the sixty-nine-position involving the edge of the bed, the floor, a small table, and four pillows, when there was a knock at the door.

"HOUSEKEEPING!"

They took a minute to process what this meant and were starting to untangle their naked body parts when the maid opened the door with her key and looked in.

"Oh, I'm sorry," she said. "I didn't know anyone was still here. You should have said something. Usually, unless there is a 'DO NOT DISTURB' sign on the door we assume the room is unoccupied. The sign hangs on the doorknob. See, it's right here hanging on the inside. Just hang it outside and you can avoid any interruption next time, okay?"

During this dissertation, Tilly and Elmer were attempting to disentangle themselves, and private body parts were shockingly exposed for close examination by the interloper.

"You do know the checkout time is 11 AM, and the management requires us to charge for an additional day if you haven't moved out and turned in your key by that time, don't you? Lots of people don't realize that and they're always angry when it happens. But there's nothing we can do. Not only that but it sets the cleaning staff back in their schedule when people are not out by checkout time. I think pretty much all the motels around here enforce an 11AM checkout time. Lots of people come up here on football weekends and they don't want to leave so early because the games start later in the afternoon. But we have to tell them we need to make the room ready for the next guest. Well, it just stands to reason doesn't it, new people will be coming in later in the afternoon."

At this moment in their disentanglement Tilly lost her balance as her foot slipped from the grip of Elmer's sweaty hand, and in her tumble from the bed and table to the carpet, her leg swept the bedside lamp off the nightstand onto the floor. Fortunately, it landed on a stray pillow, so it wasn't damaged. The maid, after making the sign of the cross over her chest, came forward to be sure, leaving the door open.

"That could have been costly!" she said, placing one of her tennis shoe clad feet between Elmer's thighs as she bent down to survey the situation.

"Guests have to pay for breakage, you know! It's amazing how many things get broken! And stolen! Do you know people have even stolen the bedsheets! It's unbelievable."

Elmer tried to squirm his scrotum out of harm's way as she continued. "I was telling my sister just last week, or was it two weeks ago, how many towels we lose every week. You wouldn't believe it! Even the knobs on the TV are missing after some people leave. Of course, those are usually due to people who don't have game tickets and watch on TV from here. If the Huskers lose, it's not pretty what people do to these innocent motel rooms. And we're the ones who have to take care of it! Of course, you two wouldn't do that because there's no game today. They don't start for a couple more weeks, thank goodness."

By now Tilly and Elmer were perched naked on the edge of the bed attempting to find the edge of the bedsheet so they could pull it over their laps as the maid began to recite dollar figures associated with the losses.

"Could you come back a little later?" Elmer asked.

"Of course," she said. "You know, you kids should be more careful, you could get hurt doing it that way. Remember, 11 AM Checkout! Have a nice day!"

Elmer got up, and hiding behind the open door, reached around and hung the "DO NOT DISTURB" sign on the outside knob.

"She'll have a good story to tell her sister tonight, don't you think? Now, where were we?"

They moved the undamaged lamp to a safe location and, as well as possible, retook their earlier position. As Tilly was about to begin once more on Elmer's now flaccid manhood, she started to giggle.

"What?"

"She was probably waiting for us to invite her to join our gymnastics troop."

After settling down to business, it didn't take long for both participants to achieve their mutual desires, anointing each other with fluids in the process, and requiring both to enjoy a communal shower.

They managed to check out with a few minutes to spare, acquire a proper breakfast accompanied by giggling which drew the attention of the other diners, and hit the road bound for the bridge over the Missouri River and into Iowa. Tilly and Elmer soon found themselves on Route 34 headed toward South Branch, and the entry into Iowa occasioned a period of silence while each was considering the future in spite of their agreement to set that aside and just enjoy each other's company for now.

Elmer was, given his newfound affection for her, dreading the prospect that Tilly would leave Iowa, and him, yet again. Acceptable candidates for his favor were few and far between in South Branch, and Tilly, in his mind, had once again reached the top step on his podium of potential partners. For Tilly's part, many of the undesirable characteristics she had superimposed on Elmer, due to her stereotypical ideas about the Midwest in general, turned out not to be applicable in his particular case. They didn't agree on everything, but he was, from her recent personal experience, good in bed, and would probably be good at doing practical things, like earning a living.

The thought-filled silence was interrupted by cautious conversation. Tilly had been sitting sideways with her left knee on the seat stretched out toward Elmer who was focused ahead.

"Where are you going, Elmer?" Tilly asked.

"South Branch, although I'm open to other ideas. I hear Paris is nice in the summer."

"I mean with your life, silly."

Elmer was taken aback a bit by the directness, and new age flavor, of her question. On the other hand, when they were dating, it was always a good thing when she addressed him as "Silly" because she obviously used it as a term of endearment and meant, more or less, "I love it when you get all silly on me."

"That's a silly question," he said.

"I didn't mean it that way. I mean do you have any kind of plan or anything for what you want to do?"

"Sure. I want to get married to a rich girl, have three children and a dog, and live happily ever after eating potato chips but not getting fat."

"What's the dog's name?"

"Rutabaga, but we call him 'Rudy'."

"Quit making me giggle, Elmer. I'm serious."

"Ok, we can name him Tinklemuffin. We'll call him 'Tink'. What do you say?"

"So, your life plan is to keep me giggling the rest of my life?" Tilly asked, a little frustrated.

"I can think of worse plans," Elmer said. "But I guess you're really asking if I learned anything in school that I can apply to earning a living, living in a community, and being a good father. And driving some girl crazy in bed every night. Is that about it?"

"Not 'some girl', but yeah."

"Well, I have a degree in business administration. I don't think farming is a good fit for me long-term, but I liked working in construction, so I'd be looking toward managing a business related to that in some way. Eddie's dad is the county road commissioner so maybe I could work for him when this draft-dodging gig is over, not that I don't like working for your folks."

"Draft 'dodging' is the right thing to do these days, Elmer."

"Don't try that theory on any of the old guys in South Branch, but I agree with you. And so do your folks as far as that goes."

"How do you feel about fatherhood?" Tilly asked, venturing out onto an increasingly thin branch.

"I think I'd enjoy the beginning part. And I suppose you learn the rest as you go along. I hear kids are expensive though. I might have to get a side job as a dog-naming consultant."

"I suppose any kid would have to be proud of a dad who was a dog-naming consultant," Tilly said, straightening her knee and rubbing his thigh with her toe.

"Really Tilly, it seems to me you have to think ahead and prepare for the future but be flexible enough to figure you can adapt to whatever comes. Planning sounds good in a general way, but not in so much detail you're stuck if something changes. I'm a little leery of the rigid five-year-plan idea."

Tilly thought back to Gary and Rocky, who had no plan beyond rustling up some breakfast, and Ira, who had planned out every week of his future career in advance. So far over the last few days, she had underestimated Elmer time and again.

"Since we landed on this subject, what's your five-year-plan, Tilly?"

"I guess it's 'marry a boy who makes me giggle, have some children, and get a dog with a funny name'!"

"Good luck with that plan!" he said, smiling at her endearingly.

"Let's think near-term for a while," Elmer said. "Have you ever done it in a church?"

"You mean 'DONE IT, done it?" she asked, frowning.

"Yes," he said. "In the 'Biblical sense' of course."

"Of course not!"

"Well, there's no time like the near-term!"

"What in the world are you talking about, Elmer!"

"Someone built a little chapel out in a field south of South Branch. The kids call it 'St. Tiny's' and I hear it shelters a lot of 'worshippers' at night. It's usually empty during the day, though."

"That makes my pussy hot and gives me the chills at the same time."

"Well, besides getting us both kicked out of Iowa permanently, what could go wrong?"

"As long as we BOTH get kicked out of Iowa, I guess it would be okay," she said, noticing how their conversations had gradually begun referring to them as though they were a couple.

"It's pretty far away. Let's just go have a look when we get there," Elmer suggested.

"Damn it, Elmer."

"What now?"

"Every time you open your mouth, I start getting wet between my legs!"

"And to think I was just trying to make you giggle."

"What am I going to do with you, Elmer?"

"It?"

This teasing, as entertaining, affectionate, and puzzling as it was, couldn't last all day and the conversation turned to the pleasures and problems of Iowa as a landscape and as a locale.

"Isn't this beautiful countryside?" Elmer opened with, looking out over the rolling hills spread with geometric blankets of greenery and punctuated with tree-lined waterways.

"I'll give you that, Elmer. Too bad all that geometry is blazing in the summer and freezing in the winter."

"All the better to get cozy by the fire. Remember that time we did it down by the creek in the middle of winter?"

"Yeah, my bare butt was in the snow and you had a warm girl to keep you from freezing."

"Well, I didn't make you freeze for too long as I recall. We had only done it for the first time a couple of weeks before."

"I doubt either of us were too distracted by the cold, but cozy would have been better," Tilly said. "Too bad my mother was in the house; we couldn't very well sneak into my bedroom right then. All right, name another good thing about Iowa."

"Your neighbors would give you the shirt off their back if you were in trouble."

"As long as you were the same color and religion and belonged to the same political party, sure." Tilly noted. "Just don't try it if you have any different ideas than they do."

"Well, I imagine California is the same, except that the accepted criteria are different."

"I suppose you're right, Elmer. At least San Francisco is a lively urban area with music and great restaurants and whatever you need within walking distance."

"It has to be because there's no place to park! And there are a million people in your way, wherever you go."

"So everyplace has advantages and disadvantages. I guess people like what they get used to," Tilly observed.

"Well, that's better than the opposite, I guess. It would be bad if everybody wanted the same things."

"San Francisco did eventually get irritating in some ways."

"You hung out with a pretty off-the-wall crowd out there, didn't you?"

"Not really. We were pretty normal for the Haight."

"Smoking dope, going topless in the park, nude beaches. I don't want to know all the places you had sex. Everyplace except in church apparently."

"We never set foot in church, Elmer!"

A few days before, this conversation would have had a tone of insulting one-upmanship. Now, after a brief forty-eight hours spent rediscovering their old chemistry, the current version of this conversation was an exercise in affectionate teasing and endearing innuendo.

"What do you think? Shall we consummate our mirage in St. Tiny's?" Elmer inquired.

"Are you proposing we get miraged, Elmer? I'm not sure I'm ready to become part of an optical illusion with someone just yet!"

"Okay, can we just have sex then?"

"Tell me about this St. Tiny's place."

"It's not clear who built it, but some religious farmer apparently. It's about the size of a garage. There are a few seats and a lectern. The idea is that people can pull in off the road if they feel the urge to pray, but I hear most of the users just feel the urge to play."

"What if you get caught?"

"Nothing happens except someone might admonish you. Mostly they just have to wait their turn. And you can see them coming in plenty of time if you're paying attention."

"I guess we could go in and see what it's like," Tilly said with a grin.

Tilly and Elmer returned to reminiscing about their high school courtship. They covered their original shyness, events that had happened between them, such as the night Tilly nearly pushed Elmer off her front porch by accident when he first attempted to kiss her and they laughed together at incidents that seemed mortifying at the time but were hilarious now. They teased about old boy and girlfriends that were too far in the past to threaten any rekindling of whatever this new attraction was going to turn out to be.

They stopped at a drive-in restaurant for lunch where they ate in the truck while sensually slipping French fries into each other's mouths and tickled one another under their clothing.

"Are we going to stay overnight somewhere tonight so we don't get to South Branch until tomorrow?" Tilly asked.

"We sure are!" Elmer announced. "I have an idea you'll love."

"We can't stay over in South Branch, if that's what you're thinking. My mom would kill us both if she thought we were that close and didn't just come home."

"We'll be within walking distance, but not in South Branch!"

"Oh my god, Elmer. I hope your idea is what I just imagined," Tilly said. "Down by the Creek?"

"That's it!"

"That's the first place we saw each other totally

naked! I had never seen a grown man completely naked before, although I had seen all your most useful body parts in the dim light of the truck." Tilly remembered.

"I had never seen a real girl naked either and I was thrilled to start with the most beautiful one around."

"Elmer?"

"Yeah?"

"That night was the first time you told me you loved me," Tilly said.

"Really?" I loved you long before that night."

"We were both too scared to just come out with it, I guess."

"I guess so," Elmer said.

They looked at each other silently for a long moment.

"St. Tiny's is just up ahead," Elmer said.

"Are we going to pray or play?" Tilly asked.

"We're going to play for pleasure and pray for privacy."

This dispelled the momentary awkwardness and started a small word game.

"Let's wiggle 'till we giggle!"

"We'll fuck for luck!"

"Let's come 'till we're numb!"

"We'll screw it 'till we eschew it."

"Do you even know what 'eschew' means, Elmer?

We're never going to eschew it!"

"I hope you're right, Tilly!"

St. Tiny's (official name, "Chapel in the Fields") was a small gabled building set back from the road in a grassy notch carved out of the surrounding cornfields. It had most likely been built starting with the plan for a garage to which the builder had added a short steeple and an arched window over a pair of French doors at the entrance. St. Tiny's was a couple of years old and was clearly a work in progress. The floor was plywood, and there was no ceiling to hide the roof trusses. No trim surrounded the windows, and the furnishings were not fixed in place. The sparce furnishings included four pews, each of which would accommodate four slim worshipers. The pews faced a lectern and a small table against the back wall.

The notion apparently was that people flying by on the highway might suddenly feel the need to interrupt their errand to spend time in prayer at a makeshift church. There was no regular clergy, although now and then very small weddings were held there with a visiting minister or officiant of some kind. Some visitors used the space for spending time alone, some visitors were just curious, and others found it a convenient place to have sex indoors during bad weather when they had no other options. It wasn't monitored in any official way and, naturally, some messages and love notes were carved into the furnishings. But this didn't detract from its function as a place for very small groups of people to gather for a variety of religious, or irreligious, undertakings.

The building was ill-suited for intimate coupling but, as many had discovered before Tilly and Elmer's arrival, where there's a will, there's a way. They arrived after the "nooner" crowd and before the evening rush, so they had the facility to themselves. Elmer had seen St. Tiny's from the road but had never stopped to appraise the amenities of the venue. To be honest, they didn't rise to the level he had anticipated. The room was so small there were no hidden areas or anterooms, and even the pews were quite exposed to any unanticipated interlopers.

The only concealment provided was the lectern. A person or two standing behind this chest-high object were hidden from the waist down and there was a view out the front windows that would allow time to become presentable if a visitor showed up. Assuming, of course that the miscreants were paying attention. Tilly and Elmer, who a few days earlier were not on speaking terms had, by now, established a regular timetable for their romantic trysts and they were behind schedule. Under these circumstances, any shortcomings of St. Tiny's would have to be worked around.

The most likely place for the regular celebration of their new religion was behind the lectern and Tilly took up the place of the celebrant behind the lectern, leaning forward, placing her elbows on the top, and resting her chin in her hands.

"Let us worship together," she proclaimed.

Elmer stepped behind her, unbuttoned her top, lifted her lower vestment, and lowered his shorts. He was quite ready to proceed without hesitation, but he loved to tease Tilly by delaying his intimate entrance with sweet touches. These he applied to her perfect breasts and bottom, advancing slowly to her inner thighs and the dripping wet area between her legs. Tilly grasped the sides of the lectern and tilted her head back as he slowly and sensuously entered her. Given the sacred surroundings, Elmer's skill at performing the required ritual, and their religious fervor, both worshippers understood that the service would be brief, and before long the young churchgoers felt that the final blessings would be flowing momentarily.

Elmer bent forward to kiss Tilly's neck, and in doing so noticed through the window, a bloated Buick turning into the gravel driveway.

"Goddamn it," Elmer said.

"You shouldn't use that language in church, Elmer," Tilly moaned, then caught sight of the unwelcome visitor herself.

"Goddamn it!" she said.

They quickly restored their clothing to its proper position, except for the fact that Tilly, in her haste, fastened her top with the buttons in the wrong buttonholes. Nevertheless, by the time an older, matronly lady entered the church they were relatively presentable, standing behind the lectern.

"What are you two up to?" the visitor asked

suspiciously.

"Ummm ... we were just about to ...," Elmer began uncomfortably.

"We were just about to discuss where each of us would stand during the wedding," Tilly asserted excitedly.

"You're getting married?" The woman asked skeptically.

"We're getting married," Elmer said, using a tone and inflection that could equally be understood by a listener as, "We're getting married?" or as "We're getting married!"

Tilly smiled at him sweetly for saving them so cleverly, and quickly added detail to the act.

"We haven't set the date yet!" she said, convincingly, "but this is one of the venues we were thinking about."

The woman studied the young couple. "Tilly? Tilly Williams?"

"Um," Tilly said.

"It IS you! I haven't seen you since the New Year's Eve party at your friend Linda's house back in 1963.

"Um," Tilly said.

"Oh, I'm Shelly Chestnut," the lady said. "I know your mother from church! And this must be your adorable young man, Elmer? You two were together at the New Year's Eve party I remember, and I thought you were such a cute young couple. And here you are getting married! Goodness me!"

Tilly squirmed as she felt a dribble of vaginal lubrication begin to tickle its way down her inner thigh.

"What a coincidence running into you," Tilly said with as much enthusiasm as she could muster.

"Well, you know, whenever I see a car up here when I go by, I like to stop and see what's going on. You wouldn't believe it, but sometimes young couples come here to engage in immoral activities! I know how shocking it sounds, but some people are just born sinners I guess."

"Shocking!" Tilly said.

By now, Elmer's erection had drooped, and he stepped out from behind the lectern.

"And just look at you, Elmer! You've grown up to be such a handsome young man. Congratulations! I'm sure you two will be very happy since you've been together now for, — it must be five or six years!"

"Thank you, Mrs. Chestnut," Elmer stammered.

"Okay, I'll leave you two lovebirds to carry on with your powwow. Have fun! Oh, and Tilly dear, it looks like you buttoned your blouse wrong this morning. Okay, toodle-oo!"

"Well, that was awkward," Elmer said as the Buick sped off in a swirl of dust.

"More awkward than you think, Elmer. Word of our impending marriage will reach South Branch before we do!"

"Still want to fuck?" he asked hopefully.

"Oh my god, Elmer, I've never been as horny in my life as I am right now!"

They retook their positions behind the lectern and completed their holy mission with passionate zeal.

Once on the road again, Elmer continued to make light of their "baptism at St. Tiny's," asserting that they could recount it to their grandchildren one day once they were old enough. Tilly loved the outcome of the assignation, but worried about the rumors that were, no doubt, already speeding toward South Branch. "How are we going to explain this, Elmer?"

"We'll just tell them we were practicing consummating our marriage to see if matrimony would be worth it!"

Tilly gave him a wry smile – and squeezed his thigh.

"What do you have in mind for dinner?" she asked.

"It's 'supper' in Iowa, and I thought we'd stop up here in the next town and get a couple of sandwiches."

"What do you say we replenish the wine supply while we're at it?" Tilly proposed.

"You're out in here darkest Iowa, Tilly. They don't stock wine in these parts. That's for weirdos from California!"

"Okay, we'll pick up some dope then!"

"I'm afraid beer is the best we're going to find, Tilly. But I think we still have enough wine left to give us a good night's sleep. We'll get the beer and ply your dad with it when he hears we're getting married!"

"Do you think he'll object?" Tilly asked.

"Well, first we have to figure out whether WE object!"

They laid in the night's supplies, including mosquito repellant, and Elmer drove to Tilly's parents' farm by the back way, opening a gate into the 'south forty' and driving the truck down along the edge of the field. He parked under the trees close to their old swimming hole in the South Branch of 'Skeeter Crick' and they walked a short way through the woods to their old private swimming spot. It was still hot at 5PM and they enjoyed a naked swim before their naked picnic.

"I wasn't looking forward to this trip, Elmer, but it's been a lot more fun than I expected."

"Same for me. I had a pretty bad attitude toward you when we left San Francisco."

"This is our last night off by ourselves, what are we going to do?" Tilly asked.

"I take that to mean 'What ELSE are we going to do?'"

"Right, what ELSE are we going to do?"

"I know what I'm going to do," Elmer said. "Try to talk you into staying here longer than you had planned."

"How much longer?"

"Fifty years."

"I'm not sure if that's part of my fifty-year plan, Elmer, but I could probably agree to another week or two depending … "

"On what?"

"On if you're going to fuck me again RIGHT NOW!"

"You mean you want to commit the sin of once again gaining, … gaining, immoral, oh my god, Tilly, … carnal knowledge of … ?"

"Yes!" Tilly said, taking his manhood into her mouth.

"Of one … another?" Elmer stammered.

Tilly was too busy to answer verbally.

August 11, 1967

The sun rose early and the flashing effect of sunlight through breeze-shaken leaves woke Tilly and Elmer up before they were fully ready. They snuggled together praising one another's skills in a sleeping bag and then got up for an early morning dip. Not wanting to get to Tilly's parents' house too early lest they realize Tilly and Elmer had spent the night close by, they dawdled, had delightful sexual relations in the open air, and finally went for a last swim before they would have to go. Around mid-morning, Tilly and Elmer gathered up their gear and walked back to the truck.

"We should make ourselves look a little bit presentable before we go over to my house," said Tilly.

Neither had brought a large supply of clean clothes

but each of them had saved one last outfit for the coming-home party.

Elmer retrieved the suitcases from under the table in the truck bed and they stripped down in the grassy road next to the open tailgate. Elmer watched Tilly remove her clothes, and for the first time, he was not associating this activity with imminent sex. She looked beautiful and ordinary. She changed clothes in a casual way that was not meant to entice him, or quickly make her body available to him, but as he imagined couples who had been together for a long time did, just to clad themselves in something new.

"You look beautiful," he said without trying to talk her into anything.

"Thanks for saying so, that's sweet," she said, rummaging through her suitcase for a clean pair of panties.

"I forgot to give these back to you. They would be a good choice for today," Elmer said, reaching into his back pocket and retrieving the panties Tilly had been wearing — was it only three days ago? – when he cut a circle out of the bottom to make a temporary fuel filter.

"Perfect," she said. "Now you can rub my ass without any hindrance. Did you throw the circle away?"

"No, I absent-mindedly washed it out and put it in my pocket. I guess I thought it might go into a museum someday." He handed Tilly the circular piece of fabric and she put it into a small pocket inside her suitcase for safekeeping. In doing so, she felt a metal object that had apparently slipped out through a small hole in the pocket into the space between the shell and lining of the suitcase. Wearing only the panties with an attractive window in the back, Tilly bent over the tailgate of the truck and attempted to retrieve the curious object from its difficult hiding place as Elmer reconsidered whether he had dismissed the idea of a last quickie too quickly.

"Oh my god, Elmer, look at this!" she said, holding up a small necklace on a chain. "Do you recognize this?"

"I can't believe you still have that!" he said, examining the half heart on a chain that he had paid 95 cents for at the airport four years ago as Tilly was about to leave for San Francisco. He gave her a kiss.

"I'll be right back," he said.

Elmer walked around to the driver's side of the truck and returned with his toolbox.

"Check this out!" he said, opening the toolbox, and rummaging around under a jumble of tools to find the other half of the broken heart necklace.

"See, I'm a hopeless romantic too!" he said.

"How did that get in your toolbox?" Tilly asked.

"I don't know. I wore it around my neck for a while but when you dumped me, I probably tossed it in there thinking I might use it as a shim or something."

They hugged for a while, forming the subject of a beautiful photograph, a loving couple wearing only a single item of clothing with a hole in the butt. No one was around to take the photo, fortunately.

"It's been a fun road trip, Elmer," Tilly said.

"Maybe next time we'll make the entire trip fun!" Elmer responded.

Twenty minutes later they drove into Tilly's driveway. As their custom became when they were teenagers, they took a minute of private time together before getting out of the truck.

"Elmer?"

"What?"

"I love you!"

"I love you too, Tilly! And you know what?"

"What?"

"Unlike the first time I said that to you in this truck, this time I know what it means!"

They walked up to the back porch as Edith emerged from the kitchen door, wiping her hands on her apron as she rushed to give them hugs. Tilly's dad joined in the festivities, asking Elmer about the trip and the road conditions out West.

"Congratulations!" Tilly's mom said looking them up and down.

"For making it across 2000 miles of wild west in the same truck as Elmer?" Tilly asked.

"Don't be coy you two; Shelly told me you've decided to get married! I'm so happy for you and I can't wait to start baking cookies for the grandchildren."

"We haven't set a date yet, you know!" Tilly said, as she gave a little tug on Elmer's ear lobe.

EPILOGUE

October 5, 2018

"Let's stop for lunch at Pearl's Downtown Diner before we go home, Elmer," Tilly proposed. "I can get the latest news from Pearl, and you can admire Molly's bottom."

"Good idea. I'll take my reading glasses in with me so I can read what brand of jeans Molly's wearing today!"

"You're never going to change, are you Elmer?"

"You should hope I don't! When I can't find anything interesting about Molly's bottom, I won't find yours that interesting either!"

"Hi Mr. and Mrs. Talbot," Molly said as she brought the menus. "Soup and a half-sandwich as usual? It's tomato soup today."

"Great," they said in unison.

"Calvin Klein! She must have gotten a raise!" Elmer whispered after Molly went into the kitchen.

"She's young enough to be your granddaughter, you know!" Tilly reminded him.

"How could that be, Tilly? I'm only eighteen."

"Good, I love younger men!" Tilly asserted.

"Speaking of our grandchildren, isn't Tommy turning eight one of these days?" Elmer asked.

"October 14th. What's the date today?"

"October 5th," Elmer said.

They looked at each other for a minute, trying to figure out what was unusual about that date.

"Oh my god, Elmer! Today's our 49th anniversary!"

"And neither of us remembered!" Elmer said. "Let's try to remember our 50th next year!"

They stood up, and attempted to kiss forty-nine times, but lost count. They actually kissed 53 times.

"All right, you lovebirds. What was that all about?" Pearl wanted to know.

"It's our 49th anniversary," Tilly told her.

Pearl gave them both a hug. "Are you going to have a party?"

"Absolutely," Elmer said, giving Tilly's earlobe a tug. "Now that we've remembered, we're going to go home and have a party all afternoon!"

ABOUT THE AUTHOR:

Gene Clements grew up in a small town in the Midwest. His father was an English teacher, his mother an artist. Gene studied architecture at the University of Illinois and MIT and, during his career as an architect in California,  dedicated a good portion of his spare time to drawing and painting the figure. Eventually, he began writing short stories that are intended to be sweet, funny, nostalgic, and a little dirty; sometimes more than a little.

Since retiring, he has written, illustrated, and published 52 short stories, three short story collections, two coloring books and two novels, including *The Great American Tilly and Elmer Novel*. His work can be found online and in each of the five most recent editions of the Literary Art Anthology, published each year in conjunction with the Seattle Erotic Art Festival.

FOOTNOTES:

Form and Thought in Prose, 2nd ed. Ed. Wilfred H. Stone, and Robert Hoopes, The Ronald Press Company, New York, 1960

Walden, Henry David Thoreau, New American Library, inc., New York